Someone Exactly LIKE ME

BOOK 1 IN THE WOUNDED HEARTS SERIES

DEBBIE CROMACK

Printed in the United States of America

Book Cover & Interior Formatting: Qamber Designs
(https://www.qamberdesignsandmedia.com/)
Developmental Editor: Sarah Pesce (https://www.loptandcropt.com/)
Copy Editor: Lynda Ryba (http://fwsmedia.net/)
Proofreader: Annie Bugeja.

The publisher is not responsible for websites (or their content) that are not owned by the publisher.

ISBN 978-1-7923-4929-4 (pbk.)
ISBN 978-1-7923-4930-0 (eBook)

This book is dedicated to YOU, my amazing readers.
Whew, what a wild few years it's been.

I hope you're all hanging in there and staying safe and healthy.
I also hope this story gives you an escape from the real world to
make you laugh, feel swoony, and forget about all the stresses of
the world, at least for a little while.

Thank you for your support. I appreciate you.

I'm sending you hugs from across the miles.

Debbie

MORE BOOKS BY *Debbie Cromack*

Standalones
Untouchable Zane

Is it possible for a gorgeous, A-list celebrity to actually find true love with someone who genuinely loves him for himself and not his status and wealth? And when he does, could one fateful night drive her away forever?

Tropes: SLOW BURN, reverse age-gap (older woman, younger man), celebrity hero, wounded / broken hero, Hollywood romance

https://books2read.com/u/47Npla

Series
Someone Exactly Like Me (Book 1 in the Wounded Hearts Series)

He's a hot Italian celebrity who wants the American dream. She's a romance author whose career is in a slump. They strike a business deal to help each other get what they want. When sparks fly, neither may get what they bargained for and both may end up with broken hearts.

Tropes: SLOW BURN, friends to lovers, soul mates, strong female friendship, wounded / broken hero, celebrity / Mediterranean hero, slight forced proximity

https://books2read.com/u/mvojwz

Kiss Away Your Pain (Book 2 in the Wounded Hearts Series)

She's not into one-night stands. He's a commitment-phobe. When sparks fly, is true love even possible?

Tropes: SLOW BURN, friends to lovers, soul mates, strong female friendship, wounded / broken hero, learning to love again

https://books2read.com/KissAwayYourPain

Someone to Watch Over Me (Book 3 in the Wounded Hearts Series)

They've been in love since they were kids, though neither will confess it to the other. One night changes everything, bringing them closer together then ripping them apart. Will their deep childhood love be the catalyst that seals their fate?

Tropes: SLOW BURN, childhood friends to lovers, soul mates, unexpected pregnancy, hidden love

https://books2read.com/SomeoneToWatchOverMeCromack

VISUAL RECOMMENDATION

I'm a very visual person. So, for each of my books, I create a Pinterest board that houses Pins of my hero, heroine, places they'll go, experiences they'll have, things from their past, and so on. To get a glimpse into the story of Nicco and Destiny in Someone Exactly Like Me, I invite you to visit their Pinterest board here: www.pinterest.com/debbiecromackauthor/someone-exactly-like-me/.

PLAYLIST

Music is powerful. It can set my mood, help me change my mood, and/or intensify my mood. Along with being a visual person, I surround myself with music. When I write, I see my stories as though they're movies. And every movie has a soundtrack. I create a soundtrack for each of my books. Below is a list of songs you may want to check out as you read certain scenes and chapters in Someone Exactly Like Me. They'll bring you even deeper into the story. You can find most of them on my playlist on Spotify: open.spotify.com/playlist/4xaPAHL0ZSYPyjtBhyX8yI. I hope you enjoy them!

Chapter 1 – "Coffee" by Hippie Sabotage

Chapter 2 – "Put Me Up" by Mike Perry

Chapter 3 – "Who Is Ready to Jump – Original Club Mix" by Chuckie

Chapter 4 – "Get Low" by Dillon Francis and DJ Snake

Chapter 5 – "Ay Mi Pendejo" by La Nevula23 Productor, La Nina23

Chapter 6 – "Temptation" by Coté De Pablo

Chapter 7 – "I Want It" by Two Feet

Chapter 8 – "Breaking Me – Acoustic Version" by Topic, A7S

Chapter 9 – "Call Out My Name" by The Weekend

Chapter 10 – "Lights Down Low" by MAX

Chapter 11 – "La Ciudad" by ODESZA

TRIGGER WARNINGS

This book contains some things that may be triggers for some readers. Those things include a panic attack, a smoking habit, a couple mentions of body image struggles, and a mention of the loss of a child.

PROLOGUE

—

Destiny

On my thirtieth birthday, I make a deal that changes the rest of my life.

I'm not much for going out, but my best friend since we were in first grade wants to take me out to celebrate. I've begrudgingly agreed to go because I barely get to see her anymore and I know it'll make her happy.

Little did I know when the night began that I was about to accept a deal from one of the sexiest men on earth.

1

—

Destiny

Candi: Happy birthday! I'm so excited we're going out tonight! Come to the studio around 5:00 and you can pick out a fun outfit to wear. No backing out. I love you. Mwah!

Crap, it's my birthday. I'm dreading that I agreed to let Candi take me out. With her crazy schedule, she hasn't been home for my birthday the last three years. Up until that time, we celebrated our birthdays together for as long as I can remember. Our celebrations have always been very different. My introverted self loves ordering sushi, eating cupcakes, and drinking hot cocoa while we curl up under blankets and watch movies until we fall asleep. For Candi's birthday, it's always party, party, party. While I don't enjoy going out to nightclubs, drinking and dancing all night, I'd do anything for her. She's my ride-or-die.

Me: Nope. No backing out. I'll see you tonight. I love you bunches!

Thirty. Thirty years on this earth. I've had a pretty good life so far. Nothing awful and nothing fabulous. My parents love me, I love what I do for a living, and I have the best friend a girl could ask for.

My fingers rest, almost paralyzed, on my keyboard as I stare out the window at the waves crashing onto the shore and spilling across the sand. I'm desperate for inspiration to crash into my head and spill onto the blank page that's taunting me. The cursor blinks relentlessly, provoking me.

The waves that used to practically sing love stories to me are useless right now. I can remember days of walking along the beach with my notebook, furiously scribbling down scenes as they popped into my head. And now…nothing. My last book was, by far, worse than the first book I ever wrote. Each word felt forced and the love scenes lacked passion. Passion? They were pathetic fizzles.

I had a pretty successful career for a while, but right now, I'm wondering if I'm going to be able to pay the rent on my little beach cottage next month. My book sales have plummeted over the last seven months and my savings account is dwindling quickly.

Being an indie author is a lot of work. Between self-editing, self-promoting, self-publishing, being active on social media to build your audience, creating a team of people to support you, writing newsletters, and everything else the do-it-yourself romance author has to do, finding time to write can feel impossible sometimes. And when you *do* have time, you pray for inspiration and the most wonderful love story to create itself in your brain.

So, here I sit, my mind blank, wallowing in self-pity.

Staring at this page won't miraculously make a love story come out of me, so I make lunch and put on *The Holiday*. Maybe it'll jolt some romance into me. I get all swoony for the character of Graham and love the scene where he, his girls, and Amanda are all lying in the girls' tent in their bedroom. Oh, my heart.

Though I didn't intend to watch the entire movie, what can I say, I got totally sucked in and did. After my laughs, my cries, and my hopeful romantic heart was tugged on, I get up from the sofa, put my lunch dishes in the dishwasher, and sit back down at my computer, determined to write. Words. I'll take any and all words that come to me right now. Something, anything.

Placing my fingers on the keyboard, I start typing away. Click, click, click. I don't quite know what I'm typing, I'm just trying to see what comes out. Several hundred words later, I take a swig of water from my glass water bottle and scroll up to read what I've written.

Crap. It's total and utter crap.

Tap, tap, tap. Tappity-tap. My taps on the faded backspace key become more like a pounding. Ugh. I grab the mouse, select everything I've written, and hit the delete button. Whoosh. Gone. The blinking cursor torments me. Blink, blink, blink.

Irritated by the blank page that's now mocking me, I grab my notebook and head to the beach. If nothing else, it'll soothe me.

My stroll on the beach is exactly what I needed on my birthday. While inspiration doesn't strike, breathing in the salt air that tousles my hair and feeling the warm sand seep between my toes is like a cozy blanket to my soul.

Several houses down from mine, there's a woman and a little girl building a sandcastle. My mind wanders to when I was little and Mom and I built elaborate, multi-level sand castles with moats. I smile at the memory. We'd spend hours building them, only to have the waves wash them away. One time I asked her if I could live in a castle someday. She told me I could do anything I dreamed of. She's always been my biggest supporter and my most devoted fan.

I check my phone and it's time to head back home to get ready for the evening. I shower and shave, do my hair, and put on a little makeup. Even though Candi has tried for years to teach me how to do my makeup better, I'm just not great at it.

Candi always has tons of different outfits at her photography studio, and sometimes, when she's in town, we play dress-up like when we were kids. Knowing she'll be letting me wear something from her studio wardrobe, I throw on skinny jeans, a white T-shirt, and sneakers.

As usual, I'm ready early. I schedule my Uber and settle into the weathered white rocking chair on the front porch. Closing my eyes, I rock easily back and forth, letting the warm summer breeze caress me.

The Uber driver honks me out of my momentary escape from reality and I jump to my feet. The instant I get into his car, I'm uncomfortable. The smell of heavy cologne stings my nostrils and the way he turns around and glares at me is creepy.

"Be sure to strap in, little lady." He doesn't wink at me, but he may as well have. Heebie-jeebies crawl up my arms, meeting between my shoulder blades, then shooting up my neck to the base of my head.

Not being a big drinker, I'm usually the designated driver when Candi and I go out drinking. Those occasions are far less frequent now that we're older. With it being my birthday, I figured I'd have a few drinks tonight. But right now, in this car with Mr. Creepyman, I'm regretting that decision.

He pulls up to Candi's studio and I can't get out of his car fast enough. I scurry into the studio as quietly as possible so I don't disrupt Candi's photo shoot. She's incredibly talented and the most driven person I know. Her career exploded about three years ago and she now travels the world doing photo shoots with all kinds of famous people and iconic brands. It makes me so happy to see how successful she's become. She's worked extremely hard to get where she is.

From our appearance to our personalities, Candi and I are polar opposites. With her waist-long cotton-candy pink hair, her screaming-sexy body, exquisite Italian-Egyptian beauty, and flamboyant style, she could be a top model if she didn't love being behind the camera so much. She's sassy, confident, and doesn't take shit from anyone. People are often surprised to learn we're best friends.

One place we're exactly the same, however, is our fierce loyalty to each other and our friendship.

She got crazy-lucky with her studio in that her uncle owned it and sold it to her for an ungodly low price. It's a huge old warehouse with exposed brick walls. It has tons of space and Candi has loads of various styles of furniture and decor for setting up different scenes. Massive windows at the top of the brick walls filter in plenty of natural daylight.

Today she's doing a shoot for Fendi. Fendi! Our lifestyles have become so different, but Candi remains unchanged by her success. She's still the goofy-ass girl with a huge heart who's been with me through all of life's ups and downs. Every failed history test, every bad perm, and every heartbreaking relationship demise.

I sneak into her office and send a text to let her know I'm here. I know she keeps her phone on silent when she's working and checks it during breaks. Within seconds, she whips around the corner through the open door.

I open my eyes wide and clench my teeth. "I'm sorry. I tried to be quiet."

"What? No. You were. You're fine." She shakes her head as her words come out rapidly.

"What's going on?" I ask as she pinches the bridge of her nose, her telltale sign that she's stressed.

"Thank God you're here." She paces, pressing her fingers into her temples, then walks over to me. "I'm going to need your help," she says, placing her hands around my shoulders. She's already a couple inches taller than me and with 3-inch heels on, she looks like a giant.

"Of course. Whatever you need. I'm here. What's happening?"

She releases me and fills me in quickly. "Gigi, she's the other model, she's running late." She lets out an exasperated sigh. "She's *always* late. I need to get this shoot in tonight because she leaves tomorrow and then she's booked for another two months. And this project is due. I have to get it done."

"Okay, tell me, what can I do to help?" I have no idea how I can possibly help in this situation, but I'm certainly willing to.

She takes my shoulders in her hands again. "I know this is totally out of your comfort zone, but I need you," she says desperately as she releases me.

"Okay." I shake my head and stretch out my palms toward her. "What? I'll do it."

"I need to test the lighting so as soon as she gets here, we can get the shots in."

Seems like a no-brainer to me. "Okay, done. How can I help with that?"

"She'll be wearing white so I need you to wear white and pose with the male model."

"You want me to pose with someone?" Surprised by her request, my voice raises a bit.

"Yes. For the lighting. I need you both in the shot. He's really nice. I've worked with him before. Actually, you know him."

"I do?" She has me searching my mind as to what male model I would know because I don't know any.

"Yeah. He's from the movie that got you all hot and bothered." Giving me a mischievous smile, she wiggles her brows at me.

My eyes widen and my face heats instantly as I take a small gasp of air. "You mean…"

She shoots me a devilish wink and shifts her gaze behind me.

I turn my body, following her gaze, and he's walking toward me, oozing every droplet of sexiness he possessed in his role in the movie Don Matteo. Like I'm in some distorted time warp, he approaches me in slow motion and I swear I can see heat waves shimmering, emanating around him, filling the air.

His dark hair is glossed in place and his chocolate eyes melt me where I stand. Tidy two-day scruff hugs his strong jaw. With each step he takes, the temperature of my blood rises, heating my cheeks even more. Every stride of his long legs in sleek black dress pants synchronizes with the thumping of my heart. Add some dry ice smoke and the song "Coffee" by Hippie Sabotage and it would be a stinking movie scene. By the time he reaches me, the perfectly groomed dark hair dusting his toned bare chest meets me just above eye-level. With his open, crisp white shirt clinging to his broad shoulders, he towers above me and I almost fall over.

"Niccolo Mancini." I breathe his name in a proper Italian accent as my body seizes in place and I look up into his gorgeous face.

Ho…ly…shit.

"I'm impressed." His deep voice with its thick, Italian accent vibrates in my ears. "You pronounce it very well." He chuckles.

My tongue is nonfunctional and all that comes out of my mouth is a bizarre, nervous giggle as I stumble back into Candi's desk. Thankfully, the desk prevents me from falling backwards.

Reaching both of his massive hands out towards me, he wraps them around my arms. "Are you okay?"

No, I'm mortified and want to disappear into thin air. "Yes." Another strange laugh weasels out of me as I tuck an unruly wisp of hair behind my ear. "I'm, I'm fine. Thank you."

Candi chuckles from behind us. "Nicco, this is my best friend, Destiny." She gestures her hand at me.

"It's a pleasure to meet you," he pauses. "Destiny." The way he says my name is so damn sexy. The man *is* sex. Everything about him exudes sex. Lowering his head, he leans toward me. *What's he doing?* The scent of stale smoke drifts into my nostrils as he gently kisses my left cheek and then my right; a traditional Italian greeting. As he draws back, I try not to contort my face from the stench of cigarette smoke still lingering in my nose.

A nervous laugh huffs out of me. "Yes, it's nice to meet you as well, Niccolo."

"Please, my friends call me Nicco." Finally releasing his grip from my arms, he takes a step back. "You're going to help us, yes?"

"Huh?" Ever since I saw him in Don Matteo, I've been fantasizing about him and Candi knows it. Now she wants me to pose with him? I can't believe she didn't tell me he's one of the models she's shooting today. Not that she had to, but a little heads up would've been nice. I could've prepared myself to not be in shock and behaving like a weirdo.

"Until Gigi arrives, you're going to help us, yes?"

"Oh, yes." I nod, further processing the situation. "No." I stammer as I shake my head and wiggle my finger back and forth.

"No? You're not going to help us?" With a furrow etched in his forehead, he looks over at Candi, then returns his gaze to me.

"Well, your model…"

"Gigi. And not mine." He smiles.

The sexiest man in the on earth is smiling at me. I think I may pass out. "Right, yes, Gigi." I clap my hands together, so nervous I think I'm going to pee my pants. "She's on her way. I'm sure she'll be here soon." My tongue behaves like it's never been used before and my embarrassment continues to burn in my cheeks. "And you'll be all set." I try to plaster a polite smile on my face.

"Okay." The pitch of his voice slides from low to high as he says it. He shifts away from me and looks at Candi, who gives him a nod. Pivoting, he walks out of her office.

As though detached from my body, my feet propel my body toward Candi. Her head is jetted forward and her arms shoot out to her sides, hands waving as if to shout, "What the fuck?"

"No." I sharply whisper.

"Destiny." Her voice is just as sharp, but she's not whispering.

"Candi. No." I cock my head to the side and wiggle my finger at her.

"Des. You said you'd help me. I *need* you." Her pleading eyes are too much for me.

"Candice Alessandra Gamal." A shit-eating grin spreads across her face as I use her full name. "You owe me."

"I do." She squeals and squeezes me.

When she lets go, I look her dead in the eyes. "Big time."

"I do. I do." She waggles her head as she holds my hands.

"How am I supposed to get through this?" The shy little girl inside me wants to hide in a corner right now.

"Mmm, I've got just the thing." She opens the freezer on her mini fridge and pulls out a bottle of Patrón tequila, her favorite. Opening the glass door on the small fuchsia cabinet on top of the mini fridge, she takes out a shot glass, fills it to the top, and hands it to me. "What better way to start your birthday?" Her smile is playfully evil.

Though I know I'm going to regret it, I down the shot because I also know it's the only way I'm going to get through a mock photo shoot with Niccolo Mancini. As the smooth liquid slides down my throat, my neck and face instinctively tighten and grimace as my tongue darts out of my mouth.

"Attractive." Candi laughs. "Just don't do that out there, okay?"

9

"Deal."

"Tina will get you set up with an outfit. She always brings extra sizes and outfits so I'm sure she'll have something that fits you." She cages me in her arms and breathes a sigh. "Thank you." Releasing me, she squeals. "Happy birthday."

As I walk over to Tina, I catch Nicco's gaze on me. I feel a little bad for being such a bumbling oaf and then telling him I wouldn't help them. Candi heads toward him and I'm sure she'll let him know I'll be helping out after all.

Tina's flipping through a bunch of dresses and jumpsuits on a clothing rack when I reach her. Candi must've already shared the plan with her about me standing in for the female model. She's been with Candi for years and is a perfectionist at her job. I haven't seen her in a year or two and spot a few gray hairs swirling through her tidy bun that's secured with an eyeshadow brush.

"Still a size two?" she asks, briefly turning toward me to smile, then continuing to flip through the rack as her glasses slide a few centimeters farther down the slope of her pug nose.

"Yup." Still as scrawny as ever.

"Oh this. This will be *per*fect." Pulling a silky white jumpsuit from the rack, she holds it up to me and looks me up and down over the top of her glasses. "I'm going to put a little more makeup on you and grab some heels. Seven and a half?"

"Um, yes, but I don't think I need the makeup. I'm just standing in."

"Yeah, it'll be fun though." Taking her glasses off her face, she lets them dangle from the chain attached to each arm and grabs a sassy pair of white heels from another rack. Then she drags over a stool to the vanity where the bright lights must be illuminating every pore on my face. "Here, sit down. We've gotta be quick so we'll just put a little on."

I sit on the stool and raise my eyebrows at her as I smile. Moving her glasses from the shelf of her breasts, she secures them snugly against the bridge of her nose and tilts her head from side to side. A big grin spreads across her face. "Yup," she says, then winks at me, saying nothing more. Before I know what she's even doing, she's put moderate false eyelashes on me, given me a slight smokey eye, and dabbed on a deep burgundy lipstick.

"Okay, now go throw this on. Be careful of your lips." She hands me the jumpsuit and points me to the curtain of the dressing area.

I put on the jumpsuit and the silky fabric feels luxurious against my skin. I don't wear clothes like this, but I'd love to. The plunge of the neckline is way lower than anything I'd wear and my non-existent cleavage certainly doesn't fill the plunge. If that wasn't enough to make me uncomfortable, there are thigh-high slits on the front of both legs. There's no mirror in here so I can't see the full effect of what's going on, but I know I can't walk out from behind this curtain.

Holding the curtain around my neck, I pop my head out. "Um, Tina? Do you have something, uh, a little less…"

"Revealing?" She finishes my thought. "No, dear. Not with me." She gives me an understanding smile. "Come on out. Let's see."

"Um, give me a sec, okay?" I shrink back behind the curtain and try to find the guts to step out and let anyone see me in this getup. I don't have the body or personality for an outfit like this. Candi would look sensational in it. Growing up, she blossomed into her body early, while puberty skipped me.

Before I can even try to plan an escape, Candi comes in with half a shot glass filled.

As soon as she sees me, she lets out a whistle. "Damn. You look fuckin' hot," she coos, handing me the shot glass. "You're wearing *this* tonight."

"I can't wear this out." I refute, adjusting the thin spaghetti strap on my shoulder.

"Oh, yes you can and you *are*."

"I look ridiculous," I say, downing the half-shot. "You're lucky I love you so much."

"Okay, come on. Let's get this moving along. We have a

birthday to celebrate." She grabs my hand and I follow her out and over to the setup where Nicco is standing and waiting.

The backdrop is a light and dark gray floral fabric and long strings of crystal baubles hang from above. A massive, 8-foot-tall mirror stands in the corner, it's silver frame intricately carved and detailed with crystals and pearls. What looks like a refurbished vintage burgundy brocade chair sits in front of the mirror on a light gray shag carpet.

As we approach him, Nicco's eyes are on me, a quick sweep from my feet to my face. His eyes blink and he pulls in his lips, then runs the barely visible tip of his tongue between his slightly parted lips. He must be holding back a laugh. I knew it. I *do* look ridiculous. Candi releases my hand and walks into her setup.

"Okay, we're almost ready. Nicco." She looks up at him. "I want you just a little bit shiny." She grabs a bottle of oil from a nearby table.

Before I can say anything, she takes my hand in hers and squeezes a few drops of oil into my palm. I look down into my hand and then back up at her. She's out of her mind if she thinks I'm going to rub my oil-covered hands on this sexy man's chest.

No...freaking...way.

"Okay, you do this. I need to make a couple adjustments to my cameras." She turns and walks away, leaving me standing there with a palm full of oil.

With my hand held open, I look up at him, pretty certain that the expression on my face reveals how terrified I am. I have no poker face.

"You look beautiful." The baritone timbre of his voice shoots a shiver from the tail of my spine all the up to the base of my head.

Right, I look beautiful. As compared to the gorgeous, voluptuous women he's surrounded by daily and probably has wild, passionate sex with. His playboy reputation precedes him. "You don't have to mock me."

He squints his eyes. "What does it mean, mock? I don't know this word."

I'm forgetting that English isn't his first language. "It means to make fun of," I say, looking down into my hands and rubbing the oil between my palms, trying desperately to avoid eye contact with him. "I'll just, uh, try to warm this up a little for you."

"Why do you say I'm making fun?"

I continue rubbing my hands and slow my pace, still avoiding his eyes. "It's just, well, you're around beautiful women all the time. And…" I'm now rubbing my fingers together as my tongue twists around inside my mouth. "I'm not…"

In one gentle movement, he curls his large index finger under my chin and lifts my face toward his. Our eyes lock. I don't move. A tiny gasp hitches deep in my chest.

"You are beautiful." His reverence stuns me.

Two arms wrap around mine from behind me, grabbing and twisting my wrists. "It's warm," Candi says as she separates my hands and smacks them onto Nicco's chest. I snap my head toward her as she walks away saying, "Let's go."

Oh God, oh God, oh God. "I'm, I'm sorry." I look back up into his smokey eyes.

"It's okay."

Returning my gaze to his chest, I lift my hands from his warm skin and delicately swirl the oil around with my fingertips. I'm living inside a fantasy right now. Then I start patting his chest with my hands like I'm patting a baby's bottom. Though part of me wants to be doing just about anything but this, I'm also incredibly aroused. I can't believe I'm touching his chest right now. I'm trying so hard to ignore the sensual visions from his movie that are invading my thoughts.

"I think you need to rub it in," he says, placing both of his large hands on top of mine, dwarfing them, and rubbing our combined hands in circles on his hard chest, erect nipples, and down his tight, rippling abs. Whether his intention is to help me feel less uncomfortable or to turn me on, I have no idea, but right now my mind is racing with wild and dirty thoughts and my salivary glands are in overdrive. My heart thumps in my ears.

He would be an amazing muse for one of my romance novels. I write scenes like this in my books, but I've never experienced one. Holy hell, this is hot. My sex life has been pretty standard, I guess. Okay, kind of boring. And recently, non-existent. But that's why I write the stories I write. I write about the kind of love that doesn't exist and the kind of passion people like me only ever read about, dream about, or see in movies. That kind of passion isn't real. It hasn't been for me anyway.

I need to get a grip on myself. This sure will feed some fantasies and inspiration though.

"Okay." Candi's voice breaks the hot moment. "Let's do this so we can go party." She hands me a wet towel.

I wipe my hands on it and offer it to Nicco. Taking the towel, he wipes his. "Thank you for your help." I don't know why, but with his playboy reputation, I keep expecting the delivery of his words to be dripping with insincerity, but it's quite the opposite.

He hands the towel to Roy, one of Candi's assistants, and Candi starts giving us instructions on where she wants us. She has Nicco stand behind the chair and tells me to sit in it. As soon as I sit, my legs slide out between the two high slits of silky material. I quickly try to figure out a way to drape the material over my legs but it's not working. The thin pieces of fabric drop between my legs, leaving them exposed.

"No, no," Candi says. "Leave it like that, it's perfect."

I look up at Nicco and see him watching me, expressionless and professional, as I flounder.

"Beautiful. Open your knees a little, Des. Don't worry, we can't see anything." The tequila is definitely kicking in because I do as she says and spread my knees wider. "Okay, I like that, Des. Now I want you to keep looking up at Nicco and lean back in the chair. Rest your left arm on the arm of the chair and your right arm by your side."

My nerves settle a little more and I do as she instructs. The clicking snaps of her camera echo in my ears.

"Now, Nicco, I want you to come around here to the side of Destiny and squat down. You're going to look directly into her eyes and I want your hand on her inner thigh. Just delicately rest it there."

What the hell is Candi doing to me right now?

Nicco places his hand gently on my inner thigh and I flinch a little.

"Is this okay?" he asks my permission which I didn't expect.

I take a stalled breath. "Yes, it's okay."

More snaps from Candi's camera. Nicco's gaze holds my eyes captive.

"Slide your hand a little higher for me Nicco. Roy, shift the key light to the left about six inches."

Keeping his eyes locked on mine, Nicco moves his hand higher up my thigh. My chest rises and falls as my breathing speeds up.

"Good, Nicco. A little higher. I want to see desire in your eyes."

As he glides his hand even farther up my inner thigh, I feel wetness between my legs.

"Yes. Nice." Click, click.

Without further direction from Candi, he inches just a little higher. My breath hitches in my chest, my knees responsively spread a little more.

"I love this." Click, click, click. "Okay. Now I want you both standing."

Nicco breaks our gaze, stands, and reaches out his hand to help me up. Between the adrenaline rush and the tequila, I'm a touch dizzy and lose my balance. He wraps his hands around my waist to steady me and heat blazes through my body.

"Are you okay?" His eyebrows draw together and concern washes his handsome face.

"Yes. I'm okay. Thank you." Holding onto his muscular arms, I try to slow my breathing and keep my knees from buckling beneath me.

"Let's move the chair." Candi motions to Roy and he moves the chair. "I want you standing in front of the mirror." She approaches us, positioning Nicco and then ushering me into the side of his body. "Nicco, I want your hand around her lower back and Des, I want your hand on Nicco's chest. Then look at each other."

We assume our positions and touching his chest again has my blood heating. I can't believe I'm in his strong arms, staring into his sultry eyes with his lips only inches from mine.

"This is for perfume guys. I want passion, desire. Nicco, pull her in closer for me."

He tightens his grip around my waist, sealing my body against his. Candi wants desire? Yup, desire is definitely what's pulsing through me right now. I could swear I hear a growl under his breath.

"I'm here." A female voice announces, shattering the moment.

We look over at the devastatingly gorgeous woman who entered the studio.

"Gigi, finally." I know Candi's doing her best to stifle her frustration and be professional.

Nicco still has his arm around me and he turns my face to meet his. "You did great. Thank you again for your help. I know you didn't want to."

"I, well." I lift my hand from his chest and step back, causing him to loosen his grip. "Candi's my best friend and, she needed my help, so…"

"Still, I want to thank you."

"You're welcome." I tuck my hair behind my ear and walk into the area behind the lights.

A flurry of activity ensues and Gigi comes out of the dressing area in a different white jumpsuit than mine, filling it extraordinarily well. Her body has curves in all the right places, her flawless olive skin is perfectly tanned, and her facial features are exquisite. She's sheer perfection and drips sexiness.

Sauntering over to me, she introduces herself. "Hello, I'm Giovanna. Thank you for stepping in to help with lighting while I was delayed," she says, stroking her long dark hair and looking at Nicco.

I guess I'm supposed to call her Giovanna and not Gigi. "I'm Destiny. You're welcome." Standing next to her, I feel like a curveless toothpick wearing a potato sack.

"Okay, let's do this." With her camera in her hand, Candi motions for Giovanna to sit in the chair where I was sitting minutes ago, gazing into the most seductive eyes I've ever seen.

Hiding in the shadows behind the light fixtures, I watch Nicco and Giovanna entangle themselves while Candi snaps her camera. The most absurd twinge of jealousy snarls inside me. They'll probably have sex tonight.

After about ten minutes, I can't watch anymore. I quietly sneak off to Candi's office and snuggle into her plush, oversized, fuchsia chair. Closing my eyes, I let my mind return to the steamy moments I shared with Nicco. Inspiration smashes into me out of nowhere and I quickly grab a notepad and pen from Candi's desk. I'm scribbling so fast to keep up with the scenes racing through my head.

Several hours later, I hear clapping and Candi's voice shout, "That's a wrap!" Within seconds, she's in her office.

"Okay birthday girl, get up, it's time to celebrate." She holds out her hand, which I grab, and yanks me out of the cozy chair. "Whatcha writing there?" She eyes the notepad and gets her purse. "Did inspiration hit?"

I nod vigorously and know I'm smiling like a kid.

"That's great. I know you've been in a slump." Though the words sting, she's not wrong and I know she says them with sympathy.

"Yeah, it felt so good. A bunch of scenes came rushing at me and I wrote them down as fast as I could."

"Des, that's so great." Her eyes sparkle with delight.

"Hey, what *was* that back there?"

"What do you mean?"

"I mean, what the hell were you doing to me? Having us all — you know." I twist my arms and legs around each other and bug my eyes out.

"What? That's my job. That's what I do. Besides, I know you're hot for him and have been fantasizing about him ever since you saw that movie. I just gave you the experience of a lifetime." She shrugs her shoulders up and down a few times, playfully teasing me.

"Um, yeah, you sure did. And why didn't you tell me he was the one you were photographing today?" I park my hands on my hips.

"I don't know. I just didn't think of it." She loops her purse onto her shoulder. "Come on, let's go. They're probably waiting for us."

I drop my hands to my sides. "Who's probably waiting for us?"

"I invited Nicco, Gigi, and the crew to join us. You don't mind, do you?"

My entire body tightens. "You mean *he's* coming?"

"Do you not want me to come?" From behind me, Nicco's deep, raspy voice climbs the length of my spine, startling me.

Shit. I turn to see him standing in the doorway of Candi's office. "Yes, yes of course I do." *No, no I really don't.*

"They'll give us a ride, then we only have to Uber back to your house later."

"Great." I grit my teeth behind my smile as I rip out the pages from Candi's notepad and tuck them in my purse.

2

Nicco

Ever since I shot to fame, what feels like overnight, about a year ago, my life has changed dramatically. I went from being a no-name actor to getting fired from my acting job to being a gardener for three years.

Now, I have ten million followers on Instagram, I've starred in a wildly successful erotic movie, and I'm making albums of my own music. My life is incredible and I'm grateful for how blessed I am.

One thing I'm learning about fame is that sometimes fans have a hard time differentiating a character from the person playing the character. Men seem to think I'm going to whip out a gun and kill them and women want me to kidnap them and have sex with them. It's very strange. Whenever I'm interviewed or talk to fans, I do my best to distinguish myself as being separate from the character that skyrocketed my career.

Outsiders may look at my life with envy and think I have it all; success, fame, wealth — the world at my feet. But, there's one thing missing: love.

My fame has brought me two kinds of women: either hot women who think they're better than everyone else or star-crazed fans who cry and tell me they love me, even though they know nothing about me. The hot ones fulfill a basic sexual desire for a while before we part ways. I learned long ago not to hope for anything more when it comes to women and relationships. That's the way it's been. And I'm afraid that's the way it will always be.

Though I've learned to accept this as my reality, a petite, fair-skinned, blue-eyed, blonde caught my attention from the moment she turned around and stumbled backwards.

Destiny's awkwardness is quite charming. The fact that she's pretty and doesn't know it makes her even more attractive. When she came out in that white jumpsuit, I had a hard time focusing. Once she stopped fumbling with the fabric of her jumpsuit and let herself relax, she was unbelievably sexy.

Though our interaction was brief, something inside me made me want to know more about her. When Candi invited us to join them, I didn't hesitate to accept.

Destiny

Candi and I get in Roy's car while Giovanna, Nicco, and Shawn, another one of Candi's crew, get into Nicco's car. The rest of her crew pile into a third car.

Roy pulls up to the valet parking at Songbird Plaza and we get out and wait for the others to arrive. Once we're gathered, we head into the club.

Candi and Nicco lead the way to the hostess stand. Several steps behind them, I see all the women and a few men near us peeling off Nicco's clothes with their eyes. How strange that must feel for him and so violating.

Candi waves at me and we all fall in line behind the hostess who leads us down a black-marble hallway to several elevators. I've never been here before so I have no idea where we're going. We get into the elevator and Candi loops her arm in mine, bending her knees alternately to the beat of the music and grinning from ear to ear.

As the elevator doors open, we're greeted by a huge private suite. I can't believe she did this for my birthday. It's a little over the top for me and she knows I don't need any pomp and circumstance.

I just want my sushi, cupcakes, a good movie, and my best friend.

We exit the elevator and I scan the room. Squeezing her arm in mine, I whisper, "Candi, you didn't have to do all this. It must be expensive to have a private suite with a bartender."

"You're worth it, but I didn't." She winks.

Then I hear the hostess. "Thank you so much, Mr. Mancini. We're happy to have you here and accommodate your request. Let Barry know of anything you need and we'll get it for you," she says, gesturing to the bartender. "Please enjoy your evening." She smiles politely at him and gets back into the elevator.

I'm so confused right now. Surely Nicco didn't do this for my birthday. I guess this is just what he's used to. But he didn't know we were coming here until sometime during the time we were at Candi's studio and he was in the photo shoot the whole time. Maybe because of who he is, they were able to get him a private suite? But this place looks like it would be booked solid.

"Come on." Candi grabs my hand and leads me to the bar.

I stop trying to figure out how we're in this amazing suite and follow her to the black marble-topped bar where we each sit on a black, buttery-soft, leather-covered stool. They sure do like their black marble. I must admit, it adds to the classy style of the entire place. With the silky fabric falling between my legs, I make sure I keep myself facing the bar.

"Good evening, ladies. I'm Barry," he says as he grabs two cocktail napkins, stamped with a silver logo of a songbird inside a diamond shape, and places one in front of each of us. "I hear we have a birthday girl in the house tonight." He smiles as he adjusts the black bow tie around the collar of his perfectly pressed tuxedo shirt.

"That we do," Candi says as she stands up from her stool and hugs me. "And she's right here."

"Well, happy birthday." He smiles broadly at me. "What can I get you both?"

"I'm thinking shots all around." Candi raises her voice as she turns and waves everyone towards us.

Oh boy, here we go.

"Nine slippery nipples please, Barry," she announces as everyone makes their way toward us. It's my favorite shot.

Barry gets straight to work and we watch him line up the shot glasses. Candi holds onto the bar top and dances to the thumping music, swinging her pink hair to the beat.

Someone is hovering next to me. I look up and Nicco's dark brown eyes meet mine. My heart lurches to a syncopated rhythm.

"Do you like it?" he asks, expressionless.

"Like what?"

"The suite." He looks around the room then returns his gaze to me.

"Oh yes, it's incredible."

"Good, I'm glad you like it. Happy birthday," he says, remaining stoic.

Wait, what? Now I have to ask.

"Nicco, did you get this suite for my birthday?" I cringe inside, unsure I should be asking because it might sound presumptive.

"Yes," he says flatly as Barry lines up the shots in front of Candi.

She passes out the shots and spins my stool so I'm facing the group that is now gathered in a circle around us. I fumble around with the fabric of my jumpsuit, trying to cover my exposed legs but nothing's working.

"Happy birthday to my best friend in the entire world," she says as she raises her shot glass into the center of the circle and everyone follows suit. "Cheers!"

"Cheers!" everyone shouts in unison and we toss back our shots.

Giovanna's position in the circle is straight in front of me and I catch her send a fake smile with a sort of side-nod in my direction. I don't know if it's meant for me or Nicco.

"Okay, what can I get everyone to drink tonight?" Barry asks as we start putting our empty shot glasses on the bar.

I spin myself back toward the bar and Candi orders us s'mores martinis.

Nicco waits until everyone has ordered. When Barry makes eye contact with him, he smiles. "Do you have a Macallan whiskey on hand?"

Barry gives him a discerning nod. "We do, sir. Coming right up."

The buzz of chatter from the group grows and I look up at Nicco.

"Nicco, I don't know what to say. Thank you so much. You really didn't have to do this."

"I know." That's it. That's all he says.

"While Barry gets our drinks, let's get a group shot," Candi says, walking over to a tufted dark red leather sofa, in a grouping of four that are arranged in an open square against a wall covered in a black-on-black damask print.

Nicco sits at one end of the sofa and Candi ushers me in next to him then sits on the other side of me followed by two more people. Giovanna plants herself on the arm of the sofa, next to Nicco. I struggle with the damn jumpsuit fabric again and Nicco grabs my hand.

"It's useless. Leave it." The man's expressionless face is infuriating. Because of his reputation, I keep thinking he has sex-on-the-brain, but I might be entirely wrong. Maybe he's trying to help me feel less uncomfortable. I don't get it.

"Nope, hold on. There's too many of us. We need to squeeze in. Lily, you sit on Shawn's lap." She waves in their direction. "And Fiona, you sit on the arm like Gigi's doing." She looks to either side of her. "Almost. Des, you're in Nicco's lap."

Before I can object, his large hands are around my waist, pulling me onto his lap. My stomach quivers. Giovanna's now looming above me, my stomach winds tighter. With Nicco's arm around my waist, his hand naturally falls to the top of my bare thigh, sending warmth through my body. His other arm is around Candi's shoulders.

Roy stands in front of us, ready to take our picture with his cell phone.

"Wait. Roy, I want you in the picture too. Hey, Barry," Candi calls out. "Can you come take our picture quickly?"

All I can think about is Nicco's hand on my thigh and I want this picture taken and over. I'm sure he's very used to touching women's bare thighs so it doesn't faze him in the least, but this woman's thighs aren't used to being touched and certainly not by the extremely hot Niccolo Mancini.

Barry comes out from behind the bar and takes Roy's phone as Roy sits on the floor in the middle of the group.

"Okay. 1, 2, 3." Barry snaps several pictures.

"Stay where you are," Roy instructs us as he gets up and takes his phone to check the pictures.

Hurry, before he feels my heart beating wildly against his chest.

Roy swipes through the pictures. "Okay, all good. Thanks man."

"You bet. Drinks coming right up. Also, let me know if you want something to eat. I can have your food brought here." Barry goes back behind the bar and continues making our drinks.

We unravel from the sofa and stand up, dispersing back to the bar.

"What did you order, Nicco?" Giovanna asks through her perfectly pouty lips.

"You know what I ordered Gigi."

"I know." She bats her thick, feathery-long lashes at him. "I know everything about you because we've been in love since we were little." Her voice is now an octave higher and she's pursed her lips into the shape of a kiss. There's no hesitation in marking her territory.

"Gigi, go mingle." Unphased by her flirtatiousness, he sends her away.

She sulks and walks away, flipping her long, shiny brunette hair and rocking her hips from side to side. I have no idea what their relationship is at this point, but there's definitely some kind of long-term connection between them.

Barry starts setting our drinks on the bar top. While everyone takes their drinks and heads to the opening overlooking the dance floor, Candi and I sit together at the bar.

"I know this is more my scene than yours, but maybe you can let loose a little. Will you dance with me? You know you love dancing with me." She gives me her little-girl smile because she knows she's right. While the club scene isn't my thing, I do love to dance, especially with her. "Besides, you look hot so let's not waste this sizzling outfit you've got on." She raises her glass and takes a sip.

"I feel very out of place." I look down at my drink while a lump grows in my throat and tears swell in my eyes.

She puts her hand on my leg and rubs gently. "Hey, hey, what's going on?"

Thankful it's just her and I at the bar, I confess. "I don't know. I guess I just thought I'd be in a different place in life by the time I turned thirty, you know?" I hold back the tears that sting behind my eyes because I don't want to start blubbering.

"Oh, honey." She takes my hand in hers and tugs a little, making me look at her. "Des, where you are is temporary. You're just in a little slump right now. You told me you had a good writing sesh back at my studio. Who knows, maybe that photo shoot was the spark of inspiration you've been waiting for."

"Maybe." I sip my martini, recalling how hot and bothered I was with Nicco's hands on me and then being in his arms.

"And, I'm sorry to say it, but you really need to let go of Henry. You don't like him and whatever it is you two are doing isn't going anywhere." She takes a longer sip.

Oh, Henry. He's not my boyfriend, but we go to dinner every now and then. I'm pretty sure he wants more, but there's just no spark. Candi thinks he's a dud and she's not wrong.

"I know." I sigh. "I *know*. I guess I just feel bad. He really is a nice guy. So he's a little boring and I'm not at all attracted to him. But, it's nice to have someone to go to dinner with every now and then." I lick a little of the chocolate syrup and graham cracker crumbs off the rim of my glass and take another sip.

"It's time to let him go and open yourself up to your soul mate finding you."

The second she lays it out there is the second I wonder if my soul mate is out there or if he even exists. Is there really a soul mate for every person? I always believed there was, especially watching my parents and how in love they still are. Recently, I've started to doubt it. I want to believe my soul mate is out there, somewhere. But I just don't know anymore.

"This is going to be an amazing year for you. I can feel it." Excitement rises in her voice as she takes a big swig of her martini.

"Oh, yeah?"

"Absolutely." She smiles so big I can't help but smile back. "Come on, drink up. We have dancing to do." She downs the last of her drink.

"Then dance we shall," I announce, then lick the remaining chocolate syrup and graham cracker crumbs off the rim of my glass and down the rest of my martini.

The group is huddled at the opening that overlooks the dance floor below us. They're dancing and drinking as they watch the crowd. Nicco's standing off to the side, a bystander, taking it all in. He's barely had any of his drink.

Holding my hand, Candi leads me into the group and we dance together to the thumping of the loud music. Sexual energy permeates the air above the sea of dancing bodies below us. The slippery nipple shot and martini kick in and Candi and I dirty-dance, like we used to back in the day. Every now and then, I catch Nicco watching us. I can't blame him. Candi's an amazing dancer and her magnetism and voluptuous body draw thirsty gazes from anyone near her.

After several songs of bumping and grinding, most of us head back to the bar for refills. Plates of fancy-looking appetizers scatter the bar top and we nibble on the delicious food. Barry serves up our drinks and everyone heads back to the opening to dance.

"Aren't you coming?" Candi asks, popping what looks like a caviar-topped scallop in her mouth.

"Yeah, I'll be right there. I'm going to rest a bit first. I'm getting older you know." I wink and smile.

"Okay, hurry up though. If you're not there soon, I'm coming to get you." She extends her arm toward me as she dance-walks away, pointing at me.

I raise my martini as if to say, "Okay." Sliding into the barstool, I've given up trying to make the fabric cover my legs and cross them. Turning toward the group, I sip my drink and watch them dance, bobbing my head to the beat.

Drink in his hand, Nicco starts walking toward me. There's that slow-motion time-warp thing again. The alcohol must be hitting me harder than I thought. Dear God, this man is hot. I take another sip of my martini.

As he walks toward me, he shifts his gaze from me to the group and then back to me. Once he reaches me, he slides into the barstool next to mine. The stale smell of smoke radiates off him and into my nose. Once again, I hold back my grimace from the foul smell.

"No more dancing?" he asks, setting his drink on top of the bar.

"I'm just taking a break." I consider getting up and joining the others, but don't want to be rude. I'm hungry so I spoon some tuna tartar onto a plate and scoop it up with a toastette, hoping to get the bite into my mouth and not drop it in my lap.

"So, tell me, Destiny, what do you do for work?" He lifts the tumbler to his lips and sips his whiskey then looks at me.

I turn my stool to face the bar and conceal my exposed legs. Wishing my body didn't react so strongly to him, I clench my thighs together. "I'm a romance author." Taking a drink of my martini, I try to breathe normally.

He nods, looking down into his drink. "What kind of romance do you write?"

"Not the kind you make movies about." Oh, how I wish the alcohol hadn't destroyed my ability to filter my thoughts before words fly out of my mouth.

He puts his glass on the bar and turns his stool toward me with a sexy grin on his face. "You've seen my work then, yes?"

Oh God. He studies my face. I hope it doesn't look as red as it feels.

I clear my throat, trying to buy time for my brain to think straight. "Um, yes. It was suggested to me."

"And what did you think?"

"Great work. Nicely done." I sound like a bumbling fool. "What I write isn't quite so — graphic."

A laugh bursts out of him that he tempers. "So, what are your stories like?"

"Well, I do have some steamy scenes." I can't look at him as I say it. "But I also make sure to build the relationship between my characters. There's a lot of heart and soul mate connection."

"You believe in soul mates?"

"Well, I write about them."

He shoots me a cunning smile. "But do you believe in them?"

"Maybe I live in a fantasy world, but I like to think there's someone specific out there for each of us." I clench my teeth, starting to feel like I have to defend my work and my beliefs, even though I'm starting to doubt them myself. I change the subject. "You don't have to babysit me, you know. Giovanna's been shooting daggers at me all night. Maybe you should go be with her." Glancing over at Giovanna, I catch another piercing stare.

"You don't want to talk to me?"

I almost thought I detected the smallest hint of hurt as he asked the question.

"No, it's not that. It's just…" I stammer. "She doesn't seem too happy that you're talking to me."

"I'll decide who I spend my time with and who I talk to. And I'm not the least bit interested in Gigi," he deadpans. "I *am* enjoying your company however." He leans in, ever so slightly, tilts his head down, and shifts his gaze quickly to my mouth then back up to my eyes. The air around us is still and somehow quiet in spite of the thumping music.

"Oh. I thought you were…together." Especially after she

basically peed around you in a circle earlier.

"Gigi?" He uprights himself, glances at her, and looks back at me. "No. Never. Gigi's been chasing me since we were kids. She's like a little sister to me."

"She doesn't look at you like you're a big brother." I shake my head and raise an eyebrow. "Still, I'm sure there's a ton of women here you'd rather spend your time with. You don't need to talk to me because it's my birthday. Besides, I'm not your type." *Mr. Playboy.*

Never releasing my gaze, he asks, "No? So, what's my type?"

I clasp together my clammy palms, wishing I could sink into the floor and slither away. I'll answer his question then excuse myself and find Candi to let her know I'm leaving.

"Someone like Giovanna or even Candi. But Candi just physically, your personalities aren't a good match." *What am I saying? Shut up and get out of here.*

"Why them?" Crinkle-lines form between his brows. "What makes them my type?"

"They're gorgeous and have ridiculously perfect bodies."

"You don't see yourself that way?"

"No, it's not that I don't see myself that way. I'm just *not* that way."

"Is that why you're hiding over here by yourself and you don't want me to talk to you?"

Ouch. "That's not true. I'm not hiding." Now the truth comes out. "I'm just — not used to people being aware of me." I finish my drink as though it will somehow erase what I just said.

"I'm aware of you." He stares directly into my eyes and the room around us disappears. "I'm very aware of you."

He releases my gaze and raises his hand toward Barry then points at my empty glass.

"Where do you get your inspiration from for your steamy scenes? I'm curious about how authors come up the scenes they write."

"Well, it's not from personal experience, I can tell you that." My face, neck, and ears grow impossibly hot as the words that spilled out of my mouth register in my head. Terrified to look at him, I try to backpedal. "What I mean to say is that sometimes we have to use our imagination, you know, to fill in the blanks, so to speak." My backpedaling is failing miserably.

He lets out a loud belly laugh that tempers into a broad smile as he looks at me.

Nothing like admitting to a confirmed sex-god that your sex life is pathetic. Ugh. Please, can the floor just open up and swallow me?

"So, if you have no personal experience, then how do you write it?" His smile is gone and he sounds genuinely curious.

I fumble with the fabric, trying to drape it across at least one leg, and failing. "Well, we research. We read books, and — and we watch movies. It's research. And then we create the fantasy with words in our stories." I'm a bumbling fool.

He rubs his index finger across his mustache. "So, you watch a movie, fantasize about someone in the movie, and then write out your fantasy?"

I think I'm going to pass out. "I'm not having sex with you." *Oh God, where are my filters?*

Another bellowing laugh erupts from him. "Who said I want to have sex with you?"

"You do know you have a reputation for being a playboy, right? Always rotating through women?" I swirl my index finger in the air.

"You know you can't believe everything you read, right?"

"True." I'll give him that. "Okay, convince me you're not a total player." Why did that sound like a dare?

3

—

Destiny

Barry clears my glass and napkin, setting down a clean napkin and freshly made s'mores martini.

"Okay," Nicco says. "I will convince you." Again, he's expressionless. And again, it's maddening. He turns my stool to face him. "You're cold."

I'm always cold. I rarely admit it because I'm usually the only one in the room who's cold and I don't like to complain about it. "No, I'm okay."

Curling his index finger under my chin and lifting it, he locks his eyes on mine. "You're cold," he punctuates.

Instantly, I know my extremely sensitive nipples are greeting him through the silken white fabric, and adrenaline runs through me, making my nipples even harder. Where I would've expected some sleezy, flirtatious, sexual reference from him, instead I'm met with discreet and respectful candor as he stands up, takes off his suit jacket, and drapes it over my shoulders.

"Thank you." I tug the lapels closer together across my chest as warmth flushes into my cheeks.

"This is your favorite drink?" he asks, sitting back down on his stool then pointing at the martini.

"Yes. I don't drink often, but when I do, I like something sweet. I have a huge sweet-tooth." I reach for my martini to take a drink and, in full Destiny-klutzery, I manage to graze the rim with the side of my hand, smearing chocolate syrup and graham cracker crumbs from below my pinky down to my wrist. Thank God I didn't knock the whole thing over. That would've been a classic move and thoroughly embarrassing.

Holding onto his jacket so it doesn't fall off my shoulders, I reach across the bar for a napkin to wipe off my hand. Nicco stops me mid-reach, takes my wrist in his hand and wraps his fingers firmly, yet gently, around it. He grabs a napkin, looking back at me with his smoldering eyes.

Lifting my wrist, he slowly wipes the chocolate syrup off the meat of my hand then moves down to my wrist. The seductive way he drags out the movement sends heat burning up my chest, through my neck, and scorching my face. The rooms spins and blurs around us. My increasing pulse thumps in my ears as he inspects his work.

"Tell me," he says, releasing my wrist. "What is your soul mate like? I don't see a ring on your finger. Maybe you haven't found him yet? Or he hasn't found you?"

"No, not yet. But I will." I pause. "Someday."

"Tell me about him. I want to know."

Triggered by him, I lash out. "Well, he has a stable job, not uncertain jobs like you and I have. He's loyal, and by that I mean he doesn't sleep around. He definitely doesn't smoke or have tattoos." With my filters betraying me, it comes out more snide than I'd intended.

Nicco looks down into his drink, then lifts his gaze forward and chuckles. Ceasing his laugh, he turns his expressionless face towards me and follows with his body. With a devious smile, he leans forward, closing the gap between us before I can continue with my description. "So, someone the opposite of me."

"Yes." My throat thickens. "The *exact* opposite of you."

He chuckles again and nods.

"Well, what about you? Have you found your soul mate?"

"No. I don't believe in such things. Besides, I'm finally building the career I want. I wouldn't have time for that even if I did. You can't have everything." Instead of the sips he'd been taking, he tosses a gulp of whiskey down his throat.

"You can if you want it. You have to want it. You can't expect to find your soul mate when you sleep around with all kinds of different women. With your physical appearance, you're going to be swarmed by beautiful women forever. Do you plan to just have meaningless sex for the rest of your life?" *Filters, FILTERS.*

"What do you know about my love life?"

I cock my head to the side. "I told you, Nicco, you have a reputation."

"And I told you, you can't always believe what you hear." He pauses. "So, you like the way I look?" He stares straight into my eyes. I'm not sure he knows.

"Women across the world are hot for you. You don't need me to validate that for you."

"Then you *don't* like the way I look?" Now I can't tell if he's messing with me or if I seriously hurt his feelings.

"No. That's not what I said. You...you're twisting my words around. I didn't say that."

"Maybe you like pretty-boys. Like Brad Pitt. Is he your type?" He air-quotes, 'type.'

I bat down his hands. "No, I don't have a type."

"So, when you make up the hero for your next book, what's he like in your fantasy?"

I draw back my head, shaking it. "I'm not telling you that."

"I already know you fantasize. I'm sure you have a vibrant imagination." He pauses, studying my eyes. "So tell me, what's he like?"

I break his gaze and spin my stool away from him and toward the bar, clearing my throat. "He's..." I hesitate. How did I get myself into this conversation? Thank goodness for those drinks or I'd be shaking from nerves right now. Will he put two and two together? "Taller than me with dark hair and brown eyes. Broad shoulders." Envisioning the man I'm describing, I let my eyes drift upward. Will he know who it is? "He's muscular yet gentle. Confident, passionate, and knows how to please a woman. He appreciates and revels in the anticipation and sensuality of foreplay."

"So." His voice breaks my reverie, bringing me back. "Someone like me."

I turn my face toward him. His gaze freezes me. "No," I say firmly. "He desires me."

He spins my stool to face him and drags it toward him with my legs between his, locking his eyes on mine. "Someone *exactly* like me."

A blaze of heat lights up my body and I suck in a breath. Yes, it's him. I've just described him to him and now he knows I fantasize about him. I open my mouth and nothing comes out. Nothing.

"Are you two going to sit here and talk all night?" Giovanna's voice extinguishes the flames combusting between us.

I'd been holding my breath and finally exhale.

"Maybe we will," Nicco says with an edge.

"Nicco, come dance with me," she whines, tugging on the sleeve of his shirt.

"I'm not in the mood for dancing, Gigi." He looks at me. "Please excuse me." Pushing his stool back from mine, he goes to the in-suite restroom.

Bouncing up and down to the beat of the music, Giovanna orders another drink and doesn't say a word to me. Barry whips up her drink and she goes back to join the others who are still huddled together and dancing.

I've got to get my head on straight so I ask Barry for a glass of water which he promptly gets for me.

Nicco comes back from the restroom, sits on his stool, and sips his whiskey. "Where do you get your inspiration from? Also other books and movies? Sitting in a park?"

I nod. "Those, sometimes. For me, I often get visions that come to me. I don't really sit down and make up what I want to write and then write. A vision pops into my head and I have to write the story of the vision. Usually I get them after I watch a movie. I know, it sounds strange. We writers have crazy things that go on inside our heads." I chuckle at my admission.

"No, not strange. Sometimes that's how my songs come to me. So, what are you writing now? What's the story?"

I pull my lips into a grimace. "Well, I've been in a bit of a slump lately."

"Ah. I can't stand when my brain is stuck like that. What do you do when that happens?"

"I used to take walks on the beach and that usually helps. But it hasn't lately."

"No?'

"No. But I did start writing something tonight while you guys were shooting."

"Really? That's good. Can I see it?"

"No." The word flies out of my mouth. "I mean, it's really very, very rough." No, no, no. I'm not letting him get his hands on these pages. Talk about complete mortification. I'd die if he read them. My fantasies about him splayed out on paper. Oh no. Not happening.

Okay, it's time to break the seal. Although I know that I'll have to pee every ten minutes after the first one, I just can't hold it. The door to the in-suite restroom is closed and I can see light shining from underneath.

"If you'll excuse me, I need to use the restroom." I stand up, remove his jacket from my shoulders and lay it over the back of the bar stool.

"Yes, of course. I'll have a cigarette. Meet you back here?"

"Oh, um, feel free to mingle. Maybe you can find tonight's conquest." I wink at him. Hah! Look at me, winking at Niccolo Mancini. Who *am* I?

"Or not. Remember, I'm on a mission to convince you I'm someone other than what my reputation has you believing about me." He winks back at me.

"Ah, right." I waggle my finger at him and head to Candi.

"Hey, I need to pee and I think Giovanna's in this bathroom

so I'm going to scoot downstairs. Can you keep an eye on my purse for me?"

"Sure you don't want to wait?"

I shake my head and give her the universal sign of "I can't hold it" by squeezing my legs together and bouncing. She laughs and I scurry to the elevator.

When it opens on the lower level, I'm met with a sea of dancing bodies and maneuver through them as quickly as I can. As I'm about to pass a group of men, I swear one of them purposefully steps into my path and I bump into him.

"Well, hey there," he slurs.

"Oh excuse me. I'm so sorry." I tuck my head down and continue on to the restroom.

4

Nicco

I walk out to the terrace attached to our suite to have a cigarette and take in the view of the city. Getting the lighter out of my pants pocket, I flip it over in my hand a couple times, losing myself in the worn design as I rub my thumb across it, the way I've done thousands of times before. It's the only piece of my dad I have left. I think he would be proud of me, of what I've accomplished and made of myself. But there's so much more I want to do.

Mindlessly taking a cigarette out of the pack, I clasp it between my lips. Swallowing the lump that's choking my throat, I flick open my lighter and watch the flame dance. Touching the dancing flame to the end of the cigarette, I watch it ignite. Sucking in deeply, I let the first drag fill my lungs with the toxic, beautiful gray death that took my dad from me.

Another inhale flows from my core out to my arms and legs, relaxing me as I stare out into the twinkling lights of the city. Los Angeles, L.A., Hollywood, the American dream. I don't know how yet, but I'm going to make it happen. I'm going to work my fucking ass off and make the right connections to build my American dream, right here in Hollywood.

Visions of my dream-life fill my head. A lavish home, luxury cars, parties with celebrities — the high life. A twinge of emptiness hollows a hole in my heart knowing I'll experience all of this alone. Another drag to fill the hole and blur the thought with a haze of smoke.

Loneliness is the cross I bear. One I've become accustomed to carrying. Though Destiny may be right and the world sees me as a playboy, it's the only way I know how to fulfill my needs given the impossibility of ever having love.

After Ana, I understood my only value to women and I've kept my relationships with them purely sexual. I get my needs met, they get their needs met, nothing more. I know how to fuck. And I'm really good at it. Sure, it's empty and meaningless, but it serves its purpose.

I'm used to women readily spreading their legs for me. Something tells me Destiny is *not* the kind of woman I'm used to. This woman non-verbally commands respect. I have a feeling when I earn my way between Destiny's legs, it's going to be very different and hot as fuck.

She's a feisty little thing. Though I know my truth and it's what I've come to accept, something about her view of me disturbs me deep inside. In a place I burned and exiled four years ago.

Destiny. She amuses me. She intrigues me. And now she's challenged me. Though part of me wants to convince her I'm more than what she perceives, I'm not sure I'm capable of following through. Proving that I'm not just a playboy would mean exposing parts of me I no longer want the world to see. Not now, not ever.

I suck the last glorious drag and tap out my cigarette in the black marble ashtray sitting on the glass-topped table.

She'll be done by now.

Stepping back into the suite, I don't see her. Candi is dancing with the group and I go over to her.

"Did Destiny leave?" I ask, raising my voice over the music, hoping she hasn't left. I'll be pissed if she left alone in her condition.

She shakes her head. "No. She had to pee and Gigi was in this one so she went down to the public one." She points through the opening and toward the restroom on the level below.

As Candi continues dancing, I step away from the group and watch for Destiny.

Destiny

After standing in line for about ten minutes, I'm finally hiding in solitude in a stall, regretting that I didn't stay in the suite and wait for Giovanna to finish, but also relieved to be away from the group, and Nicco.

With my feet sticking to the floor, I try to wrap my head around what transpired during the last hour. With dozens of women ready to be in his company, and in his pants, at the snap of his fingers, why in the world is Nicco wasting his time talking to me? In my fuzzy head, no logical answer comes to mind. As I squat above the toilet, staring down at sassy white shoes that don't belong to me, the white veins in the black marble beneath my feet begin swirling together. Yup, I'm tipsy. It's time for me to go home. Before exiting the stall, I take a deep breath and blow it out. This is thirty. Happy birthday.

On my way back to the suite, the same man from earlier steps out in front of me as his friends close in behind me. "Where you goin' so fast?" he slurs.

Adrenaline shoots through me. "Oh, I'm here with my friends." *Stay calm.* I attempt to walk past him, but he steps in front of me again.

"How's about you get your friends and bring 'em over here and we'll all get to know each other?" he asks sloppily as he sways.

"Uh, thanks, but we're actually leaving," I say, trying to conceal my trembling.

He tugs at his already loosened necktie. "Aw, come on. It'll be fun." He steps toward me and I step back. *Shit. Why did I drink so much?*

With my next shaky breath, Nicco steps between two of the men and stands directly in front of me, turning his back to me and facing the drunk man. "Is there a problem here?"

"No man, no problem. We're just talkin' to her."

"She's with me." He reaches an arm behind himself, holding me against his back. Safety replaces my fear.

"Oh, yeah?" he hurls.

I can't see what's happening, but it sounds like the situation is escalating.

"Yeah." Nicco stands firm and doesn't move, continuing to keep his hand holding me against him.

"Well, maybe she doesn't wanna be."

Nicco nods his head and, within seconds, two bouncers are standing behind the men behind us.

"Are we gonna have a problem tonight guys?" one of the bouncers asks.

"Nope," the drunk man answers. The men separate, making space for Nicco and me to walk away. "No problem."

"I didn't think so," the bouncer says.

Nicco reaches around, takes my hand in his, and ushers me in front of him as we walk between the men. My heart lurches and pounds in my chest. While I know his words were dictated by the situation and didn't mean anything, the way he claimed me as his was kind of flattering. I've never felt so protected by a man. Yeah, Henry would *not* have done well in that situation.

Nicco leads us through the crowd of dancing bodies. It takes me two steps to keep up with his long-legged strides. He marches us down the hallway and presses the elevator button. Now that we're alone, he releases my hand and paces while we wait. When the elevator doors open, he nudges me in with his hand on the small of my back. The doors close behind us and he puts his large hands on my waist, turning me to face. Towering above me, he places his hands against the wall on either side of me. His arms stiff, he hangs his head above me.

"Why did you put yourself in danger like that?" With nostrils flaring, his anger startles me. "Do you not see how sexy you are? Men like that will eat you alive and take advantage of you. You should've stayed in the suite." He withdraws his hands, turns away from me, and then turns back to face me. Curling his hand under my chin, he gently strokes my cheek with his thumb. Concern replaces the anger in his eyes. "They could've easily hurt you."

Though I'm startled, his protectiveness is comforting and my nerves temper. And sexy? Maybe he had more drinks than I saw. Maybe I'm so tipsy I didn't hear him correctly. There's no way this man looks at me and thinks, "sexy."

Nicco

I look down into her soft blue eyes. With her blonde hair and alabaster skin, her beauty is undeniable. While I'm sure she can stand up for herself, I didn't like watching her so helpless surrounded by those assholes. I'm glad I got to her in time before something happened. I'm not typically an angry person, but when she was in danger, my blood vibrated.

"Thank you for coming to get me." Her gentle voice is like soft music in my ears and I'm frozen. Frozen by a longing I haven't felt — I've denied — for years. One brief glance at her lips.

After Ana, I refused to let myself kiss a woman. Unless I'm getting paid to play a role that requires it, I don't kiss women on the lips. Sex is sex. That's all it's become for me. I don't need to entangle it with emotions or the intimacy of a kiss. Yet right now, looking down into Destiny's eyes, it's all I can do to keep myself from leaning in and capturing her lips.

The elevator doors open and I turn around to the opening. She walks past me and toward Candi as I head to the bar. Barry comes over to me and I order another whiskey and a s'mores martini then ease back into the bar stool and watch Destiny and Candi talk.

As Barry sets my drink down, Destiny takes her purse from Candi, gets out her phone, and slings her purse onto her shoulder. After checking something on her phone, she hugs Candi. I take a sip of my drink, peeking over the rim at Destiny's long, milky legs slide out between the fabric of her jumpsuit as she walks toward me.

"Nicco, thank you so much for getting this suite for my birthday. It was a very unexpected gesture and I appreciate it."

"You're not leaving, are you?" I want to know more about her and I'm not letting her out of my sight after what happened.

She looks down toward her feet and a silky curl of her hair falls forward. When she looks back up at me, she tucks the hair behind her ear with her slender fingers.

"Yes, I — it's getting late, and I — really should get home."

I'm so used to pretentiousness women and Destiny's shyness is charming.

"Stay. Let me get you at least one birthday drink."

"You really don't have to do that. You've already done all this." She spreads her arms and looks around the suite.

"I know I don't have to. I want to."

"I really think I should go. I already ordered an Uber."

"Uber? No. Cancel it. I'll take you and Candi home when you're ready to go. Please, have one drink with me." I gesture toward the bar stool.

She hesitates and her eyes shift to Candi and then back to me. "Um, okay." She slides into the bar stool and taps on her phone, cancelling the Uber.

Barry sets the martini on a cocktail napkin in front of her.

"Wow, you're fast," she says, smiling at him.

"So, tell me." I draw her attention back to me and put my suit jacket around her shoulders again. "How did you know you wanted to be a romance author? Is that what your parents do?"

"Thank you. Oh no. My dad's retired and my mom's in the film industry." She pauses. "But actually, I suppose my mom's job influenced me a little. She's worked on a lot of romantic comedy films over the years and those stories have stuck with me."

Hmm, her mom works in the film industry. Interesting.

"What does she do?"

"She's a director. Twenty-two years now. She's worked on some amazing projects. I'm so proud of her and the work she does." She runs the tip of her tongue along the edge of her glass, licking the crushed graham crackers and chocolate syrup. My eyes are drawn to her mouth with a force I can't stop. She doesn't mean it to be sexual, but holy hell does it turn me on.

As she takes a sip of her martini, a thought pops into my head. A really fucking good thought.

"So, I have an idea. And, I think maybe it's something we can both benefit from."

"Yeah?" She turns her head to the side a bit and a crinkle forms between her brows. "What in the world would benefit both of us?"

"Okay, hear me out. You could use some help getting your career back on track, right?"

"Yes."

"My agents in Italy are great, but I'm looking for connections here in America so I can transition my career here."

"Okay." She shakes her head with a blank expression.

"I have a massive audience of women who like reading romance books. What if I allow you to write a book where I'm your main character as I was in Don Matteo? Then I can promote you and your book to my audience."

"Okay. And?" Her expression is tight as she folds her arms across her chest.

"What if you put me in touch with your mom and I work with her to make connections out here for my career? I know there's no guarantee of any kind. And your only obligation is to connect us."

She leans back in her stool, arms still crossed and eyes shifting from side to side.

"I'd like to adjust the terms of this deal." She uncrosses and recrosses her sexy legs, causing a quick spurt of adrenaline through me. She's quite alluring when her guard is down.

"Okay. How?" She has me intrigued.

"How about my main character is *you*, Niccolo Mancini?"

Now I cross my arms over my chest. "Me."

"You," she states matter-of-fact. "Not you as someone else, a character, a role. Just you as you. Now, I do write fiction, so there will be elements I create that are fictional, but the hero is you, Niccolo Mancini, in as much as you'll agree to let me write. You let me interview you and I'll write a love story around what you share."

She plays kind of dirty. And while I'm amused by this sassy side of her, I'm not sure I'm willing to let the world see that much of me. I need a cigarette.

I stand up. "Do you mind if I have a cigarette?"

"Yes, I do." Her bluntness freezes me.

Looking down into her beautiful face, I'm again struck with an urge to kiss her, to taste her lips.

"I need to think about this."

"I can give you access to the world you want. All you have to do is agree," she says, metaphorically holding my balls in the palm of her hand.

I trace her delicate features with my eyes then lock my gaze on her eyes. "I'll be right back," I say, releasing our gaze and stepping away.

"I'll see if Candi wants to catch an Uber home."

My body stiffens and I turn back to face her, spinning her stool to face me. I hang my head above her so she has to look up at me. "*I'm* taking you home," I stress. "I won't be long. Don't leave."

I stalk away from her and out to the terrace. Forgoing my usual ritual, I quickly light my cigarette and consider her adjustment to the deal I suggested. It sounds like she'll only write what I agree to. So, I can keep private what I want to keep private and only share what I'm willing to share. A few long drags on my cigarette, I blow the smoke out my nostrils and decide to accept her adjustment in return for the chance at my American dream.

Two things have me excited right now, the possibility of making my dreams come true by working in Hollywood and the thought of spending time with Destiny. One thing has me nervous, sharing the personal side of my life.

5

Nicco

When I get back inside, I don't see Destiny and exasperation surges through me. I catch Candi's eye and she points to the in-suite restroom. My temper settles.

I sit back down on my bar stool and Destiny walks over and sits back on hers.

"Did you have a chance to make your decision? Do we have a deal?" She extends her toned arm out toward me, offering her delicate hand for me to shake as a contract of our agreement.

I sigh inside my head. Still somewhat hesitant about my side of the deal, I can almost taste the life I want, it's so close. I reach out my hand.

Quickly, she withdraws her hand. "Wait. What assurance do I have that you won't vanish once you get what you want? I mean, you'll have the information you need tomorrow. How do I know you won't disappear and I'll have no way of getting my side of our deal?"

"You may think I'm a playboy, but I'd never vanish on you. I have more integrity than that. You have my word." I pause, looking deep into her eyes and keeping my expression neutral so she knows the sincerity of my promise. "Give me your phone," I say, holding out my hand.

"Why do you want my phone?" she asks as she reaches into her purse. Taking out her phone, she places it in my hand.

I punch in my cell number. "Here." I touch my number on the screen and hand the phone back to her. My phone rings in my pocket and I get it out, showing her phone number on my screen. "This is my personal number. Now I can't vanish from you." I smile and a bashful smile forms on her face.

"Okay then." She extends her hand back out and I take it in mine. Our gazes lock as we shake hands, sealing the deal.

We release our hands and I take a sip of my whiskey. "Before you start writing about me, I want to read one of your books to see what your writing is like."

"No." The word launches out of her mouth like a torpedo. "I mean, they're probably not something you'd enjoy reading."

"You don't know what I enjoy reading. I enjoyed reading Don Matteo when I was preparing for the role. I really want to read one of your books. Think through all the books you've written and tell me which one is a good one for me to read."

Her eyes shift back and forth. "Sunflowers for Sarah is a good representation of my writing. I can get a copy to you."

"No. I'll buy a copy. This way I can support your career."

"Oh. Okay. Thank you. I appreciate that." She tries to stifle a yawn.

"You're tired. Are you ready to go home now?"

"I'm sorry. Yes, I am tired. Are you sure you don't mind taking us home?"

"No, I don't mind. I wouldn't have offered if I did."

"Thank you. The Uber guy on my way here really spooked me."

"You're welcome. You have to be careful with those guys. Let's get Candi and get you home." I'll feel better knowing I got them home safely, especially with both of them having been drinking.

We say our goodbyes to the group and I make sure Gigi has a ride back to her hotel. When the valet pulls my car around, both Candi and Destiny get in the back seat.

"Des, you get up front," Candi suggests. "I wanna stretch out my legs."

"Quickly," I say. "There are more cars behind us."

Destiny gets out, closes the back door, and gets into the front seat then buckles her seat belt.

As I drive away, Destiny pointlessly tries to adjust the fabric of her jumpsuit to cover her long, sexy legs and Candi bounces her torso to the beat of the music.

"Ooo, this is a good one, Nicco. Turn it up," Candi howls from the back seat.

I turn up the volume on the radio a little and return my attention to Destiny. "Where am I going?"

"Oh. Turn left out of here and then through four traffic lights."

As I drive, we don't talk much. Candi dances in the back seat and Destiny gives me driving instructions.

Pulling away from a stop sign, I'm forced to slam on the brakes to avoid hitting a car that didn't stop at the stop sign. Stop? He didn't even slow down. We're all jolted forward and I hear clatter from the back seat.

"What the fuck, asshole?" I growl. "Are you guys okay?" I look over at Destiny and then back to Candi.

"Yeah, yeah, I'm okay," Candi replies. "Our purses just fell on the floor. Whoowh! The seat belts back here work." She rubs where the seat belt crosses her chest.

"Destiny, are you okay?" I ask, placing my hand on her forearm.

"Yes, I'm okay. Just startled. Are you okay?" she asks.

"Yeah, I'm fine."

"Okay. Turn right down Sunshine and I'm the last house on the left."

"Okay." I follow her directions and pull into the driveway.

"Key, keys. Pee-pee, pee-pee." Candi bounces up and down in the back seat.

"My purse, the zipper." Destiny points.

Candi gets out, both of their purses in her hand, and shouts back, "Thank you, Nicco! Talk to you soon." Then she runs to the front door of the small house.

We get out of the car and Destiny walks in front of me down the short path to her front porch. I like watching her tiny figure move.

Arriving at her front door, she turns to me. Her beautiful face glows under the dim, warm light above us. I steal a quick glance at her lips. The same urge fills me. I lean down toward her, the faintest scent of vanilla enters my nose. I could kick myself that my sense of smell is diminished because of my smoking. Just another thing that makes me despise my addiction. I want to smell her more deeply.

I press my lips to her left cheek. When I move to face her, before going to her right cheek, I linger, blood pulsing quickly. I move and press my lips to her right cheek, hearing her breath in my ear. Her audible response to our closeness arouses me. A soft curl brushes my face.

Returning to face her, I drink in her beauty once more. "Good night, Destiny." I straighten my stance.

"Good night, Nicco. Thank you again." She opens her front door and steps inside, looking back at me before she closes it.

Destiny

As I close the door behind me, my heart rattles in my rib cage. Candi's in front of me in seconds.

"What was that?" she asks like a giddy schoolgirl.

"I think I just made a deal with the hottest man on the planet."

6

Destiny

Around nine-thirty the next morning, Candi and I wake up, feeling the effects of last night. Before I bring her back to her studio where her car is, we go to Justina's for breakfast. Though we both throw on leggings, an oversized sweatshirt, and toss our hair into messy buns, Candi somehow manages to look adorable while my red eyes and puffy under-eye pockets make me look fifty instead of thirty.

As we open the door to Justina's, we're greeted by the familiar scents of coffee, bacon, and freshly made baked goods. Reminiscent of a French country bakery, Justina's oozes of charm and has become our favorite place to get breakfast on a Saturday morning when Candi's in town. We're quickly seated at one of the small wooden tables near the back next to a window where the sun filters in, kissing the small arrangement of billowy ivory roses brimming out the top of a little galvanized pitcher.

Pencil cradled behind her ear and dark hair tucked into a bun, Vivian approaches our table. "Good morning, ladies," she says with familiarity and a bright smile. "Coffees?" We've been coming here so long, she knows the answer, but routinely asks.

"Yes, please," we say in unison.

She places menus in front of us and goes on her way. There's nothing new, but we don't mind because we love everything they have. Vivian comes back with our coffees and we both order our usuals.

"Okay, I was very lit last night," Candi confesses, leaning forward. "I know we had fun and I know we danced, but I'm gonna need you to tell me again about this deal you made with Nicco, *and* was that a *kiss* out on your porch?"

"No," I emphasize, then whisper, "it wasn't a kiss." I insist, then return my voice to a normal volume. "He was doing that Italian thing where they kiss on the cheek. It was nothing more than that, I assure you."

"I don't know, Des, from what I saw, there was some lingering in there and I know my heart would've been hiccupping." She cocks her head to the side and smiles as she grabs two sugar packets out of the rectangular ivory ceramic container.

"Okay, I admit it." I hold my hand up in defense. "For a *second*, in my drunken head, I thought he was going to kiss me. I mean, his gorgeous face was inches from mine and his lips were *right there*." I shake my hands in front of my lips. "I've had dreams about a hot moment like that. I think I stopped breathing." I laugh. "Then I realized, of course, that he was doing that polite Italian kiss-on-the-cheek thing." I blow an exhale. "How do you not end up sleeping with these extremely hot men you're surrounded by all the time?"

"One hard rule: never, *ever* sleep with clients. You know how much I love my job. I'd never do anything to jeopardize it."

"I know you wouldn't."

"Anyway, as hot as Nicco is, no one stood a chance with him, at least not last night. There was only one person he had his eye on and that was *you*." She points her finger at me.

I grab three packets of sugar. "It wasn't like that. I'm telling you," I say, opening the packets and pouring them into my coffee. Picking up my spoon, I swirl the coffee and add milk from the small silver pitcher. "We just made this deal, to help each other, that's all. Besides, I have no interest in becoming another notch in his belt."

"I know that, honey." She makes a pout with her lips then reaches over and rubs the top of my hand. "It would be the hottest sex of your life though." She draws back her hand and winks at me. "Maybe you'd finally give Henry the heave-ho if you let yourself experience the hotness and passion of a man like Nicco."

"Oh, Henry." I chuckle. "Nope. Not happening. Besides, you know I won't stoop to playboy-level, no matter how incredible the sex would be. I'll never be in the same bed with that man."

"Okay, okay." She takes a sip of her coffee. "So, about this deal. How exactly are the two of you going to help each other?"

"Well, he's looking for connections here in L.A. He wants to transition his career to Hollywood. You know my mom's crazy connected so I'm going to put him in touch with her. Then they'll take it from there."

"And that's it?"

"That's it. He fully acknowledges that I have no other responsibility after that and the rest is on him and his talent."

She shrugs and the corners of her mouth turn down a bit. "Hmh, okay. That seems pretty easy. And what's your side of the deal?"

I can't hold back a grimace as I cringe. "I get to interview him and make him, as himself, the hero of my next book. Then he'll promote me to his followers."

Her eyes open wide, crinkling her forehead. "Des, really?"

"I know, I know. I don't know what I was thinking. I wasn't thinking. I was drinking stupid martinis and I was out of my mind. I think I even winked at him at one point. Me. Winking at Niccolo Mancini. What?" I shake my head and hang it toward my lap in disgust.

"Actually, I think it's a fantastic idea."

"You do?" Now I'm surprised.

"Yeah. Do you know the kind of reach he has? And it's the perfect audience for your books. This could be just the thing to get you out of your slump."

"I don't know if I can go through with it. I mean, I was all bold and sassy last night." I waggle my head with attitude. "But, who the heck am I, thinking I can write a book about him? What if it's awful. I can't put something awful out there? I wouldn't do that to him. What have I gotten myself into?" Leaning forward, placing my elbows on the table, I press my fingers into my temples.

"Hey, take a breath. You can totally do this. You're an amazing writer. Set up your interview, ask your questions, and write your book. Let yourself have fun with it."

Vivian brings over our plates. "I have strawberry blintzes with a side of bacon," she announces, putting the plate down in front of me. "And a bacon, egg, and cheese bagel," she says putting the plate in front of Candi.

We each thank her and she smiles and heads off.

"Fun? How am I supposed to have fun when, without alcohol pulsing through me, I'll be a sweaty, jittery disaster?" I cut a piece of my strawberry blintz and shove it in my mouth as though already defeated. "Maybe he's forgotten."

"I doubt it. You're about to help him set the course for his future. He's not likely to forget that."

"Then I'll follow through on my end and tell him to forget about his side of the deal."

"Here's the thing. I don't know him intimately obviously, but I know him well enough to know that he's not the kind of guy to back out of something he's committed to. It's not his style." She takes a big bite of her breakfast bagel.

"But he won't be backing out. I'll just be letting him off the hook. Besides, I have a good start with the stuff I jotted down yesterday while you were shooting." I wiggle a little in my chair and match the wiggle with my eyebrows.

"Ooo, let me see, let me see." She wipes her hands on her napkin. "Do you have it with you?" She reaches out, clapping her fingers and thumbs together.

I finish chewing my bite. "I do," I say happily as I reach into my purse. I move around my wallet, my sunglasses, my hand lotion — nothing. My chest caves in. My pages are gone. I lift my head slowly and look at her, my heart races in my chest.

"Des, what's wrong?"

"They're gone. They're not here. My pages. I put them in my purse when we left your studio."

"Oh shit." Her eyes open wide.

"I can't think of when they might've fallen out. Other than when I left my purse with you, I had it with me the whole time. Oh my gosh. What if someone found them. That's my work." My pulse thumps in my ears as my stomach churns.

"Is your name on them?"

"No. I wouldn't put my name on them. And now they're probably either in the trash at the club or in someone's hands who they don't belong to." I'm frantic.

"Deep breaths. Even if someone found them and picked them up, chances are they're not an author and have no intention of stealing your work. They probably threw them out, not knowing what they were."

"Ugh." I cover my face with my hands, my stomach still churning. "I can't believe I lost them. I wrote a few really good scenes too."

"Yeah?"

"Yeah. Well, you had me all tangled up with Nicco. I mean, I do have a good imagination. And he's easy to write about." I fan myself.

"So, you'll write them again. And now you'll have him in real life as your muse." A shit-eating grin spreads across her face.

I take a bite of my blintz, so mad at myself for losing my pages. As Candi scarfs down her bagel, I try to trace my steps from the night before and figure out when and how I lost my pages.

My phone chimes with a text message and I get my phone out of my purse. Looking at the name on the screen, I freeze and turn my phone to Candi.

"Open it," she encourages.

I tilt back my head, tracing the grain of the wood-beamed ceiling. "I'm not ready to talk to him."

She waves her hand at me. "Open it."

I open his message and clutch my phone tightly. My heart drops to my stomach as I suck in a gasp of air.

"Des, you're as white as a ghost. What's it say?"

"It says, I think these may have fallen out of your purse in my car last night. I found them on the floor in the back seat." I turn my phone to face her and show her the picture of my folded pages.

Her hand flies to her mouth. "Oh shit."

Leaning back in my chair, I hold the sides of my head. "How? How does he have my pages?"

She gasps. "I know what happened. They must've fallen out when he had to slam on his brakes and our purses fell on the floor."

My heart races. "He's probably read them. He's read my thoughts. My thoughts about *him*."

She finishes a bite of her bagel sandwich. "They were good, right?" she asks with a smirk.

"Candi." I bug my eyes out at her. "They're my raw, unedited private thoughts, about him. They're basically a fantasy I scribbled on paper until I create a story around them." The sinking feeling in my stomach makes me stop eating. "Oh no. This is bad. This is so bad. I can't face him. Not knowing what he's read."

"You don't know that he read them."

"He said he wanted to read my work before we do the interview. Of course he read them."

"You have no proof of that."

I blow a puff of air out my mouth. "I'll call my mom to fill her in and let her know to expect his call. Then I'll text him her number. I'll have fulfilled my part of our deal and I can just walk away."

"Just like that?"

"Just like that."

"You don't even want to talk to him?"

"No," I bark. It comes out harsher than I mean it to. "Honestly, what do I say to him? Hey, thanks for feeding my fantasies, I hope you don't mind that I got off while writing about your tongue dancing across my flesh? Ugh." I sigh. "I can't believe he read the intimate things I wrote about him."

"I still say you don't know that for a fact. I think you should respond to him."

As the words come out of her mouth, my phone chimes again.

Nicco: I'd like to get your pages back to you and set up our interview.

I stare at the message.

"What'd he say?"

I look up from my phone. "He wants to give me my pages and set up our interview."

Candi's shoulders drop. "Des. Just as much as you're giving him a once-in-a-lifetime opportunity to make his dreams come true, he could very well be giving you the same chance for your life." She reaches her hand across the table, placing it on top of mine. "Don't miss out on this." There's a pleading behind her eyes.

"I promise to seriously consider it."

"You better." She winks at me.

We finish our breakfast and I drive us to her studio.

When she gets out, she shouts, "Call him! I love you!" and blows me a kiss.

I wave, blow her a kiss, and head home. Call him, huh? I have no idea what to even say. Do I come right out and ask him if he read my pages? He could easily lie and I won't even be able to see his face to see if he's lying. Do I ignore the whole thing? Ugh, I'm beyond frustrated.

I drive mindlessly along Pacific Coast Highway toward home, creating different scenarios in my head of how awful the conversation will go. I do want my pages back. They were the start of something I felt inspired to write and I haven't felt inspired in so long. I settle on meeting up with him to get my pages, give him Mom's phone number, and release him from our deal.

I call Mom to brief her on Nicco and his desire to come to Hollywood.

"Hi, my birthday girl. How was your night out with Candi?"

"Oh, you know. Drinking, dancing, very Candi. I did have fun though."

"Good, I'm glad you had fun. Are you still coming over tonight for your birthday dinner?"

"Yup, I am. I'm just calling quickly because I have a favor to ask you."

"Okay."

"I met a nice man last night. He was part of Candi's shoot and he came out with us. We got to know each other a little and…"

"I like the sound of this already."

"Mom, focus please. He's an Italian actor and he's looking to transition his career here and move here. I'd like to help him out. Is it okay for me to give him your number so you can help him get a few connections?"

"Oh." Her excitement shifts to disappointment. "That's it?"

"Yes, that's it," I say, dousing her hopes that there was anything more between us.

"Of course I'll help him."

"Thanks Mom. I gotta go. I'll see you tonight. I love you."

When I get home, I get my phone out to text Nicco. My heart pounds in my chest. *Relax, you're not talking to him, you're texting him.* I send the text with Mom's number and let him know she's expecting his call. I also wish him luck.

Before I can put down my phone, it rings in my hand. "Nicco" lights on the screen. My heart resumes its pounding and my phone nearly slips out of my clammy hand. I take a deep breath, exhale, and slide the bar on my phone.

"Hi, Nicco. I thought you'd be calling my mom."

"Hi. Yes, I will. I'll call her soon. Thank you so much for giving me her number. Now I'm ready to fulfill my part of our deal." Hearing his deep voice again triggers the flash of his face lingering inches from mine last night.

"You know, I was thinking about that. You really don't need

to. I wasn't thinking clearly last night when we made our deal. I want to earn my audience based on my writing and my marketing efforts, not sponge off of you and everything you've worked so hard for. Besides, I can do research online. It'll be fine. But thank you for being willing. I'm sure you're very busy. I *would* like my pages back though." Words sputter out of me and I have to remind myself to take a breath.

"Research online? Why would you waste your time researching online when I can give you exactly what you want?" The way he phrases it shoots a shiver run up my spine to the base of my neck.

"It's okay, really. I'm sure you have a very busy schedule."

"As a matter of fact, I don't right now. I'm staying here in L.A. for two weeks and taking some time off. I was actually calling to see what you're doing this afternoon."

Blood runs hot through my veins. "This afternoon? I'm — I'm planning to do some writing." What would possibly interest him about my afternoon?

"I have an idea. How about we get together so I can give you back your pages and you can show me a good place to have lunch? I want to spend some time getting to know my way around here. And, I can buy you lunch to thank you for connecting me to your mom."

"That's really not necessary, especially after everything you did last night."

"Last night was for your birthday. This is different." He pauses. "You're not comfortable with people doing things for you." While he's not wrong, his bluntness surprises me.

"No, it's not that. I just don't want to be a burden on people. I can take care of myself." I straighten my posture.

"Yes, that's very clear. Let me put it to you this way, I'd like your help in familiarizing myself with L.A. and I would enjoy your company over lunch. I can also give you back your pages." As he says, "your pages," heat rushes to my face. "Will you help me?"

Oh my gosh. The gorgeous man I've been fantasizing about for months is inviting me to lunch with him. This is crazy.

"Um, I suppose I have time. And I do need those pages to continue my writing."

"Perfect. Tell me when and where to meet you."

"I just came back from a late breakfast with Candi. Do you mind meeting around one?"

"That works for me."

"What are you in the mood for?"

"Well, I'm Italian so I'd love some good Italian food." He chuckles.

"Okay, I'll text you the address of Pane Carasau and see you there at one."

"Great. I'll see you then." He pauses. "Ciao, mia dolce ragazza." The timbre of his soft, deep voice is so damn sexy.

I have no idea what he said, but goose bumps pop all over my body. "Bye. Ciao."

I hop in the shower and get ready for my lunch with Niccolo Mancini.

Oh boy.

7

Nicco

I wasn't sure she'd say yes, but I knew I had to at least ask her to get together. This morning when I found her pages, I only read the first few paragraphs to see what it was and my curiosity about her was piqued. Reading the sensual scene was a massive turn on.

During the lighting check shoot, I had to stifle my arousal. I loved watching her body respond to my touch. I'm dying to know if I'm who she was writing about.

She writes with an intimacy I've long-since denied myself. It took all my willpower to not read more. She hadn't given me permission and I wanted to honor that so I stopped once I knew what they were. But, damn do I want to read more from her. Fuck, I want to act out the scenes with her.

But it's not just the physical attraction, I feel that with lots of women. There's something I can't quite pinpoint about Destiny, but it's tugging at me, making me want to know more.

I put the address she texted into my app to see how long it'll take to get there. Grabbing her pages, I head out early to make sure I'm on time.

>>>>>> <<<<<<

I arrive ten minutes early and text her.

Me: I'm early. I'll go in and get us a table.

My phone chimes immediately.

Destiny: I'm inside. When you come in, turn right and walk to the end of the aisle.

Wow, she's really early. With her pages securely in my hand, I enter the restaurant. The homey smell of pasta surrounds me, intensifying how hungry I am. The ambiance is rich with Italian flare. Brick archways, greenery draping down from the ceiling and crawling up walls, and ornate chandeliers providing the subtle glow of romantic lighting. I turn right and walk down the aisle. Sunlight streams through the window, casting a glow on Destiny's light hair and fair skin.

She sees me and waves. When I reach her, I lean down to kiss her on both cheeks. I love the way she smells faintly of vanilla. Today she's dressed more how I would expect from getting to know a little about her last night. A feminine flowery top and jeans suit her personality.

"Hello," I say, sitting down and tucking my legs under the white linen tablecloth. "It's good to see you again. Thank you for meeting me for lunch." I hand over her pages. "Here are your pages that were in the back of my car."

Her cheeks flush. "Yes, it's nice to see you," she says, taking her pages from me. "Thank you for returning these. I was freaking out wondering what happened to them." She chuckles nervously.

"They were in safe hands." I assure her.

She glances at her pages and curls her hands in toward her chest, her shoulders slightly hunched. "Did you," she hesitates, "read them?" Wincing anticipation sits in her eyes as her eyebrows lift.

"No. I only read the first few paragraphs to see what it was. When I read it, I figured out they were your pages you told me about so I stopped. You said you didn't want me to read them. I'm waiting to read Sunflowers for Sarah."

"Oh." She looks blankly at me.

"Were you expecting me to say that I read them?"

"Actually, I was." She briefly casts her eyes down and back up.

"That's because you don't know me yet. You asked me not to and I fully respect that."

"Thank you for respecting my wishes." Her shoulders release, her features soften, and she tucks her pages into her purse.

"I'll always respect your wishes." I smile. "Would you like some wine?"

"Yes, that would be nice. I confess I don't know much about wine though."

"I do." I look through the menu, pleased by the selection.

The waiter comes over, places a basket of bread and a dish of seasoned olive oil on our table, and pours water into my glass from the bottle on the table. "Welcome. Can I get you both something to drink?"

"Yes, please. One moment." I shift my attention to Destiny. "Red or white?"

"A red would be nice."

I look back up at the waiter. "Two glasses of Sella and Mosca Tanca Farra, please."

"Coming right up, sir." He turns on his heels and walks away.

"It smells so good in here. I'm hungry." I touch my stomach and her gaze follows my hand.

She smiles and looks back at my face. "I hope you like their food. It's one of the best Italian restaurants in the area."

"They have a great menu. Lots of options." I peruse the menu. "Do you know what you want?"

"Yes, I was here early and looked over the menu."

"Yes, you were early. I thought I was early, but you beat me."

She chuckles. "Yeah, sometimes the traffic is awful so I usually plan to arrive early because I'd much rather be early than keep anyone waiting."

The waiter returns with our wine and we place our orders.

Picking up my glass by the stem, I hold it between my thumb, forefinger, and middle finger, and raise it toward her. "Salute."

She raises hers toward me. "Cheers."

We both take a sip.

"Your mom is amazing, by the way." I shake my head in disbelief.

"That she is." Pride gleams in her smile. "How did your call go?"

"Incredible. She didn't just give me contact information, she set up appointments for me."

"That's fantastic." She clasps her hands together. "Who did she get you in with?"

"I have appointments on Monday with James Tank at William Morris and then I see Mick Stevenson at Creative Artists. Then on Wednesday, I meet with Vance Langerfeld at United Talent Agency."

Pride washes her face again as she nods. "She's got you in with top-notch people. You're very lucky."

"Lucky? I'm grateful. This is so much more than I expected. And it's all because of you."

Her eyes gaze down as she shakes her head slightly. "No. I just put you in touch with the person who can help make your dreams come true."

"Right. *You* did that. And you didn't have to."

"Yes, I did." She tilts her head to the side. "We made a deal. I'm happy I could get the ball rolling for you. Now you just have to show up, be your amazing self, and secure representation here. My guess is, you'll have your pick."

"Thank you. That means a lot." Hmm, that's quite a statement.

"You're very talented, Nicco."

Now the pride is mine. "Thank you." I sip my wine. "I always like to know from people who've seen the movie, what their favorite scene was. Will you tell me what yours was?"

Her chest visibly rises and falls. "I know many women like the sex scenes so you're probably expecting that."

That *is* the answer I get about ninety-nine percent of the time. She whets my curiosity. "Not you?" I can't stop my brain from flashing a quick vision of her naked in my bed.

"They were very sexy." Her impassive expression is a stark

contrast to the pink filling her cheeks. I smile inside as I shift in my seat, trying to deflate the hard-on growing in my pants. "But my favorite scene was when your character asks Lena to teach him how to be gentle. There's a vulnerability you masterfully bring forth in the character during that scene that humanizes him. Your portrayal of his desire to be something more, something deeper than the monster, the sexual god alpha-male he showed to the world was what drew me into the character."

Her words humble me, flowing into me and speaking to my heart. *If you only knew.*

"Thank you for sharing that with me." I clear my throat. "So, did you have a good birthday?"

"I did. Thank you again for everything. Honestly, that was unexpected and so generous of you."

"Good. I'm glad you enjoyed yourself. How are you feeling today?"

She lets out a laugh and bugs out her eyes slightly. "Well, I don't drink very much and definitely had quite a bit to drink last night. This morning was tough. But, I'm feeling better now."

"You have to be careful when you go to those places and have a little too much to drink. You put yourself in a scary situation."

"Last night was unusual. I rarely go out to places like that. And when I do, I'm usually the designated driver and don't even drink." She drops her chin toward her chest, her gaze follows. Then she looks back up. "Thank you again for being in the right place at the right time and stepping in."

"Of course. I was watching for you."

"You were?" Her brows pinch together.

"Yes, I was." I lift the white linen napkin that's keeping the bread warm and cut off a piece. "Would you like some?" I hold the piece toward her.

"Yes, please."

Handing her the bread, I cut off another piece, dip it in the oil, and take a bite. "Mmm, this focaccia is excellent. And the wine is very good also."

"I thought you might like it here." She smiles sweetly.

"I do. It has a nice atmosphere." I gesture my hand in the air. "All the details are just so. The decorating, the music, the candlelight, the flowers." I point to the small arrangement of burgundy hypericum, purple peonies, and red roses. Being a gardener for so many years, I learned a great deal about flowers and these are perfectly arranged. I take a sip of wine. "So, I'm here for a couple weeks on vacation and I want to learn the area. But I don't want to waste time. I'd like to hire you to show me around. That is if you have time in your schedule. I don't want to interfere with your writing. What do you think?"

Her eyes shift slowly from side to side. Then she tilts her head slightly and her right eye squints. "You want me to be your tour guide?" The pitch of her voice raises as though I've asked something crazy.

"Yes," I say flatly. "I know this will take away time from your writing so I'm willing to pay you for your time. I already know you could use the money."

"Wait. You want to pay me to show you around town for a few days?"

"Yes. You live here so you know your way around, you know good places to go. You can give me recommendations for when I live here someday. And I want to pay you for your time and knowledge. This will also give you research material for your book. It'll be more than a few days. Again, if you have the time."

She takes a slow sip of her wine. As she puts down her glass, her lips twist to the side. "I'm happy to show you around, but you don't need to pay me."

I suspected she'd refuse payment. "Then no. I'll just use Google."

My response elicits a chuckle from her. "Nicco, you can't just use Google. *That* would be a waste of time for sure."

"Well, you seem determined to refuse to help me."

"No, no. I *will* help you. You just don't need to pay me."

"Then forget it. I won't accept your help if you won't let me pay you." She's fiercely independent which I like, but it's also frustrating.

She sighs. "You're kind of stubborn, you know?" Her lips lift into a provocative smile.

"Me? I'm stubborn? Look who's talking." I chuckle and nod at her. "I want what I want and I do what I need to do to get it."

One last contemplation as she purses her lips together. "Okay, I'll show you around. And I'll accept payment for my time, a hundred dollars." She reaches her small hand across the table.

I don't agree to the hundred dollars, but reach out and take her soft hand in mine, shaking it.

"When do you want to start and what kinds of places do you want to know about?"

The thought of spending time with her over the next couple weeks fills me with a pleasure I haven't felt in ages — excitement. I'm looking forward to learning about her. It's been a long time since I've cared to learn more about a woman.

"Let's start tomorrow. Monday and Wednesday are no good because of my meetings. I want to know great places to eat, where to go for fun, and good beaches."

"Okay." She nods. "I've got some ideas already. I can make up a list for you too so you'll remember them once you're here permanently."

"That would be great. Thank you."

Our meals arrive and she begins telling me about some of the restaurants in the area. She may not be Italian, but she's very animated with her hands as she speaks. She's adorable.

We finish our lunch and make arrangements to visit the Griffith Observatory the next day.

"It's the best place to see the Hollywood sign. Have you seen it before?"

"I have, but only from far away. I've been here twice, both times for business so I'm in and out pretty fast."

"Are you up for a hike? I can take your picture with the sign behind you. We can't go right to it, but we can get close enough for a good picture."

"Okay, I'd like that."

"Did you bring comfortable shoes, like sneakers."

"No, but I can get some today."

"Okay, I suggest sneakers, shorts, and a T-shirt."

"Got it." I nod.

The waiter brings our bill, I pay, and we leave together. I'm dying for a cigarette.

I kiss her on each soft cheek, taking one last whiff of her before she leaves. I like the way her skin feels under my lips. I like being close to her. I should've said I wanted to start our touring today.

"Ciao, mia dolce ragazza."

"Goodbye. Thank you for lunch. I'll see you tomorrow."

I eagerly await tomorrow.

Destiny

The second I'm in my car, I grab my pages out of my purse. I have no idea what I even wrote on the first page. God, I hope he couldn't tell from what I wrote that it was him I was writing about. How do I know he didn't read them all? Sure, he said he didn't, but he could be lying. The way he's perfected being expressionless, I couldn't tell. Please. Please, please, please let me not have written anything identifying.

I open the pages and start reading.

I slowly slide my hand from his hard chest down to his abs, letting my fingers dip between each ripple as I go. Moving my hand lower, I trace his treasure trail with my finger, down to the top of his jeans. Exploring. Indulging. Thirsting.

Adrenaline zips through me. *Oh God.* I cringe and skip a few lines.

He curls his long tongue into my mouth, swirling, dancing, provoking.

I force down a thick swallow as my heart thumps in my chest and I try to slow my breathing. Okay, there wasn't oil on my hands here so really, it could be any man. My stomach sinks at the unknown. Did he read them? Did he tell me the truth? *Ugh.*

8

Destiny

Tour guide? My social life is pathetic and I confess I don't really know where to take him. Now I'm laughing at myself for resorting to Google.

I didn't ask how many days during the two weeks he wants me to help him so I'll put together four days' worth of itinerary and run it by him tomorrow when we meet. That should be enough. I can't believe he wants to pay me to show him around. This is nuts. But, he's also right, I could use the money.

My phone chimes.

Candi: Hey! How did it go with Nicco?

Me: Can you talk?

My phone rings.

"Tell me everything!" Enthusiasm bursts out of her. "I'm packing to head out of town so I have you on speaker."

"Where are you off to?"

"Hawaii. I've never been there before. It's an amazing shoot for Guess and I'm so excited! Come on, tell me what happened with Nicco."

"Okay." I sigh. "So, not only am I going through with this ridiculous deal we made, but it seems that now I'm going to be his tour guide here and there over the next two weeks. *And*, he insists on paying me."

"Well, isn't this interesting." I can see her tapping together her fingertips with a mischievous grin plastered on her face.

"He's just looking for someone to show him around so he has a better feel for things when he moves here someday, that's all," I say, trying to douse whatever fantastical thoughts are brewing in her head. "I don't even know where to take him."

"You're resourceful. You'll figure it out."

"I'm thinking some touristy things, you know, to give him a little taste of that stuff. And then I thought I'd take him to a few off-the-beaten-path places, even though my life is so boring I don't even know what those places might be." I chuckle. "Where do *you* think I should take him?"

"The Hollywood sign for sure. But I'm thinking you should spend a day in Malibu. You can hit the beach, a winery, and eat at Malibu Farm. That would be a fun day."

"Yeah, that would be good. Oh hey, what does dolce ricotta means? Is it some kind of cheese?"

"What?" She laughs.

"Dolce ricotta. He says it when we're leaving each other. I don't know what it means, but it sounds like some kind of cheese." Now I laugh at how silly it sounds.

Her laugh grows louder. "I think you've got something wrong in your translation. I'm pretty sure he's not saying, goodbye cheese." She laughs harder still. "Shit, I gotta go. My limo's here to take me to the airport. I love you. Tell me more later."

"Okay, Love you. Bye."

Malibu is one good idea. That'll definitely fill up a day. The beach though? I'm not about to let Niccolo Mancini see my shapeless body in a bikini. I'll wear a suit, but I'll keep my coverup on.

I change into jean shorts and a tank, grab my water bottle, and settle in at my computer to do some research and plan a few days of fun activities for Nicco. But first, I Google him.

While there are many articles about his movie and his music, there isn't much about his personal life. Hmmm. I was hoping to learn a little more about him. Well, I guess I'll learn as we go.

A few hours later, I've created itineraries for four days that I know I would have fun doing. I just hope Nicco will. Nicco. I can't believe I'm going to be spending four days with the hottest freaking man who I've been having torrid fantasies about for months. God, every time he does that kiss-on-the-cheek thing, I feel like I'm going to melt to the ground. I know that sounds childish and ridiculous, but I can't help it. He just has this sexy energy that makes my entire body tremble.

Our plan is for him to come to my house around eleven a.m. so I can get some writing done in the morning after my workout. Then we'll grab lunch, head to the observatory, hike to the Hollywood sign, and call it day.

Fueled by thoughts of Nicco, I get some words written before I go to bed. I can fill in the practical parts of the story once I've interviewed him. Right now, the steam is all I can think about.

>>>>> <<<<<

Holy hell was my dream realistic last night. I swear I could feel the warmth of his lips on my skin as he trailed hot, feathery kisses across my collarbone. Thankfully there was no smoky smell in my dream. It was just the two of us, together, alone.

His strong hands on my waist pinned me against the wall. He moved slowly, determined, trailing from my collarbone up the side of neck, nibbling, kissing, sucking.

My heart raced with each of his muted groans. When he moved his face in front of mine, the way he had that night on my porch, my heart pounded wildly in my ribcage. I was begging for his lips on mine. He lifted me up in his arms, pressing me hard against the wall. I wrapped my legs around his waist and felt how rock hard he was, grinding into me. Looping his arms under mine, he wrapped his hands around my shoulders and tugged my body down into him, letting out a guttural groan. I cradled his head in my arms and squeezed my thighs around his waist, wanting more.

That's when I woke up in a full-body sweat and scribbled the scene into the notebook on my nightstand.

How am I going to look him in the face all day and not think about that dream? I've seen him naked. I've seen how he moves his body during hot-as-fuck sex. Okay, fake sex on a movie set, but you'd never know by watching. I have to get a grip on myself. He's just a man. An ordinary man. An intriguing ordinary man. An attractive, intriguing ordinary man. Shit, he's no ordinary man.

I get out of bed, both excited and nervous about the day ahead. I power through my workout and head home. After a quick breakfast and a shower, I put on jean shorts and my favorite and softest light blue T-shirt. Then I get to work on my manuscript. I've got a bunch of good scenes written, but it's all haphazard and I need to create some structure so I know where I'm heading with it.

I start with a high-level timeline outline. It has some holes, but I can fill them in. Next, I create my character bible. With Nicco as my muse for my hero, the words flow rapidly onto the page. Though I have a heroine and I've written some scenes with her, I have yet to delve into who she is.

This is when the flow of words comes to a screeching halt. I look up at the ceiling. I look around the room. The words aren't in those places. Who are you, heroine? Where do you come from? What has your life been like until this point? What are you struggling with? What are your faults that you don't want anyone to know about?

The ocean calls me. Wanting to hear the lull of the waves, I get up and step out onto my back porch to listen to their song. Inhaling deeply, I let the salt air clear my head. Before I can move forward, I need to dig inside my heroine, get into her soul. Climbing into the pillows on my large porch swing, I close my eyes, trying to picture her face. I have to know what she looks like before I can know her heart.

"It's beautiful out here." His deep, raspy voice sends a rush of blood shooting through me and my eyes spring open.

I gasp. "Hi."

"Hello. I'm a little early. I knocked on the door, but you didn't answer. The view was too enticing not to come back here. I hope you don't mind."

"No, no, not at all. I'm sorry. I must've lost track of time." I get up from my swing, still clutching a puffy, seafoam green pillow.

"I can see why. This is some view you have." He gazes out to the ocean.

"It's the perfect place for me. And it inspires my writing, usually."

"Do you need more time? I don't want to interrupt you if you're working on something."

"No. I'm ready. I just didn't realize the time." I put the pillow on the swing. "Come in. I just need to put on my shoes." I open the screen door and he follows me in.

I walk over to the weathered, light gray shoe bench in my foyer and put on my socks and sneakers, not daring to look up at him standing in my house.

"It's nice in here. Cute. Very beachy and comfortable."

When I finish tying my shoes, I grab the small purse I prepared for today with only the essentials. "Thank you. Okay, I'm ready. How about I drive since I know where I'm going?"

"That works." He gestures his hand toward the door.

I grab two water bottles, handing one to him as we head toward the front door. "For our hike."

"Thank you. I didn't think to bring one."

My phone rings. "Karen" lights up on the screen. "I'm sorry. I need to take this."

"Of course."

I swipe the screen, putting the phone to my ear. "Karen, hi." I pause, listening. "She is? Today?" I pause again. "Now? Yes, it's taken care of. He'll be there. Okay, yes, I'll be right over." I hang up the phone.

"Do you need to reschedule us?" he asks.

"No, but do you mind if we make a quick stop first?"

"I don't mind at all."

As I drive toward the hospital, I point out places that may interest him. Thankfully the hospital's not far.

"Should I stay here?"

"No, come with me."

We enter the hospital and I walk us quickly to the maternity ward. As we approach room two, I stop far enough away to not be noticed, but close enough to see into the room.

Nicco

"What are we doing here?" I keep my voice hushed, respecting the quiet of the ward.

Keeping her voice quiet also, she answers, only briefly looking up at me, then returning her gaze to the open door of room two. "This couple has been trying to have a baby for three years. She's had two miscarriages. And today, she finally gave birth to their first child…" She stops abruptly, her right hand clutches her chest and her left hand reaches down, grabbing my hand. Though I don't think she did it purposefully, it felt so natural, intimate, and drew me into the moment with her. I like the way her soft hand feels in mine. The smallest gasp releases from her.

My gaze is lured to the open door. A man dressed in army fatigues removes his cap and turns into the room.

Destiny squeezes my hand, causing me to look at her. Tears sit in her beautiful eyes and her lips are closed tightly together.

I hear a very surprised female voice come from the room, "Patrick!"

Looking back into the room, I see the man bent over his wife who's lying in the hospital bed. She rubs his shaven head. A nurse walks in, carrying a baby, and the man turns toward her. The nurse gently places the baby in his arms and tears stream down his reddened face. I'm not sure what's happening, but I know this is a special moment for Destiny to witness based on her reaction so I don't speak and let her experience it. The tears spill out and slide down her face as she squeezes my hand once more.

The nurse exits the room and walks toward us, taking her glasses off her face and tucking them on top of her head into her gray and white curly hair. When she reaches us, Destiny lets go of my hand and the nurse embraces her. The two hug and cry. When they release each other, the nurse cradles Destiny's face in her hands.

"You did a beautiful thing," she says, smiling and shaking her head.

"I couldn't have done it without your help. Thank you, Karen."

One more quick hug and Karen smiles at me.

"Hello there," she says politely.

"Oh, Karen this is my," Destiny hesitates, "friend, Nicco. Nicco, this is my friend, Karen, she's a nurse here."

Karen reaches out her hand to shake mine. "It's nice to meet you," she says, then steps back as her eyes open wide. "Oh, *ooohhh*." Her eyes move quickly back and forth between me and Destiny. Still with my hand in hers, she shakes more vigorously. "It's *very* nice to meet you." Given the flush in her cheeks and her broad smile, I think she may have just figured out who I am. She looks back to Destiny, releasing my hand. "Where are you two off to?" she asks.

"I'm taking him to the observatory and then we're going to hike to the sign, after Trails, of course."

Karen's eyes light up. "Ooo, have a piece of that apple pie for me, will you?"

"I just might." She smiles at Karen.

"Okay, you go have a fun day." Karen winks at Destiny.

"We will. Thank you again."

"Thank *you*, honey." She looks up at me with a spunky smile on her face. "Goodbye Nicco." Giving us a wave, she turns and goes back to work.

We turn and walk back down the hallway.

"What just happened there?"

"Oh, I'm sorry. I didn't get to finish telling you before he arrived. Patrick's been deployed. When Karen told me their story and that he couldn't even be here with his wife after her second miscarriage, I wanted to do something to help them. I was able to pull some strings and get him here for the birth of their first baby." She pulls her shoulders up to her ears and clasps together her hands with a smile of pure joy spreading across her face.

I stop dead.

She stops, turning toward me, her eyebrows squeezing together. "Are you okay?" she asks.

"Yes, I'm okay," I say, processing what she said. "You mean *you* arranged for him to be able to come home for this?"

"Yes," she says, like it's no big deal.

I rock my head forward and down, getting close to her face. "Destiny, you just gave that couple a gift they'll remember forever." I force a strained swallow down my throat.

"I hope they do," she says casually, clearly not understanding the magnitude of her efforts.

"Do you know them? Do they know who you are?"

"Oh my gosh, no. They don't need to know," she says and starts walking down the hallway again.

I'm stunned, shocked if I'm being honest. What an incredible act of kindness. Anonymous no less. Who is this enchanting woman I've stumbled upon? I'm in awe and enamored of her huge heart.

"How were you able to even make something like this happen?"

"Oh, I have connections," she says with a devious smile as she winks at me.

We continue our drive and she gives me some history about the places we pass. She pulls into the parking lot at Trails and we grab a quick bite to eat in the busy café.

"I wasn't sure how many days you wanted me to show you around so I put together four days' worth of itineraries for us," she says, carrying her tray of food and weaving us through the café to a two-person table near the back. Sitting down, she puts her tray on the wooden table. "Once I know you're okay with what I'm thinking, I can print it out for you so you have names and addresses of places in case you want to visit them again."

"Wow. You're taking your tour guide job very seriously."

"Yeah, I don't do anything halfway."

"Great. So, what do you have so far?"

"Well, today is the Griffith Observatory and a hike to the Hollywood sign to take your picture. One of the days, I'd like to take you to Santa Monica Pier. We can ride bikes from my house to get there. It's like a big carnival on a pier. Then another day, we can go to Malibu. We can hit the beach, stop at a winery, and then go to Malibu Farm for dinner. It's all fresh, local, organic food and pretty much everything they have is delicious. And the last day I planned is a day trip to San Diego. We can go to the zoo and grab some lunch. Then we can come back here and go to the Street Food Cinema which is an outdoor movie theater. It's something different to do. What do you think?"

I'm impressed by how much thought she's put into our time together and showing me different places. "It all sounds amazing."

"I tried to put some variety in there. Is there anything that doesn't sound like something you want to do? Because I can change things around," she says, taking a bite of her apple and bacon spinach salad.

"No. I like the sound of everything."

"Okay. I'll print it up when we get back to my house. Do you have any preference of days to do each trip?"

I want to spend more time with her than just four days, but I'm willing to start with that.

"Let's go to Santa Monica Pier on Tuesday and Malibu on Thursday."

"Okay, then that leaves San Diego for next week. It's about a two-hour drive from here. Is that okay with you?"

"Yes, that's fine. We can figure out what day later this week."

"Okay. How's your sandwich?"

"Mmm, so good."

"Right? Great food for such an unassuming little spot."

I curl my fingers into my pursed lips then splay them out and away, making a kissing sound. "Delizioso."

She laughs her tiny, adorable laugh.

We finish our lunch and she drives us to the observatory.

"I need a cigarette before we go in. Do you mind?"

"Yes, I do. I'll wait for you by the entrance," she says, pointing up the hill. "I don't want to smell like smoke."

I can see by her toned body and how she eats that she lives a healthy lifestyle.

"Of course. I understand." My shoulders weigh me down. Fuck, do I understand. I don't want to smell like smoke either. I've tried quitting, several times, but the addiction is strong. I started sneaking cigarettes not long after these fucking things took my dad's life. Not even a teenager, I lied to myself that it was my way of coping and I could stop whenever I wanted. Nineteen years later, they're shackles, imprisoning me, killing me faster each day. My twisted connection to my dad, holding onto him any way I can.

I stamp out my cigarette in the large round concrete ashtray. *Help me, Dad.*

Taking our time, we tour the grounds of the observatory, learn from the exhibits, and marvel at the sky through the telescopes.

"What did you think?" she asks.

"Absolutely fascinating. The sky is magnificent." I look up into the clear blue sky.

"I'm so glad you enjoyed it. Are you ready for our hike?"

"Lead the way."

I'm looking forward to our hike so we can talk. I want to learn more about her and her life. She takes the lead and I follow beside her.

"Have you always lived here in L.A.?"

"Yup. Born and raised."

"Did you ever want to live anywhere else?"

She tilts her head up and twists her lips to the side. "Actually, no. I love living here. I also love experiencing different cultures and countries. Even though my parents both have demanding, successful careers, they always made sure we went on vacation once a year and traveled to wonderful places. I don't travel as much now as I'd like to, but maybe someday I will again."

"Have you ever been to Italy?"

"No." She shakes her head. "It's definitely one of the places I want to visit. It looks breathtaking on Google and Pinterest."

"Pinterest? What's Pinterest?"

My question elicits a laugh from her as she tucks a stray strand of her hair behind her ear. "It's a visual platform where you create something like a virtual vision board. I use it for my business and to share my inspiration with my readers."

"Interesting. Will you make one for the book you're writing about me?"

She pulls her lips in like she's suppressing a smile. "Yes, all my books have boards." She pauses. "Speaking of the book, should I interview you during one of our days together? Let me know what works best for you so I can be prepared with my questions."

"We'll figure that out."

"Okay, just let me know." She takes a few long steps in front of me. "It's a little narrow here and gets a bit steep. Be careful." For being tiny, her legs are long. The sexy indentation between her quads and her hamstrings shows her dedication to fitness. I'm aching to touch her tight body again. Candi having me put my hand on her inner thigh the other day was a brutal fucking temptation.

"I will." I move cautiously. "So, you're not married and I know you haven't found your soul mate. Is there a boyfriend?" I know it shouldn't matter, but something inside me wants to know. And that something is hoping she says no.

She looks back at me as the path opens wider. Already winded, I quicken my steps to walk beside her again. "No. Not officially anyway," she says looking forward.

"Not officially? What does that mean?"

"There's a guy I have dinner with from time to time. It's nothing serious."

"No? You just eat meals together?"

She chuckles. "Yeah, pretty much."

"There's nothing physical?" What kind of relationship is this?

"I think he might want there to be more —"

I cut her off. "Of course he does."

She snaps her head toward me, her questioning eyes dart back and forth.

I stop walking. She stops. Taking a step in front her, I gaze down into her breathtaking blue eyes. "Destiny." I drag my finger softly across her cheek, tucking the hair the wind blew across her face behind her ear. Her lips part slightly. "You're beautiful." She's beyond cute or pretty or sexy. She's all of them plus being kind, compassionate, and caring. I know I'm only scratching the surface of who this captivating woman is. And I want to learn more. I want to learn everything I can about her.

She ignores my compliment. "I — well." She catches a breath and continues walking. "It doesn't really matter because *I* don't want anything more."

"Who is this guy?" I take a large gulp of water from my bottle as beads of sweat gather on my forehead.

"Henry. We've been friends for a few years. He knows I don't want anything more than friendship."

Poor sap. He doesn't stand a chance with her. And he never will with me in the picture. I have to have this woman. Do *I* stand a chance with her? For me, it can only be physical. I know my strengths and I know my weaknesses. There's no way I'm good enough for anything more with her, no matter how much the feeling is growing inside me for more than just hot, passionate sex. Shit, I'm getting hard thinking about it.

She abruptly changes the subject and tells me her ideas for our trips she's planned as we continue our hike. We reach the spot designated for tourists to take pictures with Hollywood sign behind us and I'm itching for a cigarette. I excuse myself and walk away since I know she doesn't want to smell like smoke and I'm sure she doesn't want to inhale it either.

When I return to her, she's stretching her legs.

"Are you ready?" She reaches out her hand for my phone.

I tap in my password and hand it to her. "Where should I stand?"

"You stay right there. I'm going to move around to get as much of the sign in for you as I can. I'll take a couple so you have a few to pick from."

She takes some pictures, moves left, takes more, moves right, and takes more. Then she returns to me and hands me my phone.

"Take a look and make sure there's something you like in there."

I stand next to her, close, and flip through the images. "Yeah, these are good. I like them. You got some good ones. Thank you."

"Of course. Now you can say you've been to the famous Hollywood sign." When she looks up at me, the sun sparkles in her eyes.

"Here, let's get one of us together," I say, putting my arm around her before she has the chance to decline.

"Oh. Okay."

I extend my arm and snap the camera several times. Her faint scent of vanilla enters my nostrils. Picking the best one, I send it to her phone.

"Are you ready to head back down?" she asks, taking a drink of water.

"After you."

On our way back down the mountain, she continues telling me about different things to do in the area. Things we won't be doing together, but she thinks I might enjoy.

As we drive back to her house, I'm not ready to end our day together. She pulls into her driveway.

"Come on in quickly and I'll print out the itineraries for you."

I follow her in and she takes off her shoes and socks. I do as well. While she sits down at her computer, curling her leg under her, I gaze out at the ocean.

"I'm hungry. Are you hungry?" I ask, hoping she is.

"I *am*. An afternoon of hiking in the sun will do that to you."

"What do you say to ordering food?"

"You want to eat here? With me?"

"I do."

"Aren't you tired of me by now? Yammering your ear off all day."

"No. I enjoy your stories and listening to you tell me about all the things there are to do around here."

"Um, okay. What are you in the mood for?"

You. "Are there any good sushi places?"

"Oh yeah. Hana Sushi. Their food is so good. I'll pull up the menu."

We place our order and I insist on paying since it was my idea.

"Want to eat out by the fire? Sunsets here are amazing."

"I can't say no to that."

"We'll start the fire while we wait for the food." She gets up and goes out to her back porch.

Grabbing some wood, she places it in my arms and carries a few pieces herself. She heads down the few steps into the sand and out to a fire pit. Two white, weathered Adirondack chairs sit close to the circle of rocks creating the pit. Taking her pieces of wood, she forms a teepee and reaches out for my pieces.

"Do you want s'mores after we eat?" she asks.

"Sure. I know what they are, but I've never eaten one."

Placing the piece of wood in her hand onto the sand, she whips her head toward me. "You've *never* had a s'more?"

Her surprised reaction makes me laugh. "No, I haven't."

"Well, that changes tonight. We're making s'mores," she says, standing up and dusting off her hands.

"You make them?"

"Yup, you're going to toast marshmallows and make your very first s'more." She smiles at me and nods then heads back to the house.

Lifting the lid of a large round woven basket, she reaches in, pulls out two blankets, and hands them to me. Then she goes inside and comes back out with a two dinner trays and a candle lighter in her back pocket.

"It can get chilly as the sun goes down. We'll get the fire going. Food should be here soon, they're not far away."

I follow her back to the pit and put a blanket on the back of each chair while she sets a tray in front of each and lights the wood.

When the food arrives, she puts everything on plates and we bring them, a bottle of wine, and glasses out to the pit where the fire is flickering and crackling. I pour us wine as she pokes at the fire. Then we settle into our chairs to eat.

"So, I know what your mom does. How about your dad, what does he do?"

"He's retired now, but he worked for the government."

"Retired. Good for him."

"What about your parents?" she asks.

"My mom was a housewife and raised me and my brother until my dad passed away. Now that we're grown, she likes to keep busy working at a small clothing shop in the town where we live."

"I read that your dad passed. You were pretty young."

I clear my throat. "Yes, I was. Twelve years old."

"He died young then. I'm so sorry."

"Thank you. It was these." I take the pack of cigarettes out of my pocket and shake it, eager for a drag. "These took him from me." I pause. "Excuse me." I get up from my chair, walk to the shoreline, and touch the flame of my lighter to the end of a cigarette. Taking a long drag, I watch the tip burn in toward me, a tiny vibrant fireball. Half closing my eye, I send the smoke down to my lungs, relaxing into the calm that spreads through my body. I exhale out my nose, watching the smoke curl and dance in front of the sun.

Looking out to the horizon and the sun about to touch the edge of the water, my dad stands by my side. A ghost. The sun is a searing white, feathering out to a bright yellow then fading to a softer daffodil-yellow to tangerine and then orange. I watched so many sunsets with my dad after a day playing at the beach. If I stay still, I can almost feel him holding my small hand. Together, staring out at the waves as they mesmerize us.

Placing the cigarette to my lips, I suck in my death, yearning for one more day with him, making sandcastles at the beach. One more sunset.

The foamy water splashes onto my feet. I bend down and let it extinguish my cigarette. *Help me, dad.*

Dirty cigarette butt in my hand, I walk back toward Destiny. A different kind of peacefulness fills me as I watch her. She's not doing anything but eating, yet she makes me feel at peace. I toss the butt into the fire and sit back down in my chair to finish my meal.

"I'm sorry." Sorrow colors her soft voice. "I didn't mean to pry about your dad."

I wave my hand. "No, it's okay. It's," I hesitate, "it's hard for me to talk about him."

"I understand." She pauses. "I can't help but wonder, if smoking took your dad's life, don't you worry it will take yours?" Where most people ask this question in such a malevolent way, her gentleness brings compassion to her curiosity.

"Every day." I confess.

"Have you ever thought about quitting?"

"All the time. I've tried to quit, a couple times." I put the last bite of sushi in my mouth. "The desire is so strong it's unbelievable. It's a love-hate relationship. I hate knowing I'm killing myself. I hate the way I smell, I hate that I'm exhausted after climbing a flight of stairs, I hate the addiction. Then, I love the calm it brings me, and the feeling that I can take on the world and, this is so stupid." I shake my head. "But it — it makes me feel connected to my dad."

"Mmm." Her lips tighten together and she nods.

I laugh at how ridiculous that must've sounded. "I know, it doesn't make any sense. You probably think I'm crazy."

"No. I don't think you're crazy." Tenderness wraps around her words. "It sounds like you had a close bond with your dad and, even though you know it's going to kill you, because it took him from you, doing it somehow makes you feel close to him still. The mind connects things in interesting ways."

"It's true."

My smoking typically elicits judgement and criticism from most people. Destiny listens with an open heart, removing the shame I often feel when people ask me about it.

"Here's the thing, your mind is also powerful enough to break that connection. And you're the only person who can do that, if you want to."

Whomph. With empathy and respect, she puts an imaginary mirror in front of me, reminding me that my habit, my addiction, is *my* choice — and I'm the only one who can change it.

"Are you ready for the first and most delicious s'more of your life?" She stands up with a playful smile on her face.

"I *am*." I've seen pictures of them and I'm excited to make my first one, with her.

We gather our dishes and bring them inside. She opens a cabinet in her kitchen and takes out a glass jar filled with large marshmallows, chocolate bars, and another glass container filled with graham crackers. She hands both glass containers to me, opens a drawer, and takes out two long, silver forks on wooden handles. Before going back out, she grabs paper towels, two paper plates, and turns on some music.

When we get back to the fire pit, the flames of the fire have died down.

"The fire is perfect now for roasting our marshmallows." She sets down on her tray the things she was carrying and turns the tray to the side of her chair. Then she turns mine to the side of my chair and I set down the containers. "Here." She tugs her chair closer to the fire. "Pull your chair closer."

I pull my chair closer to the fire and closer to her. She

prepares our plates by snapping the crackers in two then placing half a chocolate bar on one of the halves. Taking one of the long silver forks, she pulls on the end of it, extending it to three times its length.

"Whoa. You're serious about your s'mores." I chuckle, reveling in how cute she is.

"Oh, s'mores-making is a very serious thing in these parts." She smiles and winks at me then slides a marshmallow on the tip of one of the forks and hands it to me then sits down. Sliding another onto hers, she holds it toward the fire. "Now, the genius of these s'mores sticks is that you can rotate your stick by the base." She demonstrates by twisting the wheel at the top of the wooden handle.

"Okay. How do I know when it's done cooking?"

"Well, there are full debates about that and it really comes down to personal preference. Some people like theirs more stiff and underdone, some people like to catch theirs on fire and burn them to a crisp, and some people like them somewhere in between."

"What do you like?"

Her gaze remains on her marshmallow as she slowly rotates it over the embers. "I like mine golden brown, hot enough to melt the chocolate and deliciously gooey."

I sit quietly and watch her. The lyrics from the song "Breaking Me" float softly through the air from her house. The sun dips farther into the ocean, casting its glow on her fair skin.

"Nicco!" The alarm in her voice startles me from my trance.

My marshmallow is on fire. I pull it from the pit and wave my stick wildly, sending the marshmallow flying into the sand. She doubles over in laughter and I join her.

"What happened? Did I leave it too long?"

She tempers her laughter. "Yes, you torched the poor thing. Weren't you watching it?"

"Yes. No. I don't know. It happened so fast." I chuckle. "This really is an art."

She withdraws her stick from the embers and puts a plate in her lap. Then she taps at her marshmallow, sucking in quick bursts of air as she quickly pulls away her fingers. She lays the marshmallow down on top of the bar of chocolate, takes the other half of graham cracker, puts it on top of the hot marshmallow, and slides the fork out. Picking up the gooey sandwich, she holds it out toward me.

I lean and take a bite, keeping my eyes on hers that are watching my mouth. The crunchiness of the graham cracker; the hot, gooey marshmallow; and the melting chocolate are pure bliss in my mouth. "Oh my God." I roll my eyes. "I've been deprived my entire life. This is amazing."

She giggles. "Right? Heavenly."

"Heavenly," I say, taking the rest of the s'more into my mouth from her fingers.

She slides another marshmallow onto the long fork and hands it to me.

"Give it another try," she says, taking the blanket from the back of her chair and laying it on top of her legs.

We roast our marshmallows, listening to the music. This time, I keep my attention on my marshmallow and toast it to perfection. The sun dips farther into the ocean, barely lighting the sky that's turning different shades of red as it sinks.

As I finish my last bite of gooey heaven, a little yawn releases from her. That's my cue.

I pat my stomach. "I'm so full. You were right, great sushi and the s'more were unreal," I say, standing up and picking up my containers.

"I'm so glad you enjoyed everything," she says, unwrapping from her blanket, standing up, and grabbing the plates, long forks, and chocolate bar wrappers.

We walk back to the house, putting everything in the kitchen, and then go back to the fire pit for the trays and blankets.

"Do you need help cleaning up?" I ask as she lowers the volume of the music and turns on her gas fireplace.

"Brrr, it got chilly," she says, rubbing her arms vigorously. "No, I'm good, but thank you."

The outline of her hard nipples in the glow of the fire makes me twitch in my pants.

"Okay, if you're sure," I say as I walk over to where we left our shoes at her bench.

"Positive. I'll have everything cleaned up and put away in a few minutes."

Once my shoes are on, she opens the door and follows me out to her front porch. I turn to face her and chuckle.

"What? What's so funny?"

"You have some chocolate…"

She parts her lips and grazes the thin connection of her lips with the tip of her tongue. My eyes are drawn to her mouth and I lean in toward her. Curling my fingers under her jaw, I run my thumb down the side of her parted lips, sweeping the chocolate across her lower lip, then stick my thumb in my mouth, sucking off the chocolate.

Her exhale is audible. I move my gaze from her lips to her eyes, they're flicking back and forth. The urge to kiss her is growing stronger. Her breathing is shorter and quicker. I stare into her eyes, taking a deep breath. "Don't worry, I won't kiss you. I don't kiss women on the lips." *But I'm not sure how much longer I can resist you.*

"Okay," she breathes softly.

I move to her cheek and press my lips into her delicate skin. Passing in front of her face, I see her eyes open. I press my lips into her right cheek, inhaling her faint vanilla once more.

"Thank you for today," I say, stepping away from her. "I enjoyed being with you."

"You're welcome. I'm glad you had a nice time," she says, rubbing her arms briskly. "Good luck tomorrow. Let me know how it goes."

"Yes, I will. Go. Get inside, you're cold."

"Good night."

"Buona notte, mia dolce ragazza."

Destiny

I close the door, my heart races. That's when it hits me, the heroine I've been writing, is me. No. No, no, no. It can't be me. I *cannot* write myself as the heroine. I have to create a character. She'll be the complete opposite of me.

What *was* that? No wonder women willingly spread their legs for him. Holy shit. Nothing even happened and I'm so freaking turned on right now. Of course he wasn't going to kiss me. A man like him wouldn't kiss someone like me. But, why does he get so close to me like that? It's unnerving. And what did he mean he doesn't kiss women on the lips? He kisses women all the time.

I tilt back my head. He captures my mouth with his full lips, confidently sliding his tongue in…*cut it out*. Well, my dreams are going to be interesting tonight, that's for sure.

Three more days. Just three more days. I'll ask my interview questions, give him his tours, and we'll be done. I have to admit, I liked seeing a deeper side to him. I'm honored that he trusted me enough to share a glimpse beyond what the world sees.

No. I'm not going there. I'm not going to let things get personal. I'm not going to be swept off my feet and into his bed.

9

—

Destiny

Exhausted, I roll over and look at my phone. 7:04 lights on the screen. I slept later than I wanted to. Lying under the covers, I stare at the chippy ivory chandelier above my bed, wishing I could remember my dreams. I know Nicco was sprinkled in them, but have no idea what he was doing or saying. It's best I don't remember.

I grab my phone off my nightstand and text him.

Me: Good luck today!

Nicco: Buongiorno, mia dolce ragazza. Thank you.

Hmm, now I know how to spell it. I toss off my sheet and duvet, throw my robe on over my satiny camisole and shorts, and run down to my computer. Pulling up a new tab, I type it in, mia dolce ragazza. One result: my sweet girl. That sounds like a term of endearment. It must be some kind of generic thing Italians say.

I get my coffee started and go back up to my bedroom to change into gym clothes. My head is spinning with different scenes, some driven by the time I've spent with Nicco and some driven purely by my lack of sex over the last few years and my current fantasies.

Grabbing my coffee, a notebook, and pen, I go out to the back porch and climb into my swing. With the muted sound of the crashing waves filling my ears and the smell of sea salt swirling in the air as the breeze carries it to me, I jot down words, phrases, and bits and pieces of scenes as I sip my coffee. I know more will come and some will change once I interview Nicco, but I don't want to forget them.

Once I finish my coffee, I hit the gym then get back home for, hopefully, a good day of writing. My notebook has scenes all over the place with no order or structure. It's time to create my goal, motivation, conflict spreadsheet and get into the heads and hearts of my characters.

By evening, I have a few things filled in, but there are still lots of blanks. At least I named my heroine: Emma. It feels like I'm trying to force the story and I know myself well enough to know that that approach never works well for me. So, I call it a day and make dinner.

As I'm eating, my phone chimes with a text.

Nicco: Today went well. I'll tell you about it tomorrow. What time are we meeting?

Oh right. After the whole let-me-stick-my-face-inches-from-yours-and-get-you-all-hot-and-bothered-then-tell-you-I'm-not-going-to-kiss-you thing, I completely forgot about settling on a time to meet tomorrow.

Me: That's great! I'm excited to hear about it. Let's go with 11:00 again, my house. Dress comfortably.

Nicco: Sounds good. Okay, I will. Have a good night.

Me: You too.

⋙ ⋘

I hit the gym, come home, shower, and put on jean shorts and my white eyelet tank top. Before Nicco arrives, I decide to spend a little time on research. Since he's Italian, I want some of the book set in Italy. As I Google, I stumble across Ponza Island and it looks so beautiful. A few more clicks and I find a guide for Ponza Island on Amazon. Add to cart.

Nicco arrives a little before eleven. I already have our bikes and bottles of water on the front porch. When I open the door, the smell of smoke hits me and I ignore it. He's wearing gym shorts and a black T-shirt. The man is adorable and sexy all rolled together.

"Hi."

"Good morning." The deep rumble of his voice sends goose bumps up my spine.

Damn, he has me going already. I slip into my nude-colored flipflops, grab my small purse, and lock the door.

"Is this one for me?" he asks, pointing to the men's bike.

"Yeah. I borrowed it from my neighbor since I only have two women's bikes. You may need to adjust the height of the seat with your long legs."

He takes a minute to adjust the seat. "Okay, I think I'm good."

"Great. Just follow me. It's about a fifteen-minute ride. We won't be able to talk much during the ride, but we can catch up once we get to the pier. I want to hear all about your meetings."

"Okay, I'll follow you."

I keep a mild pace since we're not in a rush and I want him to be able to enjoy the scenery. When we reach the pier, I find a visible spot to lock up our bikes and we enter the pier.

We're met with the vibrantly painted buildings and booths and the buzz of happy people. Carnival music fills the air that smells of burgers, buttery popcorn, and sweet funnel cakes. He looks up, looks around, and his mouth drops open as an expression of wonderment coats his face.

"Wow, this is amazing. It's like a child's playland." He spreads his arms out wide. "An amusement park on stilts in the water."

His childlike reaction makes me laugh. "It is."

"What can we do?"

"Anything you want. There are rides and games and food. There's so much to do."

"Let's start with one of your favorite things."

"Do you like roller coasters?" I ask.

"Yeah, I love them."

"Okay, let's go. It's not big, but it's fun." I start walking toward the roller coaster.

"Great. Hey, I wanted to take your mom to dinner to thank her for all her help, but she said she's very busy and doesn't have time right now."

"Yeah, she just started on a new film."

"I'd like to send her a gift basket. Can you tell me some things she might like?"

"That's very nice of you. How about we do that together when we get back to my house later?"

"That would be great."

We ride the coaster and play some arcade games then get big, juicy burgers, French fries, and milkshakes for lunch. After lunch, we head for cotton candy. On the way, we pass my favorite booth, the water race, and a cute stuffed pig catches my eye.

"Oh my gosh, look how cute," I squeal with delight, pointing at the little pig.

"What that?" he asks, pointing at the pig.

"Yeah, he's cute."

"Do you want it?"

"No. What am I going to do with it?"

"I will win it for you," he says, gallantly puffing up his chest.

"Nicco, you don't have to do that."

He ignores me, pays for a race, and picks his spot. A group of kids rush over, pay, and stand on both sides of him. Two of them look like they might be brother and sister. The other three are rowdy teenage boys.

He glances back at me. "I think I have some competition."

A little girl with baby blonde, ringlet ponytails stands next to him and looks up at him.

"Which one are your trying to win, mister?" she asks in her sweet, tiny voice. Her big brown eyes alight with curiosity.

"Me? Oh, I want the little pig. Which one are you trying to win?"

A big smile spreads across to her cheeks. "Me too."

"Okay then." He offers his hand and she places her tiny hand in his. "Let's do this," he says, shaking her hand gently.

The kids grab their water guns and lean over the platform. Nicco looks down at the little girl, quickly tugs up the right sleeve on his T-shirt, and winks at her. While it's completely adorable and playful with the girl, catching a glimpse of his muscular arm in real life sends my brain straight to the first sex scene in his movie and my heart rate quickens. I immediately shake away the image.

The boy behind the platform rings the bell, signifying the start of the race. Standing to the side of them, I can see the determination in the little girl's face. I can also tell Nicco is purposefully missing the target here and there, but not making it obvious.

"Come on. Go, go!" he cheers.

Meanwhile, the rowdy boys and the little girl's brother are ahead of both of them. The bell rings and the race is over. One of the rowdy boys won.

The little girl looks up at Nicco. "You tried your best," she says, patting him on his arm in consolation.

He chuckles. "So did you. Would you like to play again?"

"I can't. I don't have any more money."

"I do," he says, pulling cash out of his pocket. "Is that your brother?" he asks pointing at the boy I thought was her brother.

"Uh-huh." She nods.

He hands money to the boy behind the platform for the three of them to play. The girl looks at her brother who shrugs his shoulders and returns to the booth.

"Thank you, mister," she says.

"Are you sure?" the boy asks, looking up at Nicco.

"Absolutely sure."

"Thank you, that's very nice of you." he says quietly and stands on the left of Nicco.

The rowdy boys hadn't gotten far and are back to play again. Nicco looks at me with feigned fear on his face, making me smile.

"Come on, we can do this," he says, giving high-fives to the little girl and her brother.

When the bell rings, I know he's not messing around. He keeps his gun aimed at the target and his eyes laser focused. The bell rings again and Nicco's light beams, signifying him as the winner. The three of them cheer with arms raised in the air.

"You did it, mister. Good job," says the little girl. "Get your piggy."

The boy behind the platform hands the pig to Nicco as the little girl and her brother turn to walk away.

"Wait," he says loudly then squats down.

They turn back and step toward him.

"I have to travel on an airplane soon and I'm afraid this piggy won't fit in my suitcase. Will you take care of him for me?" he asks, handing the pig to the girl.

Her doe-eyes open wide and her mouth drops as she gasps. Taking the pig from him, she wraps her arms around his neck. "Thank you so much, mister." She releases her embrace. "I promise I'll take good care of him."

"I'm counting on it." He smiles sweetly at her.

The kids say goodbye and run off.

As he rises, watching them go, a wistfulness cloaks his face — and vanishes the instant our eyes meet.

He approaches the boy behind the platform and hands him more money. The boy gives him a stuffed pig.

Walking toward me, he hangs his head, then raises it when he reaches me. "I had to give yours away." He gestures in the direction the little girl and her brother ran off.

Was that the reason for the forlorn expression on his face? Can't be. There was something deeper behind it — pain. He's hiding something. *Hmmm.*

Witnessing his playful side with the kids, I have to admit, he's much more endearing than I thought the virile sex-god would be.

Whether he's trying to prove to me that he's more than just a playboy or not, this scorching-hot, devastatingly adorable man has just lightly tapped on my heart. Oof, I have to be careful. What we have is a business arrangement. He's basically a client and I'm sticking by Candi's rule, and adding to it: Never ever sleep with or fall in love with clients. This is an excellent rule. Plus, I made a pact with myself after Kevin and I broke up. It's better for my career if I stay single. Being single allows my imagination to be wildly creative and write steamy love scenes that come from my fantasies. Getting tangled up in a relationship would destroy that. And right now, I need to get my career back on track.

"Thank you, Nicco." I smile and take the pig from him.

"Are you ready for that cotton candy now?"

"Yes, let's go."

We find cotton candy and I pick out a pink one.

"What color do you want?" I ask.

"No, I'm not having any."

"Are you sure?"

"I'm sure. I'm full from lunch. I'll have a bite of yours."

"Okay." I get money out of my purse.

"No," he says, putting his hand on mine. "This is part of my requested tour. I'll pay."

"But, Nicco, you're not even having any. I can pay for my own cotton candy."

"Do you want to insult me?" he asks, stone-faced.

"Well, no. It's just…"

He pulls out his money and pays.

We stroll to the side of the pier and gaze out over the water. I don't like getting my hands sticky so I poke my tongue into the fluffy pink candy and curl pieces into my mouth. Since he said he wanted a bite, I figure I'd better offer before I finish the whole thing myself.

"Here." I point the puffy ball toward him.

Like a big kid, he sticks his mouth into it, yanking out a wad and eating it. Cotton candy is stuck to his mustache and scruffy chin. I can't help but laugh at him.

"What?" He looks around, pretending he doesn't know it's all over his face.

I laugh harder, then wet the napkin I grabbed with the water he bought me. I reach up and take his strong jaw in my hands.

"Here, I'll get it off." I dab at his chin and then his mustache, avoiding looking into his gorgeous brown eyes. It takes a few strokes to get it all off.

"Thank you." His seductive grumble pulls my gaze to his eyes.

"You're welcome." My words are breathier than I intend.

I continue my ritual, sticking my tongue into the cotton candy and grabbing pieces, curling them into my mouth as we quietly look over the water. I finish my last bite and I know my lips are sticky with sugar. I glide my tongue around my lips, savoring the last bits of sweetness before I wipe my mouth with the napkin.

Feeling his eyes on me, I turn toward him. He chuckles.

"You amuse me," he says, leaning against the railing and facing me while I look back toward the water.

"How do I amuse you?" I ask, returning my gaze to him.

"You're sexy like a woman and cute like a little girl."

Has the sugar gone to my head? This is the second time he's called me sexy.

Blood rushes through me and my eyes shift back and forth between his. "I — I don't know what to say to that."

"No response is required," he says flatly then looks out into the water.

We stand silently for a few minutes, listening to waves crash against the piles and seagulls sing above us.

Nicco

The more time I spend with her, the more I want to know about her. I feel like we're becoming friends. It's a strange feeling for me, but nice. How is it she's still single?

"I'm kind of surprised you haven't married yet," I say, not looking at her.

"I was engaged once."

I shift my body to face her. "Really?"

"Yeah." She looks over at me then back out toward the water. "Well, that was until I caught him the week before our wedding, lip-locked with his childhood best friend."

A sting pinches my heart. "Destiny. I'm so sorry." I know the hurt of being cheated on. "What happened?"

She turns to face me, a slight breeze tousles her ponytail. "I always had my suspicions about them. I mean, she's absolutely gorgeous, incredible body, beautiful face." She looks at me. "Someone you'd be with. And she was actually really nice. We got along great." She shakes her head. "There always seemed to be flirtatious energy between them though. They both denied anything more than friendship, but I always felt there was something more. Anyway, I'd left my wedding planner at his house and wanted to go over a few things so I stopped by to get it. That's when I walked in on him and Tessa, half naked, making out."

Thunk. My heart drops for her. "What did you do?"

"What could I do? I ran out, drove home sobbing, and cried in my room the rest of the day. Candi came over and stayed with me."

"You didn't scream? Or throw things at them?"

She laughs. "No. I tend to get hurt rather than angry. Don't get me wrong, I was crushed. And I was definitely mad for a while. But more mad at myself for not trusting my instincts."

"The women I've dated would've been enraged and tried to beat up the other woman." I chuckle.

She laughs harder. "Nope, not me. I took my broken heart and ran away. We met the next day to talk. He apologized and tried to tell me it didn't mean anything. I looked him in the eye and told him he needed to figure out what his feelings were for Tessa because there was, very obviously, something more than just friendship. He wasn't a bad guy. I mean, what he did wasn't nice, but I wanted him to be happy. I wanted both of us to be happy. Plus, I don't want to be with someone who doesn't want to be with me. Clearly, he didn't." She rests her arm on the railing.

"How were you so okay with it?"

Pain sits in her eyes. "I wasn't." She pauses, looking out at the water. "I was devastated. For a long time. He broke my heart." A sheen veils her eyes and my heart is heavy for her. "But, once I had some distance from it and really looked at our relationship, I knew it was for the best. There was never a mutual investment in our relationship." She cast her gaze downward and then back up. "And he never looked at me the way he looked at her." The sadness in her voice tugs at my heart.

"How did he look at her?"

She sighs. "With a passion that went beyond physical desire. Respect, admiration, a deep longing." She looks down at her feet, shaking her head. "I — I don't know how to explain it."

I reach out and touch her arm. She looks into my eyes. "It's okay. You don't have to explain."

We both face the water again, quiet, listening to the sounds of chattering voices and singing seagulls.

"Is there anything else you want to do here?" I ask.

"You have to ride the Ferris wheel. The view from the top is beautiful."

"Okay, let's go."

We get in line and it moves quickly. Within five minutes, we're nestled into a gondola. Ascending higher, the view is quite beautiful as she said it would be. The big wheel lazily spins twice, eventually stopping at the top. The breeze feels nice against my skin.

Suddenly, she grabs my thigh, and *not* in a sensual way. Her grasp is firm, nails digging into my skin. When I look at her, her already fair skin is ghostly pale and she's clutching her chest.

Adrenaline zaps me as I turn my body toward her. "Destiny, what's wrong?"

She stares straight ahead, her breathing is rapid and her entire body is trembling. Then she looks at me with fear sharp in her eyes. "I'm sorry. I'm so sorry." She shakes her head. "I didn't expect this."

"Expect what? What's happening to you?"

Her nails still digging into me and her breathing still fast, she continues. "I didn't think to tell you." She breaths in and out. "It hasn't happened in so long."

"What? What hasn't happened?"

"I'm —" She breathes. "I'm having a panic attack," she says, taking my hand and placing it between her breasts. Her heart beats wildly.

"Holy shit." I withdraw my hand and take her hand from my thigh, holding it in both of mine. "Tell me what to do. How do I help you? Do we need to get off? I can yell down to them."

She gazes forward again, breathing in deeply, focused. "No." She releases the breath. "I'll be okay." She continues her focused breathing as her body continues trembling. "It's okay." She nods trying to assure me, but I'm freaking out.

"What can I do? I want to help you."

She exhales. "When we spin down —" She inhales. "I want to get off." She exhales, shuddering, then clutches our clasped hands to her chest. Her other hand has a death-grip on the pig and is curled into her stomach. I sit closer to her, putting my arm around her shoulders, trying to make her feel safe. "Until then, there's really nothing you can do." She inhales. "I'm so sorry about this." She shakes her head vigorously, inhaling and exhaling, rocking her body back and forth.

"Please. No. It's okay. I'm here." I stroke her arm.

Finally, the wheel begins moving. As we get closer to the bottom, I shout to the operator.

"Excuse me, sir! We need to get off right now!"

Thankfully, he hears me and slows the wheel as we approach the bottom.

The operator opens the gondola door.

"Thank you so much," I say, getting out and holding my hands out for her.

"Man, is she okay? Do I need to call an ambulance?"

"No, I'm fine," she says breathlessly as she trembles, sweat glistening on her face. "It's just a panic attack, I know how to manage it." She breathes. "Thank you for stopping for us." She breathes. "I'm sorry for the inconvenience."

"It's fine, ma'am. You feel better now."

Wrapping my arm around her tiny, shaking body, I walk us to a bench. She clutches my other hand into her.

I sit her on the bench, release her, and squat down in front of her. "Destiny, what can I do?"

"I'd love some cold water." The quaver in her voice rips at me. I don't want to leave her, but I want to help her.

"Okay, I'll be right back. Stay here."

As I rise, she clasps her hands together tightly around the pig in her lap, her shoulders hunched inward. My heart aches. I quickly find the closest place that sells water and return to her. Opening the bottle, I hand it to her. She takes it with her trembling hands and the water spills out and down her arms.

"Oh gosh, I'm sorry."

I take the bottle from her and sit next to her. Putting the bottle to her lips, I slowly tilt it into her mouth. She sucks it in.

"Destiny, please, stop apologizing. It's okay. I just want to understand what's happening to you so I can help you."

"I'll tell you." She breathes. "I just need to focus on my breathing —" she inhales, "and calm my heart rate. I didn't bring my emergency medicine."

Taking the water bottle in both of her hands, she puts it up to her lips and sips. I sit quietly as she closes her eyes and breathes. I feel helpless. Still with her eyes closed, she reaches out to hold my hand, gripping it tightly. I slide closer to her. As the minutes pass and she breathes in and out, seeming to follow a rhythm, the tremors begin fading.

Loosening her grip on my hand, she releases a long sigh and opens her eyes. Her shoulders relax down and the color comes back to her skin. Her breathing is normal again.

"Are you okay?"

"I'm okay." Her nod assures me.

"Are you afraid of heights?"

She giggles. "No, I'm not afraid of heights. I started having panic attacks about four years ago, but I haven't had one in a long time. That's why I don't have my emergency medicine with me, I haven't needed it."

"Why did that happen to you?"

"I'm not sure, to be honest. Usually for me it's a claustrophobic thing. Like, I'm not in control of what's happening. The first time I had one, I was on an airplane and I explained to the flight attendant that I wanted to get off the plane, *that instant*. Well, we were in the air and getting off the plane obviously wasn't possible. I remained calm as I was telling her what was happening, but inside, my heart was racing, my body was vibrating, it felt like all the muscles in my body were seizing, and I thought I was dying. It was the most scared I've ever been in my life."

"That sounds horrifying." I can't imagine what it must feel like, even after her description and watching her go through one.

"I guess because we were up there and I wasn't in control of us getting down. It must've triggered something." She lowers her head. "I'm so embarrassed."

"There's nothing to be embarrassed about." I squeeze her hand. She must not have realized she was holding my hand because she releases it immediately. "I'm sorry," she says.

"It's fine." I take her hand back in mine. I like having her hold my hand. I'm glad I was with her when this happened.

"And I ruined the ride for you." The beautiful features of her face draw down into a frown.

"I don't care about that. I care about you." As I gaze into her eyes and say the words, I feel their truth in my core. I'm starting to have feelings for her, feelings beyond physical attraction and wanting to get between her legs.

"I'm okay now. They do take a lot out of me though. Do you mind if we go home?"

"No. I was going to suggest it. Are you okay to bike though?"

"Yeah, I'm fine."

"Okay, we'll take it slow."

We find our bikes, she puts the pig and her purse in the front basket of hers, and we ride back to her house. When we arrive, we park our bikes on her front porch.

"You wanted to send my mom a gift basket. How about we do that quickly and then you can go," she says, entering her house.

"I'm not leaving you alone," I say sternly.

She chuckles. "Nicco, I'm fine." She looks up into my eyes. "I promise."

Tilting my head down toward her, I lower my voice. "May I stay?"

She steps back. "Yes, um, of course."

"Good. We can order food and watch a movie." And I can keep an eye on you.

When she goes upstairs to change, I take off my shoes and socks and get a chance to really look around her home. It's cozy and beachy, decorated in neutrals, soft blues, and muted greens. The decor is tasteful with vases of white hydrangeas, a few large seashells and white coral pieces, candles in glass holders, and glass jars filled with small shells and starfish. While it's unusual to have a desk in the living room, given her work, it makes sense. And the view she has through the large bay window is something else. I grab the remote on top of her fireplace and, even though it's still early evening, I turn it on. She gets cold so easily and, after the day she had, she might like having it on.

She comes back down a few minutes later wearing black leggings and an oversized gray sweatshirt. *Damn, she's adorable.*

"I turned this on. I hope you don't mind."

"Not at all. I love having the fireplace on." She smiles.

Sitting down at her desk, she tucks her leg under her and helps me find a nice gift basket online for her mom, and then we order food. While we wait for the food to arrive, we pick out a movie, *Fast & Furious Presents: Hobbs & Shaw*. As she's loading the movie, she gasps and spins around, facing me.

"Nicco, we were so busy with all the games and rides, you forgot to tell me about your meetings. I want to hear how they went." Her excitement makes me smile.

"That's right. I forgot too."

We sit on the sofa portion of her comfortable sectional and I give her the highlights of my meetings. Given her mom's career, Destiny's met people from different aspects of the industry through the years. She spoke very highly of Vance and I'm even more excited about my meeting with him tomorrow afternoon.

Our food arrives and she starts the movie. When it finishes, we decide to binge-watch the *Fast & Furious* collection, she has them all.

"I'm surprised you like these kinds of movies given you write romance for a living," I say as she switches the Blu-rays.

"I love all the action, and there are love stories woven in. What I really love though is their dedication to each other and the family they create among themselves." She walks over to her connected kitchen. "Want a snack?"

"Sure." Joining her in the kitchen, I'm curious about what snacks she has.

There's a variety of both healthy snacks and junk food, mostly chocolate. We both opt for unhealthy snacks. I take the glass container of homemade chocolate chip cookies she'd made and she grabs the glass jar of Hershey kisses plus two water bottles.

"You're the most organized person I've ever met. I don't know anyone who keeps their food in glass containers," I say as we bring our snacks back to the living area.

She laughs. "Yeah, I'm a bit of a neat-freak. I like things organized. It helps me be productive."

We settle back on the sofa, me stretching my legs on the chaise section with a big pillow at my back, and her sitting close, but not too close, with her legs curled up on the sofa under a blanket and a pillow tucked into her side. I probably shouldn't, but I want her closer to me. I can't figure out if she feels anything for me. I still don't know if I'm who she was writing about in her pages and I don't know if I'm misinterpreting what feels to me like chemistry between us. I'm so used to women being attracted to me, but with Destiny, I have no idea. Sometimes I think she might be because of how she reacts when we're close, but then other times, it's like she resists me. I can't figure her out.

Snacks in hand, we resume our binge-watching.

Destiny

When I open my eyes, Nicco's arms are wrapped around my feet, cradling them like a stuffed animal. Carefully, I stretch my arm to get my phone off the coffee table to see what time it is. I tap my phone and 6:18 lights on the screen. Resting my head on the pillow, I gaze up at the seashell chandelier and quietly sigh.

Though I still think he's a playboy, I'm seeing a different side of him that I didn't expect. He was so sweet with that little girl yesterday. And when I had my panic attack, the way he took care of me blew me away. He's inching into my heart.

Feeling gross from not having brushed my teeth or washed my face last night, I cautiously slip my feet out from his arms. He stirs a bit and I freeze, staring at him. I can't believe he's here, in my house, on my sofa, asleep. Damn, he's gorgeous. *Cut it out.*

I quietly sneak upstairs and get a shower. As the water washes over my body, my thoughts immediately go to Nicco — naked, stepping into the shower behind me. Squirting body wash into his hands, he rubs them together and starts washing my back. With his soapy hands around my waist, he slides them up my back then around my shoulders, massaging my neck with his thumbs. Sliding his hands back down, he grazes the sides of my breasts with his fingers. When he reaches my waist again, he applies delicate pressure, and slides his hands slowly up, grazing my breasts again. I tingle between my legs.

As he glides his hands back down, he moves them around to my stomach, then down my inner thighs. His hands feel so good on me. My body arches in response and he groans as my butt presses into him. He roams again with his large hands, back around my waist, up the sides of my body, around to my breasts. Then, taking my arms in each hand and sliding his sudsy hands up them as he raises them above my head, he places my hands against the wall. Holding my hands above my head with one hand, he slides the other back down my body and around my waist then tugs me into him. I gasp, feeling how hard he is against my skin.

His mouth is at my ear. "Don't move," he whispers.

He squeezes more body wash into his hands and touches me, circling my butt cheeks with his slippery hands. He encases my waist with his arm, sliding his other hand between my cheeks. Slowly, he glides both hands up my arms still above my head, wrapping them around my wrists. I feel him move behind me, sliding himself gently between my butt cheeks, up and down, up and down. Tilting my head back, I let out a hushed moan as my breathing increases.

He returns his mouth to my ear. "Spread your legs for me, mia dolce ragazza." His whisper shoots straight between my legs.

I do.

"Don't move your arms," he says in a low growl.

He slips his hands down my body again, one hand grabbing my opposite breast, the other sliding between my legs. I squirm. He reaches his hand up to the water, rinsing off the suds. Still holding my body against his with his other arm, he inserts his finger into me, staying shallow. Sliding it out, he rubs the nub at the top of my slit. Inserting again, he goes deeper, then back out, massaging my nub. I release a whimper. He slides his length between my cheeks again, pressing my abdomen in and down, tilting me against him, groaning.

This time, he slips two fingers into me, dragging them out, and sliding them in. He quickens his pace then stops, rubbing my nub and sliding himself between my cheeks. Back in with two fingers, he slides them deeper, groaning louder. My heart races, I pant as he slides his fingers in and out of me faster. Each time he stops to rub my nub, my frenzy heightens. He plunges his fingers deep, stroking inside me. Pounding the wall with my hands, I release a squeak. He's relentless in giving me pleasure, thrusting his fingers in and out.

"Will you come for me, Destiny?" he murmurs.

"Yes," I say, between pants.

He pulls me against him, guiding my arms so my hands can reach his trap muscles. Pressing my body against his, he thrusts two fingers back inside me, ruthlessly pulsing in and out with one hand and massaging my nub with the other, waiting for me to come undone.

Tension builds inside me, my breaths rapid. The faster he moves, the louder I moan. I dig my nails into his muscles and he focuses fully on my nub, massaging at the perfect speed and pressure. My back arches in response.

"Yes, mia dolce ragazza, come for me."

My entire body explodes with tingling ecstasy as my walls pulse and contract. My clenching thighs squeeze around his hand still between my legs. I fall forward and, as my knees weaken, he slides one arm across my torso and the other around my stomach, holding me against him.

My fingers are pruney from standing under the shower for so long. I calm myself down from my fantasy and finish my shower. *Holy hell.*

Hair still wet and no makeup on, I open the bathroom door and smell coffee. How am I going to look him in the eye and not tingle between my legs?

10

Nicco

Destiny comes down the stairs wearing jean shorts and a tan T-shirt. Even with wet hair and no makeup, she's beautiful.

"Good morning. I made coffee and started some scrambled eggs," I say, stirring the eggs with a spatula. "I hope you don't mind."

"Good morning. No, not at all. Did I wake you?" she asks, getting a mug that says, "Salt Water Cures Everything" out of the cabinet.

"No, I woke up on my own. I heard the shower running and didn't want to leave without saying goodbye so I started breakfast. You have quite a collection." I smile, nodding at the mug.

She grins. "My mugs make me happy."

I stop scrambling the eggs and pour coffee into her mug.

"Thank you." She scoops in two teaspoons of sugar then adds creamer. "Do you want toast with your eggs?"

"Sure. I made enough for you. Are you hungry?"

"Starving," she says, taking a loaf of marble rye bread out of a wooden bread box.

She puts two pieces of bread in the toaster and gets butter from the refrigerator. Then she takes two plates out of the cabinet and silverware from the drawer. Once she has everything out, she lifts herself to sit on the countertop and sips her coffee.

"Ah. You make a good cup of coffee. What time is your meeting this afternoon?"

When I look at her to answer, her nipples capture my attention. The water from the ends of her long hair has darkened her T-shirt around her breasts and caused the fabric to cling to them. Catching a quick glimpse of the outline of her nipples and curve of her breasts makes me stir in my pants.

Lowering the heat on the eggs, I press down the toaster button, and stand in front of her. Placing a hand on either side of her, I lean down so we're face to face. I have to see if she shows any signs of attraction to me.

"Two o'clock." I look directly into her eyes and don't move, hovering in front of her.

Her pupils expand as she sips in a tiny breath of air.

As I rise and step away, I see teeny bumps covering her arms. Hmm, maybe she does feel something.

"Oh good," she says, taking in a deeper breath. "Then you're not risking running late."

"No."

The toaster pops up the toast and I put them on a plate then insert two more pieces. I scoop eggs onto the plate with toast and set it next to her. Hopping down from the counter, she butters her toast, and waits for me at the small dinette.

During breakfast, she shares with me a little more about Vance and I'm excited for my meeting with him today. After we finish eating, I help her clean up and know it's time to let her get to work.

As we stand in her foyer, she looks up at me. "We haven't scheduled time for me to interview you yet. Do you think we could do that soon? I have some of the structure laid out now and still have some location research to do, but I'd like to start creating the meat of the story."

"Do you have your questions ready?"

"Not all of them. I'll be doing that today."

"Okay, how about when we go to the beach tomorrow, you can ask me your questions?"

She nods. "That'll work."

I linger, not wanting to leave, but knowing I should. I give her quick cheek-kisses and turn toward the door.

"Nicco."

"Yeah?" I say, turning back to face her.

"I — uh, thank you," she says, one thumb looped into her pocket and the other hand pointing to the kitchen, "for breakfast. That was very nice of you."

"You're welcome. I'm a pretty good cook." I cock my head to the side and smile.

"And —" She rubs the back of her neck. "Thank you for taking care of me yesterday. I appreciate it."

"Of course. I'm glad I was with you. Although I don't think I did much to help."

"But you did. I…" She hesitates. "I feel safe with you."

My heart swells. "Good. I'll always keep you safe." Stepping toward her, I tuck her damp hair behind her ear and wrap my arms around her, pulling her into me. She smells like citrus and vanilla. Pressing her into me, I feel her breasts against my chest and yearn to touch them, with my hands, my mouth. I love how she feels in my arms.

Releasing her, I stare into her beautiful eyes. Fuck I want to kiss her.

Breaking the moment, she steps back and folds her arms across her chest. "Let me know how it goes today."

"I will. Eleven tomorrow?"

"Great. I'll see you then. Good luck."

I walk out the door and, as she closes it behind me, it hits me: I want to break my own damn rule and kiss her.

My brother, Marco, should be done with his photography job and I want to check in with him to see how it went and also to tell him what's been going on with me. As soon as I get back to my hotel, I sit in the chair on my balcony overlooking the city, light up a cigarette, and call him.

"Hey, how's it going? You're home now, right?" I ask.

"Yeah, bro. Hey, how's your vacation? How's L.A.?"

"I have so much to tell you."

"Yeah? Tell me."

"The Fendi shoot went great. Candi was incredible as usual."

"That's good to hear, man."

"Yeah, yeah. At the shoot, I met Candi's best friend, Destiny. It turns out, her mom is in the industry and, not only does she know people, she set me up on interviews with some of the big guys for representation here in the U.S."

"No fucking way!"

"Yeah. I had two interviews on Monday and I have one more later today. It's fucking unbelievable."

"That's incredible. Let me know how it goes today."

"Yeah, I will."

"What else have you done there? Did you drive around and start getting familiar with places?"

"Actually, I hired a tour guide." I blow smoke into the breeze.

"A tour guide?"

"Yeah, I made a deal with Destiny. Actually, we have two deals going."

"Okay, now I'm curious. What are these deals?"

"She's an author. She writes romance books. And right now, her career is having a hard time. So, I asked her to show me around L.A. and told her I'd pay her for her time since it would take away from her time writing. She needs the money."

"That was generous of you. And the second deal?"

"Actually, it was the first deal. When I learned what her mom did for a living, I suggested she connect me with her, that's how I got the meetings. In exchange, I told her she could base her next book on me and tap into my social media following since they'd probably like her books." I take a long drag. "The interesting thing is, the next day, she offered to let me back out of my end of the deal because she said she wants to earn her audience, not just sponge off me. I admire her integrity and honesty."

"I'm sorry, did you say you *admire* her?" he asks, his voice raising.

"Yeah. We made a deal that will expose her to the millions of women who follow me and that would probably explode her career. Once she was sober, she basically turned it down."

"Okay, I admit, that's admirable. I've just never heard you say you admire something about a woman before, except Mamma, that's all. It caught me off guard."

"Yeah." He's right. A quick scan in my head through the women I've dated and none of them had half the qualities Destiny has.

"So, what's she like, this Destiny?"

"She's pretty great. I've never met someone as kind as her. Does things for others without wanting anything in return, purely from the kindness of her heart. The one day, she was taking me to the Hollywood sign, but needed to stop by the hospital first. We watched a soldier get reunited with his wife for the birth of their first child. *She* set it up."

"Wow, that's pretty amazing."

"She is. She's also very compassionate."

"Yeah?"

"And she's fuckin' beautiful, man, but she doesn't even know it."

"Should I ask if you banged her yet?" He knows me well.

"Nah. I'm not saying I didn't wanna fuck the shit out of her when we first met, but no." In an attempt to smother my amplifying craving for her, I take a long drag. "First, she'd never have sex with me and second, there's no way I'm good enough for her. She's worth more than just a fuck, way more."

"Do you have feelings for her?" His voice raises again.

"No. She's just nice. I like her. I like hanging out with her."

"That's why I'm asking, shithead."

"No, man. You know I'm not going there. Not for me and not for her. I'm not gonna screw her up."

"Look, I love you. But I gotta call you out. It's time to let go of the Ana-bullshit and move on. Do you really want to be single and alone for the rest of your life?"

"No, but look, even if I wanted to see if there could be something between me and Destiny, it would never work. My career is taking off and I'm traveling a lot doing movies and singing at concerts. What kind of dating life is that when I'd be gone most of the time? Nah, she deserves more than I could give her."

"Okay, it's your life. I hope you know what you're doing."

"Yeah, it's cool. Someday I'll settle down." An emptiness sags my heart as I say the words, fearful they're a lie and I'll never have what he has, an incredible wife, a son, a family. Maybe my one chance was my last chance. My chest hurts when I think of Ana. "Okay, enough about me. How was your shoot?" I stamp out my cigarette.

"Hey, before that, Franco misses his Uncle Nicco. You should come for a visit when you get back."

"Yeah, I'd like that. I have another brand shoot when I get back, but I could come after that."

"Great, Angelina and I would love to see you."

He tells me about the photo shoot he just did and, when we hang up, I go back inside and lay on my bed. All I can think about is Destiny and my conversation about her with Marco. As much as I'm attracted to her and I'm captivated by her beautiful heart, I like her too much already to risk messing with her life.

11

Destiny

When I walk back in from the gym, I'm ready for another shower. But before I can do that, Candi calls.

"Hey, how are you?" I ask.

"Hey, girl. I have a break for a little while and took a chance you'd be around."

"I am. I just got back from the gym."

"Really? That's kinda late for you isn't it?"

"Um, it is, a little." I stall, not sure I should tell her about Nicco. I mean, she's my best friend and we share everything, but really, is there anything to share? Just because I'm having the hottest fantasies about him and finding him to be more interesting than I thought he'd be in real life doesn't mean there's anything to actually share with her, right? "How's Hawaii?"

"It's fine," she says with a mischievous undercurrent.

"Have you been able to sight-see at all? Or is it all just work, work, work?"

"So far, it's been all work, but I'm going to stay a few days longer since I have some time between jobs. Um, let's back up a bit. Why are you so late in getting back from the gym?"

"I — I just got a late start, that's all." I've never been a good liar and she knows the different tones of my voice too well.

"Bullshit. Des, what's going on?"

"Nothing, it's nothing."

"Okay, let's say I believe you, which I don't. How are things going with Nicco and your tour guiding?"

"Good. Really good. On Sunday, I took him to the observatory and the sign to get a picture. He stayed for dinner that night. We got Hana's and he made his first s'more." I laugh, recalling him flinging his flaming marshmallow into the sand. "He torched his marshmallow. And yesterday I took him to the pier. It was nice, but ugh, I had a bit of an incident."

"An incident?"

"It was so embarrassing." I drop my head into my hand. "We were at the top of the Ferris wheel and, whoosh, it hit me, a panic attack."

She gasps. "Oh, Des."

"I know. It came out of nowhere. You know I haven't had one in years. And I didn't have my emergency medicine with me. It was awful. But Nicco was," I pause. "Incredible. He was so compassionate and took care of me. Even stayed for dinner to make sure I was okay. And..." I pause.

"And?"

"And, well, we ended up falling asleep on the sofa."

"Together?" Her voice raises a pitch.

"No, not together. I mean, yes, technically on my sofa together, but not *together*," I emphasize. "Trust me, it was completely accidental."

"Hmh." For such a small sound, it packs a punch of suspicion. "So, he was there this morning?"

"Yes. He made scrambled eggs and toast."

"That was nice." I can see the wheels spinning in her head.

"Can, come on. I know exactly what you're thinking and no. Be realistic."

"Why? Why do I have to be realistic? Dreams aren't always realistic and sometimes, miracles happen and dreams come true."

"Candi," I say sternly. "He's Niccolo-fucking-Mancini. I have no business thinking or dreaming anything realistic about him. Also, he smokes. No. No, no, no. Besides, we both know my creativity suffers when I'm in a relationship. I need to be single in order to fuel my imagination." I walk out to the back porch and sit on my swing, curling my legs under me.

"Um, yeah, about that. You know I say this with love, but girl, you've been single for a while now and you're in a slump. So, I'm not sure your theory is holding up. What are you going to do, stay single until you die because you think that's the only way you can be inspired? Seems to me, the minute Nicco walked into your life, your inspiration ignited."

"Whoowh, you're telling me." Grabbing a pillow, I clutch it to my chest.

"What?" There's that high pitch again.

"Oh my gosh, I had the wildest, most vibrant fantasy about him in the shower this morning. I mean *wild*." I bury my face in the pillow and scream.

"Oooo." She squeals. "Yes, girl! See, maybe this is exactly what you need."

"Look, he's a really nice guy. Actually, a lot nicer than I gave him credit for, well, only knowing the playboy side of him I read about. But honestly, it doesn't matter. He's hot and rising to fame, and that puts us in two different categories. Someday when he realizes he's so much better than the image he throws out there and decides to show the world what a great guy he is, some hot, famous woman is going to win his heart."

"Not if it's already taken." The sincerity in her voice makes me sad because I know the truth is that Nicco and I could never be together. "Hey, I gotta go."

"Okay."

"What do you say you fly out here and spend a couple days with me?"

"Oh my gosh, you know I'd love to, but I don't have the money right now."

"What if I pay half?"

"Candi," I gruff. She knows I don't want pity-money.

"Please. I'm making a killing on this job. Besides, what else am I gonna do with my money?"

I sigh. I really want to go. "I don't even know if I can get a flight this close."

"Just try, please." I can picture her pleading face.

"Let me check on flights and see if I can borrow some money from my mom. When should I go? I'm with Nicco tomorrow and have to help my mom with a charity event Friday morning."

"Can you come Friday night? We can fly back Monday if that works for you."

"Okay, you go and let me do some research."

She squeals with delight. "I hope you can come. And, Des," she says, shifting from excitement to tenderness. "I know Kevin hurt you, but please don't close off your heart forever. You're such an amazing woman and you deserve to have an amazing love story with an amazing man."

I match her tender tone. "And maybe your love story's not over yet."

"I'm lucky. I had mine. You don't get that twice." The weight of her words sags my heart.

"I love you." As much as she keeps faith that I'll find love, I'll keep faith that she'll finds it again.

"I love you too. Let me know how you make out."

She makes a kissing sound into the phone and we hang up. Letting the warm salty breeze wash over me, I consider what Candi said. She's not wrong. Even though I'm holding tightly to my theory, right now, it's crap. Even if it is crap, that doesn't mean I have any business thinking there could ever be anything between me and Nicco. I do hope we stay friends after next week though.

Bending up my knees, I wrap my arms around my legs and take in a few more breaths of salty air, listening to the hushed waves crashing down at the shoreline. I go back inside, shower, and call my mom. Thankfully, she has airline miles I can use so neither Candi nor I have to pay for the flight. I got lucky and managed to get the last available seat on the plane. *Reminder: bring emergency medicine, Nicco won't be there to help you.* I can cover my food and I know I can sleep in Candi's bed. All in all, not bad for a last-minute trip to Hawaii. I text Candi to let her know we're on.

Still sitting at my computer, I see my Word document, minimized at the bottom of the screen, with the few questions I started writing for my interview with Nicco. I get up from my chair, walk around to the back of it, and lean over it, looking at the little W icon at the bottom of the screen, taunting me. Straightening back up, I cross my arms and pace behind the chair, eyeing my computer screen, practically staring down the W. Nope, I can't do it. I have to get out of this. But, I can't. I tried. He won't let me. Ugh.

I give the W my best evil-eye and go to the kitchen to make a late lunch. Once I finish eating, I continue avoiding writing the questions by making my priority washing the dishes. *This is ridiculous. I'm being ridiculous. I'm a professional author for goodness sakes.* I settle in at my computer and maximize the document to type up the rest of my questions. I don't have much so far.

1. What got you interested in acting?
2. What's your favorite song on your album?
3. Who do you want to do a movie with?
4. What's your favorite food?
5. Do you have a favorite tattoo? What's the meaning of it?

Good gracious, these are fine questions for a generic interview, but it's also stuff I can find online. I need to go deeper. I need to get inside his head, his soul. I need to know what motivates him, what keeps him up at night, what terrifies him. Hmm, while I know I need to know these things to develop my character, I have to admit, I want to know the answers for myself. The more time I spend with him, the more curious I am about him.

In order to have a believable story, I need to come up with

what it is he needs to attain, his "why" behind needing to attain it, and what his solution is, albeit misguided, to attaining it. Then I need to throw some obstacles and conflicts at him and help him uncover his true need and the solution that gets him to *that* thing. I can't very well come out and ask *him* all this. He won't know.

And I have no idea how to ask him about his love life without basically calling him out as a playboy again, which, I'm discovering, there's definitely more beneath the surface of this devastatingly hot, sexy man. I shouldn't have agreed to this. I'm better with fictional characters. Okay, more questions.

6. What keeps you humble with your fast rise to fame?
7. What was your childhood like?
8. What motivates you when you're having a bad day?
9. What do you want for your future?
10. What's the one thing you want the world to know about you?
11. Why do you sleep with women, but rarely have relationships with them?
12. What turns you on about a woman?
13. What scares you?
14. What scares you about being in a relationship?
15. What's your biggest fear in life?

I stare at the screen, reading the questions. Ugh, this is hopeless. I write fiction, fantasy, not reality. I inhale and blow out loudly. Okay, I think what I need to do is ask him these questions tomorrow so he feels like he's fulfilled his part of our deal. I'm sure he'll tell me things I can use. Then, I'll make up the rest just like I know how to do. Done.

I'm not in the headspace to write so I print out my questions and pack my beach bag for our trip tomorrow. Sunscreen, book to read, snacks, two beach towels, beach blanket, four rocks, notebook with question page tucked in, and a pen. I fold up a sundress to put on over my suit for the winery and dinner, and put it in a separate bag. Then I get out my small cooler that I'll pack with waters and ice tomorrow.

With showing Nicco around town, I haven't spent much time on social media. Since I'm not writing, I invest some time making a few new posts, interacting with people, making a TikTok video, and working on my Pinterest board. It doesn't take long to get lost in pictures of Nicco and Ponza Island. There isn't a whole lot else on my board.

Remembering that he took a picture of us together at the Hollywood sign, I pick up my phone and slide the bar, tapping on my camera app. Finding the picture of us, I stare at it. *What goes on inside that head of yours, Niccolo Mancini?*

My phone rings, startling me out of my mini-trance, and I drop it in my lap. It's Nicco.

"Ciao, mia dolce ragazza. How's your day going?"

I tingle between my legs, remembering my shower fantasy and him calling me that. "Hi, good. How'd your meeting go today?"

"It was great. I really liked him and we had a very good conversation. I really connected with him. We talked about work and also personal things."

"That's awesome. I'm so glad to hear it." I'm thrilled for him that he's one step closer to making his dreams come true.

"Oh, your mom called to thank me for the gift basket. She said she loved everything. Thank you again for your help in picking out things she would like."

"Good, I'm glad. You're welcome."

"So, I have a question for you."

"Okay."

"What are you doing this weekend?"

"Believe it or not, I'm going to Hawaii," I announce cheerfully. "Hawaii?"

I laugh at the surprise in his voice. "Yeah, it was totally last-minute. Candi's out there for a photo shoot and decided to stay a few days. She invited me to come join her. My mom had some airline miles and I can stay with Candi, so I'm going. I'm so excited."

"That's amazing." He shares my excitement. "When do you go?"

"I'm helping my mom with a charity event Friday morning and I leave later that day. We'll come back on Monday."

"That's a short trip."

"It is, but that's okay, it'll be fun. Oh, did you want me to show you something this weekend?" I hope I didn't throw a wrench into things for him.

"No, no. It's okay. Go have a good time. When do you want to go to San Diego next week?"

"I was thinking Tuesday. Does that work for you?"

"Okay, yeah, that works. What are you doing next weekend?"

"Next weekend?"

"Yeah."

I'm getting the feeling he wants me to show him around some more, but he's not coming out and saying it. Surely four days, and one accidental night, together is as much as he can handle of me. "Um, writing probably. Why?" If he won't get to it, I will. "Did you want me to show you something more than what we've planned?"

"No, no, it's fine. We're on for tomorrow at eleven, right?"

"Yes. I have a beach towel for you. And you'll probably want to bring a change of clothes for the winery and dinner."

"Okay, great. Got it. I'll see you tomorrow then."

Hmm, what was that about?

12

—

Nicco

When I arrive at Destiny's house, she's putting a small cooler and beach bag in the back seat of her white Acura SUV.

"Good morning. Perfect timing," she says, smiling brightly at me. I can't see her beautiful blue eyes behind her sunglasses. "Do you have a change of clothes?"

"Good morning. I do," I say, handing her a rolled-up wad of shorts, a T-shirt, and underwear that she puts in a separate bag. "Do you need to get anything else from inside?"

"Nope. I just need to use the bathroom and lock up. If you need to as well, I can go upstairs."

We both go in and meet back in her foyer.

"You can leave your keys here so they don't get lost in the sand," she says, pointing to the seashell on the small table next to her shoe bench. "Ready?" she asks, taking a large sun hat from one of the hooks above the bench.

I drop my keys in the seashell. "Let's go."

As we drive, I tell her more details about my meeting yesterday and we discuss the three agencies and people I met with, as well as who I'd like to work with.

The drive isn't long. She parks and we unload her car, I take the cooler, she puts on her hat and takes her beach bag. Finding a spot on the sand, she pulls a large blanket out of her bag and lays it down then sets her bag on a corner. She reaches in and takes out four rocks then places one on each corner of the blanket. Damn, she's right. She's one organized woman.

She takes a small purse out of her bag. "I'm going to go get us an umbrella and some chairs. Watch our stuff, okay?"

I take her arm in my hand. "Wait."

"What is it?"

"This is part of my tour, right?"

"It is."

"Then I'll pay."

She cocks her head to the side. "Nicco, you don't have to pay for everything. I know I'm in a slump right now, but I'm not poor."

There's her feisty, independent side. So cute and so frustrating. "I know you're not. This is part of our arrangement. You're bringing me here because I asked you to."

She sighs.

"Look, if we were dating, I'd let you pay for things sometimes. But, you'd never date me, would you?" I wish she didn't have sunglasses on, hiding her expressive eyes. They usually tell me more than her words. I'm not sure she'll answer the question.

She jolts back just the slightest bit.

"I..."

I save her the discomfort. I know the answer. "I'll get the umbrella and chairs."

I go to the stand where we entered the beach and pay for one umbrella and two chairs that I help the kid carry to our spot. Once the umbrella is securely in the ground, we arrange the chairs and sit down. She shows me the variety of snacks she's packed for us, some healthy, some junk food. I love that about her, she's very healthy, but has this little bad-girl inside when it comes to snacks.

"I brought my interview questions with me. Do you want me to ask you them now? Or do you want to wait until later?" she asks, taking a notepad and pen out of her beach bag.

"I'm not ready to go in the water yet. You can ask me some now."

"Okay. Most of them are probably ones you typically get."

"Then it should be easy." I chuckle.

"And, if there's anything you don't want to answer, you know you don't have to. That was our agreement."

"I'll let you know."

"Okay. What got you interested in acting?"

"Ever since I was a kid, I loved watching movies. Acting always seemed like a fun job. As I got older and began learning more about what goes into really stepping into a character and the craft of acting, it fascinated me. I liked learning about the psychology of the person I was playing. So, I auditioned for different roles, small ones, and I got a few every now and then. Nothing big, you know, just supporting roles, but never the lead. And the one time I finally got the lead, I was fired. That knocked me off my feet. I figured I wasn't cut out for acting and that's when I became a gardener. I almost didn't take the role as Matteo because of my gardening job. When they asked me to audition, I was in the middle of a gardening project for a customer and I feel bad because I never finished it."

She writes quickly on her notepad as I answer. "Well, we're all very happy you auditioned and got the role," she says, adjusting the strap on her aqua coverup and shifting her position. "What's your favorite song on your album?"

"Hands down, "Dad." I wrote it for my dad. It has great meaning for me."

"I've heard it. I love the lyrics you wrote. It's a beautiful tribute to him." She pauses. "Who do you want to do a movie with?"

"Robert De Niro," I say, without hesitation.

"Why him?"

"That guy can master so many different types of roles. He's truly inspiring."

"I've loved every movie I've seen him in. You're right, he's extraordinary in every role he plays. Okay, what's your favorite food?"

"Mmm, there's nothing better than Mamma's pasta," I say, curling all the fingertips on one hand to my pursed lips and then spreading my fingers outward as I move my hand back, making a kissing sound, and smile.

She giggles. "Good answer. Do you have a favorite tattoo? And if you do, what's the meaning of it?"

"They each have a special meaning, but this one," I hold out my left hand to show her the top of my hand with the phoenix and skull inked into my skin, "is my favorite. You see the phoenix, when it dies, it's born again. And the skull inside represents bad things. So, when bad things try to get me, the phoenix will take them and fly away with them."

More scribbling on her notepad. "Almost like a guardian angel." She has a way of bringing lightness to my dark side.

"Almost. Let's do two more questions. Then will you walk with me on the beach?"

"Okay. What keeps you humble with your fast rise to fame?"

"The thing about fame is that it can be gone just as fast as it came." I snap my fingers. "Even though I may be on the rise right now, tomorrow it can all be gone. I'm grateful for every day of this life I get to live."

"Life can change in the blink of an eye."

"This is why we must be grateful. Life isn't about money and fame. Those are things we desire and dream about having and there's nothing wrong with wanting those things. I want them. But life is about love, generosity, and living in your essence every minute of every day. It's about baring your soul and protecting the souls of those you love."

As I speak, she stops writing. She stares at me like she's hanging on to every word. I want to know what she's thinking right now.

"Um, okay. One more question here and then we can do the rest later. What was your childhood like?"

"Do you mind if I answer while we walk? Or do you need your notepad?"

"No, we can walk. If I forget something, I'll just ask you again." She stands and puts down her notebook and pen then takes off her hat, wraps her small purse across her body, and puts her hat back on. "Do you want to put your wallet in here?"

"Okay." I stand, hand her my wallet, and take off my shirt, tossing it onto my chair.

"Okay," she says, under her breath as her eyes sweep quickly across my torso and she takes my wallet, tucking it into her purse, not looking back up at me.

We walk in silence to the edge of the water.

"Your hat is cute. You need it to protect your fair skin."

"Yeah, I burn easily."

"I bet." I want to see more of her creamy, fair skin. "There was nothing special about my childhood, I don't think. My dad worked hard. He was in construction. He had the most amazing work ethic. But he also made time for family. Family was very important to him. He understood the values of life. By my age, he had a stable job, was married, and had two kids." Tightness wrings around my chest at the reality that I've not accomplished any of these things. A reality that was shoved in my face four years ago. "I always looked up to him and wanted him to be proud of me." I swallow, trying to ease the constriction in my throat. I miss him every day.

"I think he would be very proud of the man you've become." She looks up at me, the sincerity in her voice overwhelms me.

"Even though I'm a playboy?" I tease.

A wave washes onto our feet.

"Well, that's currently under debate." Her smile carries a playfulness.

"Am I allowed to ask you questions?"

"Sure."

"What's your favorite food?"

"Hmm, healthy or unhealthy?" She reaches down and picks a shell out of the sand.

I laugh. "Both."

"Healthy would be the spinach salad I make and unhealthy would be chocolate molten lava cake." Tilting back her head she lets

124

out a delicious growl that makes me wish we were alone and naked. "That good, huh?"

"Oh yeah." She nods with a huge smile on her face.

"Okay, another one. Why do you think you're struggling with your career right now?"

She takes a long inhale and blows it out, dragging her toes through the wet sand. "I really wish I knew. If I knew, I'd have a chance at fixing it." She shrugs. "I can't seem to find inspiration. My life's pretty boring these days. Candi and I used to do a lot together and many of our adventures fueled some fun stories. I have friends other than Candi, of course, but most of them have nine-to-five jobs and a lot of them have babies now so we don't get together much, let alone do things like girls' weekends away. My love life leaves a lot to be desired so my writing's been falling flat there as well."

"So, your life is lacking adventure and really good sex." I can't help but smile as I tease her.

She nudges my arm with hers. "Thanks, very helpful." She chuckles.

"What about this Henry guy you mentioned? You're sure there's nothing there?"

"I'm sure. Life would *not* be an adventure with Henry. I wouldn't date him anyway."

"So, you wouldn't date me, you wouldn't date Henry. What type of person would you date?"

"I dated my fiancé."

"How long ago was that?"

"Three years."

"That's a long time."

"I know. And Candi keeps reminding." She chuckles.

"So, based on what I know about you so far, I'm guessing you haven't had sex for three years." I get itchy when it's been three weeks, I can't imagine going three years.

"You make it sound so awful."

"I can take care of that for you." I exaggerate a sleezy voice so she knows I'm joking.

"Um, I thought you were trying to prove you're *not* a playboy." She laughs. "Not all of us want to have meaningless sex with people and then move on." She picks up another shell and hands it to me. "Here, for you to remember your trip to the beach. Ready to walk back?"

"Thank you." I take the shell from her. The sentiment tugs at my heart. I'll remember *her* more than I'll remember the beach. "Yeah."

We turn around and walk the shoreline back toward our umbrella.

"I love the sound of the waves. They make their own music," she says.

"It's very peaceful. Someday I'll have a house on the beach."

"I have no doubt that you will."

We walk the rest of the way listening to the waves sing their melody and letting the water caress our feet.

"I'm going to go in the water. Will you bring my shell back for me?" I hand her the shell she picked for me.

"Sure. Enjoy your swim."

Destiny

There's much more to this man than meets the eye. He's insightful, pensive, sincere. This is unexpected. I do hope he puts his T-shirt back on when he comes back. His bare chest is distracting. Even though I've already had the pleasure of stroking his chest and abs with oily hands, just the sight of him makes my body tingle. Sure, I've seen plenty of shirtless men before, but no one like him. His broad chest expands out to his toned shoulders and narrows toward his waist and that sexy V-line. Mediterranean skin covered with the perfect amount of hair, and hard nipples, always. Beautifully outlined six-pack without being overly rippled. He's the kind of unrealistic fantasy-man I write about, and he's so very real. Thank goodness for my sunglasses, at least he can't see me ogling him like a teenager.

I take waters out of the cooler for us then sit back in my chair, get out my book, and start reading. About ten minutes later, Nicco's walking up from the water. Oh God, here comes that slow-motion time-warp again. He's dripping wet, pushing his hair back off his face, arm muscles tensing as he does, glistening in the sun, and walking toward *me*. I can't even look away. My gaze follows a trickle of salt water that rides the center channel of his chest down his abs and is then captured by a tiny curl of hair at his naval. Holy hell, this man is hot. Whoowh. *Get a grip on yourself.*

"That was fast."

"Yes, I just wanted to cool off before our next round of questions," he says, grabbing his towel and rubbing his hair with it. "I need a cigarette."

"You'll have to go to the parking lot, there's no smoking allowed on the beach."

"Okay," he says, taking out a cigarette from his pack and grabbing a very worn looking lighter. "I'll be right back."

When he returns, he doesn't put his shirt back on. So distracting.

"Okay, I'm ready for more questions," he says, sitting back in his chair and taking a swig of water. "Can I have some of those chips you brought?"

"Of course." I hand him the bag of chips and a paper towel. "All right, here we go. What motivates you when you're having a bad day?"

"My fans. I would be nothing without my fans. They show up for me and I appreciate them so much. I must show up for them." He tosses a chip in his mouth.

"What do you want for your future?"

He doesn't answer immediately. "I want a fulfilling life. I want my life to mean something. I want to leave my mark in some way."

"Do you want a family someday?"

"I…" He hesitates. "I do, but I don't know if that's going to be possible for me."

"Why?" Surely at some point he'll want to stop sleeping around and settle down. His playboy persona, I'm learning, is quite contrary to who he truly is.

"It's my work, my lifestyle, the traveling. It's not so good for a relationship," he says, opening his hands in a sort of surrender then folding them together.

"Is that why you sleep with women, but rarely have relationships with them?"

"It's best for both of us," he says, removing his sunglasses and putting them on the blanket. He takes a breath, locking his eyes on mine. "That way there's no emotional attachment and no one gets hurt," he deadpans.

"I guess that's one way to go through life." There's something more behind this. I can feel it in the incongruence of the words he speaks and the emotions hidden behind them. His words are empty, but there's something beneath them. Pain. "What's the one thing you want your fans to know about you?"

"No, not me. I want them to know that *they* can do anything. If I have any impact on this world, I want it to be that I inspire people to never give up on their dreams. That anything is possible." The passion he has when he talks about his work and his fans is powerful, endearing.

I read the next question. Maybe I should skip it. I can make up those parts.

"What's the next one?"

"Oh um, what scares you?"

"That's what made you hesitate?"

"No, I had something else, but I don't need to ask it." *Stop talking, you're sounding suspicious.*

"What scares me? Failing. Failing scares me. When I got fired from that acting job, I felt like a complete failure. I don't ever want to feel that way again."

"Feeling like you failed at something you really want is an awful feeling." I take a sip of water and get an organic granola bar out of my bag. "What scares you about being in a relationship?"

He looks at me for a moment, saying nothing. Then he speaks. "I don't want to answer this one."

"Okay, that's fine." Yup, there's definitely something deeper here. I'm not going to push him. I said I'd respect his decision to decline to answer anything I asked. But, I'm so curious. "Here's the last one. What's your biggest fear in life?"

He leans forward in his chair a little. "That I'll never fall in love or have a family."

My heart sinks in my chest. What happened to him?

"That's the last question?"

I look down at my page and lie. "Yes."

"No, you skipped one. Ask it. I want to completely fulfill my side of our deal."

My cheeks heat up. "It's really just, uh, for the more intimate scenes," I say, clearing my throat and twisting my pen between my fingers. "So, you know, you can be as vague as you want. I can fill in around it." I wave my hands briefly, trying to indicate it's no big deal.

"What's the question?"

I take a sip of water, stalling. "Right, the question. So, the question is, what turns you on about a woman?" I tilt my head down toward my notebook, pen ready to write, avoiding looking at him.

"I have a question about your question."

I look up from my notebook and he leans farther toward me. "Physically or about her personality?"

I want to disappear. "Uh, both. Let's go with both." *I'm a grown woman for heaven's sake. What's wrong with me? I'm behaving like a lunatic.*

He leans in even more locking his gaze on me. "Physically, her response to my touch, what I see when I look in her eyes, the way her soft skin feels under my hands. For personality, her heart, the way she behaves when no one's looking, the way she treats others with kindness." He pauses. "That's a start anyway."

Though I'm under the umbrella, I think I just melted into the sand. A light gust of wind blows, breaking his gaze on me.

As I go to write in my notebook, I drop my pen. He reaches over, picks it up, and hands it to me.

"Thank you." I look at him briefly. "So that was uh, touch, eyes…" I scribble. "Skin was in there. Her heart, kindness. Okay, got it." I close my notebook, putting it and my pen in my beach bag. "Thank you. This will all be really helpful for my book." Suddenly I sound like I'm solidifying a business transaction. "I appreciate you following through with your end of the deal."

"It's my pleasure. Can we go in the water now?" he asks, standing up.

"Definitely. Go ahead."

"You're not coming?"

"No. I'll stay here and watch our stuff."

He walks away and over to an older couple under their umbrella to the left of us. Then he comes back.

"This nice couple will watch our things for us. Come on." He waves his hand.

"It's okay. Really, you go ahead."

"Why won't you come with me? I want you to come."

Ugh. Now I'm being rude. Gritting my teeth, I take a deep breath and take off my hat. *I can't believe I'm doing this.* I take off my coverup and sunglasses, trying my best to conceal any look of embarrassment that might be smeared all over my face.

"Come on."

He waves to the couple as we pass them and they wave back. We walk to the water's edge and it's a little chilly splashing up my legs. I take a few more steps in and it's still pretty cold. By the time I'm thigh-deep, he does a shallow dive under the water. Slowly wading in, I get up to my stomach.

"It's beautiful," he says, swimming back to me.

"A little cold too."

"You're cold?"

I nod. "A little."

"Just dive in. You'll get used to it."

I chuckle. "You don't know my body temperature issues."

"I know you get cold easily." Now I'm in up to my breasts and sink my arms under the surface, shivering.

He's farther out. I can't go out to where he is because I'll be under water.

He swims over to me. "Can you swim?" he asks.

"Yes, I can swim. I just don't swim in the ocean much."

He laughs. "But you live at the beach."

"I know. A lot of times it's just too cold for me so I don't go in all the way."

"Here." He takes my body in his arms. "Wrap your legs around me," he says, guiding my legs around his waist. "I can take you out a farther and keep you warm."

What is he doing? How the hell am I in this situation right now? In an ocean, with Niccolo Mancini, my legs wrapped around his body.

"Nicco, maybe we shouldn't be like this, so close. I'm sure people have recognized you by now." I nod toward the shore. "I can't imagine you want pictures taken of us like this. It would misrepresent you."

"Pictures will always be taken and always be misinterpreted," he says, as I tremble in his arms and he presses me against his body. "Are you shy about your body?"

"No." My teeth chatter as I lie. "A little, maybe."

Moving his hands to where his thumbs are just under my breasts and his fingers wrap around my back, he pushes my body back from his.

Our faces only inches apart, he gazes into my eyes. "Destiny, you are a very, *very* sexy woman. You should never feel anything less than that."

I shiver in his arms, speechless, and wrap my arms around his neck, looking back toward the shore. If I wasn't so cold right now, I'd probably be turned on.

"I like your belly ring. When did you get it?"

"That was a Candi-adventure. She wanted to go into the city for her birthday. She got a tattoo and I got my navel pierced. I think it was her twenty-third birthday."

"It looks good on you."

"Thank you. I'd always thought they looked so cute on other girls."

"It doesn't look cute on you. It looks sensuous." With our bodies pressed together, I'm pretty sure he can feel my heart racing.

Silently, we stand in the ocean, the water enveloping us.

"I like having you wrapped around me." The sincerity in his words cradles me.

I like being wrapped around him. Knowing I'll never be in this situation again, for a brief moment, I let go of how intimidated I am by him and surrender into the safety, comfort, and euphoria of being in his arms. I know the moment will pass in a heartbeat so I revel in it, etching this surreal intoxication in my mind and on my heart.

My shivers stop, I curl my neck around his, and relax into him. He sways gently with the water as it bathes us. He squeezes tighter around me, dropping his head to my shoulder. We're fused together as one.

The sun is hot on my skin and I know I need to get back under the umbrella. I don't want to let go of him. But I have to. I draw my body apart from his. Our faces so close, the intensity is undeniable. A mixture of desire, connection, and respect sits in the space between us.

His eyes move to my lips. Mine are drawn to his.

"Destiny…" His stillness sends a rush through me.

The current of the water knocks his balance, disrupting the moment, severing our gaze.

"I think I'm ready to go back in," I say reluctantly.

"Your skin is getting pink."

"You can stay out here, I'll just swim back in."

"No, I'll come with you."

He walks to where I'm able to stand and we head back into the shoreline then up to our spot on the beach. Well, I look more like a mall-walker because I'm walking so fast to get to my towel and dry off. As we pass the older couple, I wave at them and he thanks them.

Grabbing my towel from my chair, I quickly pat the beads of water off my skin so I can warm up. "Brrr." I tilt my head to the side and squeeze the water from my ponytail. As I do, I catch his gaze on my breasts. My nipples are hard as a rock.

"When we're dried off, how about we go to the winery?" he asks.

"Okay, that sounds good."

He moves his chair into the sun and lays out. Putting on my sunglasses, I sit and soak in his glorious body since this is the last time I'll see this much of it in real life.

Once we're dry, we pack up our things, wave to the older couple, and head to my car.

"Where can I change?"

"I'll throw the blanket over the windshield and we can close the towels in both doors. You can change in the car. Is that okay?"

"Hah!" he laughs. "Okay, if that's what we've got, then that's what we've got."

"Any women walking by have probably already seen you naked anyway." Well, that was bold of me. And now, I'm thinking about him naked.

He lets out a hearty laugh. "You have a point."

We cover the windows and he gets in. I can think of nothing other than Niccolo Mancini being naked in my car. My head starts on a fantasy that quickly ends as he gets out.

"Do you need me to hide you?"

I chuckle. "No, I'm a woman, it's easier." I hold up my sundress.

He helps me remove the blanket and towels. I open my door and quickly slip out of my coverup and put on my sundress. He watches me.

I drive the few miles to the winery and we don't speak. I'm thinking about being in his arms, his lips inches from mine, and desperately aching for him to kiss me. "Control" by Zoe Wees comes on the radio, the lyrics ringing true. Is he thinking about holding me in his arms? Why did he do that?

We only stay at the winery for one tasting and both end up liking the same wine. He buys two bottles and we go to Malibu Farm for an early dinner. As we eat, our conversation is disconnected, almost stilted. We've both withdrawn. Regardless of what I'm feeling, nothing more than friendship can exist between us, if that's even possible once he leaves and continues on his path to stardom. He's quieter than usual. There's more than one stolen glance above the rims of our wine glasses.

On the drive home, he remains distant, as do I.

"You look like you're far away somewhere," I say.

He shifts his gaze from staring out the window to me. "No, I'm not far away. I'm here."

"Is something on your mind? I'm a really good listener."

Reaching over, he tucks a loose strand of my hair behind my ear. "I know you are. No, nothing's on my mind." His tender smile rips at my heart as his gaze lingers on me. He might be a good actor, but he's a terrible liar.

I pull into my driveway and we unload the car. As much as he's able without knowing where things go, he helps me put things away.

"Do you have a vacuum for the car?"

"I do. It's in that closet by the stairs," I say, pointing.

"I don't know where anything else goes in here, but I can vacuum out the sand."

"Okay, thanks," I say, pleasantly surprised.

By the time he comes back in, I've finished putting everything away.

"Do you want a glass of wine before I go?" he asks.

"That would be nice."

I give him the bottle opener and get two wine glasses. Silently, he pours the wine into our glasses. He hands a glass to me, takes his glass and the bottle of wine, and walks toward the back porch.

"The sky is pretty tonight," he says, stepping onto the porch.

"Twilight is my favorite time of day." I sit on one side of my swing, leaving room for him.

"Why's that?" he asks, sitting back into the swing next to me.

"I love a beautiful sunset, but twilight is like the last few seconds before you fall asleep at night. You fluff your pillow." I fluff a pillow and hug it to my chest, curling my leg under me. "Wiggle around and get comfortable, and start to quiet your mind. Then there's that blissful few seconds where you're not asleep, but not awake, just at peace. At twilight, that's when the colors morph from bright and brilliant to soft and celestial." I sip my wine.

"I love how you describe things. This is why you're such a good writer. The way you use words conveys emotion."

I smile.

He looks out to the ocean. "You leave tomorrow."

"Yes, after I help my mom in the morning."

"Are you going to be okay on the plane?"

He remembered. "I'm sure I'll be fine. I'll pack my emergency medicine."

"Okay, good. Please text me when you arrive so I know you got there safely. Otherwise, I'll worry the whole weekend."

I'm so confused. I felt his energy shift throughout the day from friendship, to almost seductive, to tender, to detached. And now he's going to worry about me? What's going through his head?

He excuses himself and walks down to the shoreline. Though the sky is darkening, I can see the smoke trail out of him.

We spend the next hour making small talk about what Candi and I will do in Hawaii, what he'll do back here, and then we confirm our plans for our trip to San Diego when I get back.

As the sun kisses the top of the horizon, we finish the bottle of wine. I shouldn't have had the second glass, especially after having had some at dinner.

"I should let you get to packing," he says, standing up and holding out his hand toward me.

I take his hand, uncurl my leg, and rise from the swing. At a leaden pace, we go back into the house and put our wine glasses and empty bottle in the kitchen.

We stand face to face in our usual spot in the foyer.

"Thank you," he says, taking the end of my ponytail, that was lying on my chest, in his hand. He watches his fingers twirl my hair, then returns his gaze to my eyes. "I had a nice time with you today." The low, hushed timbre of his voice sends a chill up my spine.

"You're welcome. I enjoyed being with you, Nicco."

He lets out a soft chuckle. "I don't want to leave. But I know I can't stay."

What does that mean? What does he mean by that? I'm lost. My head is slightly tipsy from the wine and I'm melting under the warmth of his gaze.

He leans down and wraps his strong arms around me. I can't hold back a small gasp. I swear I hear a stifled groan as he presses me against his hard chest and audibly, yet faintly, exhales.

Releasing me, he takes a small step back, and cups the side of my face in his hand. I close my eyes in response to his touch and I tilt my head into his palm. As I open my eyes, he presses his lips into my cheek and then the other. My heart rate quickens.

Returning his face to mine, he stares into my eyes. "Buona notte, mia dolce ragazza," he hums, just above a whisper. Keeping his gaze fixed on me, he inhales deeply, almost frustrated, then moves his hand from my cheek to the back of my head and presses his lips to my forehead. His audible exhale through his nose sends another shiver through me.

Stepping back from me, he takes his keys and the seashell I gave him from the shell on my table, and walks to the door.

"Good night," I say softly as he leaves.

I close and lock the door, then turn around, standing frozen in my foyer, my heart beating frantically.

Nicco

I drive back to my hotel with a hard-on and an aching heart. *What the fuck am I doing to both of us?*

13

—

Nicco

We have one more day planned together next week. That's not enough. I've never felt this way about a woman, not even Ana. I don't know what I'm feeling right now, but it's intense. I know I want to plunge deep into her, but it's more than that, so much more. I don't know how I can feel whatever I'm feeling right now, it's only been a few days. I have to drown these feelings, but I can't. She's more addicting than my fucking cigarettes. She has to come with me next weekend. After next week, whatever is happening between us ends. I don't want to hurt her. Shit, I don't want to get hurt.

My thoughts are all over the place.

Back in my hotel room, I go out to the balcony and have a cigarette. I can't stop thinking about her and the day we just spent together. Her tiny, sexy body, the way she felt in my arms in the ocean, the smell of coconut on her skin when I kissed her cheeks. I've seen many female bodies and fucked my share of hot women, but when Destiny took off the dress covering her bikini, it took everything in me to keep from getting hard on the spot. Her skin is unspoiled perfection, I'm dying to touch her. Perky breasts, small waist, tight ass. This is torture.

I finish my cigarette and get in the shower to wash off the salt water. Closing my eyes, I hang my head, letting the water run down my body. Destiny comes to me in my thoughts. Remembering her diamond-hard nipples, visible through her wet bikini top, I'm immediately hard. Fuck, I think I've been hard since I first laid eyes on her. I've got to do something to relieve the pressure. Lathering up my hands, I close my eyes, wrapping one hand around my myself, wishing my hand was her mouth.

We're not at the beach, we're at her house. She takes my hand and leads me to the sofa. Guiding me to sit on the edge, she kneels between my knees. Hair up in her ponytail with pieces falling loosely around her face, she looks up at me with her big, blue eyes and takes me in her hand, stroking me. After a few long strokes, she leans forward and covers my head with her pretty mouth, swirling her tongue around it.

At the end of a rotation around my head, she bends lower, dragging her tongue from my base to the V just below my head, flicking at it. I groan, grabbing the back of her head instinctively as she flicks her tongue at the sensitive skin. One more quick swirl of her tongue around my head and she takes me into her mouth, all of me, sucking me.

Her hand and mouth work me in unison, slowly at first, then faster. I wrap her ponytail around my hand, resting it on her head as she bobs up and down on me, faster and faster. The pressure intensifies as my blood rages through my veins. The heat inside her mouth, her lips gripping me, pumping up and down is too much. I explode, heaving a loud groan. Finally, relief.

Fuck, I have to have her.

Later, as I lie in bed, I remember her description of twilight. She comes to me in my thoughts again. She's in her leggings and big sweatshirt, looking adorable. I turn on my side and grab a pillow, wrapping it in my arms, wishing it was her, snuggled into me. For the first time in my life, I'm aware of the few blissful seconds between being awake and being asleep, imagining Destiny tucked into me.

Destiny

Candi picks me up at the airport and we head straight to dinner. She tells me all about her photo shoot, both how much fun it was and how exhausted she is.

"How was the flight?" she asks. "Were you okay?"

"I was. I didn't need my emergency medicine so that was good." I gasp. With all the activity of getting my luggage and finding Candi, I forgot to text Nicco.

"What is it?"

"I forgot to text Nicco," I say, getting my phone out of my purse.

"Text Nicco?"

"Yeah, he wanted me to let him know I landed safely and I forgot."

Me: Hi. I landed safely. The flight went well. I'm with Candi now.

Nicco: Okay. Good. Thanks for letting me know. Have a good time. Tell Candi hi for me.

Me: I will. Have a nice weekend.

"He wanted you to text him when you landed, huh?" She gives me her side-eye as she drives.

"Yes. It's nothing. I told you I had the panic attack on the Ferris wheel. I told him about the first one I had happening on an airplane so he was just concerned knowing I was flying today. Oh, he says hi."

"So, how's that been going, by the way?"

I slump forward and drop my head. "Fuck."

She snaps her head toward me and I raise my chin from my chest. I fill her in on our day at the beach, his shifting behavior, and my confused feelings.

"Okay, that's a lot to take in. I do *not* profess to understand much about men and how their brains work, but that whole hot-cold thing makes me think he's feeling something, but he's trying to deny it."

"Well, I don't know about that, but there's something there with him and relationships and women, and I can't figure it out. When I was asking him my interview questions, he wouldn't answer my question about what scares him about being in a relationship. He didn't even go all playboy on me. He just said he didn't want to answer it and was deadly serious. But there was, something." I shake my head. "Something behind his eyes, something that felt, painful somehow."

"Des, you're pretty intuitive about things like that. There's probably something he's scared to share, scared to face. Guys don't talk about that stuff."

"I know. And I know I shouldn't care because nothing can happen anyway. He leaves next week and I shouldn't even be thinking about feeling any sort of anything for him."

"Do you?" She glances over at me. "Feel something for him?"

"I don't know. I don't know if there's anything to feel. He's hard to read, you know? He's this hot Italian guy who's just shot to fame because of an erotic movie he starred in and sometimes I feel like I'm misinterpreting that sensuality. Is it because I saw him in the film? Is it because I'm extremely attracted to him? I mean who wouldn't be? Is it because I'm getting to know the man behind what the world sees? A man who has a depth to him I've never seen in a man. I have no idea."

"What's the energy you get from him?"

"Here's the thing, that's confusing too. I know he's a passionate man by nature, but when he's close to me, I swear there's fire between us. And, I know this is going to sound crazy, but it's more than just the fact that I've been fantasizing about him and his hotness. Can, I feel something," I say, putting my hand on my heart. "I don't know if it's just part of his innate heritage or what, but he has this lure about him. He gets so close to me, Can, inches from my face and lingers. I don't know if that's just how he is with women or what? I know, it doesn't make any sense at all."

"Okay. Take a deep breath and let it out."

Together, we take a deep breath in and blow it out.

"I've known you your entire life. So first." She looks over at me with her head cocked to the side and her lips pursed together. "Honey, I've never heard you talk like this about a guy, not even Shithead-Kevin before he was Shithead-Kevin. And, second, it's okay to have these kinds of feelings, even if they feel really confusing and uncertain right now. I haven't known Nicco all that long, but from the interactions we've had and the time we've spent together, when you take away all the sexy-sexy, he really seems like a good guy. And, by the way, there's never been *any* lingering when he kisses my cheeks. All that being said, I don't know what there could possibly be between you two, but I think it's worth being open to the possibility of what *could* be. Your soul mate is out there, looking for you. I don't know if it's Nicco. But you know I believe in miracles and I know dreams can come true."

"I like him, Can. I like him a lot. So much so it scares me."

"Honey, I know it's scary to open your heart to someone, especially after what happened with Kevin."

I shoot her a side glare. "And Paul."

"Virga?" Her pitch raises an octave.

"Yes," I say sternly.

"Well, Paul Virga. I mean, come on. He *did* ask Abby before he asked you. He had no way of knowing her mom was gonna change her mind and let her go to prom with him."

"I still can't believe I helped him wash his car before he went to pick her up. Even his mom was mad at him for that one. And then I had to stand there watching them dance in the dry ice smoke while everyone formed a circle around them like it was a scene in a movie. Ugh." I shake my head. "Okay, Justin Scoggins."

"You've *got* to be kidding me," she scoffs and laughs. "That was elementary school." She bends forward, bellowing in laughter.

"Well, he kissed me and the very next day he kissed Suzie what's-her-face."

We both burst into a laughing fit.

Once we've composed ourselves, the memory of Kevin pinches my heart. "Seriously though, am I ever going to be enough for anyone?"

A pout sits on her lips. "Des, of course you are. You're a total catch."

"I don't know. I seem to be stuck in a pattern of guys picking someone else over me. And with Niccolo Mancini having his pick of the litter, there's no way he'd ever pick me." I shake my head. "I'm so afraid of getting hurt."

"I know. And that's the risk. That's the chance you take. But I think it's a chance worth taking. Please, just open your heart and let God lead the way."

After dinner, we go back to her hotel, order room service for desserts, and watch movies until we fall asleep.

⟫⟫⟫⟫ ⟪⟪⟪⟪

Candi and I spend Saturday being tourists, shopping, eating, hiking, and taking in the beauty of the island.

Sunday is a beach day. I read my book under our umbrella and Candi works on making her already-tanned skin more golden.

My phone chimes.

Nicco: Hi. How is your trip going? Having fun?

I wasn't expecting to hear from him. My heart pumps a little faster.

Me: Hi! It's great! We did touristy things yesterday and we're on the beach right now.

Nicco: Don't get sunburned. The sun is very strong there.

Me: I'm under my umbrella. ☺ What are you keeping busy doing?

Nicco: Right now, I'm reading your book.

I gasp.

Candi rolls to her side and pushes her sunglasses on top of her head, peering at me. "Who is it?"

"It's Nicco, he's reading Sunflowers for Sarah." The words spill out of my mouth as adrenaline spurts through me at the thought of him reading my words.

Me: I hope you enjoy it.

Nicco: I am so far. I picked up a few of them. ;)

I lurch forward in my chair, gasping again. My hand flies to my chest as I stare at the screen.

"What? What's happening?" Candi's now sitting on the edge of her lounger.

"Apparently he got several of my books."

"Hmmm. He wants to learn about you."

I whip my head toward her. "I don't want him reading too many of my books."

"Why?"

"Because, they're like, glimpses into my soul. You know that." My stomach twists.

"That might be a good thing."

"No. That's not a good thing. I don't care about strangers reading my books, but I don't want him knowing that much about what goes on in my head. What if he got one of the more sensual ones? I don't want him reading my intimate thoughts. What do I say back?"

"Take notes, baby." She laughs playfully.

I erupt into laughter. "You're no help."

"Hey, here's what I'm getting, he's thinking about you. He's reading your books. He's texting you. You're on his mind."

"I think he's probably just bored."

My phone chimes.

Nicco: I miss hanging out with you.

My mouth drops open slightly as I stare at the screen.

"What? What'd he say?"

I look at her. "He said he misses hanging out with me."

She squeals, leaning back in her lounge chair, lifting her knees in the air, and tapping her toes alternately in the sand. "Just sayin'." She winks at me then takes her sunglasses off her head, puts them back on her face, and lays down again.

⋙ ⋘

Thankfully the flight home is uneventful. I'm so glad I went on the trip. It's been a while since Candi and I got to hang out together, just the two of us.

Hmm, just the two of us. Tomorrow will be just the two of us. Me and Nicco spending our last day together.

Why did you have to come steaming into my life, Niccolo Mancini, only to walk right back out?

14

—

Destiny

My conversation with Candi replays in my head. I honestly don't know how to feel. I don't want to misinterpret something that's not there, but I'm terrified for there to be something between us. Even if he does feel a little something for me, there's no way, logistically, it would work.

Before going to bed, I settle on enjoying our last day together without letting my confused feelings interfere. Excited about seeing him tomorrow, I drift off to sleep with the memory of being wrapped around him in the ocean, our heads tucked into one another.

Nicco

She's back safely and I get to see her today. Not only do I get to see her, but I also have to make sure she agrees to come to Ranch Inn with me. Today won't be enough, I need to see her again before I leave.

As has become our meeting time, I get to her house at eleven o'clock. When she opens the door, the tension that's been sitting in my chest the last few days releases. Today she's cute and sexy melted together. Part of her hair is pulled into a small clip behind her head, she wears dark gray shorts, a V-neck lavender T-shirt, and a delicate gold necklace.

Leaning in, I touch her lightly on the arm and kiss each of her soft cheeks. Stepping back, I take her in again. She has no idea what she does to me with her long, creamy legs and the outline of her hardening nipples through her shirt. It's so fucking hot how responsive she is to my touch. I have to focus intently on not getting hard.

The drive is about two hours to the San Diego Zoo and she tells me about her trip to Hawaii with Candi. Along the way, she continues to be diligent in her tour-guide duties, pointing out landmarks and things to do. We stop for a quick lunch before we get to the zoo.

"You'll want to have your cigarette now because you can't smoke on the zoo property at all." Though she never judges, there's always a disapproving sadness in her eyes when I stop whatever we're doing to go have a cigarette.

Cutting my ritual short, I have my cigarette and return to her car where she's waiting inside for me. As soon as I get in, she puts the windows down.

"I don't want my car to smell like smoke." Her words, still void of judgement, pinch at me.

I don't apologize, I can't. Though it's an addiction, it's also my choice, I know that. I hate feeling powerless to it.

"Does it ever bother you, the things you miss out on because you need to smoke?" She tilts her head slightly, her eyebrows raised as her lips press together.

Tension coils around the muscles in my neck. "A lot." I know it would break my dad's heart to know I'm smoking.

"My friend, Heidi, works with people to help them quit smoking. Obviously, there's a big part that's the addiction, but I also know how connected you feel to your dad when you smoke. She does things like matrix reimprinting and EFT tapping that could help you if you wanted to try quitting again. I confess, I don't fully understand what's involved or how it works, but I can give you her number if you wanted to ask her some questions about it."

Her kindness and compassion continue to inspire me. "I do want to quit someday, for good. I want to be free from craving something I know is killing me."

She gets her phone from her purse and messages me her friend's contact information. "She's helped so many people with the work she does. I believe she could help you if that's what you really want."

"Thank you. I appreciate it." While I do appreciate her giving me her friend's information, I don't think I'll call her.

When we arrive at the zoo, we're just in time to catch a bird show. After the show, we weave our way down different paths to see the animals. Watching her behavior and interaction with them, I can see her love of animals. If there's an opportunity to pet one, she's right there with loving strokes and a gentle voice.

There's a section in the elephant sanctuary where you can get close enough to feed them. As she steps toward the wall that separates us from them, a massive elephant approaches, one lethargic step after the other. It stands right in front her, shifting its head so its eye is looking directly at her. She affectionately gazes into its eye and smiles. They stay like this for a few seconds. Then the elephant reaches out its long trunk toward her. I almost pull her back, but she doesn't look scared. Though people are nearby, sounds fade and the air is still as I watch them.

The elephant stretches its wrinkled, gray trunk a little longer, putting it close to her face, sniffing. She lifts her chin, still smiling at the majestic creature. It curls its trunk and she slowly reaches up, cradling the trunk in one hand and gently rubbing it with the other. Then she whispers. I'm not close enough to hear what she's saying, but as she whispers, the elephant's marble-like eye closes and opens slowly.

She lengthens her strokes, still whispering. Then she leans in. The elephant reaches as far as it can and tucks the end of its trunk into the crook of her neck. She rests her head on it and a tear falls from the elephant's eye. I stand there, motionless, frozen, my eyes fixed on them. Raising her head, she takes the large gray trunk in her hands and kisses it, then releases it and steps back. Wiping tears from her cheeks, she steps back again. The elephant backs away from the wall, flaps it massive ears, and releases a loud, trumpeting sound.

Turning away from the wall, she walks toward me. I rub my chin with my hand, both confused and amazed by what I'd just witnessed. There's still some moisture under her eye that I wipe with my thumb.

"What just happened there? Do you know this animal?"

Looking up at me, she smiles. "I do."

"Are you some kind of elephant whisperer?"

She chuckles as she starts back down the path. "No. When I was in high school, I thought I wanted to be a zoologist. My aunt and uncle live out here and I'd visit them on weekends a lot during the summer. They know the people who own the zoo and they helped me get a part time job here. I was here the day Jo-Jo was born. As much as I was able to, I came to the zoo to take care of him and play with him. And now, I visit him when I can."

"That was one of the most incredible things I've ever seen." My entire body is swarmed by a strange mixture of calm and exhilaration. "Was he angry that you were leaving just now?"

"No, that was a happy sound he made. He was happy to see me."

"He misses you."

"I miss him."

As we head toward the large cats section, my phone rings, it's Vance. "Excuse me, I have to take this."

Destiny

It was so nice to see Jo-Jo. He looks healthy and happy. I love watching Nicco with the animals, he's like a big kid.

Walking back toward me, he has the biggest smile on his face and his eyes are wide. He stands in front of me with his mouth partially open, but says nothing.

"What? What is it?"

"They want me," he says, shaking his head. "They want me," he says a little louder, bending his knees and shaking his hands.

"Who, who, which agency?" Goose bumps break out all over my body.

"Vance." Blindsiding me, he scoops me into his strong arms and spins me around, laughing. When he puts me back on the ground, he holds me, lingering, eyes darting back and forth between mine. "This is unbelievable. Thank you, Destiny. You made this possible." His gratitude warms my heart.

"I only helped set it up, you did all the hard work."

"We have to celebrate." Excitement radiates from him as he throws his arms out to his sides.

"Absolutely. Do you want to skip the movie tonight and go to dinner?"

"No. I want you so come to Ranch Inn with me tomorrow."

What?! "What?" A wave of heat rushes from my head to my toes.

"I have to leave earlier than I planned. During my meeting with Vance, he told me about Ranch Inn and I booked a room for Wednesday to Thursday. I have to leave on Friday. We can go together and celebrate."

I want to spend more time with him, but that will only make ending, whatever this is, harder. Conflict spins like a twister inside me.

"Will you?"

"I don't know, Nicco —"

"Please. I have a suite and you'll have your own bedroom. I mean, technically, we've already slept under the same roof together." He winks at me, putting his hands on my waist, increasing my body temperature. "It's beautiful there. Have you ever been?"

"No, I haven't, but I have friends who have and they've told me how beautiful it is."

"Then let's go. We can experience it together and celebrate the start of my future."

"I —" My head is spinning.

"I'll bet you'll even find some inspiration there." The way he smiles at me is like he knows the power it has over me and he's using it to its full potential to wear me down.

It's working. My yearning heart makes the decision. "Okay, I suppose I can go." Did I really just agree to spend the night in the same suite with him on a getaway to a romantic destination? I've lost my mind.

"Yes!" he cheers, picking me up in his arms again, then putting me down.

"After the large cats, we should probably start heading back so we can get to the theater on time."

As I drive, we talk about what we liked at the zoo and he tells me how fascinated he was by my connection with Jo-Jo. And then, he brings up the topic I was hoping to avoid talking about with him.

"So, I enjoyed reading your books."

"Oh good. I'm glad." I keep my response short and brief. The thought of him reading my books, my innermost thoughts, makes my stomach churn. Before I can change the subject, he continues.

"I like the way you write, it's very expressive. The characters feel real, like I'm getting to know them through your words. And the way you describe things around them, I feel like I'm in the room with them."

"That's something I work hard on."

"You do it well. I also like how each of the main characters has something to learn or change about themselves to become who they want to be, a better version of themselves. And then you also have them grow together by helping each other. The way you intertwine their journeys strengthens their relationship in such a powerful way."

Knowing how he likes getting inside the mind of the characters he plays, I appreciate him recognizing this in my writing. "Thank you. That's one of my goals as I create my characters and their love story."

"And the sex scenes weren't what I expected."

I grip the steering wheel as my heart races.

"Oh." I know he read Sunflowers for Sarah, but I don't know what else he read. I didn't ask. I don't want to know. I can't bear knowing.

"Your words and descriptions are very sensual. Even the way you describe a kiss. The intimacy, the passion. It made me want to feel what you describe."

A tingle sweeps between my legs and I shift in my seat. It's impossible to *not* want his lips on mine this instant. I'm trying to breathe normally as my heart pounds beneath my ribs.

"You must feel *something* similar when you kiss women."

"I told you, I don't kiss women on the lips."

"You did. But why?" Will he tell me? Will he let me in?

"I just don't," he says, his words icy.

Nope, he's not budging.

"We all have our boundaries, I suppose. I don't kiss men who smoke." Which, I continue to remind myself, he does. So, I really need to stop thinking about him kissing me, wanting him to kiss me, and fantasizing about him kissing me. Ugh, I'm pathetic. But, now it's out there. Maybe he'll stop torturing me and lingering sexily in front of my face like he wants to devour me, when I know he doesn't.

He releases a low, wicked chuckle as he looks at me. "But you like kissing." It's more of a statement than a question.

"Well, a kiss is intimate, intense, vulnerable. Some might say kissing is more powerful than sex." Deep breath. Stop talking. We've moved from kissing to sex. I can't breathe. My knuckles are white with my suffocating grasp on the steering wheel.

"The sex you write is pretty damn hot."

Only knowing what he could've read, I'm stripped of my guards, completely exposed. I focus on the road, trying not to lose my grip with my sweaty hands. "It's, uh, well, I'm good at my research."

"Yes, you are." That low timbre of his voice rattles through me. I feel his eyes on me and stare straight ahead.

Oh God. Change the subject, now. "What's the next step for you with Vance?"

Thankfully, he drops the subject of my books, and sex, and tells me about his next moves with Vance and the agency.

We arrive in good timing at the theater to find a spot and get some food. I grab the blanket from the back of my car and put it between us. During the movie, I catch him stealing glances at me. Thankfully, the movie is fun and lighthearted. I love listening to him laugh.

About halfway through the movie, he touches my arm.

"You're cold."

I hadn't noticed until he said it, but I was starting to get cold. When I look at him, he quickly looks from my breasts to the blanket. Ugh, my nipples must be hard. They're so damn sensitive. Opening the blanket, he drapes it across me, tucking it in as best as he can.

"Better?"

"Yes. Thank you."

As soon as the movie is over, I drive us back home, kind of tired from the day.

"What do you want to do at Ranch Inn? I need to know what to pack."

"I thought we could go hiking or do something on the grounds during the day. On the website, the nature looks amazing. There's a hot tub so bring your swimsuit. And maybe a dress for our celebration dinner. I thought on Thursday we can go to one of the art galleries. And the rest, we'll figure out."

"Okay, that gives me a good idea," I say, pulling into my driveway.

"I'll walk you in."

I love that he makes sure I'm safely inside. Our goodbyes are becoming my favorite and my saddest part of our days. We stand in our usual spots, facing each other in my foyer, him looking down into my eyes, making my pulse race.

"Thank you for another nice day. I had fun. I especially enjoyed watching you with Jo-Jo."

"I'm glad you had a good time. I did too." I wrap my hands around my cold arms.

Instantly, he steps in, caging my body with his arms, holding my head to his chest. Without thinking, I sink into him, listening to his heart beat. He releases an audible exhale, uncages me, and steps back.

"I'll see you in the morning." Cupping my face in his hands, he kisses both cheeks, then closes the distance between our faces. "Good night, Destiny," he murmurs, barely above a whisper.

I take a deep inhale. "Good night, Nicco."

He leaves and I close the door behind him, happy it's not our last goodbye, but sad because I know it's coming.

I don't have it in me to pack tonight so I'll pack in the morning. I'll pack for an overnight trip with a man who's not mine and could never be. A man who I'm growing to like more each day. A man who unravels me in my fantasies and is starting to unravel me in real life.

A man who's inching into my heart.

15

Nicco

The drive along Pacific Coast Highway is magnificent. Though I don't want to leave early, I'm glad to have these last two days with Destiny.

We check in and go to our suite. The instant we step into it, we both marvel at the luxury surrounding us. Each room we walk into is more lavish than the last.

"This place is bigger than my entire house." Her excitement is that of a child, making me smile. I'm so happy she came with me.

We both have king-size beds and fireplaces in our rooms, at opposite ends of the suite. Mine even has a sofa in it. The kitchen and living area separate our bedrooms. With all the windows and glass doors, it feels like we're outside. And the view is spectacular. We go out to the balcony and the ocean spreads for miles below us. The hot tub is deeper than any I've ever seen. There's even a cozy spot for her to sit and write if she wants.

"Are you hungry?" I ask.

"So hungry."

"Okay. Let's unpack our things and meet back in the living room. We'll get a bite to eat and then we can go exploring for a few hours until we're ready for dinner."

"Perfect."

We spend the day enjoying the outdoors and head back to our suite when we're both hungry again. Being sweaty from our hiking and adventures, we get showers. I'm ready before her and stand on the balcony, smoking a cigarette, soaking in the view.

From behind me, I hear the clicking of heels and turn around. She's fucking breathtaking. I have to consciously not let my jaw drop open. For a few seconds, I'm speechless, scanning her from head to toe. Her classy black dress hugs her slender frame, accentuating her delicate curves. At the base of her long neck rests a string of diamonds that wraps fully around her neck.

I approach her and stop in front of her. "You're beautiful."

"Thank you," she says quietly, glancing down toward her feet, then back up at me. "You look very handsome."

"Thank you." I've gone with my signature black suit, black vest, and white shirt. I'm usually told I'm hot. I like the sound of handsome, especially the way she says it.

At the restaurant, we're seated at a table with another impressive view of the ocean. I order a bottle of Prosecco and we look through the menu. When the waiter comes back with our wine, we place our orders.

I outline the profile of her face as she looks over the water. "Destiny."

She returns her gaze to me.

"You're good with words. I'm not as much, especially with English." I smile. "I don't know the right words, strong enough words, to thank you. Thank you for everything you've done for me. Two weeks ago, I didn't know you and now, you've helped me on the path of making my dreams come true. And you've given me so much of your time to show me around. Thank you can't even begin to express how grateful I am for you."

The way she smiles at me makes the hairs on the back of my neck stand up. "You're so welcome, Nicco. I'm happy I could help you."

I lift my glass toward her, "Sarai sempre nel mio cuore, mia dolce ragazza."

"I don't know what that means."

"It's okay, I do." I nod.

Without pressing me for a translation, she raises her glass toward me. "Cheers." We clink our glasses together. "I hope you get everything you desire."

Together we sip our wine and take in the view.

As soon as I speak, her gaze returns to me. "The other day at the beach, you asked me what scares me about being in a relationship and I didn't want to answer your question." Still not wanting to answer it, I feel like she deserves an answer. An answer she may not want to hear, but an answer that may help her understand. "I'll answer it for you, but I don't want it in the book."

Intently focused on me, she agrees. "Of course." She shakes her head.

"What scares me is that I know I'll never be a good husband or a good dad. So, I don't bother getting involved in relationships and wasting anyone's time. It's not fair to the other person to invest their time, their effort, their heart in something that has no chance of becoming anything."

Sorrow coats her beautiful eyes as they roam my face. "Why would you say that?"

"Why, isn't important. It doesn't matter. It's what's true and it's something I thought you should know." I look out the window and she doesn't push me for more.

Dinner is delicious. She shares stories about her and Candi growing up together and the adventures they used to have. I tell her about the trouble me and Marco used to get into, and still do sometimes. I don't usually have these types of conversations with women and I'm thoroughly enjoying getting to know her. I can't get enough of her.

After dinner we go back to the suite. The sun is beginning its descent into the ocean.

"What do you say we get changed and meet at the hot tub?" I'm thirsting to see her in a bikini again. I'd rather see her naked, but I'll take what I can get.

"Sounds good."

Destiny

Candi texted while we were at dinner. I give her a quick call.

"Hey, did I text at a bad time?"

"Hi. No. We were at dinner. We're about to go in the hot tub."

"Hot tub? How romantic."

"Ugh, I know. And I'm enjoying myself more than I should." I slump my shoulders.

"Des, why do you punish yourself?"

"Because —"

"Because what?" I can see her now, shaking her hands in frustration at me.

"Because. Because he leaves Friday. He leaves and that's it. Even if we stay friends, we won't see each other like we have these last few weeks. And, he's — he's on his way to stardom. And I'm —" I sigh. "I'm me and I'm here."

"You can't predict the future, Des, so, please, stop trying to and just be open. Be open to whatever, to possibility, to a chance at who knows what. You keep closing yourself off with him and shutting down, not even giving things a fair chance."

"That's just it. In slightly different words, he flat out told me he doesn't get into relationships, period. Tonight, he answered the one question he didn't answer on the beach. Basically, he said he's not good enough so he doesn't even bother. Someone really hurt him. I swear I felt my heart sting when he said it."

"Okay, let that go for a minute, that's guy-crap. Strip away all this bullshit about what you think and what you shouldn't be thinking or feeling. Just," she blows an exhale. "tell me what you *feel*."

"I — I don't know. I mean, I'm going to miss him when he leaves. Spending all this time together, he's not at all what I thought he'd be like. He's charming and funny and playful. He's kind and protective. He's very diligent about his work, whether he's getting into the mind of his characters or writing lyrics for his songs, he commits, goes all in." I blow a huff of air. "He's open-minded, humble, affectionate. And I've never seen a man communicate the way he does, it's refreshing and, unexpected." I pause. "Can, my body fucking melts with how passionate he is. Arm's length away from him, I can remain feisty and fierce, but when he invades my personal space, I lose all control of myself. I can't think straight. I feel like I've downed ten shots of whiskey. Speaking of which, I'm supposed to be half naked in a hot tub with him right now." I pause. "I should probably go."

"Okay." She sighs. "Let go of the shoulds and the shouldn'ts and just be. Be in the moment and let yourself feel what you feel. Stop judging and condemning it."

"I'll try. I love you."

"Love you. Bye."

I change into my bikini, twist my hair up into a clip, and go out to the hot tub. Nicco isn't there yet. I thought he would be since I took a while talking with Candi. He's probably having a cigarette. He went our entire dinner without one.

I turn on the hot tub, tap my Yoga Music playlist on my phone, and step into the hot, bubbling water. It's pretty deep. The scenery is truly heavenly. I cross my arms on the wall overlooking the ocean, my toes barely touching the bottom. Closing my eyes, I rest my head on my folded hands. Candi's words are in my head, be in the moment. I focus on my breathing, inhaling, exhaling, inhaling, exhaling. Be in the moment.

He's behind me, barely touching his chest to my back. My breathing quickens. He must be squatting down because his mouth is at my ear.

"I can't get over how beautiful it is here."

Opening my eyes, I see his arms, spread wide, on either side of me. "It really is." I turn my face up toward him. "Thank you for bringing me here. I don't come to places like this. It's quite a treat."

"You're welcome. Thank you for coming with me. Do you want

more wine? I had some sent up."

"Oh no. I had two glasses at dinner." That's just what I need, to be tipsy in a hot tub, half naked with this scorching-hot man I'm falling for and shouldn't be.

"You're not driving."

Candi's voice pops into my head, be in the moment. "True. Okay, I'll have a glass."

He pours us each a glass at the side of the hot tub. Not speaking, we hang on the wall, side by side, sipping wine, watching the waves crash below us and the sun sink into the ocean. Half an hour must've passed as we were mesmerized. The bubbles stopped a little while ago.

"Your music ended. Do you want it back on?"

"Yes, please."

He goes over to my phone.

"Just hit the button and it should play."

The music starts again. It's not my Yoga Music playlist. It's my Sensual Massage playlist.

"I was curious what you have on this one. Do you mind?" he asks, getting back to his spot on the wall. *Oh boy.*

"No. It's fine."

"Do you listen to this while you write your sex scenes?"

The man is trying to kill me. "Sometimes."

He dunks under the water, staying down for a few seconds. When he rises, he tucks himself in behind me, spreading his arms on either side of me again. He's close, closer than before, pressing against me.

"This is nice," he says, putting his hands on my waist, turning me to face him.

With the depth of the hot tub, I move my arms to rest on the wall again so I can hold myself up. As I adjust my body, I accidentally graze the length of his hardness with my pelvis. I inhale, strangling a moan.

"Sorry about that." He spreads his legs, submerging his torso

160

into the water, bringing his face level with mine. Those chocolate-brown eyes of his are hypnotic.

"It's okay, I know any female body will do that to you. I know it has nothing to do with me." I deadpan, wishing it *was* me who elicited his body's reaction. But I know better.

"No." He heaves a breath as his nostrils flare. "Not every woman has this effect on me." I can't decipher if hurt or anger sits behind his dark eyes as they bore into me. He takes a deep inhale and releases it slowly. "So, I have an idea."

"Yeah? What kind of idea."

"A way for us to help each other."

"Another deal?"

"No."

"Help each other how?"

"You can teach me about the tenderness and sensuality of sex." Rising above me, he tilts gently into me, pressing himself against me, causing me to gasp. "And I can teach you about the passion and heat." He pauses, staring into my eyes. "For your research."

My entire body ignites at the thought as an intense tingle zips between my legs. What is he even saying right now? If this was thirteen days ago, I'd say he's pulling a playboy trick to get me to sleep with him. But, after everything that's happened over the last week and a half, the intimate things we've shared with each other, and the earnestness brushed across his face, I think this is anything but a sleazy playboy maneuver.

He lowers his voice. "Will you? Teach me to be tender? Teach me how to make love, not just fuck? The way you write about it."

"Nicco, there's something you need to understand."

His gaze searches my face, patiently waiting for my next words.

"You don't love with your dick. You love with your heart." I pause. "When you first love with your heart, you don't have to figure out how to love with your body, it just happens."

"What if," he takes a long pause as he stares deep into my eyes, "my heart is empty?"

The ache in my soul consumes my body. The tiniest bit of moisture glosses his eyes. He blinks it away.

I shake my head gently, shifting my gaze between his eyes. Wrapping one arm around his neck, I place my other hand on his heart. "Your heart isn't empty. You just need someone to help you open it."

He wraps his arms around me, I curl myself around his body. Never having experienced such a deep and profound moment with a man, I'm shaken to my core.

I'm falling.

Releasing each other, we breathe in the same air that hangs between our mouths.

"We should probably get some sleep," I say quietly.

"Okay."

We get out of the hot tub and towel off. I wrap my towel around my body and unclip my hair as we enter the suite. Neither of us had thought to turn on any lights before we went outside. He walks me to the door of my bedroom, adjacent to the living area where the fireplace is lit, casting a glow over the room.

Before going into my room, I turn to face him. "Good night."

"Buona notte."

His hands pass my jaw as he snakes his fingers through my hair, imprisoning my head in his grasp. This time, as he moves his lips from my left cheek to my right, he stops, nose to nose, staring into my eyes, exhaling into my parted lips. Unable to stop myself, I heave a breath into his mouth. My heart thrashes around my rib cage.

Kiss me.

16

Destiny

I open the door to my bedroom, watching him go back out to the balcony, likely to have a cigarette. Closing the door behind me, I clutch my chest, filled with wild, intense emotions; my heart aching for whatever happened to him that makes him feel incapable and unworthy of love juxtaposed against the explosion of passion that's blazing through every inch of my body, yearning for one kiss from his lips.

I wish tomorrow wasn't our last day together. But the reality is that it is. I'm going to enjoy every last minute of our time together before he's gone from my life. We may not have known each other long and we may not be dating, but this is the most powerful connection I've ever had with a man and I'm going to cherish it forever.

As I drift into sleep, he visits me.

>>>>> <<<<<

In the morning, he knocks on my door. I open it to his disheveled hair, bare chest, and green and navy plaid pajama bottoms. He's completely adorable and disturbingly sexy.

"Good morning. Do you want some breakfast delivered?" he asks.

"Okay."

"There's a menu here next to the phone."

"Okay, I'll be right out. Let me just clip up my hair." I'd already showered, but hadn't dried my hair.

Clipping up my hair, I join him on the leather sofa in the living area. We look through the menu and he calls to place our order. While we wait for our breakfast to arrive, he showers and I finish getting ready. When breakfast arrives, we bring it out to the balcony, soaking in the view one last time.

As we eat, we engage in small talk…How did you sleep? The weather's beautiful for our drive today…neither of us bringing up last night.

We pick an art gallery to stop at before our drive back. Finishing our breakfast, we pack up and head out. He thoroughly enjoys the art gallery and, as we drive home, he tells me which pieces were his favorite and why.

After we stop for lunch, I pull out a book I'd brought with me. Somewhere along the drive, I fall asleep.

⇉⇉ ⇇⇇

A soft finger caresses my cheek.

"Destiny."

I open my eyes, blinking.

"Destiny, we're home," he says.

He'd covered me with a sweatshirt and I was snuggled into it. I get out of the car and stretch then grab my purse and tote bag. He already has my overnight bag.

I unlock the door and we go inside, standing in our usual spots in my foyer.

This is our last goodbye. My heart aches.

"I'm sorry I fell asleep on you. I guess I was more tired than I thought."

"It's okay. I enjoyed watching you sleep."

I don't want him to leave. When he leaves, that's it. All this ends.

"Do you want to stay for a late dinner?" I ask.

He steps toward me and strokes my cheek with his thumb. "I want to, but I have some calls to return and an early flight. I have to go."

My heart sinks with the gravity of this reality. "Okay. That's fine." I wrap my arms around my body.

"Thank you," he pauses, "for *everything* you've done for me these few weeks." He chuckles. "I think I made out better on our deal." He smiles. "When your book's ready, I'll put it on my Instagram and hopefully that'll help. We'll stay in touch between now and then, okay? I want to know how your writing's going."

"You're welcome. There's a saying that goes, people come into our life for a reason, a season, or a lifetime. I believe we met for a reason and I'm so happy I could help you. And thanks, I really appreciate your willingness to do that for me. Let's stay in touch." As the words leave my mouth, I know in my heart that we probably won't. He's going to be much too busy to keep in touch.

Stepping in closer, he tucks my hair behind my ear. I'm going to miss that. "I don't know what happens from here. I hope we can stay friends."

A lump lodges in my throat, unshed tears sting behind my eyes. "Of course we can." I force a smile. "I'll watch you soar to fame on social media and cheer you on."

He chuckles. "I know you will." He pauses. "I don't know when I'll be back here, but you know my goal is to live here. I just don't know when that'll be. When I do, maybe we can get together for lunch or dinner sometime."

"I'd really like that." I swallow, trying to dislodge the lump.

Inching in still closer, he lingers above me. "Destiny, I…" His gaze sweeps across my face. "I care for you. I don't know this feeling well." He softly chuckles. "I…" He pauses, then releases a low growl, hesitating. "Last night at dinner, when we toasted and you didn't know what I said, I said, you will always be in my heart, my sweet girl." Curling his hand under my jaw, he runs his thumb across my lips. As his eyes watch the motion of his thumb, he skims his own lips with his tongue.

My breathing is audible. I can't douse the desire winding its way through my veins.

He lowers his head, his voice just above a whisper. "If I don't kiss you before I get on that plane, I'll regret it for the rest of my life."

My chest rises and falls with each breath I take. "But you don't kiss women on the lips." His face inches from mine, my heart hammers in my ears. We breathe each other's breaths.

"I know," he says, lowering his head farther, lacing his fingers through my hair. Taking my face in his hands, he tilts it up, then touches his warm lips to mine. A faint groan churns in his throat and thunders through my body.

Nicco

The second our lips touch, my body fucking ignites. Her luscious lips I ravage in my fantasies are pressed softly against mine. Releasing them, I go back immediately, wanting more, so much more. I catch her top lip with my lower lip. Holding her head still in my hands, I graze back and forth across her barely parted lips with mine. Her light, panting breaths feather against my skin.

She parts her lips more, inviting me in. I cover her lips with mine, dipping my tongue into her mouth. A tiny whimper escapes her as she presses her hands against my back. I twitch in my pants. I should stop now, but I'm craving her. I can't stop. Dragging my tongue between her lips, I sweep a little deeper into her mouth. I groan. Desire pumps through my veins.

Her faint scent of vanilla drifts into my nose as her skin heats beneath my touch. Claiming her mouth again, I slide deeper with my tongue, curling it around hers. Her whimpers grow louder, making me harder. Our tongues dance to a song that belongs only to us. I pick her up, she wraps her arms around my neck and her legs around my waist. Fuck she feels good pressed against my hard-on. Walking into the kitchen, I sit her on the counter.

Gliding my arm around her back, I cradle her head in my other hand, drawing her mouth to mine again. I curl my tongue shallowly in and out of her mouth, then run it across her top lip. Her breathing is jagged, nails pressing into my back. I go back for more. Her open lips wait for my entry. Closing my mouth over hers, I extend my tongue deep into her mouth, groaning, clutching her head, swirling my tongue around hers.

I pull away from her, my breath heavy and hard, hers rapid and wanting. Spreading my arms wide on the counter I gaze into her eyes, seeing fire, passion, desire. My heart beats fast in my chest. I want her, right now, so fucking badly. I watch her eyes follow my tongue as I run it across my lip. Grabbing her ass, I pull her, hard and fast, to the edge of the counter, making sure she can feel, between her legs, how hard I am. She gasps.

I drill my eyes into hers. "*You* do this to me, Destiny, *you.*" Slamming my mouth onto hers, I plunge my tongue deep into her.

Her whimpers are pleading as she digs her nails into my lower back, tugging me into her, squeezing her thighs around me, driving me wild. I growl deep in my throat.

Lips locked together, tongues coiling around each other, hearts racing, we kiss, lost in each other.

Fuck I love kissing her. I want to peel off her clothes and kiss every silky inch of her skin. As the thought enters my mind, guilt replaces craving. I should never have kissed her. I crossed a line I shouldn't have. I'm selfish. I know this can't go any further and that's not fair to her. *Fuck.*

Releasing her lips, I hover above her, my breathing still labored. Will I ever be able to look into her beautiful eyes again after tonight?

"Destiny, I'm sorry." I shake my head. "I — I shouldn't have done that."

She touches her hand to my cheek. "I know the reality of this. I wouldn't have let you if I didn't think I could handle the aftermath," she says through heavy breaths. Her words don't match the sadness behind her eyes.

I step back and lift her off the counter, seeing a book on the corner, *Travel Guide for Ponza Island.*

"What's this?" I ask, picking up the book.

"I found it on Amazon," she says as I flip through the pages. "What do you think? Will it be good for my research?"

"No."

"No?"

"No."

"Why?"

I have a brilliant fucking idea. "You need to experience it to write about it. You'll come to Italy and I'll show you Rome and Ponza."

She shakes her head. "Nicco. That's very kind of you to offer, but I can't go to Italy."

"Why not?"

"Well, because, I — I can't just fly off to Italy. Besides, I can't afford a trip like that right now."

"I'll pay for the plane ticket. My brother, Marco, has a large villa on Ponza and we can stay there so you don't have to pay for a hotel."

"Nicco, I can't do that."

"Says who? Don't you want your book to be realistic?"

"Of course I do. That's why I got the guide."

"This?" I hold it up. "This is crap."

"Come, let me show you in real life."

She shakes her head. "I don't know what to say."

"Say you'll come. And tonight, we say goodbye for now."

Folding one arm across her body, she rests her opposite elbow on it and touches her finger above her lip. Her eyes shift back and forth between mine. "I'll think about it."

"I have projects the next two weeks. You'll come after that."

"I'll *think* about it."

"You know this is the best way to do your research. Please come."

"You have phone calls to return and an early flight."

Leaning in, I cup her face in my hands, my heart feeling lighter, and kiss her left cheek then her right. "Ciao, mia dolce ragazza."

"Ciao. Have a safe trip home."

As I head to my car, I feel a little guilty. Though I know I should leave her alone, I can't. Now, having kissed her, tasted her, I'm so fucking addicted. I'd forgotten what it feels like to kiss a woman. Destiny isn't just any woman and that was far from just a kiss. She consumes me.

Having basically invited us to Marco's villa, I call him when I get back to my hotel to make sure he's okay with us staying for a few days.

"Hey, bro. What's going on?" he asks.

"Hey, not much." I sit in the chair on my balcony and light a cigarette, sucking in, and blowing the smoke out my nose. "I'm getting ready to come back. I have to come back early for work so I'm leaving tomorrow instead of Sunday."

"Okay. So, how was the rest of your trip?"

"It's been amazing, man. I fuckin' love it here. I told you I was taking Destiny to Ranch Inn to celebrate me getting representation over here and it was beautiful. When you and Angelina come here to visit me someday, you'll have to go there."

"Fuck bro, it's happening. You're on your way."

"It's all because of Destiny."

"Yeah?"

"Well, Destiny and her mom."

"Seems like you're into this woman. How'd you leave things now that you're coming home?"

"Actually, that's part of why I'm calling. I told you I have that brand shoot when I get back. When that's over, I invited Destiny to come here so she can experience Italy as research for the book she's writing. I'm thinking to show her around Rome for a few days and then I want to bring her to your place for a few days, if you're okay with that. What do you think?"

"Hell yeah, that's okay. We'd love to have you. I'll double-check with Angelina to make sure we don't have anything else going on, but I'm pretty sure the timing is good."

"Thanks, that's great."

"So, tell me more about Destiny."

I take a long drag of my cigarette. "I don't know, man. She kind of fucks me up."

"Whoa. What happened?"

"She's unlike any woman I've ever met. She's remarkable." Another long drag as I scratch my eyebrow with the thumb of my hand holding the cigarette. "I fuckin' kissed her."

He's silent for a second. "On the lips?" He knows about my pact with myself.

"Bro, I couldn't fucking stop myself."

"Shit." He pauses. "Good for you. It's about time you stop punishing yourself and let someone in." He's always been straight with me, sometimes even brash, but his statement comes out with compassion.

"I didn't say I was letting her in." I lie to myself, because admitting it means that when she leaves after her visit, I've not only hurt her, but I've crushed my own heart. Maybe this wasn't such a good idea. Maybe I made a rash decision in the heat of the moment.

"Bro, it's okay if you are. That's all I'm saying. Let me know when you have your plans set and I'll check with Angelina."

"Okay, I will."

"Have a safe trip back. It'll be good to see you, man. And I'm looking forward to meeting this woman who's chipping away at my brother's frozen heart." He chuckles.

"Fuck you." I laugh, blowing smoke out my nose and mouth. "I'll see you soon."

"Love you, man."

"Love you too."

Now I have to make sure she comes to Italy. I'm not ready to give her up.

17

Destiny

Holy shit. I've *never* been kissed like that in my life. He had me worked up into such frenzy, I was intoxicated. If we kissed much longer, I probably would've had a freaking orgasm just from him kissing me.

Italy? He wants me to go to Italy? There's no doubt it would be the opportunity of a lifetime. But, I just don't know. Can I keep my brain focused on it being research and not let my heart continue to have feelings for him? Would I be able to shut off my emotions? After that kiss, could I seriously be with him and not want more, even knowing I'd probably be just another meaningless conquest, which I refuse to be? My thoughts whirl around in my head like a tornado. I have no idea what to do.

I need my best friend.

Me: Call me when you can. No rush. Not urgent.

Candi: Call you tomorrow afternoon?

Me: Perfect.

Candi: Mwah!

The next day, I'm back to a normal routine, getting up at six, hitting the gym, and spending the day writing. Having spent time with Nicco and him graciously answering my questions, scenes are brewing in my head and a story is forming.

Getting gloriously lost in my writing, I lose track of time. My phone rings and it's Candi.

"Hey." I get up from my desk and sit on the sofa.

"Hey, how are you? How was Ranch Inn? Did you love it?"

"Oh my gosh, it was amazing. So beautiful. I could've stayed for a week."

"And do I need to *ask* for details or are you going to tell me so I don't have to pull them out of you?"

Laying down, I put the heel of my hand on my forehead. "Can, this man. *This man.*"

"What? Tell me." Her eagerness to know what's going on in my love life, even when it's not really what I'd call a love life, has always made me laugh.

I chuckle, pause, then sigh. "Okay, so we know I've never been on a romantic getaway for two, even when I was dating someone. For *not* dating Nicco, it was the most romantic two days I've ever spent with a man."

"Details, please." I can picture her crossing her legs then crossing her hands over her knees, tapping her foot.

"I don't know any details, but what I *do* know is that someone broke his heart, enough so that he thinks his heart is empty."

"I wonder what happened to him."

"So do I. He's a closed book. He's been really open with me about some things, but this, nothing. Whatever happened hit him deep." I pause. "Then there was a hot tub moment."

"I'm listening."

"I kind of, accidentally grazed his penis and it was *very* hard."

"You touched his dick?" she shouts.

"No," I insist. "I didn't touch his dick. I just, grazed it as I was adjusting my position."

"Well, what happened?"

"It was kind of odd, but he said he had an idea of how we could help each other. When I asked how, he said he wanted me to teach him how to be tender during sex and he'd teach me about passion."

"I'm sorry, he offered you sex? Is that what you're saying?"

"I mean kind of, but it wasn't like that. It wasn't sleezy or anything."

"So, did you?" The pitch of her voice raises.

"No," I punctuate.

"Okay, keep going. Then what?"

"Then nothing. I'm *not* going to have sex with him."

"Nothing?"

"No, nothing. We got out of the hot tub and he did one of his linger-in-front-of-my-face things. It was a long linger. I almost thought he was going to kiss me."

"But he doesn't kiss women on the lips."

"Uh, that *was* true."

She squeals. "Tell me!"

"Can, oh my God. I don't know if he was caught in a moment or it was because he was leaving or what. Before he left last night, he kissed me. I thought I was going to pass out. It was hungry, it was sensual, it was passionate, it was emotional, it was so damn hot. I think we kissed for like half an hour. I'm telling you, my panties were soaking wet, that's how intense it was."

"Yes, girl! That's how you should be kissed every damn day."

"I'm not sure I could handle that." I laugh, putting my hand over my face.

"So, what happened then?"

"Well, after we stopped kissing, he was about to leave and saw my Ponza guide on the counter. I asked what he thought and if it would be good for my research. He pretty much said it was crap and told me I needed to go to Italy so I could have real-life experience for my book."

"Do it! Go!! I'm gonna pee my pants."

I hurl a loud laugh. "Calm down. I can't go."

"What? Why? Why can't you go? You have to go. Is it money? I'll lend you the money, you can pay me back. I promise, it'll be a loan, not a hand-out."

"No, it's not the money. Well, it's sort of the money. He offered to pay my airfare and said we can stay at his brother's villa on Ponza Island so I wouldn't have to pay for a hotel. But —"

"But, what? Des, you have to go. You can't not go."

"It's not that I don't want to go, but a part of me thinks maybe it's not a good idea. Plus, I'm really not comfortable with him paying for my airfare. I don't even know what that would cost. And I'm pretty sure I used up most of my mom's miles when I went to Hawaii."

"Don't let that stop you. We can figure that part out."

"I'm kinda scared, Can."

Her excitement turns to compassion. "What are you scared of?"

"I'm scared if I see him again and spend more time with him, what I'm feeling right now will only get stronger. And then I'm left in the same position I was about to be left in, him continuing to shoot to fame, forgetting about me, and me coming back home, brokenhearted."

"Des, we talked about this. You can't predict the future. You're trying to write the end of the story when you don't yet know what's going to happen."

I tug the blanket off the arm of the sofa and drape it over me. "I just don't want to knowingly set myself up for another kick in the face when I have the ability to prevent it from happening."

"If you keep going through life with that iron wall around your heart because you're afraid of what might happen when you let it down, honey, we're going to be eighty years old and you'll have missed out on ever letting your soul mate find you. The immense amount of love you have in your heart is a beacon for that man to find you. But if you keep that wall up, you'll block him from ever seeing that beautiful beacon of light."

All I can do is sigh.

"Hey, I gotta go." She pauses. "Don't let this pass you by. Promise me."

"I can't promise. I'll let you know what I decide to do."

"If I'm in town before you go, we can go shopping, okay?" She loves to get new clothes specifically for vacations.

"*If* I decide to go, I'm sure what I have will do."

"I'll talk you into it."

I chuckle. "You probably will. I love you."

Hanging up with Candi, I tuck the blanket around me, trying to decide what to do. When I close my eyes, my mind wanders, back to that passionate kiss. Why *did* he kiss me? Was it because I wouldn't sleep with him and he had to get *something* from me? It didn't seem like that though. There was something deeper driving him than an unfulfilled sexual desire. Something more connected.

>>>>> <<<<<

My phone rings, startling me awake. I must've dozed off. I look at the screen: Nicco. Sitting up, I keep my blanket wrapped around me, and answer.

"Hi. You're home safely."

"I am. How are you?"

"Good. I got some writing done today."

"That's good to hear. Hey, I wanted to let you know that I spoke with Marco and he and his wife, Angelina, are happy for us to stay at their villa when you come. Have you decided to come?"

"No, I haven't decided yet. I'm not comfortable with you paying for my airfare. I'm going to see if I can borrow money from my mom."

"Then you're seriously considering it?" A tinge of excitement weaves through his voice.

"I'm thinking about it."

"My break is over, I have to go. Let me know when you decide."

"Okay, I'll talk to you later."

>>>>> <<<<<

The next day, when I log into my email, I have a PayPal notification. It's from Nicco. The description says, "Tour guide duties." and it's $4,000.00. *Holy shit.*

I grab my phone.

Me: Nicco, this is too much. We agreed to $100.00.

Nicco: I never agreed to that. Now you don't have to borrow money. Come.

I'm in shock. I don't even know what to think. Though I'm not comfortable accepting this much money from him, I know he won't take it back, and I can definitely use it.

That's when Mom calls to update me on the charity event and how much money they raised. Then she brings up Nicco.

"He called to let me know about how his meetings went, specifically his meeting with Vance and that they have an agreement to work together. He wanted to thank me. He's an impressive man. Very professional, quite a gentleman. Strikingly handsome too. I had to Google him," she confesses.

I laugh. "Yeah, he's a really nice guy."

"He said you'd been showing him around town and told me about some of the things you did. Sounds like you spent quite a bit of time together." She's probing.

"We did. I got to know him pretty well."

"You're being vague which I know means there's more to the story. Fess up, young lady. Do you like this man?"

Ever since I was little, I couldn't hide anything from her. "Well, I do, but it doesn't matter. We're from two different worlds, going in different directions. But, it's okay. He did invite me to Italy though."

"He did?" Her voice raises. "Well, that's kind of bold for two people going in different directions."

"No, it's not like that. The book I'm writing features him as the hero and is partially set in Italy. He's offered to show me around so I can have real-life experience for my research."

"That's nice. Are you going?"

"I haven't decided yet. It's the opportunity of lifetime. I wasn't going to go because of the money, but he just sent me $4,000.00 for my time in showing him around."

"So, the man you like, whose life is going in a different direction than yours, has invited you to Italy to show you around and he's sent you $4,000.00?"

"Mom, cut it out. I hear that thing in your voice."

"What thing?" She tries to feign innocence and deny it.

"The thing that's all curious and hopeful."

"Can I help it that I want my daughter to find love and be happy? It's been years since that idiot fiancé of yours broke your heart and I worry about you. As your mother, that's my job."

"Well, I appreciate that, Mom, but Nicco isn't my Prince Charming. He's become a friend and that's all he can be."

"Fair enough. I don't want to meddle. You know, sweetheart, Creative Artists has a few openings. I know it's not ideal and you don't want to be cooped up in a building, tied to a desk all day, but it would be steady income. And you could still write on the side. You know I can put in a good word for you."

I sigh. The thought sours my stomach. I know she's trying to help and I love her for it. The one thing I never wanted to do in life is have my career be tied to making someone else rich.

"I know, Mom, and I appreciate that, I really do. I'm not ready to throw in the towel just yet. With this book and access to Nicco's audience, I might just be able to climb out of my slump."

"Okay. If you change your mind, I'm here to help."

"I know."

"And sweetheart, God has prepared your Prince Charming for you and sent him on his way to find you. He'll find you when you're ready to open yourself up to him."

"Thanks, Mom. I love you."

"I love you too. Let me know if you decide to go."

﹥﹥﹥﹥ ﹤﹤﹤﹤

That night before I go to bed, I get a text from Nicco with a beautiful landscape of the location where he's working.

Nicco: It's beautiful here. It reminds me of Ranch Inn. I wish you could be here to see it.

Me: So beautiful.

Nicco: Have you decided? We should get your ticket soon.

Me: Not yet.

Nicco: What's making you hesitate?

My fear of not being able to *not* have feelings for you and *not* want you to kiss me again.

Me: I don't have a good answer.

Nicco: Then come.

I stare at my phone. "Then come." stares at me, tugs at me. Going to Italy would be such an incredible experience. My research and my writing would be so authentic. *Ugh.* My heart wants to be with him again.

Me: I'll come.

Nicco: That makes me happy.

Me: When should I come?

Nicco: Come next Friday and plan to stay until the following Sunday. Fly into Rome. Let me know your travel plans when you have them.

Me: I will.

Nicco: I have to go. Ciao.

Me: Bye.

I close my chat with Nicco and find my conversation with Candi.

Me: I'm going.

Candi: When are we going shopping? ;)

Me: I don't need new clothes.

Candi: Yes, you do. It'll be fun. When do you leave?

Me: You're stubborn. Next Friday.

Candi: Perfect. I'll be home that Wednesday. We can go shopping Thursday and I'll stay over and help you pack. We'll have a girls' night.

Me: Mule. Okay. I have to go buy my ticket.

Candi: Mwah!

Putting down my phone, I go to my computer to search for flights.

Please don't let this be a bad idea.

18

Destiny

The days pass quickly. Candi and I are meeting today to go shopping for clothes I don't need, though I admit, it would be fun to have something new to bring with me. She meets me at my house and we head to the mall for lunch and a fun afternoon.

After lunch we wander the mall, stopping in a few shops. I pick up a cute tank top and some new flip flops.

"Do you know what you'll be doing yet?"

"Actually, I don't. I didn't ask. I'm figuring we'll go to dinner a few nights and do some sight-seeing so I'm planning to bring comfortable clothes and maybe a couple dresses."

"You'll probably do some swimming too so bring a suit."

"Right. Good thinking."

As we approach her favorite trendy boutique store, she tugs my arm and we go in. The style is a little sexier than clothes I usually wear, but sometimes they have a few things that are cute. We flip through the racks and both pick out some pieces to try on.

"Ooo, I like this," she says, holding up a white, two-piece outfit of a long skirt and strapless, lacy, midriff top.

"Oh, Can. That's cute. Try it on."

"No. Not for me. You're going to try it on."

I laugh. "Me? And where am I going wearing something sassy like that?"

"Italy." She pumps her shoulders up and down while wiggling

her eyebrows at me with a shit-eating grin on her face.

"No." I wave my hand at her and shake my head.

She gives me her pouty face. "Fine, okay. Then just try it on for fun." Handing it to me, she continues flipping through clothing racks.

Once we've been through the store and picked out a few things to try on, we head to the fitting rooms, getting two side by side.

I mostly picked out tops since I have plenty of pants and shorts. After trying on everything I brought in, I decide to get a black, open-back, short-sleeve top. It's not something I'd normally wear, but the front is tasteful and modest.

"Did you try on the outfit yet? I wanna see it."

"Nope. That's next."

I put on the two-piece outfit. It's certainly pretty, but with a side-slit all the way up the thigh, wearing it in public would be way out of my comfort zone.

"Do you have it on yet?"

"Yes, but I'm not coming out."

"Then I'm coming in," she says, pulling back my curtain and coming in, wearing a sexy red dress that plunges to her navel.

"You look amazing in that." I scan her from head to toe.

"Thanks. I think I'm gonna get it. Here," she says, handing me a black bikini. "This didn't fit me, but it'll probably fit you."

"But I don't need another suit."

"I know. Just try it on. I like the style of it." She looks me up and down then sweeps my hair up in her hand, putting it on top of my head. "Des, I love this on you. It's classy with just a tiny hint of sexy."

"It's pretty, but I have nowhere to wear something like this."

"You don't know what you're doing in Italy. Just bring it with you. You might find you have somewhere to wear it." She winks and leaves. "I wanna see the suit when you have it on," she says from outside my curtain.

I take off the white outfit and put on the bikini. It has a thong back. No way I'm wearing this and definitely not in front of Nicco.

"I'm not wearing this," I call out.

She pokes her head inside the curtain, then comes in, holding a pink halter top.

"Oooo, it fits you so good. Your boobies look amazing the way the top is cut."

"Um, no. It's a thong."

"So? Turn around."

I turn around.

"It looks cute."

"My entire butt is hanging out."

"You've always had such a nice body. I don't know why you're so shy about it." She turns around, showing me the top she's wearing. "What do you think of this? Too much?"

It's black with two thin strings that halter at the neck. Across the bust, there are slits in the fabric, exposing at least three-quarters of her D-size breasts, barely covering her nipples.

"Nope. You can totally pull that off."

"Okay, I'll get it." She tilts a shoulder up and puckers her lips, flashing her long lashes upward. Then she holds up the pink top. "What do you think about this one?"

"I like that. You don't wear a lot of pink. I like how it's flowy at the bottom."

"I know, I don't wear a lot of pink. With my hair, I always feel like it's too much. I'm not sure." Holding it up in front of herself in the mirror, she tilts her head from side to side. "Hmm, I'll think about it." She looks at me in the mirror. "I'm done."

"Me too."

We grab our clothes and put the unwanted pieces on the bar.

"You're not getting it?" She grabs the white two-piece outfit off the bar.

"No. I'll never wear it. It'd be a waste of money."

She shoots me a scowling look of disappointment.

My phone chimes and I get it out of my purse.

Nicco: I'm looking forward to seeing you tomorrow. Let me know when you're boarding the plane.

"Nicco?" she asks, leaning in and peeking at my screen.

"Yeah."

"Thought so by your smile. He's looking forward to seeing you, huh?"

I playfully glare at her, shaking my head. "You're as bad as my mom."

We both chuckle and head to the register to check out.

"Ready to go home?" I ask.

"Yeah. Sushi?"

"Definitely."

About halfway to the car, she stops.

"You know what? I'm gonna run back and get the pink top."

"Okay."

"You wanna pull the car around?"

"Yup."

She turns to go back to the store and I get the car, meeting her at the mall entrance. Back at my house, I do a quick load of laundry to wash my new tops and we order dinner.

While we wait for it to arrive, she helps me pack for my trip. I lay out pajamas, a few outfits of shorts and tops, a couple pair of jeans, tops to go with the jeans, a sweatshirt, my black dress for dinner, my cute floral dress with cap sleeves, and my gray and white tie die bikini. I'll pack my toiletries in the morning in the morning as I'm getting ready.

We go back downstairs and she pulls out her laptop.

"Come here," she says sitting on the sofa. "I want to show you something."

I sit next to her and she pulls up pictures of Nicco and Giovanna from the photo shoot.

Though I know she doesn't do it to be hurtful, my stomach twists. "Oh, Can, these are incredible. Your talent never ceases to amaze me."

"Well, thanks, but what I really want to show you are these," she says, scrolling down to the shots she took of me and Nicco.

I suck in a breath.

"Exactly." She looks at me. Then she scrolls up and back down, and up again. "Do you see this?" she asks, pointing at a picture of Nicco and Giovanna. "Do you see the vacancy in his eyes?" She scrolls back down to shots of me and Nicco. "And this?" She points at the screen. "This right here is connection, chemistry, desire." She looks me in the eyes. "This isn't something you can fake, Des. A picture is worth a thousand words."

I'm speechless. I can't deny seeing what she's pointing out.

"And you'd only just met. Now you know each other. I'd love to see what shots of you two say now."

The doorbell rings. She closes her laptop.

"Be right back," she says. "I gotta pee."

She goes to the bathroom while I get the door and prepare our plates. Knowing I have a long day of traveling tomorrow, we go to bed pretty early.

"Get a good night's sleep. You have your emergency medicine for the flight, right?" she asks.

"Yup, it's in my purse already."

"Okay, good night."

"Good night."

She turns to head to the spare bedroom which is basically hers since she's the only one who ever sleeps in it.

"Can?"

She turns around. "Yeah?"

"Thanks. I had fun today." I smile.

"Me too." She smiles back at me. "Take a chance." She winks. "Night."

The flight went well and I didn't need my emergency medicine, thank goodness. I text Nicco to let him know I landed. He texts me back to let me know where he's going to pick me up. Butterflies flutter inside my stomach, the same way they did when he kissed me.

As I wait for him, I pop onto Instagram to check my messages and notifications. Something makes me go to Giovanna's Instagram. Three images back, there's a picture of her and Nicco. He's sitting in a chair, gazing up at her, with his arm wrapped around her waist and she's standing beside him, affectionately looking down at him. The butterflies are burned by stomach acid. Forget the fucking kiss.

They look cozy and intimate and his eyes don't look vacant here. Though I feel a little queasy, seeing that picture was a good reminder that I'm here on business and that's all. Deep breath. I go back to my account, but I can't get that image out of my head.

It's not long before he pulls up.

Nicco

Destiny's here and I'm excited to see her. I've missed her. I've missed the way her eyes sparkle when she looks at me. I've missed her laugh. I've missed our easy, and sometimes intimate, conversations. I've missed her kind and gentle heart.

She was so great in showing me around L.A. and now I get to show her Rome and Ponza. I have some fun things planned for her time here. Experiencing it all in real life should really be helpful for writing her book, and I'm eager to spend more time with her.

I'd be lying if I said that's all I was eager about. I haven't had sex since I met her. After that kiss, I'm fucking craving her. I haven't masturbated this much since I was a teenager.

I don't know what the fuck happened to me when I kissed her, but I was hooked. Hooked on more than just the kiss and her soft, sweet lips. I was hooked on her. I haven't been able to stop thinking about her. Damn, I want to kiss her again. I need to kiss her again.

But if I do, I don't think I'll be able to stop myself from wanting more. I want her body wrapped around me. I want to be deep inside her. I want to make her come undone with a pleasure I know she's never experienced. I want to be the one to do that for her.

Shit. I have to remind myself that losing control like that will only end up leaving us both hurt. Plus, she's made it clear that she won't have sex with me. Masturbation it is. It's going to be a long ten days.

I pull up to where she's waiting for me and get out. She's so damn beautiful.

Fuck I want her.

"Ciao, mia dolce ragazza. Welcome to Italy. It's so good to see you."

When I hug her, she's stiff in my arms. I draw back, kissing her on each cheek.

"Can you not call me that?"

I recoil slightly at the bitterness coating her tone. It's the first time I've ever heard her be terse. "Of course, I'm sorry."

She shakes her head, casting down her gaze, then looks back up at me. "I'm sorry. I think I'm tired. It's been a long day of traveling."

"Yes, I understand. Was the flight okay?" I take her luggage and put it in the trunk, then open the passenger door for her.

"Yes, it was, thank you," she says, sounding very formal, as she gets into the car.

Something's up and I have no idea what it is. Maybe she's not as happy to see me as I am to see her. Maybe I misread things back in L.A. It's probably best anyway. I have to keep my head on straight so I don't fuck up either of us by the time she leaves.

"I thought you might be hungry after traveling all day. Would you like to go to dinner?"

"I *am* hungry, but would you mind if we got food and ate in? I'm kind of tired and don't feel like going out."

"We can do that. There's a place near my house. We can order now and pick it up on the way back."

"Okay. Thank you."

"Of course. It's Italian food." I chuckle. "As you would expect. Do you know what you'd like without seeing a menu?"

"I'd be okay with spaghetti and meatballs."

"Okay, I'll order for you."

I call and place our orders. Then she gives me the highlights of her day of traveling. I know how tiring it can be. Honestly, I'm glad she'd rather go back to my house than go out. It'll be nice to be alone together again.

After I pick up our food, I drive us home and show her to her room.

"Is there anything you need to unpack before we eat?" I ask, setting her suitcase near the bed.

"No. I can unpack after we eat. Let's eat it while it's hot." She sets her purse and small bag on the bed then looks around the room. "It's beautiful in here. Did you decorate it?" Her side-eyed glance tells me she wouldn't believe me even if I said yes.

I chuckle. "No. I asked Angelina to help me when you said you'd come. You'll meet her when we go to Ponza. I think you'll like her."

"You, did this for *me*?" I love the way her voice gets higher when I've done or said something she's not expecting.

"Yes." I turn and head toward the kitchen. "Come on, let's eat."

I put on some music and transfer our meals onto plates while she looks around my house. I'm a pretty neat guy, but I cleaned up a lot knowing she was coming to stay with me. Her house is extremely tidy and I want her to feel comfortable.

"Is the floor okay?" I ask, setting our plates and silverware on the glass top of the coffee table then grabbing two large pillows from the sofa, putting them on the floor.

"Perfect." She squats down then sits on her pillow, crossing her legs.

"Okay, good. Let me know if you get uncomfortable and we can sit at the table."

"Okay, I will. Mmm." She inhales deeply as her cheeks rise on her face with a smile. "It smells delicious."

"I hope you like it."

"I'm in Italy. I can't imagine *not* liking spaghetti." She raises her eyebrows, softening a little from earlier. Picking up her fork, she twirls the noodles around its prongs, looking through the glass top of the coffee table. "Is it weird seeing yourself on all these magazines?"

I chuckle. "Actually, it is. It's hard to get used to. I feel like they're trophies I won. I display them here to remind myself to stay humble."

"I like that." There's that sparkle I've missed.

"I have some ideas of things we can do and places I want to take you while we're here, before we go to Ponza."

"Great. I'd love to hear what you have planned."

"Tomorrow I'll take you to Quartiere Coppedè. It's a very small neighborhood with some beautiful buildings and a large fountain I think you'd like to see. Then we can go to Trastevere. There's an outdoor food market and we can have lunch before touring the area."

"I like the sound of things so far." She smiles.

"When I told Mamma you were coming, she insisted you come for supper. I hope that's okay."

She puts down her fork and glances down into her plate, then looks at me. "Um, okay," she says, tilting her head slightly like she's confused.

"You don't want to meet my mamma?"

"No." She's quick to answer. "It's not that — I, just, I'd be happy to meet her."

"Okay, good."

"Um, when you..." She pauses, twirling spaghetti around her fork, not looking at me. "Call me mia dolce ragazza, is that like, a general term of endearment you use for women here, like say Angelina, your mamma, or maybe Giovanna?" Looking over at me, she shrugs her shoulders. Her forced attempt at seeming casual with her body language tells me there's something more behind her question.

"No," I say flatly. "You're the only one I've ever called mia dolce ragazza."

Her eyes scan mine. "Oh." She blinks and continues eating.

As we eat, I tell her more of my ideas for her time here. She seems excited and I'm relieved. We finish supper and clean up in the kitchen.

"I don't have quite the selection of snacks that you have, but here's what I have." I open a cabinet, showing her two different flavors of biscotti, several kinds of chocolates, and a container of Mamma's homemade pizzicati pinch cookies. "Or." I open the refrigerator. "Tiramisu." I stand back and smile, watching her ogle the tiramisu.

"You're going to make me fat while I'm here, aren't you?" She looks up at me from under her lashes with a playful smile dancing on her lips.

I chuckle, getting the two pieces of tiramisu out of the refrigerator. "No, I promise."

"Those pictures you sent me were beautiful. Where were you?"

"I was on the Amalfi Coast. Gigi and I had a photo shoot there."

"Oh." Her posture stiffens, very slightly, but I noticed. "Yes, I saw a picture of you both on her Instagram."

"Really?"

"Yes." Her terse tone from earlier has returned.

I pull my phone out of my pocket and go to Gigi's account, finding the picture. Huh, it makes sense now. *She's fucking jealous.* Though I have zero attraction to Gigi or emotional connection and I've told Destiny this, I kind of like that she's jealous. Although if she's jealous, that means she does feel something for me. Which means I have the potential of hurting her and I really don't want to hurt her. *Fuck.*

"Yeah, that's from the shoot we were on. The surroundings were so beautiful. If I was still a gardener, I would've loved to work there." I focus on the scenery and avoid talking about the ridiculous picture Gigi posted, hoping to ease Destiny.

It doesn't.

"You know, I'm kind of tired. I think I'll go to bed instead. I'll have my tiramisu tomorrow. Thank you for dinner." She walks out of the kitchen and down the hall to her room. No kiss on the cheek, no good night. She is a feisty little thing.

Destiny

After getting washed up, I lie in the bed in Nicco's spare bedroom, staring at the ceiling, questions swirling in my head. He had his sister-in-law decorate this room for me? His mom wants to meet me and have me over for dinner? I'm the *only* one he calls mia dolce ragazza? I want to pretend these things don't mean anything to me. But they do.

Then on the other side of him inching into my heart, it's like he's rolling over it with a dermaroller, stabbing it with tiny little pricks.

He may not think there's anything between him and Giovanna, but body language speaks volumes and their body language says there's chemistry between them. Hot, sexual chemistry. It may not have shown in the pictures Candi took, but there's no denying it in the picture on Giovanna's Instagram.

Maybe this was a bad idea. A really bad idea. If I can't turn off my emotions, I'll never make it through this trip. Maybe I can get a flight back tomorrow.

19

Destiny

When I open my eyes, it takes me a few seconds to remember I'm in Italy, in Nicco's house. I'm surprised by how well I slept. Stretching my body across the bed, under the floral sheets and cozy cream-colored comforter, I bathe in the sunlight filtering into my room through the ivory lace curtains. My room is a stark contrast to the decor I saw in the living room last night. The furniture is a light-colored wood with soft edges and carved details. A vase of bright flowers sits on the nightstand along with a small ivory lamp adorned with a champagne-colored shade. It's feminine and calming. I can't believe he did this for me.

I'm being ridiculous. I'm in Italy. Who knows if I'll ever have a chance like this again? I'll really get a sense of it from a local person's point of view and it'll be invaluable research for my book.

A local person. No, not a local person. Niccolo Mancini. Nicco. I can do this. I just have to keep reminding myself that this little fairytale ends.

Getting out of bed, I open my suitcase and grab my sweatshirt that's on top. I should probably hang my clothes today. I was so flustered and tired last night, I didn't unpack anything but my toiletry bag. Putting on my sweatshirt over my camisole and shorts, I go look for Nicco to see what our timing is for today.

The house is quiet. He's not in the kitchen or living room. I peek out on the patio off the living room to see if he's out there having a cigarette. He's not.

"Nicco," I call out, peeking down a hallway I think leads to his bedroom.

No answer. Maybe he didn't hear me. I walk cautiously down the hallway, the terracotta tile cold under my bare feet.

"Nicco?"

Still nothing. Where is he?

His bedroom door is open. I know I shouldn't go in, but I can't stop myself. The view of the headboard on his bed sucks me in. Spanning the length of his king-size bed is a massive, intricately carved, gold woodwork frame that curves and turns, crawling up the wall. There's a crest at the top with a garland of flowers beneath it. The fabric inside the frame is a royal, burgundy-red and gold Renaissance pattern that matches the spread draped over the bed. It's stunning and fit for a king.

Nightstands adorn either side of the bed and are as striking and regal as the headboard. *Is that...?* I step closer to the foot of the bed. Resting on top of one of the nightstands is a notebook and pen. Sitting next to them — *it is* — is the seashell I picked up and gave him on the beach.

As I'm admiring the regal-ness of his bed, my mind goes in the wrong direction. *I wonder how many women have been in his bed.* More than I want to know about, that's for sure.

"Do you like it?" That deep, low hum of his voice startles me, causing every hair on my body to stand up.

I gasp and spin around, stepping on his feet and crashing into his chest. He grabs hold of my arms.

"Nicco," I say, stepping back off his feet, trying to catch my breath. He releases his grasp on my arms. "I'm — I'm sorry. I — I didn't mean to invade your privacy. I just — I couldn't find you and I came down here and — and the door was open. I shouldn't have come in."

"It's okay." He smiles, heating the air in the room. "You're welcome to be in here." He digs his hands into his pockets and shifts his eyes from me to his bed. "It's beautiful, isn't it? Like a piece of artwork."

I turn to look at it again. "It really is. Exquisite."

"It's the first big thing I bought for myself when I got my first paycheck from the movie."

"I'm sure you've put it to good use." That came out a bit more spiteful than I meant it to.

"No."

I turn back to him.

He towers above me. His face, expressionless. His eyes burning into mine. "I don't bring women here."

The air grows thick around us.

"Are you hungry?" he asks. "I went down to the bakery and got some cornetti and fette biscottate."

"I don't know what they are, but they sound good."

He turns, unblocking my path to the door, and extends his hand toward the doorway.

We eat breakfast and I go back to my room to unpack and shower. As I start hanging things in the beautifully carved wardrobe closet, I can't find one of the dresses I thought I packed. My bikini is also missing. I dig farther in case they got shuffled around in transit. When I get to the bottom, I pull out a two-piece white outfit and a black thong bikini. *Candice!*

When I'm dressed and ready, I meet Nicco in the living room. He scans me from head to toe.

"What? What is it?"

He smiles. "You kind of look like a tourist. It's my fault. I didn't tell you. Most women in Italy wear dresses. You don't have to wear one if you're not comfortable. But you would look nice if you wore one."

"Oh. Well, I had a dress, but it seems Candi switched out a few of my things. So, all I have is a dinner dress and a less suitable dress Candi snuck into my suitcase."

He laughs. "Candi has good taste in dressing models. I'd like to see it on you."

"Uh, it's not really for a day walking around town."

"Okay, then I'll take you shopping first."

I hadn't planned on spending money on anything but food while I'm here. I suppose it would be kind of fun to get a new dress, *in* Italy. It'll be a souvenir from my trip.

"Okay. A new dress would be nice. And it seems I have some extra money to pay for it." I squint at him.

He shoots me a wicked smile. "I thought you meant $100.00 an hour."

"No, you didn't. You knew exactly what I meant."

"Well, it's done now." He shrugs and smiles.

He drives us to a little town close to where we'll be exploring and takes me straight to a small boutique shop. When we walk in, the shop is quiet with only two women shopping. The woman behind the counter looks up, stops what she's doing, and smiles broadly as she steps out from behind the counter.

Walking toward us, she opens her arms and embraces Nicco as they kiss one another on both cheeks. Then they engage in a quick chat in Italian.

"Destiny, this is Maria. She's my mother's best friend's daughter and she owns this boutique." He then says something in Italian using my name so he must be introducing me.

I smile at her and she beams back at me saying something to him. I have no idea what she said, but she seems very excited. She steps in toward me and kisses me on both cheeks, holding my shoulders in her chubby hands.

"Pleasure," she says, still beaming at me.

"Sì, pleasure."

They start rattling off in Italian again, both of them eyeing me up and down. She makes different hand gestures, sizing me up. It sounds like he's explaining to her the things we'll be doing because I hear some of the words he said last night. She says lots of, "ah"s.

She tilts her head and cinches her hands together around my imaginary waist. "Lei é cosí piccola."

He chuckles. "Sì." Then he says something else I don't understand.

"Sì, sì," she says and scurries off, her thighs swishing together under her dress.

"I told her a few of the things we'll be doing and she's going to pull some dresses for you. She said you're tiny, but she has some things that will fit you. You'll need a sweater to cover your shoulders when we go to the churches. Did you bring one?"

"I brought a sweatshirt." I cringe a little, thinking that a sweatshirt probably isn't suitable.

He chuckles. "Okay, we'll get you a sweater. Feel free to look around while Maria gets some dresses."

"Okay." I wander through the boutique. It's filled with so many pretty dresses from casual dresses to full length gowns you'd wear to a ball. There's a whole separate room with stylish shoes, classy jewelry, and beautiful handbags. Though I don't need a dress, I have to admit that walking around the Italian boutique feels like I'm living in someone else's dream life.

"Destiny," Maria sings out my name and waves me toward her.

I walk over to her and Nicco meets me there. She talks excitedly in Italian and gestures to the dresses in the fitting room, holding up a few to show me the backs of them.

She walks out and I walk in. "Grazie." I tried to learn a few important words and phrases before I came.

"Prego." She claps her hands together, her smile spreads across her full cheeks.

Nicco sits across from the fitting room in a large fancy chair that's covered in red velvet. "Come out when you try them on. I want to see them on you."

"Okay," I say, closing the curtain. Out of the ten dresses, there are two I don't like.

As I put on the first dress, nude sandals are slid under my curtain. I put them on and they fit perfectly.

When I come out in a red, wrap maxi dress with white polka

dots, he stands up. The dress has a low V-neck and ties at the waist.

"I like this one."

"It's pretty. I don't know if I'd wear it again when I get back home though."

"Try on the others," he says, sitting back down.

I try on the rest, liking two floral ones and the one I have on. It's a pretty green halter with tiny white flowers.

"I like this one," I say, as I spin in front of him. "But I like the two floral ones too. I'm not sure which one to get."

"Why don't you try them both on again and then you can decide?"

"Are you sure? You must be getting bored."

"I'm not bored. I'm enjoying my fashion show." He smiles that sexy smile that melts me.

"Okay, I'll be quick." I gather the dresses I don't want and hand them to Maria. "Can you tell her I won't be taking these?"

They talk back and forth as I close the curtain and change into one of the floral dresses. I come back out and spin. He nods. Then I put on the second one along with the white cardigan Maria put in the room for me. I come back out again. He nods again.

"What do you think?"

"I like them all," he says, rubbing his scruffy chin with his index finger.

"You're no help," I tease, spinning once more in the mirror. "I think I like the green one best." I go back in the room and change back into the green halter dress. Then I show him once more.

"You look very pretty," he says, standing up.

Maria walks over and says something, her face bright with a smile. I hand her the two floral dresses.

"Can you tell her I'll take this one I'm wearing?"

"Of course."

They chat and she walks away.

"Turn for me? You can't walk around with a tag on your dress."

I turn my back to him. He sweeps my hair across my back and

over my shoulder, grazing my skin with his fingers. My inhale is slightly audible. I see him smile in the mirror as he snaps off the tag.

"Thank you." I step forward, away from him and back into the fitting room. "I'll be right there. I just need to change my shoes."

He goes toward the register while I change my shoes. With my clothes and the white cardigan in my arms and Maria's sandals in my hand, I head to the register.

She has a hint of a frown on her face and starts waving at my feet, then gestures up and down at me, sputtering Italian.

Nicco laughs. "She says you can't wear your sneakers with that dress. You must wear the sandals."

"Oh. I'd only planned to buy the dress and cardigan." I look down at my feet, realizing my sneakers do look a little silly with the pretty dress.

"It looks better with the sandals."

"Um, okay. Can you have her ring them up for me? I'll go put them back on," I say, handing her my credit card.

"Yes. I'll wait here."

I find a chair and change out of my sneakers, putting on the sandals. So, I didn't plan to buy a dress, a cardigan, and shoes. Oh, well. This is a once in a lifetime trip. I'm not going to overanalyze it.

Going back to the register, I hand her my sneakers for the bag she has ready with my clothes in it. She takes my sneakers and wraps them in tissue paper before putting them into the bag, making sure to put the white cardigan on top.

"Grazie, Maria."

"Prego, Destiny." She smiles, handing me my credit card. She drops the receipt in the bag and hands the bag to Nicco. Then she comes out from behind the counter and gives each of us kisses on our cheeks.

Nicco drives us to Quartiere Coppedè where we wander the small town and I marvel at the impressive buildings. The architecture is breathtaking. Massive arches trimmed with intricately carved stone figures, every window embellished with more carvings, and huge statues that look like they're holding up the building. There are influences of Greek, Baroque, and even touches of Gothic and Medieval design. A splendor of antiquity. Weaving through the streets, we come upon the Fountain of the Frogs in the middle of the town. Five streets meet at the circle of the grand fountain.

"It's magnificent," I say, in awe at the enormity of it.

Human figures adorn the base, spitting water from their mouths, while the top of the fountain houses eight stone frogs separated by chunks of green moss.

"Can we throw coins into it?" I ask.

"No, but you can still make a wish if you want."

When I close my eyes, I feel him lace his fingers between mine. *I don't want this to end.* Taking a deep breath, I open my eyes and let it out.

Still holding my hand, he turns to me. "Are you hungry?"

I squeeze his hand gently. "Nicco, people will see. You're very recognizable here."

"I don't care. Are you hungry?"

"I am." Having no idea why he's holding my hand, I love the way it feels.

"Then let's go eat."

We walk, hand in hand, back to the car where he opens the door to let me in. He drives us to Trastevere where we have a light lunch and walk around the narrow cobblestone streets. Each ochre-colored building has arched passageways, flower-filled balconies, and doors with antique doorknockers.

Once we've finished looking through the markets, he takes me to Janiculum Hill where we hike our way up to the top. While these sandals are very cute and have been pretty comfortable for much of the day, the hike is starting to hurt my feet and my pace is noticeably slower the higher we go.

"Are you okay?" he asks.

"I am. My feet are just starting to hurt a little with all the walking in these sandals."

He looks down at my feet. "Oh." He raises his eyebrows and rubs his chin. "I didn't think about that. I don't know how women wear these shoes. We're almost at the top. Do you think you can make it? I promise the view is worth it." He smiles.

"Yes, I can make it." I've come this far. I'm not stopping now.

"When we get home tonight, you can soak in my tub and then I'll rub your feet." A flirtatious smile spreads across his cheeks as he continues walking, slowing his pace to match mine.

About five minutes later, we reach the top and the panoramic view is stunning. A bird's-eye view of Rome and picturesque terracotta and white buildings that spread for miles, blending into the mountains.

"We can stay here for a while until your feet feel okay to go back down."

We gaze over the view of the city, quietly, breathing in the sun as it descends. He steps away to have a cigarette and I take a few pictures.

"I'll take your picture," he says as he returns to me and gets out his phone.

"Here." I hand him my phone. "You can take it with mine so it's not on your phone."

"You don't want your picture in my phone?"

"No, I just..." My tongue twists inside my mouth.

"I already have a picture of us at the Hollywood sign." He reminds me.

"Um, okay. That's fine." As I put my phone in my purse, a light breeze blows my hair around my face and I tuck the stray pieces behind my ear. "Tell me when you're ready."

"Okay, smile."

I smile and I think he takes a couple pictures. He comes over to me, stands next to me, and flips through the pictures.

"Nicco." I look up at him. "There are so many." He was taking pictures while the wind was blowing my hair.

He shifts his gaze from his phone to my eyes. "You're a beautiful subject to photograph, mia —" He stops himself and looks deep into my eyes. "We should start going back down now. The sun will set soon. We can decide which ones you want when we get home."

We start back down the hill and my feet are aching. Just as I'm considering taking off the sandals and going barefoot, he scoops me up in his arms.

Caught off guard, I gasp as I instinctively wrap my arms around his neck. "Nicco, you don't have to carry me."

"I know I don't have to. I want to. This was my idea and I didn't think about your feet." He continues walking.

A few minutes later, we reach the bottom of the hill and go directly to the car. On the way home, we order food for dinner.

I'm so grateful to be back at his house so I can take off my sandals. He goes to the kitchen to put our meals onto plates and I go to my bedroom to put away my things. When I empty the shopping bag, the two floral dresses and the red dress with white polka dots are in the bag. Sitting on the bed, I scan my mind of our time in the boutique. I know I asked him to tell her I wouldn't be taking these. Did he misinterpret what I said? Did she misinterpret what he said? Ugh, I really need to learn the language a little more if I ever visit another country again.

He knocks on my door.

"Come in."

He opens the door and walks in. "Dinner's ready. How are your feet?"

"Okay, great." I chuckle. "They hurt a little, but they're okay. Um, I think maybe Maria got confused about the dresses." I gesture to the three dresses I've laid on the bed. "I only wanted to buy this one," I say, placing my hand on my chest.

"Don't you like these?" He opens his hand toward the dresses then crosses his arms at his chest.

"I do, but —"

"Good, then they're yours. I bought them for you for your birthday."

"For my birthday? But, Nicco, you already got me something for my birthday. Something extravagant that really wasn't necessary," I say, standing from the bed.

"I gave you an experience, not a gift. These are a gift. And before you tell me you can't accept them, you should know it's considered rude to not accept gifts here."

I glance at the dresses on my bed and rub my finger across my lips. "Um, thank you. That's very generous of you." While I don't feel right accepting them, I already know how stubborn he is and let it go.

"Come on," he says, walking toward the door. "Let's eat. I'm hungry."

We enjoy dinner, sitting on our pillows at the coffee table in front of his white leather sectional and talk about the day's adventures.

"Do you want to soak your feet before we eat our dessert?" he asks, taking the last bite of his lasagna.

"I'd love to, but there's no tub in my bathroom."

"Not in yours, no, but I have one in mine. It's nice and deep too. You can take a bath if you like."

Oh, jeez. Naked in Niccolo Mancini's bathtub. I don't know. My feet sure would feel better. I'll be quick, in and out.

"Okay, I'd like that."

"I'll get it started for you."

"I'll clean up out here."

When I'm done cleaning up the kitchen, he comes to get me and we walk back to his bedroom. *Don't look at his bed.* As I enter the bathroom, it's like I've been transported to a luxurious spa. The white marble tub is brimming with bubbles, the chandelier casts a dimmed glow over the room, and calming meditation music surrounds us. A tray sits near the tub, holding a gold, three-arm candelabra with lit candles, a sea sponge, and a white towel.

"Do you need anything?"

"No. This is perfect. Thank you."

"You're welcome. Take your time. I'm going to have a cigarette and maybe write some music."

He closes the bathroom door and I undress, twist my hair up into a bun, and dip a toe into the water, testing the temperature. Just right. I step in and sink into the bubbles. As my body relaxes into the heat of the water, the painted floor-to-ceiling mural draws my gaze. The cobblestone street is lined with stone-façade apartments. Flower pots line the walkway, every arch is adorned with a garland of colorful flowers, and every window sill is dressed with a window box full of more flowers.

Closing my eyes, I let my body fall limp as the music sings softly in my ears. About fifteen minutes later, I remember the sponge on the tray. Dipping it into the water, I drag it across my arm, squeezing it and letting the water fall back into the bubbles. Another few minutes of sponging and soaking and I'm ready to get out, tired from the long day and wanting to get some sleep.

Getting out of the tub, I towel off. *Shoot, I didn't bring in anything to change into.* Maybe he's still having his cigarette out on the balcony and I can sneak across to my bedroom unseen.

I wrap the towel around me and walk quickly toward his open bedroom door.

"How was your bath?" He's sitting on his bed with a notebook and pen.

I gasp, startled, and tug my towel tighter. "Very relaxing."

"Good. Come here," he says, spreading his knees.

My heart pounds as I try not to breathe loudly. My steps are hesitant. Standing between his knees, I look down at him.

A sultry smile dances on his mouth as he reaches up and twirls a piece of my hair around his finger.

"I like these wet curls around your neck." He moves his eyes to my hair wrapped around his finger. Whether he does it intentionally or not, he quickly runs his tongue across his upper lip then his lower lip. "Are you ready for dessert now?"

Breathe! "Yes, I — I just need to get changed. I forgot to bring pajamas in with me."

"I see that," he says, releases my hair from his finger. Goose bumps cover my body. "Go get changed and I'll meet you in the living room."

"Okay." I turn immediately and walk quickly out of his bedroom, down the hall, and across to my bedroom.

Closing the door behind me, I flop back on my bed. It was nothing. I can do this. Sitting up, I take off my towel and put on my camisole and shorts. Grabbing my sweatshirt, I put it on and go back out to the living room.

Our tiramisus from last night are on the coffee table and he's sitting on the sofa with the TV remote in his hand.

"Do you want to watch a movie?" he asks.

"Sure. You pick something."

Grabbing a plate, I sit in the corner of the sectional, tucking my legs under me. Finding a movie, he sits back and takes the other plate.

"Oh my gosh, this is so good," I say, eating my third mouthful.

He chuckles at me, blowing air through his nose. "I'm glad you like it."

When we're both finished with our tiramisus, I take our plates to the kitchen and rinse them in the sink, then put everything in the dishwasher.

I'm not sure how long I'll last watching the movie, but I sit back down in my corner.

"Lie back and give me your feet," he says, moving closer to me. "I said I'd rub them for you."

"It's okay, they feel much better now." I don't think I can handle him rubbing my feet.

"You are stubborn." He reaches out both arms, wraps his hands around my ankles, and tugs them, laying my calves across his thighs.

Oh God.

Looking forward at the TV, he starts massaging my feet.

"Ooo. Gentle, they're still a little tender."

He immediately lightens the pressure of his strong hands. "Better?"

"Yes, thank you."

While he watches the movie, I can't focus on anything but him rubbing my feet. His strokes are long and slow, downright sensual. Every now and then, he looks down into his lap at my feet as he rubs them.

After a few minutes, my body finally relaxes and I lie back into the cushions, closing my eyes, wallowing in the bliss my feet are experiencing. His kneading into the arch of my foot feels so good. He focuses on my left foot, rubbing and kneading. Then he moves to my right, massaging with long strokes. He moves his hands to my ankle, his thumbs rest on my shin as his fingers move up my calf. Inching farther up my calf, he slowly works his fingers into my muscles.

As he moves his hands farther, passing my knee, pressing his thumbs into the bottom of my thigh muscle, his long fingers extending up and around the back of my thigh, I'm a mixture of relaxed and completely turned on. I can't open my eyes. I can't know if he's watching me. I focus on steadying my breath.

His slow strokes reach farther up my thigh. My breath stilts as it leaves my mouth. I tingle between my legs, choking down a moan.

20

—

Nicco

Seeing her standing in front of my bed earlier today, I had to shove my hands in my pockets to keep myself from picking her up, tossing her onto it, and ravaging her. Then she was standing between my legs in nothing but a towel. And now, wrapping my hands around her silky legs, I'm going fucking insane.

Working my way back down her smooth, toned leg, I travel up her other leg, wanting to plant my face between them. She squirms a little, but doesn't stop me. Her tiny breaths tell me she likes it. I'm so fucking hard right now.

When I reach the top of her thigh, a small sound escapes her. Sucking in a gasp of air, her eyes fly open and she sits up, clearing her throat.

"I, uh, thank you. My — my, feet feel a lot better now," she says as she stands. "I'm getting tired. I think I'll go to bed. What time are we starting tomorrow?"

I chuckle to myself. I love that I get her flustered. "Sleep as long as you like. We're in no rush." I stand, stepping toward her, wanting to kiss her cheeks and inhale her intoxicating vanilla scent.

She brushes quickly past me. "Okay. Good night then," she says then goes straight to her room and closes the door.

I don't know how much longer I can be around her and not fuck her. But I can't. She won't let me. With a burning need to relieve the pressure in my pants, I head to bed and take care of business, fantasizing about plunging inside her three different ways.

⋙⋙ ⋘⋘

She looks so cute in the morning, no makeup, hair up in a mess on top of her head. Her long, sexy legs extend down from her oversized sweatshirt that hides the fact that she's wearing shorts underneath.

We eat a quick breakfast and shower. Today she wears one of her flowered dresses and sneakers.

"I know they don't look as nice as the sandals, but I want my feet to last the day and not hurt. I'll put on my sandals when we go to your mamma's house for supper."

"Good thinking." I guess my massage was too much for her to handle last night. "Remember your sweater, we'll visit a few churches today."

Once she has her sweater, I drive us to Aventine Hill where we spend the day visiting historic religious structures and churches. Our last stop before we leave is to the Knights of Malta keyhole to see the exquisite dome of Saint Peters Basilica through the shrubbery tunnel. Having visited all of these places many times myself, I'd lost my appreciation for the richness and beauty of it all. Watching her be truly mesmerized gives me a whole new experience and reminds me to be grateful for where I live.

On the drive home, she excitedly tells me some of her favorite sights of the day.

"Nicco?"

"Yes?"

"You've shown me some beautiful places and I've loved them so much."

"Good, I'm glad."

"But, I want to see *your* Rome. Places that have meaning to you. Like maybe where you went to school or places you went with Marco."

"I'll show you. Tonight, we go to Mamma's and the house I grew up in. Tomorrow I'll take you on my motorcycle to a few places and we'll drive along the coast for you to see the beautiful ocean. There's a beach we'll stop at also."

"That sounds nice. I look forward to it."

When we get back home, we still have some time before we're due at Mamma's.

"I think I'll do some writing out on the patio before we go to your mamma's."

"Okay, I have a song I'm working on. Do you mind if I join you?"

"Not at all. Do you want to have your cigarette first? I'd rather not be out there with you while you smoke."

My heart sinks in my chest. Her strong dislike of my addiction continues to remind of how badly I want to quit. *Fuck, these cigarettes.*

"Yes, I understand. I'll let you know when I'm done."

I head out to the patio, sit in my usual chair, and mindlessly engage in my ritual. As I light the tip of my cigarette with Dad's lighter, I talk to him.

I miss you, Dad. There's a woman in my life, but I don't know for how long. I wish you could meet her. Mamma will meet her tonight. She's unlike any woman I've met. She's kind and loving, and so pure of heart. She's nothing like Ana. I'm sorry, Dad, I'm angry with you. I needed you after Ana. I needed you and you weren't here.

I need you now. I'm so confused about what to do with this woman. My feelings for her grow stronger the more time I spend with her, but she leaves soon. And I don't know how she feels about me. There's chemistry, but I know she's scared.

She sees me as nothing more than a playboy. I have been, Dad. You wouldn't be proud of me. I turned into the kind of guy I always despised. The kind of guy who uses women for sex but will never give them my heart. Ana ripped out my fucking heart, chewed it up, and spit it at me. I let her destroy me. I don't want that kind of pain ever again. So, I shut off my heart, my feelings. But I can't keep myself from Destiny. I can't. I have to prove her wrong. I used to be a one-woman guy. I want to be the man I once was. For her, I can be and I will be. I want to give my heart to her. Fuck, I'm scared. Help me, Dad.

Sucking in long and deep, I hold the smoke in, a little longer than I should, then release it through my nose, blowing the last remnants out my mouth. I shift my gaze to the sky before going in to get Destiny. When I stand up to go into the house, she's sitting on the end of the sofa, clutching her computer, watching me. I sit back down and wave her toward me.

"Come here," I say, patting the top of my thigh when she comes out.

I wasn't sure she would, but she approaches me and sits on my thigh.

"I'm writing a song for you."

"For me? Why are you writing a song for me?"

"Because it came to me and now I have to write it."

"Can I hear it?"

"No. It's not ready yet."

"Okay." She pauses. "You seemed very far away just then. Were you writing lyrics in your head?"

I shake my head, looking down into her lap. "No." Lifting my head, I meet her eyes. "I, talk to my dad a lot when I smoke." I shrug my shoulders and shake my head again. That must sound ridiculous to her.

With the touch of an angel, she places her hand on the side of my face, locking her gaze on me. "I know you feel closer to him when you smoke. But you can feel close to him in other ways. Ways that aren't harmful to you." She moves her hand to cover my heart. "He lives here, and he'll *always* be here." She gently presses against my heart. The intensity of her gaze nearly brings tears to my eyes. I swallow the lump in my throat and push back unshed tears.

Rising from my lap, she pulls out a chair and opens her laptop. I go inside and grab my notepad, pen, and guitar, ready to let the lyrics and notes fall into place.

Destiny

On the way to his mamma's house, my stomach churns. Not only does it feel strange going to meet his mom, but I have a feeling I'm not going to know ninety-nine percent of what's going on.

When he opens the door, the smells of fresh pasta, baked ricotta cheese, and buttery garlic fill my nose, making my mouth water. We enter through the living room, sparsely decorated with a vintage sofa and chairs that are covered in a faded green and red vertical-striped fabric. Voices chatter in the room beyond where we entered and he leads us there. As we walk into the kitchen, we're met with a surprise, well a double-surprise.

"Ay, bro. I didn't know you'd be here." They kiss on the cheek then hug with a loud, manly pat on the back. "Angelina." He kisses her on each cheek. "And my favorite nephew in the whole world." He picks up the little boy in his arms and nibbles on his cheek as he growls. The boy giggles in delight. Putting down his nephew, he introduces me to each of them.

I receive and give cheek-kisses then squat down to the little boy's eye level. "Hello. It's nice to meet you, Franco."

"Hello," he greets me. "It's nice to meet you, Destiny."

When I stand up, Nicco's mamma is waiting patiently.

"Mamma." Respect mixes with joy in his voice.

She wipes her hands on her apron and reaches up to cradle his scruffy face in her hands. Bending down, he kisses her on each deeply wrinkled cheek.

"Mamma, questa é Destiny." He places his hand on my shoulder. "Destiny, this is my mamma, Antonietta."

"Ciao, Antonietta. Thank you for having me." I smile.

He translates for me, she smiles and nods, then comes in for the cheek-kiss. I guess that's a good sign. Once we release, she says something as her hands fly around.

Whatever she said makes him laugh. "Mamma." His tone shifts to playfully reprimanding.

He must see the puzzled look on my face. "She says you need to eat pasta, lots of pasta." He chuckles again.

All I can do is smile politely.

"Don't forget about me," Giovanna sings her flirtation while batting her lashes at him.

Great, Giovanna's here. As if I wasn't already feeling nervous and uncomfortable.

"Gigi. I didn't know you were coming." Always the gentleman, he kisses her cheeks.

"Mamma told me you were coming for dinner."

She calls his mom, Mamma? *Simmer down.* I call Candi's mom, Mom because I've known her since I was a kid. This is no different, not that it matters.

"Hi, Giovanna." I really don't want to kiss her.

"Oh, Destiny." She tilts her head, forcing a fake smile. "How nice to see you again," she says, lacking sincerity, as she purses her filler-filled lips and leans in for more of an air-kiss which is fine by me.

His mamma has made delicious stuffed shells, a salad, and the best garlic bread I've ever eaten. They all chatter in Italian during dinner and Nicco tries to fill me in on a few things they're talking about. Watching Giovanna tease him and flirt with him turns my stomach, though it really shouldn't. I don't belong here. Unable to physically vanish, I sit quietly and eat my meal.

After dinner, I help clean up the dining room and kitchen while Nicco and Marco play with Franco in the living room. Nicco kneels down and lets Franco climb onto him, riding him like a pony. With each demand of, "Go, go, go" from Franco, he neighs and circles the room weaving in and around the few pieces of furniture. When he passes the sofa, he grabs a rose-embroidered pillow with his teeth and shakes his head around like a dog, causing Franco to erupt into laughter. I love his playful nature and watching him with kids. It's a side of him I never would've expected. A side that's quite sweet.

Giovanna walks in to join them while Angelina and I finish drying the last few dishes. His mamma pulls out a large tray of tiramisu, homemade no doubt, sets it on the counter and goes to the living room.

"How long do you have here to visit?" Angelina asks in somewhat broken English.

"Not long. I leave next Sunday after we stay at Ponza Island with you." I wipe the plate in my hand and place it on the counter. "Thank you so much for letting us stay."

"It is too bad you can't stay longer. Sì, of course." She smiles warmly. "We are happy for you to come stay."

A boom of laughter explodes from Giovanna, drawing our attention. She's clinging to Nicco's arm, stroking her long hair. Marking her territory again.

I've never been great at keeping my emotions from painting themselves all over my face.

"Psh," Angelina rolls her eyes and makes a hand gesture that doesn't look at all complimentary. "Do not concern yourself with her. Even *I* know Nicco would never go so low."

"Oh, it's fine." I shake my head. "Nicco and I are just friends. He's helping me with some research for my book."

She turns her head to the side, lifting only one side of her mouth. "Friends? Is that why his eyes twinkle when he looks at you?" The other side of her mouth rises.

They do? I have no answer. All I can do is shrug and shake my head. Once the dishes are done, she and I go to the living room.

"Does everyone want wine with dessert?" Nicco asks.

Me, Angelina, and Giovanna all say yes. He and Marco go to the kitchen to get the wine.

The three ladies chatter in Italian while I sit quietly, watching Franco entertain himself. Feeling a little out of place, I go help Nicco and Marco bring the wine glasses in.

As I approach the kitchen, I hear Marco. "It's been four fucking years since Ana, Nicco. It's time to let it go," he half-shouts, slamming his hand on the counter.

"I know how fucking long it's been!" Nicco spits, rage steaming out of him, the vein in his neck swelling.

Before I can sneak backwards out the doorway, Nicco sees me.

He says something in Italian to Marco and they drop whatever it was that had them both heated.

"I — I'm sorry. I just came to see if you needed help bringing out the glasses."

"No, it's okay. I'm sorry you heard that," Nicco says, forcing a smile.

"It's my fault, Destiny. I apologize," Marco says, handing me two glasses of wine.

Once we finish dessert, Marco and his family leave and Giovanna heads out as well. Nicco's mamma turns on an ancient-looking TV and nestles into a worn chair that's partially covered with a dark red knitted blanket.

"Come," he says, taking my hand in his. He walks us down a dimly lit hallway, passing an open door on the right to a bedroom. "That was Marco's room." Walking a little farther down the hall, we enter a small room on the left where I feel like I've been transported back in time. "And this is my room."

He guides me in and releases my hand. Walking slowly around the room, I take it in. He sits on the edge of his single bed.

"You upgraded." I smile. He looks huge sitting on the small bed.

He chuckles. "I did."

Everything is perfectly tidy and looks like his mamma hasn't changed a thing since he left home. Next to the bed is an old wood dresser topped with nine trophies and a picture that looks like it's him and Marco as young boys.

"You played soccer?"

"Yes, football. I'm a very good player."

"I see that."

"Of course I don't play anymore."

There aren't any decorations on the walls. Even through the house, the decor is minimal and humble.

"Is there anything else you would like to see? I will show you."

I walk over to him on the bed and look down into his handsome face. Being here in his childhood bedroom, I can see the little boy behind his eyes.

"No." I pause. "Thank you for showing this to me."

He stands and I tilt my head up, keeping his gaze as he rises above me. "It's my pleasure."

We stand, silent, eyes fixed on each other in the quiet of the room.

"Nicco, who's Ana?" I ask, keeping my voice hushed.

"No one. She — she's no one." He purses his lips as he glances down.

"It didn't sound like she's no one. But it's okay if you don't want to talk about it."

"No, I don't." The anger from earlier is gone, replaced by something more like sorrow. He exhales through his nose. "Are you ready to go?"

"Yes."

Taking my hand in his again, he leads me back down the hall to the living room and must tell his mamma we're leaving because she gets out of her chair.

He releases my hand and lowers toward her. When she reaches up and clutches his face in her hands, she speaks softly and tears come to her eyes as she smiles. After their cheek-kisses, she wraps her arms around his waist, burying her cheek into his chest. He cages her in his arms, resting a hand on her silver curls. My heart tugs watching this virile, shooting-to-fame, seemingly-sex-god so tender in the embrace of his mamma.

Unwrapping from him, she turns to me.

"Grazie, Antonietta." As I go in for the cheek-kiss, she speaks.

"Per favore, chiamami, Mamma," she says, then cups my face in her soft, weathered hands.

Clueless, I nod my head and smile, trying to be polite.

Nicco chuckles. "She likes you. She wants you to call her Mamma."

"Oh." That's unexpected.

"Buona notte, Mamma," he says as he takes my hand and leads us to the door.

"Buona notte," she says, blowing us a kiss and waving.

"Buona notte, Mamma." I wave back.

It's close to eight o'clock by the time we get back to his house. We decide to do more writing, me on my book, him on his song.

I change into leggings and my sweatshirt then grab my laptop and go back out to the living room, sitting in the corner of the sectional I sat in last night. He comes over with his notepad, pen, and guitar.

As I type, he strums and jots things down on his notepad. Watching him create gives me inspiration.

He catches my gaze on him.

"I'm sorry, does my music interfere with your writing?"

"No. Not at all. I like it. It's pretty, whatever you're writing."

"Thank you."

"You're really good with kids. I enjoyed watching you with Franco tonight."

He jolts back, his eyes fly open, and his jaw lowers. Then his eyes move rapidly from left to right. Given his reaction and the expression on his face, I fear I've said something either alarming or upsetting, but I can't imagine what.

He leans his guitar against the sofa and stands up, pacing and rubbing his neck.

What the heck did I say?

"You — you think I'm good with kids?"

"Yes, you *are* good with kids."

He paces a little more, rubbing his hand across his forehead.

"Excuse me," he says then grabs his pack of cigarettes off the coffee table and walks out to the patio.

Have I somehow insulted him? What's going on?

I grab a bottle of water from the kitchen then tuck back into my spot, legs under me, and continue writing.

When he comes back in, he still looks flustered. I set my laptop aside and stand up, approaching him.

"Nicco, I'm sorry for whatever I said —"

"No. No." He cuts me off, shaking his head and waving his hand. "Please, don't apologize. I, um…" He pauses, rubbing his finger across his mustache. "Please, sit." He goes to the sofa and sits, folding his knee up onto the cushion. I follow him, mimicking his body position so we're facing each other.

"Tonight you asked who Ana is, and I said she's no one." He pauses. "That's not true." He looks down to his clasped hands, rubbing his thumbnail with his other thumb. Looking back up at me, he continues. "Ana and I were together, for a while. And, we… didn't end on good terms." His Adam's apple moves up and down. Watching him struggle twists my heart.

Standing up, he walks over to a tall, dark walnut bookshelf and opens a wooden box. He takes out a piece of paper and returns to the sofa. "One day, out of nowhere, she left. No goodbye, no explanation, nothing. This letter was in my mailbox."

Slowly, he reaches out his hand with the letter in it and gives it to me. The tattered paper looks like it's been crumpled and uncrumpled dozens of times. Gently, I unfold it and read.

Nicco,

I'm pregnant with your child. I don't want anything from you. Your work and income are unsteady and your dream of becoming a big star is a fantasy that will never happen. Your life is going nowhere. You aren't capable of being a good father or a good husband. I release you from any responsibility. Don't try to find me, you won't be able to.

~Ana

Despair and heartache shatter me. When I look up at him, the pain in his eyes steals the breath from lungs.

"I tried to find her. For a year, I tried to find her. But I couldn't." As he inhales deeply, his shoulders rise. His exhale is controlled, like he's trying not to burst. "Somewhere, I have a child. A child I don't know, I can't hold or kiss or play with. And it fucking kills me." He swallows, looking down into his hands, rubbing his palm with his opposite thumb.

I reach out, placing my hand on top of his, and lean toward him. "Nicco. I'm so sorry." I squeeze. "I'm sorry this happened to you." I pause. "As the child's father, you have rights. And this letter?" I hold it up. "She's wrong." I shake my head. "She's so wrong." I lean in farther, locking my gaze on his eyes. "You're going to be wonderful dad someday. And the woman who captures your heart? She's going to be so lucky you found her."

He stares blankly at me. Silence echoes through the room.

"Why do you have this letter? Why do you keep it?" I ask softly.

His swallow takes effort. "I keep it to remind me. To remind me of the pain. To remind me of the truth." He breaks our gaze, looking down at our hands. "I keep it to remind me to close my heart so I can't be a disappointment to anyone else, and I can't get my heart broken again."

Clarity smashes me in the face. My chest caves, goose bumps cover my skin, and pain lacerates my heart.

Tilting my head, I search his eyes. "Nicco, this is not your truth." I hold the letter toward him, shaking my head. "This is *not* your truth."

When I squeeze his hands, he pulls his lips in tightly, his eyebrows pinch together, and mist coats his eyes. He heaves an inhale and swallows, releasing a stilted exhale.

"How can you know?"

"I know," I say, my voice just above a whisper.

His jaw clenches as his eyes shift, searching mine.

Rising from the sofa, he takes the letter from my hand and returns it to the wooden box.

"I think I won't write tonight. I'll go to bed." He grabs his guitar. "Tomorrow you'll not want to wear a dress since we'll be on my motorcycle. Jeans will be good."

"Okay."

His tall body hunches, looking physically exhausted. I close my laptop and get up from the sofa then walk across the cool tile to my room.

He walks behind me, our steps slow, heavy. We reach my room and, as I turn to face him, he's close. I step back and I'm against the wall. He leans an arm above me, smelling of stale smoke, and strokes my cheek with his thumb.

"Buona notte, mia dolce ragazza." The phrase holds a depth in the fragility of his voice. "Thank you." Moving his arm, he holds my face in his hands then kisses my forehead.

"Buona notte."

Closing the door, I walk over to my bed, sit down, and lie back, taking in a deep breath. So much makes sense now. All I want to do is hold him in my arms and ease his pain.

Nicco

After a cigarette to calm myself, I go to my bedroom, having to consciously exert effort to move the weight of my legs. I sit on the edge of my bed, raking my hands through my hair. I hadn't intended to ever tell her about Ana. Maybe I shouldn't have. But when she said I'm good with kids, she knocked me fucking upside down. I felt safe telling her.

Having her in my childhood home, meeting Mamma, and hearing her tell me Ana's words aren't my truth, keeping her out of my heart is impossible.

Reminding myself that she leaves soon is fucking torture.

21

Nicco

My night was restless. Though I'm tired, I'm excited for our drive along SP601. When she comes out of her room for breakfast, the sight of her catches my full attention. Snug jeans encapsulate her long legs, her black top is open across her entire back with a tie that wraps around her narrow waist, and her hair is in a single braid. She doesn't see it, but she's so damn sexy.

We eat breakfast and get ready to head out on the motorcycle.

"Nicco." She stops me before we leave.

"Yeah?"

"Would you mind bringing Ana's letter with us? I'd like to try something if you're open to it."

Ana's letter? I don't know that I want to have it with me on our day together. "What do you want to do?"

"You said we're going to a beach, right?"

"Yes."

"Okay. Do you trust me?"

Unquestioningly. "Yes."

"Okay. Bring the letter. I'll tell you more later."

I get the letter out of my wooden box and tuck it into the pocket of my leather jacket. "Do you have any kind of jacket with you? You might want it for the ride."

"I don't. I just have my sweatshirt."

"Hmm. I have one. It might be just a little big on you." Getting

218

my other black leather jacket out of the closet, I hand it to her.

As she puts her arms through, the sleeves are too long and the bottom hangs below her butt. She's fucking adorable.

I chuckle. "Perfect fit."

Catching her reflection in the mirror, she laughs. "Right."

We go out to the garage and I turn the key on my motorcycle. The roar of the engine makes me smile.

"Where I'm taking you, the speeds aren't fast, but I want you to hold onto me, okay?"

She nods, with a look on her face that tells me she's a little scared.

We mount the bike and she wraps her arms around my waist. I love the way she feels against me. As I drive through the small streets of town, I point out shops and interesting things she might want to see. Then I take her by my high school, as requested.

Once we're on SP601, I increase my speed on the open road, but not too much. The straight stretch hugs the coastline. Above us, the sky is a clear, bright blue with a few clouds floating by. Ocean water stretches beyond what our eyes can see. She rests against my back and I lay my arm down on her leg. She feels so right. *Damn I don't want her to go.*

The wind in my face, a woman who's sneaking into my heart wrapped around me, and empty road for miles, I ride. About half an hour in, I pull off the road to a spot where we can walk down onto the beach. She unwraps from me and carefully dismounts the bike.

"It's so beautiful," she says, taking in the view. "Is this where we'll go on the beach?"

"Yes. We go down just over there." I point. "This is a perfect spot because no one really comes here."

"Okay." She takes off her shoes and socks.

I do the same. Taking her hand, I lead her down to the sand where we walk close to the water's edge. Together we stare into the ocean, letting it soothe us. The beach is my sanctuary. Having Destiny here with me, makes it heaven.

She turns to me. "You have Ana's letter?"

"I do."

"If you're open to it, I'd like to do a burning ceremony with you."

"What's that?"

"It's a way of releasing things that no longer serve us. I fully respect if you don't want to. And if we start and you change your mind at any point, we'll stop. I'll help you with what to say."

I've never heard of such a thing. But I trust her, more than I've trusted any woman outside of Mamma.

"Okay, I'm willing to try. What do I do?"

"Hold the letter."

I get it out of my pocket and hold it in my hand.

She reaches out and holds my other hand in both of hers as she faces me, the sun lighting her face.

"I'll say some things and you repeat them."

"Okay." I take a deep breath.

"These words I hold are not my truth."

I don't speak. She doesn't push. She holds my gaze. I breathe.

Swallowing, I push the words out. "These words I hold are not my truth." I exhale.

"They are a past I held onto as my truth."

"They are a past I held onto as my truth."

"I let them hold me captive."

I breathe. "I let them hold me captive."

"But they do not serve me."

"But they do not serve me."

"I no longer want to be their prisoner."

I choke down the swelling lump in my throat. "I no longer want to be their prisoner."

"I no longer want to punish myself with these untruths."

I suck in a stilted breath as tears burn behind my eyes. I want to run. I squeeze her hand. Her gaze holds loving space for me. She caresses my hand with her thumbs, assuring me there's no rush for my words.

"I no longer want to…" My swallow is like a dagger dragging

down my throat as I force out the next words. "Punish myself with these untruths."

She waits a moment before continuing.

"I want to open my heart to love, to joy, to possibility, to freedom."

I breathe. "I want to open my heart." I swallow. "To love, to joy, to possibility, to freedom."

"You have your lighter?"

"Yes," I say, releasing my hand from hers and taking my dad's lighter out of my jeans pocket. The rough fabric brushes against my skin.

"When you're ready, if you're ready, I want you to light the letter on fire."

Holding Ana's letter in one hand and my dad's lighter in the other, my breath shakes out of my lungs. I flick the lighter, the flame quivers beneath the letter as my hand trembles.

I touch the flame to the corner, watching the letter ignite.

"With these flames, I release these untruths from my soul and set myself free."

"With these flames, I release these untruths from my soul and set myself free." I inhale then exhale through my nose.

As the paper turns to ashes before my eyes, my flesh shivers.

It burns. I breathe.

Just like the gray death, smoke floats into the air. I twist the paper and turn it, catching each section aflame. With the last corner lit and dying, I release it, watching it blow away in the gentle breeze.

It's gone. The words that gave me so much pain are gone. Destiny did this for me.

She has my heart.

Standing behind her, her back against my chest, I wrap my arms around her and she holds onto my arms, resting her head back.

I close my eyes and breathe.

Time passes, yet it stands still as we gaze at the ocean in silence, the sun warming our skin, the grainy sand seeping between our toes. I was dead inside for so long. She unraveled the barbed wire caging my heart, exposing my scars. Pain I hid from the world. She wrapped my wounds with her healing love.

I'm free.

Destiny

Before we leave, I turn to face him.

"Back in L.A., you asked what my parents do for a living."

"Yes."

"My dad is retired from the CIA, and he has connections. I didn't give him any details, but I emailed him last night to see if he might be able to find Ana and your child."

He steps back from me, covering both sides of his nose with his hands. "Can he do that?"

"He can try. I didn't want to go any farther without your permission." I pause. "There's no promise that he can find her. Is this something you want me to ask him to do?"

Clasping his hands around the back of his neck, he paces left then right. He stops in front of me, holding my shoulders in his large hands. I can't decipher if his expression is that of hope or fear.

"Yes, please." He shakes his head. "I understand if he can't find her. But I would be so grateful for him trying."

I smile and nod. "I'll email him when we get back to your house."

He takes my hand in his and we go back to his motorcycle. The drive back home is just as stunning. Ocean for miles, the fiery sun blazing in the sky above us, my body wrapped snugly around him.

Together, we agree to eat in again and, since it's an early night, we decide to make lasagna and garlic bread. We stop by the store on the way home and get only the essentials since the bag needs to fit between our bodies on the motorcycle.

When we arrive back at his house, he turns on some music and starts immediately on the preparations. I go to my room and email my dad. When I go back out to the kitchen, he's started the water heating for the noodles and is working on the sauce. I grab the cheeses and start on the cheese mixture then the garlic bread. I've never cooked dinner with a man before. It's kind of fun. He's quite entertaining to watch, the way he dances to the music as he stirs the sauce, stopping every now and then to sing into the spoon like a microphone. I can't help but smile at him.

My cheese mixture is done and the garlic bread is ready for the oven when the timer dings, telling us it's time to strain the noodles.

"The strainer is in the cabinet above your head," he says as he shakes his hips to the beat, stirring the sauce.

I open the cabinet and see it on a shelf above me. Stretching onto my tiptoes, I reach up as high as possible, but can't touch it with my fingers. As I bring down my arm, he's at my back, extending his arm easily above me, and taking it off the shelf. A shiver runs up my spine.

He sets it in the sink and dumps in the pot of noodles and boiling water. Steam billows into the air and he ducks his head out of its path. On the counter near the sink, he's laid out parchment paper. As he goes back to stirring the sauce and gyrating his sexy body, I wait for the steam to settle and lay out the noodles on the paper.

With the last noodle laid out, we're ready to begin our lasagna assembly. He places a deep dish in front me on the counter then puts the pot of sauce on one side and the bowl of cheese mixture on the other. Then he tucks himself behind me. Every time he's this close to me, my body heats.

"I'll do the sauce and cheese layers, you do the noodles."

"Okay," I say, trying to ignore how flustered I am.

He spreads a layer of sauce on the bottom of the dish. Methodically, we build the layers, our arms grazing past each other several times. I can't stop the goose bumps from trailing up my arms at the touch of his skin on mine. He loads on the final layer of sauce then reaches for the parmesan cheese. The stale smell of smoke enters my nose as his torso presses into me. A few sprinkles of cheese and it's ready for the oven.

I move out of the way and he takes the dish, putting it into the oven. Turning my back to the counter, I suck off the tiny bits of sauce that got on my fingers, fold my arms, and watch him. I love that he cooks, not that it matters. When he rises from putting the dish in the oven, he stands in front of me, resting his arms above me on the cabinet. My inhale quavers and I release my arms from across my chest, laying them on the counter as I look up into his dark, seductive eyes framed by his thick, bent brows.

"What should we do while we wait?" he asks, glancing from my eyes to my lips.

The memory of our kiss shoots to the front of my mind. I remind myself that this is a business trip, as my eyes drop to his full lips and my pulse pounds in my head. *Breathe.*

I tear my gaze away from him and look at the mess on the counter. "We, uh, should probably get this cleaned up."

"Mhm." He nods slightly, but doesn't move. After a few breaths, he takes a deep inhale then moves back from me. "I'll have a cigarette first."

He grabs his pack of cigarettes and goes out to the patio. Blowing an exhale, I start cleaning up. I'm not sure how much longer I can resist his subtle seductions.

When he comes back in, he puts the garlic bread into the oven and helps me finish cleaning up the kitchen. I wash the dishes and he gets a towel and dries them.

"When you're not busy flying around the world, making films and singing in concerts, what do you do for fun?"

"I paint."

"You paint?"

"Yes. You seem surprised."

"Not surprised, impressed. You're very talented. What do you paint?"

"It's abstract. Beautiful monsters."

"Beautiful monsters? What does that mean?"

"People are beautiful, but sometimes we also have monsters inside. When I paint, I bring the monster to light," he says, putting away the last bowl. "Many of the paintings in my house are done by me."

"Really?" I've wondered about his choice of wall decor.

For me, it's dark, ominous, sinister. Empty faces atop distorted bodies, debauched features of a face entangled with devil-horns and hair that drips like blood. Hearing this explanation, I'm starting to understand the artwork now.

"Yes. Some are gifts and a few I purchased. But most are my creation."

I wander through the living room with a renewed perspective, taking my time as I examine the pieces. Though they disturb me, they also reveal his pain, which makes me hurt for him. Once I've circled the room, I sit next to him on the sofa.

"Was Ana one of your beautiful monsters?"

"She was. She haunted me every day. She was a reminder to me that I'm a monster." He pauses. "Now, because of you..." He takes my hand, encapsulating it in both of his. "My chest is lighter and she no longer haunts me."

Eyes locked on mine, he raises my hand to his lips and kisses it.

The timer chimes on the oven.

"Will you paint with me tonight?" he asks, releasing my hand and getting up from the sofa.

"Oh no. I'm not artistic in that way. I'm better with words."

"You're brilliant with words. Come on, I'll help you." He turns, looks back at me, and smiles.

I'm not prepared for his compliment. "Okay. I'd like that," I say, getting up and joining him in the kitchen. "How about we sit out on the patio tonight?"

"Of course."

We dish out slices of steaming lasagna and he puts the loaf of garlic bread onto its own plate. Before we head out to the patio, he changes the music to something less pelvis-pumping. His patio is peaceful with shrubbery that must be twenty feet high. Pulling out cast iron chairs, we set our plates onto the mosaic tilework that tops the table. As we eat, we talk about our trip over to Ponza Island tomorrow and he tells me about a few things we can do.

After dinner, we clean up together and he takes me down the hall past his bedroom to a fully dedicated painting room. Taking an easel from the corner of the room, he sets it up, back-to-back from one where he's in the middle of a piece. He grabs a blank canvas from a stack and sets it on the easel then walks over to a long table that houses dozens of colors of paint. Taking a paint brush out of a large carousel of brushes and a wooden painter's palette from a small pile on the end of the table, he comes over and hands them to me.

"Create anything you like. If you get stuck, tell me. I'll help you. Use any of the paints you want." He gestures to the table of paints, then walks over to a music tower and turns it on.

I stare at the blank canvas, a little intimated. It reminds me of the days my cursor blinks at me on my screen, begging me to do something. Then the vision comes. I know exactly what to paint. Palette in hand, I walk to the table and squeeze paints onto it: red, orange, yellow, white, black, several shades of blue, brown, and a tan color. I also grab a few more brushes of different sizes.

Though I have no idea what I'm doing, I allow the vision to guide me. He's busily painting away. As I swirl the paints together on my palette and brush the colors onto the canvas, I get wonderfully lost. More than an hour passes.

Consumed by the scene I created in front of me, I don't hear him approach me.

"It's beautiful," he says, standing close to my back, looking at my canvas over my shoulder.

"It's the beach from today."

"Our beach." A sentimentality washes over me as he says the words. "May I add something?"

"Of course." I step aside and he takes the palette from my hand, dipping his brush into the black paint.

Delicately, he dabs the canvas, creating two shadows, one taller than the other. Setting down his brush, he stands behind me and wraps his arms around me. "Us," he says, kissing the top of my head. *Ugh, my heart.*

"Now it's complete. May I see yours?"

He releases me. "Of course."

The image is representative of a female with a large face and huge blue eyes, but no other facial features. Her breasts are lopsided and her torso sensually curves down to her spread, feet-less, legs. Some kind of white ring is above her head.

As I gaze at the picture, he trails his finger lightly down my back. My shoulders squeeze together at his touch on my bare skin. I suck a quiet inhale.

"Does it frighten you?" His breath is hot against my ear.

"No." I breathe. "It confuses me. My eyes want to see the face."

He traces his finger back up my spine and again, my body responds, slightly arching, as I close my eyes. He presses his lips softly into my neck, just below my ear. My chest rises and falls with my labored breaths.

I wrap my arms around my waist, he follows with one arm, pulling me to press against him. Laying feathery kisses, he moves slowly down my neck, holding my jaw gently up and away with his other hand, elongating my neck. I can't stifle my gasp when his hot lips reach my collarbone.

Pulling away from him, I heave an exhale, and try to catch my breath. I glare at him.

"Why do you resist me so much?" He shoves his hands into his pockets then tilts his head down and to the side, looking up at me.

"To teach you that you can't just take what you want." My momentary desire shifts to frustration.

"I know you feel something. I can see your body respond to me." He looks down at my nipples that I'm sure are poking through the fabric of my top without a bra on.

Whether or not I feel something, right now I'm mad. "I'm not a prize you get to win just because you're intolerably hot," I bark. *Shit. That flew right out.*

A devilish grin turns up the corners of his mouth. "So, you *do* think I'm hot." He steps toward me, closing the gap between us, scorching the air.

I don't move. I want him close. I want him to fully feel my next words. "The only reason you want me is because you can't have me." I turn on my heels to walk away.

He grabs my arm, pulling me to him. Holding my shoulders in his hands, he stares down at me, nostrils flaring, eyes boring into me. His eyes move from mine down to my lips like he's going to devour me. Curling his lips inward, he sucks air in through his nose.

"I'm not one of your conquests, Nicco," I say softly, holding his gaze.

"I know that. You're —" He pauses. "You could never be." He pauses again. "You're unattainable on every level." Stifling what sounds like a growl, he releases me.

Going to my room, I close the door and throw myself onto the bed. This is agony. Why did I agree to do this? What was I thinking? While refusing to have sex with him, all I want is for him to consume me in every way possible. Just the thought of having his hands on me, his lips on my flesh, his body pounding into to me is enough to give me an orgasm. And the more we're together, the more I learn about him, the deeper he seeps into my heart. I'm falling for him. But I can't. I just can't.

I won't.

22

Nicco

Another restless night as Destiny dominates my every thought. More powerful than my physical desire are the emotions pulsing through me. She's wrong. I don't want her just because she won't let me have her. I want her because she makes me see the world differently. She makes me see myself differently. She has a way of bringing out the beauty in everything and everyone around her. She's fucking addicting.

And she's leaving. Worse than that, I can't make her stay. I have no right to think I could.

The air between us is polite, tense, as we eat breakfast. After we clean up the kitchen, we meet in the living room, bags packed. I drive us to where we're meeting Marco with his boat to bring us over to Ponza. She's uncomfortably quiet. I went too far last night. Resisting her is growing increasingly difficult. But I have to. I told her I'd always respect her wishes.

When we board, Marco and I take our bags below deck and Destiny sits on one side of the cockpit. As we get underway, I sit next to Marco, giving her some space. He and I chat as he drives while she looks over the water, her beautiful face etched with sadness. About an hour in, I can't take the ache in my heart.

Sitting next to her, I take her hand in mine, expecting her to withdraw it. She doesn't.

"I'm sorry." I turn my body toward her, putting my other hand

229

on top of hers. "I sometimes find it hard to control myself around you." I look briefly down at our hands and chuckle softly, returning my eyes to hers. "You don't make it easy on me."

She shakes her head. "You don't need to apologize." The sweetest smile lifts her mouth. "Let's enjoy the next few days."

I smile and nod. "We'll be there soon." I lean in and kiss her forehead.

⇒⟩⟩⟩⟩⟩ ⟨⟨⟨⟨⟨⇐

When we arrive at their house, Angelina has lunch prepared for us and invites Destiny for an afternoon of shopping after they drop Franco at her sister's house for a sleepover. Once they're gone, Marco and I pour ourselves some wine and play a game of pool.

"So, what's going on with you two?" he asks, cracking the cue ball into the two-ball, knocking it into the corner pocket.

I groan. "It's so fucked up."

"Fucked up how?" He takes a drag of his cigarette. "Seems like things are good with the hand-holding I've seen. What's the last few days been like?"

"She's unbelievable, this woman. I told you, I've never met anyone like her."

"You do have a track record for dating gorgeous but nasty women who treat you like shit."

"Don't I know it." I get out a cigarette and light it. "You know what she told me?"

"What?"

"She told me I'm good with kids."

He snaps up his head from his bent over position to line up his shot. "I could've told you that because you're great with Franco, but I know after Ana, you didn't believe it." He takes a drag.

"Bro, I fucking know. I ended up telling her about Ana and showing her the letter."

"Holy fuck." He straightens himself then sits on the edge of the pool table, scratching his forehead with the thumb of his hand holding his cigarette, staring at me. "What happened?"

"It just came out of me and then yesterday, I took her to the beach and she had me do some kind of burning ceremony thing and I burned the fucking letter." I hold an imaginary piece of paper in my hand and flick my lighter beneath it. "She had me say some phrases and I almost lost my fucking shit. It's gone." I shake my head. "I've never felt anything so powerful." I suck in my gray death. "Her dad is going to try to find Ana and my child. He has connections from his job."

"No way. That's amazing."

"I know. I can't believe it. And last night, we painted together. I never painted with anyone before. I liked it."

"What's happening to you?" He chuckles, getting up from the edge of the table. "Seriously, it's great to hear you like this, man. I'm happy for you." He goes back to lining up his shot.

"Don't be too happy. It all ends when she leaves." My heart pinches as I say the words.

With one smooth stroke, the cue ball tips the three-ball into the side pocket. "Why?"

"Because it does. It has to. That's what she wants. It's what I'm supposed to want. But I don't."

"Then tell her."

"There's nothing I can say. Trust me."

"You're going to give up? Just like that?" He glares at me.

"She lives halfway across the world. What do you want me to do? Besides, she won't have sex with me so she can't be too into me."

He jolts up from eyeing his next shot. "You still haven't fucked?" One eyebrow raises high above the other.

"No, man. She won't let me. My balls have been fucking blue since I met her. I'm fucking craving her." I shake my head, for the first time realizing I don't want another woman. I only want Destiny. And I can't have her.

"Damn, bro."

"Tell me about it."

"Look." He spreads his legs, holding his stick in both hands in front of him. "You're my little brother and I've seen you go through a lot of shit. I haven't seen you this happy since we were kids, flying down the middle of Vicolo del Malpasso in our wobbly go-karts with Lorenzo and Marcello, lucky we didn't split our heads open on the cobblestones." He chuckles. "Tell her how you feel. Figure out a way to make it work." He leans down, eyeballing his shot, and clacks the five-ball into the corner pocket. "And for fuck's sake, fuck each other." He blows smoke out as he laughs.

>>>>> <<<<<

When Angelina and Destiny return, we have dinner together and they tell us about their afternoon while I have to confess that Marco whooped me at pool. As we clean up from dinner, Angelina suggests we meet back at the pool for a night swim and drinks.

Marco and I are at their bar, pouring wine for ourselves and lining up shots of amaro when Angelina comes out and lights candles around the patio. She opens a chest and takes out four towels, putting one on each lounge chair. When she's done, she joins us at the bar. Destiny walks out, covered in her oversized sweatshirt, her hair twisted on top of her head, and joins us.

"Would you like your s'mores martini?" I ask Destiny.

"I don't know what that is, but I like the sound of it," Angelina says. "Will you make me one?"

"Yeah."

"Okay, I'll have one," Destiny says.

Stepping behind the bar, I make their martinis and put them in front of them next to their shots.

Angelina wiggles in her seat. "I want to say the toast," she says, holding up her shot glass.

Marco nods and gestures his open hand toward her.

"I want to toast Destiny." She smiles warmly. "Thank you for coming here to be part with our family. Salute."

With the ladies in their chairs and Marco and I standing in front of them, we raise our glasses in the center, saying, "Salute" in unison then down our shots.

Marco and I get in the pool while Angelina and Destiny sit at the bar sipping their martinis. After a few minutes, Angelina brings her drink over to the pool, sets it on the edge, and gets in. Destiny follows, also setting her glass on the edge of the pool. When she lifts her sweatshirt over her head, I'm grateful my body is under water because I'm immediately hard.

"Your suit is so cute," Angelina says.

"Oh, thank you. My friend Candi snuck it into my luggage," she says, quickly getting into the pool, but not before I get a look at her sexy body and the thong up her tight ass.

Fuck me.

"You guys, this is amazing," she says, sinking into the water, looking out at the view.

Marco and Angelina's villa overlooks the ocean with mountains to the right. Stonework and lush greenery surround the pool and patio. And the most unique part is the front glass wall of the pool. From under the water, you can look out into the ocean. As the sun is almost fully down, the candles Angelina lit earlier cast a warm glow across the patio.

"Thank you," Angelina says. "This view and the pool are one of the main reasons we bought the villa."

"I can see why."

"Come." Angelina takes her martini and glides through the water to the glass wall.

Destiny does the same, meeting her at the wall. They sip their drinks and Angelina points out some things in the village below. After the ladies finish their drinks, Angelina announces she's going in and Marco goes with her.

Before he gets out, he looks at me, looks toward Destiny, and cocks his head to the side. I know exactly the message he's sending, but I'm not going there, no matter how hard I am or how much I desire her. Destiny's made herself very clear.

Moving through the water, I stand next to her. "Do you want another martini?"

She looks up at me. "That's probably not a good idea." A devious smile lifts her cheeks. "We both know I don't make the best decisions around you when I'm tipsy and I've already had wine with dinner, a shot, and a martini."

I chuckle, take my wine in my hand, and slide closer to her. We rest our arms on top of the glass wall, I let my body relax deeper into the water.

"How are things going with Vance? Do you have any projects lined up yet?"

"He has some leads on a few parts and I'm waiting to hear about audition possibilities."

"He's really good. I have a feeling he'll have you lined up with something soon."

"I hope so. I'm excited to keep moving my career forward." I sip my wine.

"What speaks more to your heart, acting or your music?"

"I love acting. I love putting myself into a character. But, when I'm acting, I'm playing a role someone else created. When I sing, it's my words, my music, my soul. Nothing can really compare to that. Music was my first my passion, it grounds me."

"Mmm. Your passion definitely comes through when you sing. When do I get to hear your new song?" Sinking her arms beneath the water, she pushes herself off the wall toward the center of the pool.

Setting my wine aside, I move toward her. "Soon. It's not ready yet."

"Okay." She tilts her head back into the water, extends her arms, and brings her knees up, pushing the water back and forth with her hands and arms.

"What are you doing?" She looks like a squirmy fish.

"This is how I float." She continues pumping her arms against the water. "I can't float, I just sink, so this is the best I can do."

"This is not floating." I can't help but laugh a little, she's so cute. "When you float, you're relaxed. This is not relaxed." I point at her, shaking my head and crossing one arm over my chest, resting my other arm on it and stroking my chin.

She stops pumping the water, lets her legs sink, and stands on the bottom of the pool, the water hitting just below her shoulders. "Well, it's the only way I know how to do it."

"Here." I step toward her. "I'll help you."

She tilts her head, pressing her lips together into a thin line.

"I promise to behave." *Even though I want to touch every inch of your body.* "Lean back."

Without another word, she leans back. I place one hand on her back and the other on the back of her legs. She's stiff at first, moving her arms in the water.

"You don't need to push the water. I'm holding you. I won't let you sink."

It takes her about a minute to fully relax into the water, into my hands. She closes her eyes, surrendering. Making my movements slow, I glide her body through the water, watching the ripples extend away.

Burning the time that passes into my memory, I focus on the music filling my ears, the feel of her skin on my hands, the sight of her nipples atop her breasts cresting out of the water.

When she finally moves, I slide one arm up on her back and the other under her knees, cradling her. She loops her arms around my neck, the movement brings her face close to mine.

Fuck, I want to kiss her.

With her body curled into my arms, I swish her gently through the water, desperate to feel her lips on mine again. I promised to behave. I can't break that promise. I don't want to lose her trust.

"I was thinking for tomorrow, I could take you into town during the day and then we can go to supper."

"Okay. I'd like to write in the morning. Will I have time for that?"

"Yes, of course. We have no schedule."

"Okay." Her eyes flick to my lips. "I should, probably get some sleep," she says, but doesn't move from my arms. "Thank you." She pauses. "I enjoyed this."

"So did I." All I'd have to do is bend my neck down to capture her lips. My pulse races.

"Buona notte," she hushes, pulling herself up to kiss my cheek. My fingers tense into her flesh as she does.

It takes all my willpower not to kiss her. She unwraps her arms from my neck and I release her body.

"Buona notte."

"Are you coming in?"

"Uh." *Not with my hard-on ready to rip through my swim trunks.* "I need a cigarette first."

"Okay." She climbs the steps out of the pool.

Every movement of her body has my attention. When she reaches the top step, she turns, catching me staring.

She towels off and goes inside. I grab my cigarettes and focus on deflating my dick.

Destiny

I swear my heartbeat sounded like a sonar ping under the water when he held me floating. Thank goodness for the alcohol or I probably would've been trembling in his arms from my nerves. He had several opportunities to cross my boundaries and he didn't. I'm impressed. With my arms around his neck, our lips so close, and his gaze steaming with desire, I wanted to cross my own damn boundaries.

I dry my hair, put on my pajamas, and turn out the light. Waves of candlelight reflecting off the pool dance on my ceiling. Going over to the window, I carefully move the curtain aside, peeking out. It's strange to think about who he is and the fact that, ten minutes ago, his arms were wrapped around my body. Millions of women would kill to be me. During our moments of tender intimacy, it's like he's all mine. The world fades and the women lusting after him aren't even a thought in my mind. It's just me and him.

But the painful truth is, he's not mine.

23

Destiny

Fueled by a night of sensual dreams, succumbing to his seductions and my unbridled desires, I wake up excited to write. It's early, and I'm the only one up. I throw on leggings and my big sweatshirt, grab my laptop, and snuggle in to one of the chaise lounges by the pool. The sun's just breaking through the ocean, painting the sky in radiant hues of orange and yellow.

Before I begin writing, I take a deep breath of crisp morning air into my lungs, absorbing the beauty surrounding me. We're high enough above the ocean that the crashing waves pacify into a soft hum. A bird visits me, sitting on the glass wall of the pool, tilting its head as it tweets a greeting of good morning.

Another deep breath as my bird friend flies away and I open my laptop. Words fly out my fingers through the keyboard and onto the page. As I write, I fall more and more in love with my characters and their story. Engrossed in my writing, I have no idea how much time passes. Around eight, Nicco comes out to let me know Angelina has made breakfast.

The four of us eat together, then I get showered and ready for my day with Nicco. I take the red dress he bought me out of the closet and put it on. When I look in the mirror, turning to view each angle, I can't help but smile. I feel pretty and I do love the dress.

The smile spreading across Nicco's face when I meet him in the kitchen tells me he's happy to see the dress he liked on me.

We spend the day exploring the village below their villa. Large stones pave the paths through the village and many of the shop's wares are sprinkled outside the entrance of each shop. Clothing hangs from thatched makeshift walls and baskets billow over with bags and shoes. Brightly painted façades bring the village to life. A group of men stand on the sidewalk, playing delightful, folksy, Italian music. The jolly accordion player wears a broad smile, filling the air with nostalgia.

Nicco takes me into every little shop, knowing we have nothing to buy, but just giving me a feel for the local culture.

Food is a very big thing on the island. As we stroll through the village, everything from fresh pasta, to fish, to spices floats in the air. It's impossible not to be hungry surrounded by the delicious aromas. For lunch, he takes me to Osteria which oozes of Italian charm. Greenery and richly-colored flowers crawl up stone walls and around archways. Dim lanterns cast romantic shadows through the small eatery. Cozy two-person tables are adorned with candles and small vases of flowers.

After we eat, we get gelatos and he takes me down a side street that leads to an opening overlooking the ocean. Bistro sets provide a spot to sit and enjoy the view. We sit down at one.

"How long were you and your fiancé together?" he asks.

I'm caught off guard by his question. I wouldn't have thought he'd be interested in knowing anything about my relationship with Kevin. He's been so open with me about his life, I don't mind sharing a little about my own.

"We dated for ten months before he asked me to marry him. Looking back, I probably should never have said yes."

"Really, why?"

"It's kind of hard to explain. I guess I didn't feel the way I thought I'd feel when someone finally asked me to marry them. I mean, I liked him and he was a good enough guy, but there was always something missing. A deeper connection. When he asked me, I honestly wasn't excited and didn't even cry, and I'm a crier with stuff like that. That should've been my biggest clue."

"But you said yes."

"I did." I pause, taking a scoop of my chocolate gelato, the best I've ever tasted. "This is going to sound so stupid." I shake my head, embarrassed by what I'm about to admit. "I think I worried that if I didn't get married soon, then I'd never get married. Ugh. That's not a good reason marry someone. I guess, I just didn't want to be an old maid. I told you, stupid." I lift my shoulders toward my ears.

"No, not stupid. We all make mistakes, have regrets."

"I should've broken up with him long before he ever asked me to marry him. Outside of my suspicions about him and Tessa, I wasn't a priority for him. In a relationship, you show up. You pay attention to what your partner needs. He was never there for me."

"Relationships aren't easy. Sometimes we want so badly for the person to be the one, that we're blind to the things that are missing."

Knowing about Ana, I get the feeling his statement comes from experience.

"Exactly. I think I lost sight of myself, who I was, what I wanted. I was so focused on how old I was and how much time and energy I'd invested in the relationship. I'd given up on the idea of soul mate love and settled for what I thought was good enough."

He stops eating his gelato and looks at me with an intense seriousness I haven't seen before. He leans his body toward me, holding my gaze captive. "Never settle, Destiny. You're worth more than that."

My entire body tingles as the words spill out of his mouth.

Sitting back in his chair, he takes another scoop of gelato. "What do you want in a relationship?"

The night we met, we talked briefly about soul mates. I was tipsy and he was in full-on Mr. Playboy persona. Right now, he seems genuinely interested.

"I suppose I want what most people want. A relationship built on mutual respect and open communication. Someone who's my best friend and I can be totally myself around, who loves me even with my faults and awkwardness. I want someone who shares similar values and life goals as me. Someone who has at least some common interests as me and actually wants to spend time with me. I want for us to challenge each other and push each other forward. To bring out the best in each other and be each other's biggest fans. I want to feel his pain along with his passion. For me, a soul mate isn't someone who completes me, but someone who inspires me to be complete, in and of myself."

As I speak, a lump grows in my throat at the thought that I've never had these things in a relationship and maybe I want too much. I swallow, holding back the tears I know he can see welling in my eyes. "I want someone who I can rely on and trust with my life. Someone who will always be there." I swallow again. "Someone who will fight for our relationship because they believe in our love."

A tear escapes, trailing down my cheek. Before I can turn my face away from him, he reaches out and catches the tear with his thumb, his hand cradling my jaw.

"Don't cry, mia dolce ragazza. You will have all of this and more."

His tenderness is in direct contrast to the tension and disappointment twisting inside me. Though my heart wants to keep hope that I can have this kind of relationship and I want to believe my soul mate is out there looking for me, the realistic side of me has lost faith. "I don't think so." I shake my head and stand up, fearing if we keep talking about this, I'll break down entirely.

Thankfully, he takes my cue, dropping the subject and walking with me. We spend the afternoon walking through the rest of the village, popping in and out of shops. At the end of one of the cobblestone streets is a small jewelry store. It's empty when we enter except for a gray-haired gentleman behind the counter, reading a newspaper. He stands up to greet us and he and Nicco exchange pleasantries in Italian while I smile. Taking our time, we look at the beautiful pieces through the glass cases and curio cabinets.

A silver locket catches my eye. It's delicate with intricate etching on it.

"It's a stunning necklace," Nicco says from over my shoulder.

"Isn't it? It's a locket. You can put pictures in it or even an inscription. I've always thought there's something so sentimental about lockets."

"How so?"

I turn to him. "Well, usually, they house something very dear to the person. Their children, their parents, their spouse, or a quote that has a deep or personal meaning to them. Lockets are very special. I think they are anyway."

"You should get it."

"Oh no. I don't need it. Besides, I've spent more money on this trip than I planned to." I pause, looking at the locket one last time. "Where to next?"

We spend the next few hours browsing through the rest of the shops in the village. By late afternoon, we head back to the villa. Angelina and I chat about the day we had while Nicco plays with Franco.

Earlier in the day, he suggested we leave at 5:30 for our dinner reservation so I excuse myself to get ready. I haven't yet worn the two-piece white outfit Candi snuck into my luggage. I put it on, touch up my makeup, and twist my hair up into a loose bun, leaving some pieces around my face.

When I enter the kitchen where Nicco and Marco are talking and Angelina is preparing their dinner, Nicco stops mid-sentence. His eyes travel from my head to my feet and back up. I catch Angelina and Marco steal a quick glance at each other, the corners of her mouth turn up slightly before she returns her attention to the stove.

Dressed all in black with several buttons open on his shirt, exposing the top portion of his furry chest and his gold necklace, Nicco is fiercely hot.

"I, uh." He clears his throat, turning back to Marco and Angelina. "We're going to go to supper. We'll see you later."

"Enjoy your supper," Angelina says as Nicco approaches me.

"Thank you." I wave in their direction.

We walk out to Marco's car and Nicco opens the passenger door for me, lingering by my side. "This is the outfit Candi packed for you?" he asks.

"It is."

"I told you she knows how to dress her models. You look beautiful." The tiny hairs on the back of my neck stand up. The way he looked at me earlier makes his words feel true.

When we enter the restaurant, I'm awestruck. The hostess takes us through the main dining area which is the opening of a mammoth stone cave. The rough, stony walls and ceiling lead to the open-air edge of a scenic cliff that overlooks the sea below. We're seated at our table, suspended above the water. The view is breathtaking as the water kisses the sky. A delicate lamp curls above our crisp, white-linen draped table, providing warm lighting. Subdued live music sets a romantic mood.

The menu offers an impressive selection. I order spaghetti alle vongole that's flecked with sharp capers and topped with a breadcrumb crunch and Nicco gets fresh swordfish with stewed friggitelli peppers and cherry tomatoes with marinated anchovies.

"Do you see that beach over there?" He points to a stretch of sand below and behind me.

"Yes."

"That's Frontone beach. I'll take you there tomorrow and we'll go for a ride on a jet ski, okay?"

"Okay, that sounds fun. I've never been on one."

"I think you'll enjoy it."

Once our stomachs are full, we sip our wine and enjoy the view of the never-ending sea. It's so peaceful.

"When we first met, you said your career is struggling. But when I researched you, you seem very accomplished. Even a best-selling author. How is it you're struggling?"

"You researched me?" I didn't expect that.

"Yes. I wanted to learn about you."

Interesting. "I've been blessed. My career was booming for a long

243

time. It's just, the last three to four years, I don't know. It's like I lost something, my spark, my passion. I don't know how to explain it."

"It was after Kevin?"

Well, that was blunt, but he's also right. "It was. I went on dates after him, but nothing ever lasted. My books were pretty bad during that time. If I'm being honest..." I swirl the wine around in my glass, avoiding his eyes. "I think that's around the time I kind of gave up on the idea of love. I mean, what kind of romance author can't even have a solid, romance-oozing, passion-filled relationship, you know?"

"Could it be that maybe you gave up on more than just love?"

"What do you mean?"

"Is it possible that you gave up on yourself?" Though his tone is tender, the words sting.

They sting because they're true.

I take in a breath and let it out, determined not to cry.

"I think —" I look up at him and swallow. "Somewhere along the way I stopped believing in myself. I lost my footing somehow. I think I was so mad at myself for being so stupid and not seeing what was happening right before my eyes. I just got lost. And then I made up this ridiculous thing that the only way I'd get back to myself was to be alone. No men, no relationships. That's how I planned to regain my success."

"I take it that hasn't happened yet?" A question that could've been asked with a lick of judgement is spoken with compassion.

I chuckle softly. "No, not yet."

"Your plan is flawed."

"Yes, I know."

"You blame yourself for something you had no part in. You said yourself he wasn't the one for you. It wasn't going to work regardless of his behavior. And you *are* successful. You didn't *lose* anything. You just let your view of yourself get clouded for a while. I don't think you see yourself clearly. You've captivated me, since the moment you turned around and nearly fell backwards onto Candi's desk."

Someone Exactly LIKE ME

The world around us blurs as I'm enraptured by every word he speaks to my soul.

"I've read some of your books. You're a talented author and you write with depth and skill and imagination. You bring your characters and stories to life. Your heart is pure and kind and generous beyond anything I've ever witnessed. You're an independent, capable woman who's open-minded and respects others. And you don't compromise where your values are concerned, I admire that. Through your writing, I feel your passion. Through your actions, I see your compassion."

I can't move. I can't look away from him.

"And you're the most beautiful, sexy woman I've ever had the pleasure of getting to know." He stops. His brows pinch together as the intensity behind his eyes changes. The warmth of his energy shifts to indifference. "Someday, a man worthy of you will come along and see all of these things I see in you and you'll have your soul mate love. But first, you need to see them, believe them, in your heart." He takes a sip of wine then shakes his head. "None of what you thought was lost is lost. Everything is there, inside you. You just need to believe in yourself again."

I'm speechless.

I'm trying to process his words.

I can't even form a coherent response.

I sip my wine.

"Thank you. That's very kind of you to say all that. I appreciate it."

"You don't need to thank me. Every word I said is true."

Our waiter comes by with our bill. Nicco pays and we go back to the villa. Neither of us says much on the drive. I'm still processing what he said.

Does he really feel that way? Was he simply being nice? His words sounded deeper than friendship. Am I misinterpreting something? Does he have feelings for me? I felt him shift, distance himself, like he was trying to protect himself, or me.

When we get back to the villa, he pours us wine. I excuse

myself to use the restroom and put my purse in my room. Before I rejoin him, my phone chimes. It's a text from Dad that he sent me an email. I open my laptop and read the email.

When I walk into the living room, Nicco hands me a glass of wine and we sit together on the cognac-colored leather sofa.

I have no idea how to say what I need to say. But I need to tell him.

Shifting my body toward him, I start. "I just got an email from my dad. He found Ana."

His eyes fly open and his jaw drops. "You're kidding me. How? Where?" His eyes flit back and forth.

"That, I don't know. He's not allowed to share that with me. But I do have some information that I can share with you."

"Okay, what is it?" There's a tremble in his voice.

"Ana had a little boy."

He springs up from the sofa, raking his hands through his hair. "A boy," he says, shaking his hands excitedly toward the ceiling. "I have a son." The joy on his face as he turns back around to face me gnaws at my heart. He's not ready for the rest of what I learned. I have to tell him, now.

Chills prick my skin. "Nicco."

"Can you believe it? I have a son." He shakes his hands again, toward me this time, taking a heavy breath.

"Nicco," I say a little louder.

"And you found him for me. How can I ever repay you?"

"Nicco!" I say much louder, trying to halt his increasing excitement.

"What?" He looks at me with his brows pinched together, probably wondering why I'm not celebrating with him.

"Nicco, your son, he — he didn't make it." I choke out the words, swallowing chards of glass.

"What do you mean he didn't make it? What are you talking about?" Confusion paints his face.

The lump in my throat chokes me. "He had some problems

with his heart and the doctors did everything they could, but," my swallow is excruciating, "he didn't survive." I can't stop the tears forming in my lower eyelids. "He passed away two weeks after he was born."

Nicco falls to his knees before me, anguish overtaking the momentary joy. The man who I once thought was nothing more than a testosterone-oozing, single-minded, sexual playboy crumbles into my lap like a broken little boy. He wraps his arms around my waist, gripping the fabric of my skirt in his fists, and cries. His entire body jerks as he sobs.

Tears flood out of me. I curl my body over his head, draping my arms over his back.

24

Nicco

The pounding in my head throbs behind my burning eyes like a bad hangover. It's been a long time since I cried like that. Probably not since Dad passed. Though I'm grateful for Destiny's dad finding Ana, the news that I had a son and he died rocked my fucking world.

I thought it hurt when Ana vanished with my child in her belly, leaving behind a note basically telling me I'm worthless. That was nothing compared to this. My heart aches with a pain I've never experienced.

I can't imagine being with anyone other than Destiny to receive that information. Her comfort and compassion drew her deeper into my heart, making the next few days even harder.

By the time I drag myself out of bed and to the kitchen, Marco's gone to work, Angelina's out by the pool with Franco, and Destiny is tucked into her lounge chair, typing on her computer. I walk out to the pool area, squinting from the sun beaming into my sore eyes.

"Good morning," I say, scratching my head.

"Good morning." Destiny's voice is like sweet nectar. I catch her eyes sweep quickly down my chest to my abs as she shifts in her chair.

I love that, no matter how many times she's seen my bare chest, she gets flustered.

"Angelina has breakfast waiting for you if you're hungry."

"Mmm, I am. Did you eat then?"

"Yup, I ate earlier. It's almost lunchtime for me." She smiles a playful, adorable smile.

"Thank you, Angelina," I call out. She waves as I turn to go back inside.

Destiny rises from her lounge chair and walks in with me. She heats my plate and sits next to me on a stool at the kitchen island.

"We don't have to go to the beach today if you'd rather stay here and relax. I know last night was tough for you."

"It was." I sigh. "I'll always mourn my son. But now I'm truly free. I'm free from Ana because of you and now I'm free from anything that tied me to her." I reach out, taking her hand in mine. "If it wasn't for your kind heart and your dad's help, I would've always wondered. I would never have been at peace. And now, I can start to find a way. For this, I can never repay you."

She reaches out her other hand, cupping my face, love penetrating her eyes. "Nicco. There's nothing to repay. That's not how I work." She pauses, moving her hand to my heart. "Your son is with your dad, in your heart forever."

Placing my hand on top of hers, I close my eyes.

"Thank you." I take a breath before releasing her hands.

"Do you want to stay here today?"

"No." I scoop some scrambled eggs onto my fork. "I want to take you out for some fun." I smile.

"Okay. As long as you're sure."

"I'm sure."

"Should I shower if we're going to the beach?"

"No. We'll shower when we come back. Just put on your suit and sunscreen. Angelina will give us towels."

I finish eating, we pack our things, and head to the beach. Since I slept so late, we're off to a later start. I stop to get us lunch before we get to the beach. When we arrive, we find a spot to set up for the day. Wearing her coverup, Destiny sits in her chair and eats lunch under the umbrella, reading a book while I lie out in the sun.

When I open my eyes and look at her, she's finished eating and her book rests against her body. She's fallen asleep. About an hour later, she stirs.

"Are you ready for some fun?" I ask.

"Absolutely."

"Make sure you have your sunscreen on."

"Yup," she says, taking off her coverup and grabbing her sunscreen.

Through my sunglasses, I watch every stroke of her hand, rubbing the lotion into her milky-white skin.

"Will you make sure I got my back thoroughly?" She hands me the bottle of lotion.

Standing up and taking the bottle, I squeeze a little into my hand, rubbing my hands together. Reminding myself we're in public, I smooth the lotion across her shoulders and back, massaging the last of it into her lower back. Fuck, I want to grab her sexy ass.

Without moving her body, she turns her head, looking up at me. "Thank you."

Taking in a deep breath, I exhale, stifling my desire. "You're welcome."

We walk to the hut where I rent a jet ski for us. Putting on our life jackets, we get on and I drive us slowly out into the open water. The sky is clear of clouds and glints of sunshine sparkle on the dancing peaks of water.

I turn my face back toward her. "I'm going to go faster now. I want you to hold onto me tightly. I won't go too fast. Sometimes it gets choppy in the waves."

She squeezes her arms tighter around my waist. "Okay. I'll let you know if it's too fast."

"Yes, let me know and I'll slow down. This is meant to be fun, not scary. It's tough to hear out there so squeeze me hard so I know."

"Okay."

With her securely holding on, I pick up speed, zipping us through the water. Keeping to straight lines as much as possible, I make any turns slower and wide. We cut through waves and bounce around in the choppy spots. After about twenty minutes, I stop to check in with her and see how she's doing.

Undulating in the water, we bob with the waves. I turn my head so she can hear me over the hum of the engine. "How are you doing back there?"

She loosens her grip around me. "I'm good. This is fun. I wasn't sure if I'd like it, but I do."

"That's great. I rented it for an hour, but we can go in anytime you feel like you're done, okay?"

"Okay. I can probably go for another ten or fifteen minutes."

"All right. That sounds good. You ready?"

"I'm ready," she says, cinching her arms around my waist again.

With that, we're off again, skimming the surface, water spraying around us. I'm so happy she's having fun.

From behind us, a cigarette boat speeds in front of us. The wake is huge and I turn the handlebars, trying to avoid smashing directly into it. My turn is too sharp and Destiny's arms jerk off my waist. I turn my head to see her body hurtling through the air, crashing into the water.

"No! Fuck! Destiny!" I turn as fast as I can back to her, careful not to collide with her limp body. Adrenaline rages through me.

The waves bump her against the jet ski. I'm able to grab hold of her life vest and pull her out of the water into the foot well.

"Destiny!" I shout.

I rest her head against my thigh. Her eyes spring open, filled with panic. She clutches her chest with one arm and latches tightly onto my shin with her other. Her mouth hangs open.

Fuck, she can't breathe!

"Sit up." I hold my arm across her chest, straightening her body. "Push your stomach out and breathe in slowly. Now!"

Her fingers dig into my skin as she does what I say.

"Blow it out, pull your stomach in. Do it. I'm here." Keeping my arm across her chest, I wipe her wet hair off her face.

Finally, a deep, gasping inhale followed by a labored exhale.

Bouncing in the waves, I hold her while she finds the rhythm of her breath.

Releasing her death-grip on my shin, she wraps her arm around my leg and leans against it.

"Are you okay? Are you hurt?" I ask, stroking her head.

She looks up at me, a sluggish blink to her eyes, and nods. "I'm okay. I don't think I'm hurt. I don't feel hurt. I think I just got the wind knocked out of me."

As she goes to get up, I help her maneuver, sitting her on my lap facing me.

"I think I'm done now." She smiles, making me laugh.

"Yes, we're done now." I get my phone out of the small waterproof container around my neck and call Angelina. "I need you to get Dr. Mastrogiovanni to the house. Destiny fell of the jet ski and was unconscious. She's fine, but I want her checked out. We're still in the ocean, but going back in now. We'll be there soon." I pause, listening to Angelina. "Thank you." Hanging up, I put my phone back into the container.

"I don't think I need a doctor. I'm not hurt."

"I want to make sure." Pressing her against me, I kiss her head. "I'm so glad you're okay."

Wrapping her arms around my back, she leans her head on my chest. I take a slow pace back to shore. Once we're back on the beach, we go directly to our umbrella, I gather our belongings and we go to the car.

When we arrive at the villa, Dr. Mastrogivanni is already there. He and Angelina greet us as we walk in.

"Dr. Mastrogiovanni, thank you so much for coming out on short notice. I really appreciate it. I don't think we need the hospital, but I want her checked out. This is Destiny."

He nods at her and smiles.

"Hello," she says quietly.

As I explain what happened, we all walk to the living room and sit on the sofa.

"We were in the ocean on a jet ski and she fell off. She was unconscious for maybe 20 seconds and got the wind knocked out of her. I need to make sure she's okay."

"I understand." He smiles. "Let's check things out."

He takes her pulse, flashes light into her eyes, asks her a bunch of questions, and has her move her body and head in different ways.

Once he completes his evaluation, he looks at me and nods, then looks back at Destiny. "The good news is, you're fine. And, there's no bad news." He smiles. "For tonight, I want you to rest. Can someone watch over you while you sleep?" he asks, looking at me and Angelina.

"Yes. I can," I say.

"Good. You don't need to watch her the entire night. Just set an alarm for every couple of hours and ask her simple questions: what's your name, where are you? Those types of things. I'm certain she doesn't have a concussion, so this is just extra precaution."

"Yes, I can do that. It's not a problem."

"If her condition changes or you're at all concerned, call me. If she changes dramatically, go to the hospital first, then call me." He looks back at Destiny. "I'm sure you won't need to though."

"Thank you again, doctor. I really appreciate your time." I stand up, extending my hand.

"Any time, Mr. Mancini. It's my pleasure." Standing, he shakes my hand.

Angelina sees him to the door as I sit down next to Destiny.

"Thank God you're okay." I take her hand in mine and kiss it. "So, it looks like we're in for the night. What do you say to supper and a movie in bed?"

"I like the sound of that." She nods. "I think I'll take a shower first."

"I'll sit in your bedroom, listening. I don't want you falling in the shower," Angelina says, walking back over to us.

"I'm sure I'll be okay, but if it makes you feel better, that's fine."

Together, they go to Destiny's room.

Destiny

I grab my pajamas then head to the bathroom.

"I won't be long," I say, passing Angelina sitting in the cozy chaise.

"Take your time. I'm going use the time to read." She smiles, settling into the chair.

The warm water feels soothing on my skin. Though I'm a little shaken, I really do feel okay. They're so sweet to worry about me.

I close my eyes, letting the water run through my hair, down my body. Nicco's words from our conversation last night play in my head. He said things I could never have imagined him saying to me. *Someday, a man worthy of you will come along and see all of these things I see in you.* What did he mean? Those aren't words you say to someone without some emotions behind them.

Ugh. I leave in a few days. What does it matter anyway?

I wash my hair and body, towel off, and put on my pajamas. A quick blow dry of my hair and I'm done. Walking out of the bathroom, I go to where Angelina is on the chaise and sit on the floor next to the bookshelf. She closes the book she's reading and puts it back on the shelf.

"I love that you have all these books for your guests. This is such a cozy corner."

"I love reading. Now I have to get some of your books." She smiles.

"Well, I'd be honored."

"How are you feeling?" she asks, putting her feet on the floor and her elbows on her knees, clasping her hands and leaning forward.

"The shower felt nice. I'm okay, I promise. And I promise to let you and Nicco know if I don't feel okay."

"Good." She pauses. "He told me what you did for him.

Finding Ana." She looks down, shakes her head, then lifts her gaze. "You took such a heavy burden from him. He carried so much pain. Thank you for what you did."

"It was really my dad. I'm just happy we could give him closure."

She tilts her head with a little side smile. "He cares for you."

"He's a good man." I smile.

"I think maybe you care for him?" She leans her head toward me.

I pull in my lips with a shrug of my shoulders. "It doesn't matter if I do."

"Of course it does."

"I leave in a few days. Besides, look where his life is headed. There's no room for me. He's on a path to fame and he'll have his choice of the millions of women who swarm at his feet."

She shakes her head. "You have much to learn about his heart, ragazza dolce." Standing, she holds out her hand to help me up. "Come, let's find some movies for you to watch."

I quickly put on my sweatshirt. When we go into the living room, Nicco's sitting on the sofa, strumming his guitar, with his notepad and pen on the coffee table. Franco sits next to him, watching him. He stops strumming when he sees us.

"How are you feeling?"

"Good. Honestly, I feel fine. The shower felt good."

"Yes, I showered too. I'm just faster." He winks. "I got some movies for us to pick from," he says, pointing to a stack on the coffee table.

"Okay, great."

"Thank you for your help, Franco," he calls out as Franco runs to Angelina. He hands me the stack of movies then takes his notebook, pen, and guitar and walks toward my room.

"Thank you, Angelina." I wave to her in the kitchen where she's helping Franco with a toy.

"I've been working on your song," he says, sitting on the side of my bed.

"Can I hear it yet?" I ask, closing the door.

"It's not finished yet."

"That's okay. Can I hear what you have so far?" I sit on the chaise across from my bed.

He strums his fingers over the guitar strings and smiles at me, lifting his knee to rest on the bed.

"It's called, 'Blood in My Veins.' Ready?" Hanging his head slightly, he looks down, positioning his fingers on the neck of the guitar. As he strums, his body sways. "I was told my fate long ago. I'd never measure up. I didn't have what it takes." Glancing up at me, he shakes his head, still swaying. "I'd never be enough. I believed it all. Down to my core. Down to my core. Until I looked into your eyes." Lifting his head, he gazes into my eyes and strums. "Eyes that told me a different truth. I shared my deepest secrets. You opened my heart." Looking down briefly to change his finger position, he returns his gaze to me. "You're the blood coursing through my veins. You're the breath filling my lungs." He strums and sways, nodding his head to the rhythm he's created.

Tingles cover me as I listen to his words. Words he wrote about me. I can't keep him out of my heart.

Doing a rapid strum, he slaps his hand across the strings then smiles at me. "That's it. That's all I have. What do you think of it?"

"I — it's beautiful, Nicco." My heart hurts at what can never be.

He lifts his shoulders and gets off the bed, leaning his guitar against the dresser. "It needs work." He takes his notepad and pen and puts them on the dresser then grabs the movies and lays them out on the bed. "Do you like any of these?"

The variety ranges from romantic comedy to action-packed. I pick *Mission: Impossible*.

Grabbing all the movies, he puts them on the dresser then loads the disc into the player.

We fluff up pillows and sit close to each other on the bed.

"Do you need a blanket?"

"Oh yes. That would be nice."

He gets off the bed and takes a blanket from the basket next to the chaise. Before getting back onto the bed, he drapes the blanket over my legs.

"Thank you."

As the music plays on the movie, he jets his head back and forth to the beat. He's impossibly cute. By the time the credits roll, we're both hungry.

"I don't feel like cooking and I'm not going to have Angelina cook for us. Let's order something."

Before he can ask what I want, "Pizza?" comes out of my mouth.

"You want pizza?" He laughs.

"It feels like a pizza night."

"Then pizza it is. I'll be right back." He leaves to place our order.

As I wait for him to return, my emotions are torn. I do care about him. I can't help myself. I'm scared I care for him more than I'm willing to admit. I love being with him. But reality tramples whatever it is I feel about him. In a few days I leave and go back to my life. He continues on his path to fame and everything that comes with it. Nothing can exist between us.

His phone chimes. I'm not one to be nosey, but it's right there on the bed. A text — from Giovanna. I can only see the first line that's lit on the screen, "Call me." followed by a kissy-face emoji.

Reality stampedes again, resurfacing my insecurities and reminding me why I'm here.

He comes back in. "About twenty minutes."

"Your phone chimed." I point to his phone as my chest burns.

He picks it up and reads the text then puts it down. "It's not important."

Hmmm.

"Okay. Your pick," I say, confusion swirling inside me.

Standing in front of the dresser, he surveys the movies. "This one."

"Which one?"

"You'll see." He switches the discs. "You'll like it." Looking back at me, he winks.

As he jumps onto the bed, smelling of smoke, *The Proposal* lights on the screen.

"For a playboy, you have a wicked romantic side." I tease.

He leans on his side, facing me, propped up on his elbow. "You have a lot to learn about me, mia dolce ragazza." His eyes drift back and forth between mine before he sits back into his pillows.

About twenty minutes into the movie, Angelina knocks on the door. We look at each other with wide eyes, saying in unison, "Pizza."

He pauses the movie and we go to the kitchen where Angelina has set out trays, plates, and napkins for us. He comes out of a back room with a dinner tray, grabs the pizza boxes, and goes back to the bedroom. Angelina and I follow with the smaller trays. As we enter the room, he leaves, coming back with Cokes and glasses of ice.

Before Angelina leaves, he takes her in his arms and plants a loud kiss on her cheek. "You're the best."

She shakes her head and laughs as she closes the door.

"Thank you." I call out.

I put two pieces of pizza on each of our plates on our trays and he pours our drinks. Then we climb onto the bed, slide our trays in front of us, and watch the rest of the movie while eating our pizza. We laugh at the same spots. He smiles at me when I cry at the end. This is the perfect night.

After we finish eating, we bring our trays and dishes to the kitchen. I put the dishes in the dishwasher while he puts away the trays.

"I'll be right in," he says, grabbing his pack of cigarettes.

I look at the pack in his hand then back up into his eyes. He looks at the pack in his hand then back into my eyes. Not a word is spoken, just an exchange of glances. I don't know what that addiction feels like. From the way he curls in his lips at the corner and casts down his eyes as he turns to go outside, I know he's disappointed in himself.

I go back to my room, brush my teeth, and get under the covers of my bed. For the first time, it hits me that he's going to be sleeping beside me all night.

He enters the room and closes the door.

"What did you pick?" He looks at the movies on the dresser and then at me.

"I didn't." I pause. "You know, I feel completely fine. You don't have to stay and watch movies with me. And I'm sure you don't need to wake up all night long to keep checking on me. I promise, I feel fine."

He takes slow strides to me and sits on the edge of the bed, facing me.

"It's my job to take care of you," he says softly, tucking my hair behind my ear. "I want to."

Standing back up, he walks back to the dresser, loads a new movie, and turns off the lights. As he sits on the bed and puffs his pillows, *The Vow* starts playing. I sink lower under the covers while he lies down, his head propped up on his pillow.

➤➤➤➤ ◄◄◄◄

I wake up overheated from falling asleep wearing my sweatshirt. Sitting up, I rip it off over my head. It takes me a second or two to get acclimated. Moonlight streams in the window, casting a soft glow through the room. A fake fire crackles on the TV screen making me laugh inside. Nicco lies next me, on top of the covers, his head cradled in his hands and his elbows resting on the pillow. He must've gotten changed after I fell asleep. His pajama bottoms cover his long legs as the moonlight highlights the curves of his bare torso.

I've fantasized about him for months. That's what you do when actually being with the person is out of the realm of possibilities because of who they are. Now, here he is, not on a movie screen, not in my head, but lying next me, watching over me, taking care of me.

When we first met, he probably would happily have screwed me and moved on, keeping with his playboy reputation. Our connection has grown deep over the last couple months. Words have been spoken, tears have been shed, emotions have intertwined. He's opened up to me in a way I could never have fathomed. I see him physically struggle to suppress himself when we're close, respecting my boundaries.

How could I have possibly known my thirsting desire for a scorching sexual experience that only existed in my head would turn into a craving to be with him because of his heart? He's made me a priority in his life. He's made me feel like I matter.

He's shown me a man the world doesn't get the privilege of knowing. A man I can't stop myself from falling for. A man I'll probably never see again after I leave.

Be in the moment.

Candi's words ring in my head. I breathe in, and with my exhale, I release everything. I release my fears, my nervousness, the sadness I know will come in the aftermath — all of it.

Kneeling, I scoot close to him, gazing at his gorgeous face and sexy body. Though I've touched his chest before, I was so flustered, I didn't get a chance to actually enjoy it. This time, I let my lips do the exploring. I lean over him, my body flooding with anticipation, and touch my lips to his furry chest, working my way down the left side of his body with feathery kisses. He tenses when I reach the top of his V-line.

"Mmhh." The sound comes from deep in his throat.

I woke him.

When I look up at him, his head is bent toward me, his hands release slowly from behind his head, and his eyes meet mine, longing entangled with lust. I've never been looked at this way before. He's like a caged animal, salivating at his prey.

I rise from bending over his body and straddle him, pelvis to pelvis. Pulling my camisole over my head, I take his hand and place it on my breast, giving him permission.

His lips open, speechless.

Releasing my breast, he sits up, presses his forehead to mine, and laces his fingers into my hair. Hunger sparks in his eyes, intensifying my desire. His grip tightens as his shoulders lift and he heaves an exhale. He must've brushed his teeth when he changed into his pajamas because he smells more like mint than cigarette.

"Destiny," he breathes my name, capturing my lips with his, moving his hands to hold my face.

Tenderly, he kisses me, releasing and recapturing my lips like he's tasting them for the first time, savoring them. Sealing his lips to mine again, he slides his tongue in my mouth with a grunt. As his probes into my mouth grow hungrier, my heart beats faster.

Pulling back from my face, he breaths heavily, staring at my lips as he runs his thumb across my lower lip, licking his own. He returns his gaze to my eyes.

"I've been desperate to feel your lips again," he rumbles, low and wanting.

His next capture of my lips is eager, confident, greedy. I've never felt so desired. Aggressively, he slides his tongue in and out of my mouth as his fingers press into my face. Leaving my lips, he tilts my head and sweeps my hair from my neck. Leaning in to my exposed skin, he runs his nose from behind my ear, down my neck, to my collar bone, his breath hot on my skin. Blood rushes through me. Then he travels the same line up with his mouth, sucking, nibbling. My breathing increases, as I roll my head back.

With both hands, he grabs my breasts, grunting. I arch my back and he accepts my invitation, clamping his mouth on one nipple and twirling the other between his fingers. I gasp as my breasts tingle and wetness builds between my legs. Arching more, I hold myself up with my arms behind me. Switching his mouth and hand, he takes my other nipple into his mouth, swirling his tongue around it. A whimper escapes me between stilted breaths.

He leans back onto his elbows, his eyes roaming my body. "You're so fucking beautiful, mia dolce ragazza."

Holding his gaze, I lift myself off of him and slide my knees between his legs. Leaning forward, I place soft kisses on his chest, working my way down the curves of his abs. I tug down one side of his pajama bottom, exposing his V-line, trailing it with my tongue.

"Ah," he growls, taking a fistful of my hair into his hand.

Nibbling and kissing back toward his naval, I bypass the bulge peeking out the top of his pajamas, and tug down the other side, licking and nipping his skin. Kissing my way back up to his naval, I lift the elastic waist of his pajamas, pulling it down, revealing his full length. He's magnificent, every single inch of his body.

He releases my hair, staring at me. Refocusing my attention, I take him in my hand, running my tongue from his base to the little V at the top of his head, flicking at it. He flinches a little. I do it all again. This time he grunts. I do it faster and swirl my tongue around his head.

His body jolts up and I lift to sitting on my knees. Wrapping his hands around my shoulders, his eyes pierce into mine. "Destiny," he says, shaking his head, breaths heavy. "I don't think I can control myself."

"Then don't," I hush. I want him out of control. Unhinged, with me. For one hot night, I want him to be mine, all mine. I want to be the object of his desire.

Pushing him back, I lower down, taking him in my hand again, circling his head with my tongue. Closing my lips together, I insert just his head through them, and back out. In again and back out, adding a swirl of my tongue. Several more times and I curl my lips over my teeth, thrusting my mouth down his shaft to the base.

"Oh cazzo," he blurts as his body tenses.

I slide him out and thrust down again, and again, bobbing up and down. With a shove of my knees down into the mattress, I let them bounce back up, increasing my rhythm. Holding my head steady, I let the motion propel him into and out of my mouth.

With a growl, he lunges up, pulling me off him, heaving breaths. "You're going to make me come," he says, searing me with ravenous eyes. "I'm not ready yet. Come up here."

I crawl up toward him and he takes off his pajama bottoms then slides my silky shorts off me. In one swift movement, he flips me onto my back, his body hovering above me. I inhale sharply.

Arms straddling my head, he lowers, claiming my lips. Our tongues dance to the same yearning beat as I run my fingers through his hair. His rapacious kisses feed my desire. Leaving my lips, he weaves his fingers through mine, exploring my neck and breasts with his mouth. Every touch of his lips on my skin ignites me. The way he looks at me, touches me, it's like he's worshiping me.

Letting go of my hands, he moves his body between my legs, I raise my knees. Wrapping his hands around my waist, he bites gently at the skin on my stomach. He holds my leg in his hand and licks my inner thigh, outlining the edge of my panties with his tongue. Kissing where he'd just licked, he runs his fingers between my legs. I gasp, gripping at the sheets.

He looks up at me with molten eyes. "You're so wet for me," he says, stroking again.

"Yes." It's the only word I can form. I bite my lower lip.

Kneeling back, he rolls my panties down my hips. I lift up and back down then raise my legs so he can remove them. With my legs still raised, he folds one leg over his shoulder and holds my other calf in his hand, kissing my ankle. It tickles. Then he licks down my calf, opening my knee to the side, and kisses up my thigh. A quick glance at me and he runs his tongue between my folds. I inhale sharply.

Scooting off the edge of the bed to kneel on the floor, he grabs my ankles, yanking me toward him. He lowers his face between my legs and takes a breast in each hand, squeezing. With hunger staining his eyes, he runs his tongue slowly up the full length of my folds, curling it at the top. Going back for more, he dips his tongue in deeper. I squirm, holding my breath. He goes back again and again, deepening his reach and quickening his pace. Inserting his fingers in place of his tongue, he flicks my nub with the tip of his tongue. My back arches in response and my heart pounds faster. As he slides his fingers in and out of me, his flicks grow stronger and faster. I pant and groan. I'm not sure how much more I can take. My inner thighs tingle as my knees draw in toward his head. He pulls out his fingers and presses both my knees down, burying his face into me with a growl.

I grab his hair with one hand and the sheets beneath me with the other. "Nicco." I pant, whimpering.

Rising from his knees, he wipes his mouth on his forearm and climbs onto the bed, sliding my body up. Lying on top of me, he grabs a breast, sucking voraciously, moaning. I arch, heaving loud breaths. Then he comes to my face, thrusting his tongue into my mouth.

"Destiny." A look of desperate desire smears across his face. His hard-on presses into me.

"Yes," I say, my breathing erratic. If he slides down, he'll be at my entrance. He has me in a frenzy right now.

"I'm sorry. I'm unprepared." He leans off of me and slips his fingers into me, kissing my neck.

I pant. "Unprepared?" I ask tilting back my head.

He returns his face in front of me, shaking his head. "I have no protection."

"You're kidding me." I writhe at the movement of his fingers gliding in and out of me.

"No. I haven't been with anyone since we met. And you told me no." He flutters his fingers inside me, causing my arms to splay out to my sides. "I didn't think to bring anything here. You told me *no*."

I can barely focus my thoughts. "Okay. It's okay." I run my hand through his hair, trying to console him. "We don't have to. We don't have to." My breath shakes.

"Fuck that." He kisses me, rubbing his thumb against my nub. "I have to have you." He's so close, his breathe heats my skin. "I need you, Destiny." Wanton lust radiates in his eyes as he rolls on top of me, his head perched at my entrance.

My pulse pounds in my ears, breaths spew rapidly out of me as I stare into his eyes. "I'm yours."

With that, the animal is uncaged.

He thrusts into me, growling with greed. Gasping with pleasure, I feel every bit of his length inside me. He hoists onto his knees, supporting my back as he does so he stays inside me. I wrap my legs around him, cradling his head into my chest, as he pulses up into me, grabbing my butt then tilting back his head. Every blissful pump intoxicates me.

I push him back and he untucks his knees from under him. Bracing my body with my hands on his chest, I lift up and down, riding his shaft, then scoop my pelvis up and in. He grabs my hips, grinding up into me, rocking me back and forth.

"Mio Dio." Sitting up, he lifts me off him, wraps an arm around my body and flips us. Laying me on my back, he assaults my mouth with passionate, confident kisses. My body rages with desire, fire pumping through every vein of my body.

Getting onto his knees, he plunges back inside me, his body moving like a snake. He pounds his pelvis into me as his shoulders hunch and his torso waves with his movements. I groan with each crazed thrust. Rising up, he lifts my legs up, hugging them to his chest, sinking himself deeper into me. Plowing again and again as his jaw tenses and he bites his lower lip.

Then he flips me over, spreading my legs with his knees, sliding into me from behind. Grabbing my breasts, he kisses down my back then straightens, pushing me against the bed, grasping my hips and pulling me, hard and fast, into him. This is far beyond any of my wildest fantasies about him. I can't get enough of him. My entire body is aflame and ready to explode.

25

Nicco

Her sexy ass slaps against me as I slam into her tight cave. She feels so fucking good. If I don't pull out, I'm going to erupt. I want to make her come. I want to see her beautiful face as she does.

Pulling out, I sit at the top of the bed, resting against the headboard. On her knees, she watches me, catching her breath. I hold out my hand and she takes it, climbing onto my lap. She lifts, arching her back, presenting me with her breasts for a quick suck before she grabs my dick and slides down it. I take her face in my hands and kiss her luscious lips. I could kiss her for hours. I could kiss her for the rest of my life.

With our lips locked, she squeezes her walls around me. My eyes fly open as adrenaline races through my body and I pull back. "The fuck." I breathe out.

Flashing a wicked smile, she squeezes again. I groan, my muscles tensing. She does it again, pulsing her walls rapidly around me. I grunt, my body jolting forward, weaving my arms under hers and curling my hands around her shoulders.

"If you keep doing that, I'm going to fucking explode." My breaths are loud, choppy.

Moving my hands to her hips, I yank her into me. She whimpers, it's the sexiest fucking sound. Leaning back, resting her hands on my thighs, her body undulates. I wet my thumb and rub her nub back and forth slowly, then faster. Leaning back farther, she holds onto my shins, still writhing her body. She's a fucking goddess. Quickening my pace with my thumb, I pinch her nipple. She moans, breathing heavily. I press a little harder with my thumb, rubbing faster.

"Nicco," she says, breathless, looking at me with need in her eyes. Labored breaths escape her open mouth as her eyebrows pinch together.

"I want you to come for me, mia dolce ragazza."

Swirling and pressing, I can see her on the brink. I don't let up. Her breaths are fast and frantic. Her whimpers grow loud, intense, begging.

"Nicco. Oh God. Nicco."

With the release of a lust-filled cry, her body hurls forward and her walls clench, pulsing around my dick. Her body convulsing, she wraps her arms around my head, pulling me into her chest, breathing, panting, moaning. Her sounds drive me fucking wild.

"You're so beautiful, Destiny." I wrap my arms around her trembling body.

Watching her come and feeling her body's response, I'm seconds from exploding. I lift her up and flip her around, laying her down. Holding her hips, I pound into her relentlessly, fast and furious, throwing back my head when my release finally smashes into me. Holding her tightly against me, I shudder, pulsing inside her, heaving breaths, groaning with pleasure as my body electrifies and stiffens. *Oh fuck.*

Pulling out, I collapse on top of her body, exhausted. She wraps her arms around me, stroking my hair softly as we both catch our breath.

We lie body to body, heaving breaths, basking in the bliss of our ecstasy. My breath finally normalizing, I kiss her.

"I'll be right back," she says, getting off the bed and scurrying to the bathroom.

I take a deep inhale. Not using a condom was careless, risky. I know better. *She's not Ana.* If I got her pregnant, she wouldn't run.

We'd figure it out, together.

After a few minutes, she comes back with a warm washcloth and wipes me off. It's the first time anyone's ever done that.

"Thank you."

The moonlight glows on her angelic face.

"You're welcome." She nods toward the TV and smiles. "I like the fire."

"I thought you might."

She goes back into the bathroom and comes out, then climbs onto the bed.

"I'll be right back," I say, standing up and putting on my pajama bottoms.

"Do you have to?" The disappointment in her eyes makes my heart sink.

"You want me to *not* have a cigarette after *that?*" I try to ease her with humor, but it doesn't work.

Her expression is empty as she crawls under the covers.

I grab my cigarettes and lighter and go to the pool area. *Holy fuck that was hot.* As I light the end of my cigarette, I stare at the flame of my lighter. *I need to quit this shit.* I draw in a slow inhale, filling my lungs with the gray death, then rub the heels of my hands into my temples, exhaling.

I need you, Dad. What did I do? What did I just do to her? What did I do to us? Why did she let me have her? Her body is mine now. And that's not enough. Not nearly enough. I want her heart. I want her soul. I want all of her. But she's leaving, Dad. And I don't even know how she truly feels about me. Is she feeling what I'm feeling? Do I have the right to even ask her? I'm so confused. I wish you were here.

I blow the last exhale through my nose and tap out my cigarette, going back to her bedroom.

"May I?" I ask, lifting the edge of the covers.

"Yes," she says quietly.

When I get under the covers, she cuddles into the side of my body and looks up at me.

"Is this okay?"

It's more than okay. I drape my arm around her, tucking her in closer. "Yes, it's okay."

She lays her head on my chest, resting her arm across my body. Stroking her hair, I kiss her forehead. *Fuck. I want this. Every night.*

"Why did you let me have you tonight? You kept telling me no. And I honored that, as painful as it was." I chuckle. "But tonight…"

"I've, been afraid. I'm not one of your many women and I didn't want you to look at me that way —"

"I don't." I cut her off, sounding harsher than intended, and tilt her head to look up at me. "Destiny," I say, softening my tone then pause. "What we've had these last few months is something…" I pause again, trying to find the right words. "It's something I never could've imagined for my life." The right words don't come. "I'd — closed off my heart. I thought that's how I'd survive. But, you helped me forgive myself. You gave me closure." I take a deep breath. "You, melted the walls around my heart."

She lifts her head so we're face to face. "That's why I let you." Leaning in, she kisses me, then rests her head back onto my chest.

"Il mio cuore é tuo, mia dolce ragazza," I say, caressing her hair.

She tilts her face up toward mine. "What does that mean?"

"My heart is yours, my sweet girl."

With Destiny resting on my chest, I feel at peace, content, happy. I have everything I could ever want.

The alarm chimes on my phone. We both laugh.

"What's your name?"

"Destiny," she says softly.

"Where are you?"

"Ponza Island." She chuckles. "I think I'm good," she says, smiling, then returns her head to my chest.

Destiny

I can't believe that just happened. I've never felt so desired in my life. And I've never experienced such intense pleasure. I wasn't even in my body. Every sensation was fierce, powerful.

His words gripped my heart. "My heart is yours." What am I supposed to do with that? I leave in a couple days. I don't want to fall for him.

I already have.

26

Nicco

I wake up before Destiny. She lies sleeping on my chest, her arm around my body, her leg slung between mine.

I'm doing work I love, my career is moving forward, I have more money in my bank account than I ever dreamed possible, and I have the most incredible woman lying by my side, in my arms. I'm so grateful for my life right now.

She stirs, squeezing me, and releases an adorable yawn. "Good morning," she says, looking up at me.

"Good morning. Did you sleep well?"

"I did. You?"

"I did." I kiss her forehead. "For today, I was thinking I could take you out on Marco's boat for a few hours. We can decide the rest of the day later. How does that sound?"

"Sounds like a fun way to start the day," she says, sitting up and smiling.

"Great. Let's eat and get showered."

"Mmm, yes, food. I'm hungry."

"Me too." I roll her onto her back, climbing on top of her with my legs between hers. "You took a lot out of me last night." Leaning down, I kiss her lips, giving her a quick little thrust of my pelvis.

She whimpers. The sound makes me want to have her again, right now.

Her stomach growls, I lift my lips from hers and raise my

271

eyebrows. "Okay, okay. I'll feed you."

We laugh and get out of bed. When we go out to the kitchen, Angelia lets me know I had a delivery. Taking the small, burgundy velvet box off the island, I open it toward Destiny.

Her hands raise quickly, covering her mouth as she gasps, staring into the box. "The locket." She looks up at me with her big blue eyes.

"Open it."

Taking the locket out of the box, she opens it and reads the inscription. "I believe in you," she says, whisper soft. Her gaze oscillates between me and the locket. Then she wraps her arms around my neck.

I wrap mine around her tiny body. God, I love holding her.

"Thank you," she says softly in my ear.

"You're welcome, mia dolce ragazza." I don't want to let go.

With Angelina's eyes on us, we release each other. After breakfast, we shower, and I wait for her on the veranda.

As I'm waiting, Gigi slinks across the terracotta tiled floor, her heels clacking with each step. She's holding a large envelope in her hands. *What's she doing here?*

I stand to greet her. "Gigi, what brings you here? I wasn't expecting you."

Approaching me with her arms extended, she grabs my hands, leans to my left and kisses my cheek, then leans to my right for a second kiss. "If you would've called me last night, this wouldn't be a surprise. Mamma said you'd come to stay with Marco for a few days."

"Yes, I'm here with Destiny."

"The little blonde woman?" she sneers, turning up her nose and rolling her eyes. "What's *she* doing here?"

She's such a brat. "Gigi, what do you want?"

"I don't like the way I look in these." She shoves the envelope at me as she pouts like a child. "I'm sure if I talk to Silvia, she'll approve a reshoot." Pulling a chair out from under the table, she faces it toward the chair I was in. She sits down, crossing her long, tanned legs that are completely exposed due to the high center-slit of her black dress. "I can see if Nima is available to do the shoot."

Sitting back down in my chair, I open the envelop and flip through the proofs. "I don't see anything wrong with these Gigi. I think you're being too picky." I do my best to not sound condescending, although I think she's being ridiculous.

"I was feeling rushed and it shows in these pictures." She pulls her chair closer to me and pokes at the pictures in my hands.

"Gigi, honestly. You look gorgeous. You always look gorgeous. These are stunning."

"You think I'm gorgeous?" She looks up at me from under her fake, dark lashes with that provocative stare she's been giving me for the last couple of years.

"Gigi, stop." I know exactly where she's going and I won't have it. I'm not playing her flirtatious games, especially not with the feelings I have for Destiny growing more intense by the second.

"Stop what?" She tilts her head and bats her lashes.

"Gigi, no."

In one smooth movement, she uncrosses her legs and stands up. With one tug of the belt on her dress, it falls into a puddle of fabric on the floor. Now wearing only a red lacy bra and G-string, she takes one step toward me and straddles her legs around me, sitting on my lap and draping her forearms on my shoulders. "Come on, Nicco. After all these years, you can't tell me you haven't thought about it."

"Gigi, stop. You know you're like a little sister to me. It's never going to happen." Two months ago, if a gorgeous woman was sitting on my lap wearing nothing but a bra and G-string, I'd be hard as rock and ready to go. But now, there's only one woman I want and that's Destiny. I've got to get Gigi out of here.

"If I was your sister, would I do this?" Before I can stop her, she crashes her lips to mine, shoving her tongue in my mouth.

Destiny

Marco is sitting at the kitchen island, reading, when I come out of my room.

"Good morning."

"Good morning." I smile. "Thank you so much for letting us take your boat out today."

"You're very welcome. It's a beautiful day to be out on the water."

"Do you know where Nicco is?"

"Yes, he's out on the veranda. I'll come with you."

Together, we head toward the veranda.

"Do you have any specific plans for the day?" he asks.

I turn toward him. "Nope, no specific plans. We're going to see where the day takes us." I know I probably look like a giddy schoolgirl with a huge, dopey smile on my face and I don't care. I'm happier than I've ever been and I'm excited to spend another day with Nicco. Be in the moment.

As I spin back around and turn the corner out to the veranda, I see them. Giovanna is straddling Nicco wearing nothing but a red bra and panties, and black stilettos. Their lips are locked together. A tsunami crashes into me, knocking me back. My heart rips inside my chest as adrenaline pounds through me, heating my blood.

I turn around, trapped in a simultaneous speed-of-light time-warp, crashing into Marco's arms. Hot tears sting behind my eyes, ready to burst out of me.

I can't hide the fury and anguish in my face. I watch his eyes, as if in slow motion, catch Giovanna and Nicco over my shoulder.

"Oh fuck," he whispers, looking back at me, his brows squeezing together like he can feel the pain stabbing me.

"Marco, can you please take me to the ferry?" I ask, breathless.

"The ferry's not running now."

"Please." I insist. "I have to leave, *now*."

"I'll take you."

I run to my room and pack my things, haphazardly throwing them into my suitcase.

Within minutes, I'm packed and meet Marco back in the kitchen. By the disappointed look on Angelina's face, I know Marco told her what happened. I quickly hug and thank her.

Marco and I go immediately to the boat and board it.

"Destiny, I know you're upset. I don't know what we saw there."

"You don't?" I ask, sitting in the seat on the other side of the boat from the helm. "I do. What we saw was Nicco being Nicco and Giovanna finally getting the man she's always wanted." My mouth tastes bitter.

"I don't think so." His compassionate eyes don't soothe me.

"No?"

"No." He shakes his head. "Nicco isn't the man he used to be. I've seen a change in him over the last few months. A change for the better. He's not the man he once was. And it's because of you."

I can't hold back my tears any longer. "It doesn't matter." Looking out into the water, I let the tears fall.

He starts the boat and takes off. The wind thrashing at my face can't numb the pain in my heart.

Nicco

Reflexively reaching under her arms, I lift Gigi up, pulling her off me and stand up. "Enough, Gigi. No," I say with finality as I pick up her dress and hand it to her. Impatience pulses in my neck.

"Why?" She pouts. "We're perfect together. We've known each other forever. We want the same things. And we're both gorgeous," she says, batting her lashes, tilting her head, and raising her shoulder to her chin.

"We're so far from perfect together." I point back and forth between us. "And we may want some of the same things, but for very different reasons. You expect the world to drop at your feet and shower you with luxury because God made you gorgeous. I want to earn my luxury and be an example to others of what's possible for them if they work hard and never give up on their dreams. I want to make a positive impact."

"I can't help that God made me gorgeous. What do you want me to do about that?" she asks, wrapping her dress around herself.

"Nothing." I shake my head. "You asked me why Destiny's here. She's here because I asked her to be here. Because I want her to be here. She lives her life with integrity and kindness. With purpose. She helps others out of the goodness of her heart, not because she expects something in return. She's the kind of person I want to surround myself with. You could learn a lot from her."

Her pout turns bitter. "With your career taking off and me by your side, you could've had it all," she seethes, blind to her self-serving attitude.

"You and I are never going to be together. Never. Go, Gigi. Now." I point my finger in the direction she came from.

Like a sulking child, she stomps off, her butt bouncing with each pound of her steps into the tiled floor.

I have a cigarette to calm my frustration while I wait for Destiny. By the time I'm done, I go back into the house to check and see if she's ready. Her bedroom door is open so I go in.

All her things are gone.

Fear, rage, and panic intertwine and combust inside my chest. I run out to the kitchen. Angelina glares at me, the corners of her lips turned down, her brows pinched together.

"Gigi?" She shakes her head with a pained look of disapproval that quickly interlocks the puzzle pieces in my head.

One of them saw Gigi kissing me. Destiny knows. She's gone.

My body ignites. "No!" I fume. "Where is she?" I ask, stalking toward her.

"She packed her things and Marco's taking her to Naples. How could you?" She shakes her hands at me, scowling.

"No, I didn't." Blood curdles in my veins.

"Marco saw you."

"No. It wasn't anything. She kissed me and I pulled her off of me and told her to leave."

"Well, all they saw was you and Gigi kissing."

"Destiny saw?" My face burns as my heart jackhammers in my ears.

"Yes, she saw. Why do you think she left?"

"Cazzo." Shoving my hands through my hair, I pace.

I grab my phone and call her. It goes to voice mail. I call Marco. It goes to voice mail.

"Fuck! They're not answering their phones." I continue pacing as my mind races. "I have to get to her. I have to explain. It's not what she saw." Stopping, I turn to Angelina. "Who else do you know who has a boat?" I ask, my words frantic.

"Only our neighbors down the street, but they've taken theirs back to Naples for the weekend."

"I can't believe this is happening," I husk. "I can't just sit here doing nothing."

"I don't think you have a choice. You will have to wait until Marco returns. By then, how will you find her?"

"I don't know, but I have to try. Maybe he'll know where she is. I can't let her leave like this."

Going to my room, I get my laptop and bring it back to the kitchen island. I quickly open it and check to see what flights are going out.

"She can't leave today. There are no flights. I have a chance to catch her."

"What will you say if you find her?"

My thoughts are scrambled. "I — I don't know. I'll tell her the truth."

"I think you broke her heart." Her tone is gentle. "She may not be ready to hear what you have to say after what she saw."

I drop my head. My heart is a hundred-pound weight in my chest.

Marco walks in the house and I stand from the stool at the kitchen island. He slams a folded piece of paper onto the island. "You fucking asshole," he blasts. "Angelina told me that yesterday and last night, you two were behaving like a couple who were head over heels for each other. What the fuck happened?"

"We were. We are." My words stumble out of my mouth as adrenaline races through my veins. "We had the best day, cuddling and watching movies. Laughing together. We even made love —"

"Fucking wait," he cuts me off, holding up his hand. "So, let me get this straight. You finally make love to her and the next day you fucking kiss Gigi, of all people?"

"No! I didn't kiss Gigi!" I roar.

"Bro, I fucking saw you with my own eyes!" he shouts.

"It wasn't like that. She took off her dress and sat in my lap and fucking kissed me. I threw her off me as soon as she did it."

"How'd she even get that far?"

"It — it happened so fast." My brain rushes through the motions of what happened, making me dizzy and furious.

"Well, all Destiny saw was you kissing your long-time childhood friend, which I believe you said is exactly what happened with her ex-fiancé."

"Cazzo!" I thunder, thrusting my hands into my hair.

"Please tell me you aren't this much of a dick. What the fuck is wrong with you? Do you even care about this woman?"

"Yes, I care about her! I love her." As the words leave my mouth, my knees weaken and I drop back down onto the stool. I break out in tiny electric zaps all over my body, stunned by the words that just flew out of me.

Marco stops talking as his body jolts back. His eyes widen and his eyebrows raise. He shakes his head, calming his voice. "Then bro, you better fucking figure out how to fix this. She's special. Don't lose her." Laughing, he steps toward me, pats me on the shoulder, and squeezes it. "My little brother is finally in love. I never thought I'd hear those words roll off your tongue." He laughs again. "Read the letter, bro. And go get your girl." He taps the folded piece of paper, puts the boat keys on the counter, and walks away.

"Wait. Where is she?"

He turns back toward me and shakes his head. "I don't know. I dropped her off at Naples. She didn't tell me her plans and I didn't ask. I doubt she had a plan."

She left, without saying goodbye, leaving behind a letter. Though I understand why she left and what she thinks she saw, this feels like Ana all over again.

Slowly, I open the letter, terrified to read it.

Nicco,

Thank you for your generosity of time these last few weeks. I appreciate you showing me around Rome and Ponza Island. I have everything I need for my book. I'm changing the direction of my story so please consider that you've fulfilled your side of our deal. There's no need for you to share my book with your following.

I also want to thank you for the kindness you've shown me. I enjoyed our time together. You helped me more than you'll ever know.

I'm glad you and Giovanna figured out your feelings for one another and I wish you both all the happiness. You're a good man and you're going to be an incredible husband and father.

Good luck in your career. You're really on your way. I hope all your dreams come true.

Destiny

A teardrop smears her name. My heart rips open. *Fuck.* She saw Gigi kiss me, now she thinks I'm with her. How do I explain this? Would she believe me? How can I fix it? I have to fix this. At this point, I've probably lost her trust, her respect, *her.*

Unknowingly, she gathered the shattered pieces of my heart and mended them back together with her love. She's left an indelible mark on my soul. All I want is to be with her. And now she's gone.

I can't let her go like this. I won't.

I grab the keys and go to the boat. Taking it to top speed, I slice through the choppy waves.

I have to find her.

Destiny

Marco kindly dropped me off in Naples. I hugged him goodbye and thanked him for his hospitality and for making the trip to bring me here. With my suitcase in one hand, my carryon in the other, I stand on the sidewalk, frozen as the world buzzes around me. I'm a confused ball of anger, sadness, and emptiness.

I take a deep breath. What's done is done. It's time to go home and get back to reality.

Finding a café, I open my laptop and look for the first flight I can get back home. I'm out of luck for anything flying out today, but manage to switch my original Sunday flight to Saturday. Next up, I find a hotel room in Rome for the night and figure out transportation from Naples to Rome. By the time I get to my hotel room, my head is dizzy and my body moves at a lethargic pace.

Though I have time to write, I'm *not* in the right headspace — at all. I get room service and watch a movie, ignoring the texts and calls from Nicco. I can't imagine what he could possibly want from me. If I forgot something, I don't really care.

Before getting ready for bed, I check my emails and send an email to Candi to see if she'll be around when I get home. I'm in desperate need of my best friend.

Hmm, an email from Bev. She doesn't email me very often. I open it.

> Hi Destiny,
>
> Tom and I hope you're doing well and having a good summer.
>
> I'm reaching out to let you know that, after a lot of thought, we've decided to sell the house. As we're getting older, we're going to be releasing some of our properties and downsizing from all the things we have our hands in.
>
> Since you've been such an amazing tenant for so long, we'd first like to consider a negotiation with you before listing the property with a Realtor. Please give it some thought and get back to me to let me know if you're interested.
>
> Take care,
> Bev

I can't believe this. This day is turning out to be one big, bad omen. I close my laptop and go to the bathroom to get ready for bed.

Looking in the mirror, I see the locket around my neck and hold it between my fingers. In the chaos of the day, I'd forgotten I put it on this morning. A strange mixture of comfort, confusion, and melancholy spreads around my heart.

Comfort from the sentiment behind it and Nicco's thoughtfulness. Confusion because I don't know why he'd give me something like this when his heart is with Giovanna. Melancholy because it meant so much to me when he gave it to me, but it clearly didn't mean anything to him.

Neither do I.

27

—

Destiny

Carefully unfastening the clasp on the locket, I tuck it into an inside zipper-pocket of my purse. Drained from the day, I move slowly, getting ready for bed. When I finally lie down, sleep doesn't come. Even though I'm tired, my mind is all over the place, filled with images I don't want to remember and emotions I don't want to feel. This cuts so much deeper than Kevin. Tears erupt and I sob until I finally succumb to the fatigue of the day.

$$\nrightarrow\!\!\!\!\nrightarrow\!\!\!\! \cdot \!\!\!\!\nleftarrow\!\!\!\!\nleftarrow$$

Waking before my alarm, I shower, pack, and go to the airport. Thankfully my flight is on time. I board and settle in, ready to write. Once we're in the air, I pull out my laptop and open my manuscript. I have some big changes to make and lots of flight-time to make them.

The cursor blinks at me.

I stare out the window, eat a snack, and stare at the screen.

The cursor stares back. Blink. Blink, blink.

Getting my purse from under the seat in front of me, I unzip the pocket inside and take out the locket. The locket Nicco gave me. My locket. My reminder of a passion I've never known, a connection I've never experienced, and a love I've never felt. I open it, reading the inscription to myself. "I believe in you."

Fastening it around my neck, I close my eyes, seeing his face. I want to be angry. I want to cry. But I know none of that will help me.

Regardless of his feelings, he believed in me, when I didn't believe in myself.

Holding the locket between my fingers, I let the crazy range of emotions whirling inside my body fuel me.

I gather the tears raining on my soul and scoop up the broken pieces of my heart. Letting it all pour out of me and onto the page, I write and write and write.

Prologue

On my thirtieth birthday, I fell in love. I fell in love with a man who could never be mine.

No hesitation, no holding back. I'm unstoppable.

Pausing only to eat and use the restroom, I make the changes that need to be made to shift the story away from being about Nicco to being about my heroine and her journey. Her journey to love. Her journey back to herself. By the time we're ready to land, all I have left to write is the ending. I'll spend the next few days finishing it, editing, and then send it off to my beta readers. I'm pleased with how it turned out, and nervous.

As soon as we land, I check my emails on my phone. Candi's in town and can come over tomorrow. *Thank goodness.* I text her and we finalize our plans. By the time I get home, it's late. I dig my toiletries out of my suitcase, wash up, and pass out within minutes of my head hitting the pillow.

⤐⤐⤐ ⬳⬳⬳

Candi arrives with sushi and, as we eat, I tell her *everything* that happened. I also reprimand her for the sneaky clothing switch to which she chuckles with glee, knowing I can't stay mad at her.

"I think I got caught up in it all, you know? I was on this wild adventure with a hot man, just like the stories I create. Italy is so romantic and Nicco, he — well, he was…" I release an exhale. "But, it was obviously nothing. None of it meant anything to him. I mean nothing to him." My heart weighs heavy in my chest as the truth rings in my ears.

"Des, are you absolutely sure? I mean, from everything you just told me, it really seems like there was *something* on his end. Opening himself up to you, the locket, the things he said. If I'm being honest, it kind of sounds like he was falling for you. I mean, my heart is yours? That's not something you say to someone you don't have feelings for."

"Well, if he was, he got over it really fast. And maybe, it was all nothing. Maybe once he finally got to fuck me, he punched the notch in his belt and moved on."

"Oh, Des. I can't believe that's true."

"I thought I was going to vomit when I saw him kissing Giovanna." A quick wave of nausea sours my stomach as the image flashes through my head.

"I just don't see it." She shakes her head, popping a piece of soy sauce-drenched shrimp tempura roll into her mouth. "I don't see the two of them together."

"I knew better. I've been through this before. Experience should've taught me this lesson." I choke on the boulder lodged in my throat as tears sting behind my eyes. "You told me to be in the moment, open myself up to possibility. I did, Can. And here I am, my heart shattered, just like I knew it would be." I put down the sushi I was about to eat, not feeling hungry anymore, and curl my leg up onto the sofa, my shoulders hunch. "It's never hurt this much before. Will I always feel this way?" My lower lip trembles as I speak. I can't stop the tears from pouring out.

Candi stops eating immediately and wraps her arms me. "No, honey, you won't always feel this way. You'll heal." Letting me sob, she strokes my hair.

Once my crying subsides, we release our embrace.

"Do you want me to beat him up? I can, you know. And I will."

I laugh and shake my head. "No, that won't be necessary." I sigh. "I can't believe how badly I misinterpreted everything. After we made love and he gave me the locket, I actually thought he had feelings for me." Blowing a puff of air, I get up from the sofa and grab two pints of ice cream out of the freezer and two spoons. "Oh, and on top of everything, Bev and Tom are selling the house."

"What?" Her eyes open wide and her pitch raises.

"Yup," I say, putting the mint chocolate chip pint in front her and handing her a spoon.

"What does that mean for you?" she asks, grabbing the spoon.

"I don't know yet." Taking the lid off my mocha chip, I scoop a spoonful into my mouth. "Bev said they'd like to negotiate something with me first since I've been such a good tenant for so many years."

"Well, that's good, right?"

"I don't know." I shrug. "I don't think I can afford this place on my own as far as buying it. I certainly don't have any kind of down payment saved up. I have no idea what I'm going to do. I emailed her back today saying I'm open to discussing it with them, but I honestly don't think I can swing it."

"Des. I'm so sorry. Can I help at all?"

"There's really nothing you can do. But I love you for wanting to help. My mom told me about a few openings at Creative Artists. I called today and have an interview next week."

"Ugh. You don't want to do that."

"I don't, but what choice do I have? I can't believe what a mess my life is right now."

"Your life isn't a mess," she says finishing the last bite of her fried rice and lifting the lid off her mint chocolate chip ice cream. "You're just in the midst of some challenges. You *will* get to the other side of all this. And your life will be better than you imagined. I know it. I know it in my soul."

"I hope you're right." I take another scoop of ice cream. "On the plus side, I finished the book today and I'm sending it to my betas tomorrow after I make sure the formatting looks okay. I'm really happy with how it turned out."

"Ooo, that's amazing! When will you publish it? I wanna read it."

"Next month. Your signed copy will be waiting for you." I wink at her.

She squeals, drumming her feet on the floor. "I can't wait!"

The next week passes quickly. My betas absolutely love my book and I'm thrilled. My interview at Creative Artists goes well. Though I'm not looking forward to hearing back from them, I probably need to suck it up and get some stable income coming in. While my beta readers, editor, and advanced copy readers love the book, that doesn't mean anything about what my sales will look like. Bev and Tom are out of town so we set up time to talk when they get back.

Nicco has finally stopped trying to reach me. It's for the best. There's nothing to say. Still, he invades my thoughts more often than not. His tender side, his depth, his kiss, his passion.

He's in every breath I take.

28

—

Nicco

I searched for her, all over Naples. I went to every hotel I could think of. It was useless. I searched for hours and couldn't find her.

Maybe I should leave her alone. Maybe I'm no good for her. But I can't stop thinking about her, about our time together, about how I feel about her. I can't just let her go without fighting for her. At the very least, she deserves to know what happened with Gigi and that it wasn't what she thinks.

My current project has me so busy, by the time I'm in my hotel room, I'm exhausted and go to sleep. I don't want to try to talk to her when I'm tired like that. Today we travel to a different location and I have some down time. When I call her, it goes to voice mail, again. I haven't left messages before. Why won't she answer? *I've hurt her, that's why. Fuck.*

"Destiny, it's Nicco. Please let me talk to you. I need to explain things to you. I don't want to leave a message. Please. Call me." I hang up. My heart aches for her.

I need a fucking cigarette. Sitting out on the balcony of my hotel room, I grab my pack, staring at it in my hand. *Fuck.* I take out a cigarette, but don't put it in my mouth. Instead, I rest my elbow on my knee and roll the cigarette between my thumb, index, and middle fingers. I gaze at the tobacco tip, staring down the barrel of a loaded gun. *Enough.* Dad's voice echoes in my head.

Putting the cigarette back in the pack, I get out my phone and call Destiny's friend, Heidi, to make an appointment and see if she can help me finally quit smoking. It's time.

Destiny

There was something in Nicco's voice when I listened to his message. I can't decipher it. But it tugs at my heart.

I feel bad not getting back to him. We'd become friends. And now I'm letting my wounded heart make me childish and ignore him. He has plenty of friends and now he has his relationship with Giovanna. I'll be a distant memory soon enough.

⟫⟫⟫⟩ ⟨⟨⟨⟨

The next few weeks fly by so fast my head is spinning.

I'm called in for a second interview at Creative Artists. While the interview goes well and I can do the job, the thought of being chained to a desk for eight hours a day makes my chest tight.

I publish my book and have the highest sales I've ever had on a release day, even earning #1 Best Seller once again. Not a day passes where I haven't had sales. *I'm back!* Though I'm riding the high of success and a burst of income, I'm still on the fence about whether or not I should take the position at Creative Artists if they offer it to me. I don't want to be reckless.

Bev and Tom make me an offer I can't refuse. Taking out the formalities of going through Realtors makes the transaction pretty simple. They've also offered owner financing because of our long-standing relationship, making the deal manageable for me.

To celebrate, Henry invites me to dinner. With Nicco haunting my thoughts day and night, going to dinner with Henry might be what I need to start getting over him.

Henry takes me to Vespertine where we enjoy a delicious meal and I do my best to pretend to be interested in whatever it is he's talking about. He's a nice man with a good heart and he's very well-meaning. I'm really trying to give him a chance. Forcing myself to pay attention to him isn't working. My mind drifts easily, to Nicco. *Let him go.*

When Henry brings me home, I invite him in, which I've never done before.

"Would you like a glass of wine?" I ask, taking off my shoes and setting my purse on the bench.

"Yeah, sure. What do you have?" he asks, leaving his shoes on and following me into the kitchen.

"Honestly, just one red and one white."

He releases a stuffy laugh. "I'll take your red. Did you know that the grapes for cabernet sauvignon are…"

His voice mutes as the memory of Nicco's adorable expression when he took his first bite of s'more enters my head. I pour our wine and we go out to my back porch.

"Would you like to go down by the water as the sun sets?"

He tugs on his suit jacket and adjusts his glasses on his face. "The sun's almost down and I'm not really dressed for that. How about we sit here?" he suggests, sitting on my swing.

Nicco would've taken off his shoes and socks at the door and he'd be tossing his jacket on the swing, rolling up his pant legs, and running to the edge of the water, holding my hand and bringing me with him. *Stop it.*

"Yeah, I suppose you're not."

As the sun sinks into the ocean, liquified orange merging with the horizon, Henry drones on about the intricate process of how grapes become wine.

Setting his glass on the ground, he straightens the peaked lapels on his jacket and turns his body toward me.

"Destiny, we've been kind of seeing each other for a while and, uh, I — I'd like to know if it's okay for me to kiss you."

Oh boy. "Thank you for asking, Henry. I think that would be fine." This couldn't be any more awkward.

Adjusting his stiff posture, he leans toward me, bumping his nose into mine.

"Oh, I'm sorry." He takes off his glasses and tucks them into his jacket pocket.

"It's okay."

He tries again and my mouth is cavity-searched by his tongue. Trying to give this a chance to improve, I close my eyes. The instant I do, Nicco floods me. Drowning out Henry's inexperienced tongue probing in and out of my mouth and slobbering all over my lips, erotic images of Nicco making love to me overtake my thoughts. *I can't do this.*

I push Henry off me.

"Henry, I'm sorry," I say, standing up, dabbing at his saliva around my lips with the side of my index finger. "I can't do this."

The eyes of a wounded puppy stare up at me. "Did I do something wrong?"

I pull in my lips and shake my head. "No, you didn't do anything wrong. You've been so kind to me and I've enjoyed spending time with you." I pause.

He stands up, hurt eyes shifting back and forth between mine. "Then what is it?"

I take his hands in mine. "The truth is, my heart belongs to someone else. And, until I can get over him, it's not fair to you if we continue down this path."

"Oh." He looks down at his feet then releases my hands. "I understand."

We go back into the house, his tail hanging between his legs. I walk him to the door and he turns to me. We stand in the spot where I'd gaze into Nicco's eyes and he'd kiss my cheeks.

"When you're over him, you know where to find me." A hopeful smile strains his face.

"I do." *Though I'll never look for you.* After feeling what I felt for Nicco, our connection, our intimacy, our passion, I won't settle ever again.

"Good night then."

"Goodbye, Henry."

Shutting the door behind him, I get our wine glasses from the porch and lock up. Putting his glass in the sink, I refill mine and turn on the fireplace and some music.

I go upstairs and change into my pajamas, grab my stuffed pig and journal, and go back downstairs. Taking the blanket off the corner of the sofa, I sit down and wrap it around me. Desperate to erase the last few hours, I close my eyes and try to meditate.

As I focus my breathing, Nicco's face appears. The wind blows his hair and his smile I've grown so fond of warms me. I open my eyes, blowing a heavy exhale. *Please go away.*

Nicco

I've been watching Destiny's progress from my private Instagram account and I was so happy to see her hit #1 Best Seller all on her own. I knew she could get her success back without my following. I've been so busy with my projects, I didn't have time to read her book. With hours of flight time to L.A., I finally get to read it. While I know her work is fiction, the second I read the prologue, I know it's me. And now, I'm going to fix the mess I made and tell her how I feel.

⟫⟫⟫⟫ ⟪⟪⟪⟪

As I pull up the street toward her house, a man walks down her driveway and gets in his car. *Henry? Fuck.* I didn't stop to think she might be with Henry. Is it even Henry? The thought of someone else being with her twists a knife in my soul. Maybe her book *was* completely made up and I'm fucking wrong. Does she feel nothing for me? Are we to be strangers now?

The man drives away and I pull into the spot in front of her house. Maybe I shouldn't do this. Maybe I *should* leave her alone. Fuck that. I'm not giving up. She wants someone to fight for her? That's exactly what I'm here to do.

I get out of the car and walk around to her back porch, taking off my shoes and socks before stepping into the sand. She's sitting on her sofa with her eyes closed. Standing in the cool sand, listening to the distant lull of waves, I watch her. She's so fucking beautiful.

Taking my phone out of my pocket, I call her.

Startled, she picks up her phone and stares at it, then looks up at the ceiling. Putting her phone back down, she drops her face into her hands. The call goes to voice mail.

I call again.

Lifting her face from her hands, she picks up her phone again, running her finger across her upper lip as she stares at the screen. She swipes.

"Hi, Nicco." She stands, putting her blanket on the sofa. "I, uh, I'm sorry I missed your call. I was, upstairs." Pointing up, she lies then puts the palm of her hand on her forehead. "How are you?"

"Thank you for answering. I've been trying to reach you."

"Yeah, I — I've had a lot going on here." She paces, biting her lower lip.

"Destiny, I need you to know that what you saw with me and Gigi isn't what you thought you saw."

She covers her eyes with her hand. "It really doesn't matter. I'm happy for you," she says, her words contrasting her body language.

"No," I say sharply. "It does matter. I need you to know the truth. I didn't kiss Gigi. She took off her dress, sat on my lap, and kissed me. It happened so fast. But it was my fault for even letting her sit on my lap. I take responsibility for that. I'm sorry. She was mad about us and jealous. I'm not with Gigi. I told you, I will *never* be with Gigi."

She paces. "Is that what you've been wanting to tell me?" she asks, raising her voice. "That she kissed you and it wasn't you kissing her, even though your lips were locked together?" She thrusts her hand through the air.

"Yes, but—"

"Okay." She cuts me off. "Now I know." She stops pacing and rubs her forehead. "I have to go." Her voice gags.

"Destiny, wait."

"What?"

"I read your book."

"Why?" She sits back on the sofa, covering her eyes with her hand.

"Because I wanted to." I pause. "Is it me?"

Tilting her head back, she takes the stuffed pig I gave her into her lap.

"Destiny, I have to know. Is it me you wrote about in your book?"

Her breath comes before her words. "What does it matter?" she asks, defeat coloring her tone.

"It matters. Was it a made-up person? Or was it me? Do you feel nothing for me?"

Standing up, she tosses the pig on the sofa. "It makes no difference what I feel for you, Nicco. You're going to be surrounded and tempted by beautiful women like Gigi for the rest of your life. I can't compete with that," she says impatiently, pacing again.

"You *do* feel something for me. I know you do."

"Nicco, please." Her strangled words answer me. "I have to go."

Blood runs hot through my body. "Tell me. Tell me you don't want me. Tell me it's over. Tell me I mean nothing to you."

She drops back onto the sofa, silent, burying her face in her hand.

"Tell me." I quiet my voice. "Tell me and I'll walk away."

Uneven breaths pass through the phone as I watch tears trail down her face. "I can't." Her faint voice tears my heart. "Goodbye Nicco." Click.

She curls her body into itself as she clutches the pig.

No. It doesn't end like this. I grab my shoes and run to her front door. Ringing the bell, I'm ready to crash down the door.

She opens it and stumbles back as her eyes spring open.

293

"Nicco. What — what are you doing here?" She wipes her fingers under her lashes.

Stepping in and flinging the door closed behind me, I toss my shoes on the floor. I gently cup her face, sweeping my thumbs across her mascara-smeared cheeks.

"I came here for you, mia dolce ragazza. I came here because I have feelings for you, Destiny. And I think you have feelings for me." I pause, releasing her face and looking down at the locket around her neck. "You're wearing my locket."

She takes it in her hand and looks into my eyes. "It reminds me of you."

Taking a breath, I think about my next words. Terrified about the risk I'm about to take, but knowing I have to. "Destiny, my heart fell in love with you before I knew how to love."

Her brows squeeze together as her watery eyes search mine.

"You taught me how to love." I shake my head. "You showed me what it looks like, what it feels like. You woke up a part of me I'd closed off long ago." I pause. "These last few weeks have been torture with you not talking to me. I almost gave up, thinking it was best if I left you alone. I never saw you coming and I wasn't prepared for you. But sometimes love finds you when you least expect it. And if you're with Henry now —" I point to the door.

"You were here?"

"Yes. I saw a man leave here. I'm guessing it was Henry. If you're with him and he makes you feel the way you feel when you're with me and he makes you happy, I'll walk out your door and never bother you again." Closing the gap between us, I gaze into her eyes. "But I'm not leaving here without you knowing how I feel. The song I wrote for you? It's not just a song. You *are* the blood coursing through my veins. You *are* the breath in my lungs that gives me life." I pause, pressing my lips together. "I know this is going to sound crazy, but I think my dad sent you to me somehow. To save me." I shake my head gently. "I don't want to live without you. You know that saying you told me? I want you in my life for a lifetime. *You* are my destiny. You've captured my heart and I'm in love with you."

Tears spill over her lashes as she reaches her arms around my neck, drawing my forehead to touch hers. Squeezing her eyes, more tears release.

She opens her eyes and looks into mine. "I've been falling in love with you since you rescued me from those jerks in the club the night of my birthday."

I pick her up in my arms and she wraps her legs around my waist. Cradling her body in my arms, I claim her mouth with mine, overflowing with love.

29

———

Destiny

I'm in Nicco's arms. He came here to fight for me. He's choosing me.

He carries me up to my bedroom and we make the most emotional, passionate love I've ever experienced. Our souls connect on an ethereal level. Our bodies ignite in ecstasy.

>>>>> <<<<<

I wake in the morning to soft kisses on my shoulder, down my arm. He's tucked in behind me, propped on his elbow. A yawn sneaks out of me as I roll my body toward him.

"Good morning," his deep voice rumbles through me as he smiles down at me.

"Good morning."

He kisses my forehead.

"You didn't have a cigarette after we made love last night." I hadn't realized it until we were almost asleep.

"No, I didn't." His smile broadens proudly as he tilts his head a bit. "I called your friend, Heidi, and she's helping me quit."

"Nicco, that's wonderful."

"You once told me that a soul mate doesn't complete you, but they inspire you to complete yourself. You do that for me." He traces his finger from the top of my forehead, down the side of my face, and across my jaw, then touches his lips to mine.

My heart swells with happiness that's quickly overtaken by

melancholy. Though our feelings are now out in the open, I don't know how a relationship could work between us.

"Nicco?"

"Yes?"

"What happens now? With us."

"What do you want to happen?"

"I don't know. A lot's happened in the last few weeks that I haven't even told you about."

"Okay. So, tell me." Shifting his eyes from mine, he watches his fingers trail over my shoulder and down my arm.

"Well, my book's doing really well, but there's no guarantee I'm on my way back to stable income. And I'm buying my house so I need stable income."

"You are?" he asks, returning his gaze to me.

"Yes, Bev and Tom sold me the house. They made me an amazing offer and they don't even want to make money on it. They're just downsizing the number of properties they have to manage."

"So you're going to own your house now?" Squeezing my hip, he wiggles me.

"Yeah. Well, I hope so."

"That's awesome," he says, leaning down, kissing my décolletage.

"It is and I'm excited, but I'm also a little nervous. I've been interviewing at Creative Artists —"

"A desk job?" Lifting from my décolletage, he looks at me with narrowed brows. "You wouldn't like that at all."

"I know, but it would be stable income and I can write when I'm not there."

He leans back down and kisses my neck with tender pecks. My skin warms beneath his lips as I sip an inhale.

"That won't make you happy." Sliding the strap of my camisole down over my shoulder, he moves his kisses to the top of my breast.

A tiny gasp escapes me as my eyes close. "I know, but it's what

I need to do."

"I have another idea," he says, dropping a kiss on my nose and swirling his finger around my nipple over my silky camisole.

I sharply inhale in response to his touch. "What's that?"

"I'm going to be doing some traveling for my career," he says. Lifting the bottom of my camisole to just below my breasts, he kisses a line down my stomach. "And I want you to be with me," he says, dragging his mouth across my heating skin to the side of my waist above my hip bone and taking a nibble.

I squirm and he digs his teeth in, just a touch, making me whimper. "But how will I do that if I take a job at Creative Artists?" I ask, sinking my hands into his hair.

"Forget the job." Tugging down one side of my satiny shorts, he places whispery kisses from below my hip to the top of my landing strip.

My back arches slightly. "I can't just forget the job," I say on a moan.

Moving back up, he rests against my lower body, leaning his torso so his face is above mine. "I'm serious. I want to be with you. I'm not going to let anything get in the way of that. We have my home in Rome, your home here, and we can travel for my concerts and acting projects, and have incredible adventures together. If we want to stay in a city for an extra day, I'll arrange it. You can tour the cities we visit for inspiration and research and write your books. Together we'll have plenty of money." His eyes sparkle. "What do you think?"

With this sexy, kind, loving man hovering above me, I quickly think back to when we first met. How dull and uncertain my life was. How lonely, empty, and uninspired I was. Now, a man I only ever fantasized about has melded with who I dreamed about as my soul mate and he's in love with me. And I'm in love with him. I'm living inside one of my books. Goose bumps cover my body.

"Destiny?" His soft, husky voice brings me back to the moment. "That's really what you want?"

Without a smile on his face, he nods, his gaze boring intensely into my eyes. "Yes. That's what I want. I've been waiting for you my whole life," he says, brushing his thumb across my cheek. "Sii mio per sempre, mia dolce ragazza."

"What does that mean?"

"It means, be mine forever, my sweet girl." Softly kissing my lips, he encases me in his arms, burying his face into the crook of my neck.

Do I believe in soul mates? Yes. Yes, I do.

On my thirtieth birthday, I fell in love. I fell in love with a man who would be mine forever.

EPILOGUE

—

Nicco

Walking into our suite at the Mandarin Oriental Jumeira hotel, I see my wife relaxing on the chaise out on our private balcony, reading a book.

I set my guitar by the sofa in the living room and go straight to her, kneeling next to her and putting my ear on her swollen belly, waiting.

"Did he kick today?"

"Not yet," she says, running her hand through my hair. "He's waiting for his daddy to sing to him."

I look up at her and smile then sing part of a song I'll be performing at tonight's concert in Dubai. "Will you have your mother's smile? Will you have my eyes? None of it matters. I'll love you 'til I die."

She sits forward. "There. Did you see it?" she asks, taking my hand and placing it on her belly.

I feel it. A powerful kick from my son's tiny foot in the palm of my hand. I can't imagine being any happier than I am right now.

"I think he might be a football player like me."

"We'll teach him that he can be anything he wants to be. I just hope he turns out to be someone exactly like you."

ARE YOU READY FOR CANDI'S STORY?

Turn the page to read the prologue.

Get the full book here...
https://books2read.com/KissAwayYourPain

PROLOGUE

—

Candi

Lost love is the most painful, soul-crushing, gut-wrenching love of all. Trust me, I know. I was lucky enough to find my soul mate. And then he was gone…

>>>> <<<<

"Niccolo Francesco Mancini, do you take Destiny to be your wedded wife, to live together in holy matrimony, to love her, to honor her, to comfort her, and to keep her in sickness and in health, forsaking all others, for as long as you both shall live?" asks the priest.

"I do," Nicco answers, his lips lifting into a smile that melts me. That man was head over heels for Destiny the moment he laid eyes on her.

"And do you, Destiny Louise Cardone, take Nicco to be your husband, to live together in holy matrimony, to love him, to honor him, to comfort him, and to keep him in sickness and in health, forsaking all others, for as long as you both shall live?"

Standing behind Destiny, holding her bouquet, I can't see her face, but the gleam in Nicco's eyes as he focuses on her warms my heart.

"With all my heart, I do," she says.

"By the power vested in me, I pronounce you husband and wife. Nicco, you may kiss your bride."

As they seal their love with a kiss, I can't ignore the ache throbbing deep in the cavern of my soul at the loss of my once-in-a-lifetime love.

AN INVITATION

This is a special invitation for YOU. Yes, you. I know you can join thousands of author's newsletters and I know that can be overwhelming. The readers who choose to join my free newsletter are friends to me, people who actually want to be with me in my little corner of the world.

Of course, I share updates about my books, and I also share personal stories, tough times, funny times, goat/chicken/bunny pictures, do special giveaways no one else gets, give you the first look at covers and chapters, and more.

So, this is my personal invitation to you to jump into my world and join my free newsletter. When you do, you'll receive free chapters of some of my books.

Head here:
debbiecromack.com/newsletter/

DEBBIE UNTETHERED

For a deeper connection with me, join my paid newsletter. It's the place where I get to feel most at home and comfortable with people who truly want to get to know me and are excited about my books. It's also where I get a chance to get to know you.

I send emails once a week-ish and some include links to private YouTube videos where I share what's going on with me because that feels more personal to me.

Head here:
debbiecromack.substack.com/

MORE BOOKS BY *Debbie Cromack*

Standalones
Untouchable Zane

Is it possible for a gorgeous, A-list celebrity to actually find true love with someone who genuinely loves him for himself and not his status and wealth? And when he does, could one fateful night drive her away forever?

Tropes: SLOW BURN, reverse age-gap (older woman, younger man), celebrity hero, wounded / broken hero, Hollywood romance

https://books2read.com/u/47Npla

Series
Someone Exactly Like Me (Book 1 in the Wounded Hearts Series)

He's a hot Italian celebrity who wants the American dream. She's a romance author whose career is in a slump. They strike a business deal to help each other get what they want. When sparks fly, neither may get what they bargained for and both may end up with broken hearts.

Tropes: SLOW BURN, friends to lovers, soul mates, strong female friendship, wounded / broken hero, celebrity / Mediterranean hero, slight forced proximity

https://books2read.com/u/mvojwz

Kiss Away Your Pain (Book 2 in the Wounded Hearts Series)

She's not into one-night stands. He's a commitment-phobe. When sparks fly, is true love even possible?

Tropes: SLOW BURN, friends to lovers, soul mates, strong female friendship, wounded / broken hero, learning to love again

https://books2read.com/KissAwayYourPain

Someone to Watch Over Me (Book 3 in the Wounded Hearts Series)

They've been in love since they were kids, though neither will confess it to the other. One night changes everything, bringing them closer together then ripping them apart. Will their deep childhood love be the catalyst that seals their fate?

Tropes: SLOW BURN, childhood friends to lovers, soul mates, unexpected pregnancy, hidden love

https://books2read.com/SomeoneToWatchOverMeCromack

Thank You!

Thanks so much for reading Someone Exactly Like Me.
I hope you loved it!

If you did, I'd love your review on Amazon, GoodReads, and/or
BookBub. Your review not only gives me valuable feedback,
it also helps other readers find me.

Please come connect with me on my **social media accounts.**

Here's my Linktree link where you can find **ALL** my links:
linktr.ee/Debbie_Cromack_Author

WHERE DID THE IDEA FOR THIS BOOK COME FROM?

After I wrote Untouchable Zane, my debut novel, I was terrified I didn't have another book in me. And I really wanted to make writing romance books my career. After all, I'd let go of my corporate job and was unemployed so I needed to find a way to earn a living.

Being a little vanilla when it comes to writing love scenes, a friend suggested I watch the Netflix movie 365 Days. NOT something I'd normally watch. LOL! I'd already written Untouchable Zane, so I looked at it as research for any hopeful ideas I might have for another book. Peering at the screen through my fingers, I took notes. Yes, I believe I'm the only person in the world who watched that movie with a notepad and pen.

A few days later, scenes started flying into my head along with the question: What would it be like to date Michele Morrone in real life?

And so, Someone Exactly Like Me came to life with Michele Morrone as my muse. While this story is a complete work of fiction, I did research him and tried to include some realistic elements into the story.

I hope you enjoyed reading Destiny and Nicco's love story. Be sure to check out my other books for more romantic stories!

ACKNOWLEDGEMENTS

My readers who choose to be in my world, thank you for your excited and loving messages you send me. You make my heart smile. Thank you for the beautiful graphics and edits you create and share with your friends and audience, encouraging them to read my books. I appreciate you so much!

The writing community and my author friends, "I appreciate you" doesn't convey my deep gratitude. I've been in this community a short time and wouldn't even be able to list all the names of the incredible people who support me and share my posts EVERY day. So many of you have become friends of my heart and I'm incredibly grateful that God has merged our life-paths. I love this community!

My wonderful beta readers, **Courteney Tunstead, Lea Batt, Melissa Johnson, Colby Bettley, and Savannah Carlisle.** I'm massively grateful for your honest feedback and your generosity of time. I appreciate you so much!! Thank you for making this story better than I could've done on my own!

My ARC and Street teams, bloggers, and bookstagrammers, THANK YOU so much for your devotion and dedication to help spread the word for me and all the authors you help and support. I could never reach new people without all of your time and effort. You are the heartbeat of this community.

I'd like to thank some incredible women who I've never met, but who love and support me pretty much every single day: **Christy Erasmus, Julie Soper, Annie Bugeja, Lea Batt, Courteney Tunstead, Nikki Summers, and C. D'Angelo.** Thank you for the laughter you share, thank you for drying my tears, thank you for your support and guidance when I'm ready to pull my hair out, thank you for your love. You're a warm blanket around my heart.

And **YOU, my new reader.** I'm so happy you took a chance on getting my book. I hope you love it!!! Without you, I wouldn't be able to do this fabulous work I love. Thank you!

ABOUT the Author

Once you get to know me, you'll start to see bits and pieces of me in each of my books. From life experiences to heroine characteristics and quirks. This is my way of giving a tiny bit of myself to you.

I believe we all feel a little damaged or broken at times.

And while we may FEEL this way for days, weeks, months, or even years, it doesn't mean we ARE damaged or broken in our soul. I believe that our ability to feel broken is what binds us together. It connects us. It helps us feel compassion for each other.

It's important to share. Share our stories. Share our battles. Share our fears. Share our scars.

When we share, we allow others to see us for who we are, real and raw. When we share, we become vulnerable. And through that vulnerability we connect.

In vulnerability there is strength. In vulnerability there is healing. When we allow ourselves to be vulnerable and share ourselves with others, they feel empowered to share and be vulnerable as well. This is how we come together. This is how we unite.

We are human beings. I believe we are nothing without each other. We need each other. I know I wouldn't be where I am today without the support, guidance, and love of the people I surround myself with.

I write realistic characters who find each other at a time when they're feeling a little broken. Through the process of helping the other person grow, heal, or become a better version themselves, they, in turn, move beyond hurt, beyond pain, beyond feeling damaged and broken and step into a better version of themselves.

My heroes tend to be virile and masculine with hidden romantic sides and huge hearts. My heroines are often awkward, feisty, and struggle with their self-worth. Through the journey of their love stories, which are never smooth, they bring out the best in each other while stepping into the person they're meant to be.

The personal side of me...

I live in an old farmhouse and I have a dwarf bunny named Nutmeg, two Nigerian dwarf goats named Patches and Tiny, and lots of chickens. I love hot cocoa with marshmallows and usually only watch either the Hallmark channel or cooking shows.